Acclaim for
Chemistry

"In this lyrical and intensely moving novel, Lewis DeSimone writes with passion and calm assurance about two men trying, not always successfully, to find a way to love each other. The obstacles are formidable: one man's depression that leads to attempted suicide, the other's subtle but debilitating need to be needed. Though the physical attraction they have for each other is powerful, they find it difficult to negotiate the boundary between the pleasure of caring and the danger of caring too much. Through it all, DeSimone's astute psychological analyses come to us in one beautifully written sentence after another. It's an irresistible combination."

—Robert Taylor
Author, *Whose Eye Is on Which Sparrow?*,
All We Have Is Now,
Revelation and Other Stories,
and *The Innocent*

"Beautifully written, Lewis DeSimone's *Chemistry* deals with mental illness with an honesty that is painfully real. 'Chemistry,' says Neal the narrator, 'is about reactions, two elements coming together and creating something new . . . Two elements come together, and neither is the same again.' Readers of this novel will not be unmoved by the story of Neal and Zach, and of Martin, Neal's friend. We should all wish for a friend like Martin."

—Dale Edgerton
Author, *Goneaway Road*

"DeSimone skillfully maps the everyday romance and unexpected roadblocks between new lovers. This is a brave and engaging novel, deftly blending yearning, confusion, compassion, and heartbreak."

—Jameson Currier
Author, *Where the Rainbow Ends*

"*Chemistry,* by Lewis DeSimone, is a love story and so much more. This sensual, erotic novel explores, with unusual honesty, the nature of romantic chemistry. What is it about a certain someone that attracts—his special qualities? our vulnerabilities? both? To what extent should we follow our hearts? Should we ever question whether a man who seems too good to be true actually is? DeSimone handles these issues with grace, insight, and wit while exposing his characters' deepest intimacies. A thoroughly enjoyable read."

—Daniel M. Jaffe
Author, *The Limits of Pleasure*

"*Chemistry* is about attraction and repulsion—finding new love and nursing broken hearts. This wonderful, touching gay novel, set in the age of Prozac and AIDS, offers readers real characters they will care about and think about long after the story ends."

—Gary M. Kramer
Author, *Independent Queer Cinema:*
Reviews and Interviews

Chemistry

HARRINGTON PARK PRESS®
Southern Tier Editions™
Gay Men's Fiction

Elf Child by David M. Pierce

Huddle by Dan Boyle

The Man Pilot by James W. Ridout IV

Shadows of the Night: Queer Tales of the Uncanny and Unusual edited by Greg Herren

Van Allen's Ecstasy by Jim Tushinski

Beyond the Wind by Rob N. Hood

The Handsomest Man in the World by David Leddick

The Song of a Manchild by Durrell Owens

The Ice Sculptures: A Novel of Hollywood by Michael D. Craig

Between the Palms: A Collection of Gay Travel Erotica edited by Michael T. Luongo

Aura by Gary Glickman

Love Under Foot: An Erotic Celebration of Feet edited by Greg Wharton
    and M. Christian

The Tenth Man by E. William Podojil

Upon a Midnight Clear: Queer Christmas Tales edited by Greg Herren

Dryland's End by Felice Picano

Whose Eye Is on Which Sparrow? by Robert Taylor

Deep Water: A Sailor's Passage by E. M. Kahn

The Boys in the Brownstone by Kevin Scott

The Best of Both Worlds: Bisexual Erotica edited by Sage Vivant and M. Christian

Tales from the Levee by Martha Miller

Some Dance to Remember: A Memoir-Novel of San Francisco, 1970-1982 by Jack Fritscher

Confessions of a Male Nurse by Richard S. Ferri

The Millionaire of Love by David Leddick

Transgender Erotica: Trans Figures edited by M. Christian

Skip Macalester by J. E. Robinson

Chemistry by Lewis DeSimone

Friends, Lovers, and Roses by Vernon Clay

Beyond Machu by William Maltese

Virginia Bedfellows by Gavin Morris

Seventy Times Seven by Salvatore Sapienza

Going Down in La-La Land by Andy Zeffer

Independent Queer Cinema: Reviews and Interviews by Gary M. Kramer

Planting Eli by Jeff Black

Chemistry

Lewis DeSimone

Southern Tier Editions™
Harrington Park Press®
An Imprint of The Haworth Press, Inc.
New York • London • Oxford

For more information on this book or to order, visit
http://www.haworthpress.com/store/product.asp?sku=5501

or call 1-800-HAWORTH (800-429-6784) in the United States and Canada
or (607) 722-5857 outside the United States and Canada

or contact orders@HaworthPress.com

Published by

Southern Tier Editions™, Harrington Park Press®, an imprint of The Haworth Press, Inc., 10
Alice Street, Binghamton, NY 13904-1580.

PUBLISHER'S NOTES
The development, preparation, and publication of this work has been undertaken with great care.
However, the Publisher, employees, editors, and agents of The Haworth Press are not responsible
for any errors contained herein or for consequences that may ensue from use of materials or information contained in this work. The Haworth Press is committed to the dissemination of ideas and
information according to the highest standards of intellectual freedom and the free exchange of
ideas. Statements made and opinions expressed in this publication do not necessarily reflect the
views of the Publisher, Directors, management, or staff of The Haworth Press, Inc., or an en-
dorsement by them.

This is a work of fiction. Names, characters, places, and incidents either are the products of the
author's imagination or are used fictitiously, and any resemblance to actual persons, living or
dead, business establishments, events, or locales is entirely coincidental.

Interior molecule illustration by Jason W. Wint.

Cover design by Lora Wiggins.

Library of Congress Cataloging-in-Publication Data

DeSimone, Lewis, 1962-
    Chemistry / Lewis DeSimone.
        p. cm.
    ISBN-13: 978-1-56023-559-0 (pbk. : alk. paper)
    ISBN-10: 1-56023-559-4 (pbk. : alk. paper)
    1. Gay men—Fiction. 2. Mentally ill—Fiction. I. Title.

PS3604.E7583C47 2006
813'. 6—dc22

                                                                    2005021267

For my family,
biological and otherwise

part one

bonding

One of the few things I remember from my college chemistry class—my first and only foray into laboratory science—is the professor's desperate attempt to make the periodic table sexy. "Magnesium loves oxygen," he would say, his grin ripe with double entendre, and I couldn't help imagining a voluptuous molecule in a tight Mg sweater batting her eyelashes at a studly clump of O_2. It seems that oxygen is never quite safe from magnesium's advances: whenever the opportunity arises, she makes a beeline for him, with incendiary results.

That's the thing about chemistry. You can't choose whom you're going to be attracted to, even when you know that eventually it will all blow up in your face.

At least that's how it had been with Adam. All the red flags were there, practically from the start, but I was just listening to the magnesium side of my nature. Adam was my oxygen; I needed him to breathe. The explosion, when it finally hit, sent me flying all the way across the country. I ended up in San Francisco—where everyone ends up, according to Oscar Wilde—and on the doorstep of Martin Blake.

I met Martin through his sister, Natalie, an old friend in Boston. She had insisted that I call him as soon as I arrived in town, if only to allay her own fears: images of me sitting alone in an empty apartment, nursing a freshly broken heart. And she was right—Martin didn't give me time to grieve. He was my Auntie Mame, constantly pushing my nose into the banquet.

I'd been in town less than a month when Martin took over my life. He was around forty-five when we met—practically another generation, with me barely out of my twenties. He took me everywhere,

Chemistry
Published by The Haworth Press, Inc., 2006. All rights reserved.
doi:10.1300/5501_01

from the most touristy parts of town—Fisherman's Wharf on a
crowded Saturday afternoon—to quiet coffee shops on tree-lined
streets that the locals kept hidden from glazed Midwestern eyes.

The first thing you learn in chemistry is that some elements carry a
positive charge and others a negative. (Unlike humans, chemical elements are all basically heterosexual: opposites attract.) Fortunately
for my damaged electrons, Martin and I were too similar for a spark,
but it didn't take long for us to see that we would be bound in another, more durable way—as close, eventually best, friends.

But sometimes he really pushed his luck.

"What are those?" I asked, as a pair of steel-tipped cowboy boots
flew from his hand and landed at my feet. Martin was crouched in the
door frame of his closet, where he had located the culprits after a minute or so of rummaging.

"Boots," he said, rising from the floor.

"Master of the obvious," I said, picking up one specimen—worn
black leather stitched with a curlicue pattern from the top to the
pointed toe. The boot was soft in my hand, luxurious. "What am I
supposed to do with these?" I asked. I stood behind him, the boot
flopped over my arm like a dead fish waiting to be skinned.

"Dance in them," he said, picking up the boot's mate and handing
it to me.

"I have perfectly good dancing shoes on already." I stuck out a
sneakered foot for inspection.

"We're not going to a high school hop, Neal."

"Where are we going?" I asked, sitting down to try on the boots.
They slipped on fairly easily but still had to be yanked over my heels.
The hardest part was rolling my jeans back down over them.

"The Rawhide," he said. "You'll love it."

"Sounds like something out of a Clint Eastwood movie."

"Don't worry. He wouldn't set foot in the place."

"Why isn't that a comfort?"

Country-western dancing had been a trend for years, but I'd successfully avoided it in Boston. I'd never been able to take the music seriously—to me, it was just twanging guitars and whining laments
about lost love and dead dogs. Besides, Adam had kept me busy

enough with minilectures on Bach and Mahler. (Even Aaron Copland wasn't good enough for him—too American.)

As Martin led me inside, I felt all my suspicions being confirmed: a yearning female voice singing out of tune, garish streamers suspended from the ceiling, an occasional ten-gallon hat towering over the other dancers. I was still stumbling a bit in the boots, not used to the height or the sway they threw into my hips. It was as if I had to get to know the entire lower half of my body all over again.

We passed the bar and stood together at the edge of the dance floor. Couples went spinning quickly by in an elegant ellipse, counter-clockwise all the way to the back of the room and around again. They seemed to be moving together, all part of a single mechanism, swept along by the music. I'd never seen men in formal dance holds before, hands clasped in the air, bodies locked together. Their feet shifted rhythmically toward and away from each other—a predictable game of seduction, the leader backing off, the follower stalking seamlessly behind.

"Beautiful, isn't it?" Martin asked. He gazed in admiration, one foot tapping to the beat. "Let's get a drink." He grasped my hand and pulled me along the side of the room, past the wallflowers, to another bar, in the back.

We watched from the corner for a while, drinks cradled in our hands. The music was different than I had expected. The country of Loretta Lynn seemed to have merged somehow with rock and blues. Despite my best efforts to remain disinterested, something in its rhythm pulled me. I didn't have the first idea of what to do, but I found myself bouncing on my toes, longing to try.

"Come on." Martin laid my nearly empty beer bottle on the shelf behind us. "It's time to take the plunge." He took my right hand and placed his on my back. "Put your hand on my shoulder," he said. "Okay, now just relax. It's very easy." He began to move. "Quick quick, slow slow," he said, drawing out the last two words. I stumbled backward. "Right left, right left," he said, again letting the last two words linger an extra beat. He repeated as we began to move into the circle. He caught my eye, held it, wouldn't let me look down at my struggling feet.

"I'm not very coordinated," I said, laughing nervously.

"Shut up," he said. "You're a musician. Mozart or Dwight Yoakam, it's still got a beat. Just try to feel the rhythm. Quick quick, slow slow. Quick quick, slow slow."

I ignored the men floating beside and around us and concentrated, looking only at Martin, hearing only his words, barely catching the music itself. Martin's thin lips began to mouth the words silently, his eyes wide and encouraging. The song ended and we stopped in position, but he wouldn't let me go. "Let's just hope the next one's not a waltz," he whispered. The music began again and he pulled me back into the two-step rhythm.

At the end of the next song, the deejay announced a couples' line dance, and Martin and I pulled away from the dance floor. "Well," he said, leading me toward the wall, "not bad for somebody with two left feet."

"Beginner's luck," I said, watching two concentric rings of dancers form on the floor. As the music started, they danced in pairs, then drew back for a couple of individual steps and changed partners, the outer circle moving in the regular direction, the inner one clockwise. Each new couple smiled broadly, like old friends rediscovering each other, and the leader spun the follower under his arm.

"When can I learn that?" I asked Martin, leaning back toward his ear while keeping my eye on the dancers.

"I'm a florist," he said, "not Annie Sullivan."

On the dance floor the circle slowly shifted, and a tall man in a plaid shirt approached and smiled our way, arching his eyebrows. "Hey!" Martin called out, waving.

"Who's that?" I asked, still watching. The man was in the leaders' line, confidently grasping his new partner's hand and twirling him around. Their heels hit the floor in perfect sync as they promenaded and then released each other. Martin's friend drew back and clapped his hands once on the beat, waiting for his next partner.

"Zach somebody," Martin said. "I don't know his last name. We've danced together a few times. I haven't seen him around for a while. Nice guy."

Zach smiled back at Martin before turning the corner. His cheeks were round, the smile wide, infectious. He moved deftly, as if his feet did everything of their own accord, as if he didn't have to think about a thing.

The next dance was a swing. "Let's try that one next week," Martin said. "We'll stick to the two-step for tonight." We stayed in the corner and watched.

"Martin!" Zach came toward us, his boots tapping out a rhythm that cut across the music. He reached an arm around Martin's shoulder and kissed him on the cheek. Up close, he looked younger, not much over twenty-five. His face was smooth, pale, like virgin parchment still untouched by a pen. "How are you?" he said, pulling away but taking hold of Martin's hand.

"Just fine. Where have you been?"

"Oh, around. It's been a crazy time." He let his gaze fall from Martin for a second. His eyes were a bluish gray, softening pink cheeks. Thick light brown hair fell languidly over his forehead. Smiling, he pulled it back with one hand.

Martin introduced us.

"Nice to meet you," Zach said, extending a thick hand. His words carried almost a country twang—part of the atmosphere, I thought— and his grip was strong; I felt the bones of my fingers coming together.

"How's the shop?" he asked.

"We're doing great," Martin replied. "And Macy's?"

Zach smiled widely, heavy dimples slicing into his cheeks. "I've moved up to men's shoes," he said. "Tomorrow, who knows, maybe lingerie."

"That might come in handy around Halloween. Listen, can I get you a drink?" Martin was still looking at Zach, though his hand fell lightly onto my shoulder.

"Sure," I said. "Another beer would be great."

"Zach?"

"Club soda, please."

Martin nodded and headed back to the bar.

"So, how do you know Martin?" Zach asked.

A black ten-gallon hat passed behind him; I could barely make out the body beneath it. "I knew his sister," I said, "in Boston."

"Oh, you're just visiting?"

"No," I said abruptly, "I moved here recently." Looking up, I could almost see myself in his eyes, a faint outline dancing in his pupils.

"Here you go." Martin sidled up beside me, clutching our drinks in an unsteady triangle. I slipped my beer bottle out, careful not to send the whole arrangement tumbling to the floor.

Zach lifted his glass into the air. "To new friends," he said. "Welcome to San Francisco." A wedge of lime floated in the glass as he drank.

"So you've discovered Neal's secret," Martin said. "Does it still show, after all my hard work?"

Zach giggled. His eyes were huge. They were beginning to make me uncomfortable. "So what brings you to the land of Oz?"

"Well, the house began to pitch, and the rest is history."

"Oh, that's Zach's department," Martin said. "He's the one from Kansas."

"Come on," I said. "No one's from Kansas!"

"Scout's honor." Zach crossed his heart and raised three fingers.

"I'm sorry," I said. "I didn't mean—"

"Don't worry, I get it all the time. At work, they call me Dorothy."

"Too bad they don't carry ruby slippers in men's shoes."

Zach laughed. "Oh, he's funny, Martin. You should keep him."

The deejay broke in to announce another line dance. "My favorite!" Zach said. "Do you—" He gestured toward the dance floor.

"No," I said hastily. "My feet are all thumbs."

He laughed again. "Okay, just hold this for me?" He pressed his half-empty glass into my open palm. Still smiling, he dashed off and found a place in one of the forming lines.

I watched the routine, studying the steps—the heel brought back and tapped by a dangling hand, the toes skidding nonchalantly across the floor. It looked so fluid, as if the entire dance were contained in the gentle movement of the dancers' hips. Zach rested one hand on his belt buckle, the other swinging gently at his side. His shirt was open at the collar, just enough to reveal a smooth patch of skin beneath his throat. His broad shoulders floated with the music, keeping his upper body straight, while his legs, jeans tapering down to his dark boots, kicked their way through the dance. He looked indifferently ahead, at nothing in particular, as though he were concerned only with the dance, carried off by the music to a place where those steps were all that mattered.

Zach drifted toward the far side of the room when the song ended, near the other bar. I spotted him through the crowd of new couples forming on the dance floor. His smile beaming, he leaned in to talk to someone.

"He's a character," Martin said flatly, moving closer to my side.

"What do you mean?"

He gestured with his glass. "Look at the way he works the room. It's as if he knows everybody. As if they're all old friends."

The group around Zach had grown larger. One of them, a slim man in a hat, led him onto the floor. They merged deftly into the moving circle, like a sports car slipping into a rotary.

"He's just acting like a Californian," I said, trying to sound merely observant rather than defensive. "Everyone out here is friendly. At least on the surface."

"Not me!" Martin protested facetiously, eyes wide in mock horror.

"No, not you. You've got too much of that New England reserve."

"Always," he said, straightening his shoulders. His white shirt stood out starkly against the dark paneled wall. We toasted, the beer foaming up into the neck of the bottle before I drank.

Zach passed blindly by us. His partner, though an inch or two shorter, was leading, right hand pressed snugly against Zach's lower back, his pinky dangling over the belt. He gazed sternly over Zach's shoulder, eyes riveted on some imaginary point in the distance. Natalie had taken ballet lessons as a child and later told me how hard it had been to keep her eyes fixed on the same, otherwise unremarkable spot on the wall as she pirouetted. If she struggled to find it after each split-second turn, she would inevitably lose her balance and crumble into a humiliated heap on the studio floor.

"Did you go dancing much in Boston?" Martin asked.

"Once in a while."

As they looped around the far side of the circle, Zach's face finally came into view—his gaze freer, less fixed than his partner's.

"I've never been much of a dancer, though," I added, turning back to Martin. Someone jostled against me, Zach's ice clinking in my hand. "And of course, Adam couldn't bear it."

"Nothing less than a Strauss waltz for him, I suppose."

All I had told Martin about Adam so far was his taste in music and the fact that he'd broken my heart. That was enough. I was learning by Martin's example, his reticence about his own history: the past was dead.

We watched the dance floor through two or three more songs. The breaks between songs were more discernible here than at other clubs, where the beat hardly changed from one piece to another. Though there was still barely a pause in the music, the overall effect was episodic, unlike the hypnotic prolonged sameness of disco or house music. Country songs, after all, were known for telling stories—with beginnings, middles, and ends.

Zach finally emerged from the thickening crowd, winded but still smiling. Retrieving his drink, he laid his other hand on my shoulder. "Thanks," he said, glancing back at the colorful swirl behind him, couples rising and falling with the steady grace of carousel horses. "Sometimes I get so caught up, I lose track of time." He drained the glass in one sip. I had long ago finished my beer.

"You're very good," I said. "I couldn't help noticing."

"Give me a few minutes, and I'll take you out for a test ride." He rattled the ice in the glass, as though to release the soda trapped between the cubes. Gazing disappointedly into the glass, he said, "Can I freshen anyone's drink?"

"No thanks," Martin replied. "Actually, I think it's time I got going. I'm not as young as I used to be."

"You underestimate yourself, Martin." Zach poked Martin's ribs playfully. His gaze drifted smoothly from Martin to me, his smile more cryptic now, as though caught between emotions.

"Anyway," Martin said, "you boys have fun."

"Wait," I said suddenly. "I'm kind of tired, too. I might as well hitch a ride."

"Are you sure?" Martin asked.

Zach's lips fell over gleaming teeth, like a curtain closing on a still-occupied stage.

"Yeah. It was nice meeting you, Zach." I reached out a hand, and he took it warmly in his. I exerted more pressure this time, my palm stiff against his skin.

Outside, in the cold, we raced each other for the car.

"You hungry?" Martin asked, hunched over the wheel as he revved the engine.

We pulled abruptly out of the parking space and toward the intersection. I was still looking back at the door, still hearing a two-step rhythm. "It's kind of late for food, don't you think?"

Martin tapped one hand on the wheel. "I repeat: Are you hungry?"

We turned right on Harrison and I let my stomach answer. "Yes," I said, giggling as I noticed the sensation. "Yes, I am."

"Listen to your body, Neal," Martin said, still watching the road. "If I've taught you nothing else, remember that."

There was an all-night diner on Church Street. I was shocked to see how many people crowded into its booths. In Boston you'd be hard-pressed to buy so much as a doughnut after 10 p.m.

"So, what did you think?" Martin asked when we were settled.

"About what?" I was still studying the menu, trying to resist the temptation for something heavy.

"Have I converted you into a card-carrying cowpoke?" Martin added, a nasal twang to his voice.

I laughed and affected a similar accent. "Maybe, pard'ner. May be."

"Of course, you'll have to work on your form. It's like dancing with a tree, you know."

"Why, thank you, Martin. You say the sweetest things."

I settled on a garden salad. Martin gasped and ordered a cheeseburger and fries.

"I think you made quite an impression on Zach," he said later, stirring sugar into his iced tea.

I felt myself blushing and tried to suppress it—calm breaths to stem the tide of magnesium. "He was just flirting," I said.

Martin didn't respond. The waitress came back with our food and he poured ketchup onto the burger bun.

"How well do you know him?" I asked.

"Not very. Why? Do you need references?"

"I'm just cautious, that's all." I tossed the salad with my fork to spread the dressing evenly.

"He really burned you, didn't he?" Martin said.

"Who?" I speared a slice of cucumber.

"Adam."

I swallowed and stabbed the next bite. "You could say that."

"How long were you together?"

"Adam and I were never exactly together," I told him. "But we dated off and on for a year. He was having trouble making up his mind about things."

"What things?"

I took a long sip of tea. "Boys or girls."

"Oh. Bicoastal, huh? I've never believed in them. The two great myths of American culture—the Easter bunny and bisexuality."

I was grateful for the laugh. "Yeah, well, Adam would disagree."

"Did he ever make up his mind?"

"God knows. I didn't stick around long enough to find out."

"Smart move." He lifted his glass in a toast. "Mixed marriages never work."

"How'd you meet him?" he asked, picking up a french fry. He'd smothered the pale thin sticks in ketchup and had to lick it off his fingers after every bite. He pushed the plate toward me in invitation.

"At Tanglewood." I hesitated, searching for a fry still wearing its mottled skin. "I went there to study the cello, and Adam was teaching a workshop."

My stomach churned. I hadn't told anyone else the details before; it had all seemed too shameful. But I was three time zones away now. It was safe.

"What a bitch, though," Martin said. "Toying with you like that."

"No," I countered, "not at all. Adam's very sweet. He's just a little confused."

"I'll say. What's his girlfriend like?"

"I hardly knew her. We met at a couple of parties. She seemed nice enough."

"Did she know?"

"About us? No, she couldn't have."

"What about him? Did she know about him?"

I took another forkful of greens and tried to identify the song on the jukebox. I hadn't listened to popular music for ages; it could have been the number-one song of the year and I wouldn't know.

"I'm sorry," Martin said, "I'm prying. You have to stop me when I get like this; sometimes I can be extremely rude."

"It's okay." Martin's curiosity was unflagging, but I didn't mind. It might have been my own voice echoing in my head, asking all those questions. Questions I had asked Adam myself, lying beside him, staring into his eyes, trying to reach whatever pain was inside. He had given me his body, freely, without inhibition, but he kept the rest of himself hidden, guarded, as if it were fragile, as if he weren't quite sure he could trust me to treat it gently.

Still, telling Martin all this, going on so much, I couldn't help feeling self-conscious, whiny. Martin never talked about *his* problems—lovers, past or present, issues unresolved. In fact, he slyly deflected my attempts to steer the conversation in that direction. He wanted to keep the focus on me.

I was flattered, but curious. He had fit me into his life so smoothly—always making himself available to show me the sights, to keep me busy on the weekends. It seemed odd that he should have so much free time. He never talked about other friends, never seemed to have other obligations, besides his work.

"I think you should call him," Martin said.

"Adam?"

He smiled slyly and lifted the burger with both hands. "No."

The Rawhide became a Saturday night ritual. Martin was determined to get me in touch with my own feet. "I guess cellists only have rhythm in their fingers," he said as I stumbled into his knees once again.

He taped some music for me—everything from Tammy Wynette to Billy Ray Cyrus—and I practiced the few steps I knew on the kitchen floor, trying not to bump into the stove every time I changed direction.

We saw Zach again the third week. He swept Martin away for a waltz and, when he brought him back to the corner where I stood, eyes down, dreading being asked to dance, he pulled my right hand and led me onto the floor. The music was familiar—Tina Turner, of all things. If she only knew.

"Don't worry," he said, pushing me along the circle. "Martin told me you're new at this. I won't try any fast moves." He winked. His hand was light on my back, holding me at a polite distance.

We sped around the corner to avoid a bottleneck by the bar, and I fell back against his hand. "I gotcha," he said, smiling. It seemed an odd combination—that confident air set against baby-fat cheeks. His fingers fanned out between my shoulder blades, warm and strong, as though imprinting their shape into my skin.

I still couldn't talk while dancing—my feet required all my attention—so I just smiled back, trying not to look nervous, trying not to act like I was on a tightrope rather than a thirty-foot-wide dance floor. When the song ended, he released my back and spun me out. I was shocked to find myself standing right beside Martin.

"Well, if isn't Fred and Ginger," Martin said, lifting his glass in a toast.

A man about Martin's age, mustache graying at the sides, tapped Zach on the shoulder and gestured toward the dance floor. "Sure," Zach said. He smiled back at us briefly and blended into the circle.

"Had enough?" Martin asked. He looked at his watch.

I'd lost track of Zach. It was a fast song and they were already on the other side of the room. "Sure," I said.

Martin put his half-empty glass on the shelf and led me along the side. A crowd was gathered around the billiard table, studying the layout of the balls. A cheer rose when one of them made what must have been a pretty difficult shot.

It was cool outside; the temperature had dropped at least fifteen degrees in the past couple of hours. "The coldest winter I ever spent," Martin said.

"What?"

"A summer in San Francisco. God, Neal, you really have to learn these clichés!"

I laughed, shaking my head. "I will, Mr. Baedeker, I will." My boots tapped noisily on the sidewalk as we made our way to the car. Martin had lent them to me indefinitely, until I decided to commit to country-western and buy my own pair. "It's you," he'd said last week, picking me up in my 501s and a new plaid shirt. "All you need is the hat."

I got paid for staring at the walls of my cubicle. Chin resting in my palm, I would gaze into the gray fabric, waiting for an idea. When someone passed by, I would immediately hunch over some papers on my desk or type random characters onto the screen. Few people understood that staring into space was an essential part of the creative process.

So far, that staring had paid off pretty well. Somehow or other, despite a level of computer illiteracy that would have made the Unabomber proud, I had produced several pieces of ad copy about software that a few months ago would have completely boggled my mind. I considered myself a staunch humanist, above all the jargon and rigmarole of the technological age. But, as I discovered after a few desperate weeks of job hunting, you take what you can get if you expect to survive. And in the mid 1990s, for good or ill, computers were the new gold rush. But marketing is marketing, whether it's software or potato chips: learn what your audience wants, and pretend to give it to them. The hard part was figuring it all out for myself. That was where Diana came in.

Diana, the only other copywriter I'd been able to befriend—or wanted to—had saved my professional life more than once in the past couple of months. After poring over an engineer's opaque description of a product, I would peek over the wall into Diana's cubicle for a reality check. Unlike me, Diana had at least studied computer science in college, so she wasn't floundering nearly as much. She was one of the few technical types I'd ever met who could handle an ordinary human conversation. I teased her that she had missed the nerd seminar in college, the class where they strip you of all social skills and hypnotize you into considering the microchip your best friend and Mr. Spock your undisputed master.

She drew diagrams to explain things. "Okay," I said, huddling in her cube over her latest illustration—a series of boxes linked by dotted lines, "so the CD searches the Web? Without your even knowing it?"

"Exactly," she said. "The user's going to think all this stuff is on the disk itself."

"Isn't that . . .?"

"Misleading?"

I was going to say *unethical,* but I could live with *misleading.*

Diana sat up and massaged the back of her neck, lifting straight black hair that fell lithely over one shoulder. "Not really. Everything's interfacing today; people know that. All they want is the information; they don't care where it comes from."

I still felt a catch in my throat when I heard words like *interface.* One of the challenges of my copy was to avoid jargon. I'd gotten away with it so far: nobody had yet noticed that, in my work, *impact* was only a noun.

"You know what you need?" Diana said, closing a window on her screen. "You need lunch."

I checked my watch. "It's twelve-twenty."

She scoffed, a grating cackle bursting through her nose. "Like anyone's going to notice if we skip out ten minutes early."

"You love to live dangerously, don't you?"

"Is there any other way?" She reached under her desk and pulled her purse up by its long strap. "Come on," she said. "I'm starving."

The elevator zoomed us down to the first floor, nonstop. "Where to?" I asked. Diana was already marching toward Market Street. It was a stupid question, actually. Diana was practically addicted to Big

Macs; she had one at least three times a week, with fries and a shake, usually chocolate. ("We all have our rituals," she'd once said. "So mine's a little unhealthy. At least I don't smoke.")

"So how's your love life?" she asked a few minutes later, licking the excess special sauce off the side of her bun.

"What love life?" I had decided on a Filet-O-Fish today, my attempt at health food. I couldn't get past the first bite, and now I was scooping up french fries by the handful.

"That bad, huh? You should get out more."

"And how are things on your side of the dating scene?" I asked. I loved turning the tables on Diana, poking holes in her Dear Abby veneer.

"It's hardly comparable," she said disdainfully. "Straight men are shits. That's a fact of life. Can't you see I long to live vicariously through you?"

"That's pathetic."

"It wouldn't be if you'd indulge my fantasies by getting a date." Her cheeks hollowed out painfully as she sucked on the straw. She loved her shakes extra thick, though I worried she'd have a stroke from the effort.

Vicarious living was more than a hobby, Diana had told me during my first week on the job. Copywriting was only her day job; she was really an actress, though she'd hardly done any stage work since college. Imagining the hidden lives of her friends was as close as she could get to greasepaint.

"Isn't there anyone?" she asked, finally coming up for air. Her cheeks were flushed, like a swimmer's after a long dive.

"Well, there is a guy I met at the Rawhide a while ago, a friend of Martin's."

Diana poked her head at me, eyes wide in expectation. "Is he cute?"

"I guess you could say that."

"Sounds gorgeous." Diana had a knack for hearing what she wanted to hear.

"Gorgeous is out of my league."

"Don't sell yourself short. You're very good-looking." She turned her bag of french fries upside down to spill out the tinier pieces. "So what's his name?" she asked. "What's he look like? Is he rich?"

"The three most important questions, I take it?"

"Not necessarily in that order."

"Well, he's not rich. He works at Macy's."

"Downtown?" She gripped the table, and her tray nudged mine, my Coke trembling slightly.

"Yes."

"Are you finished?" She gestured at my tray. Her own was already empty except for the crumpled paper and half a shake.

"Yes."

"Good, let's go."

"Where?"

"Don't be a doof," she said. "It's right around the corner." She took both trays and emptied them into the trash. They clattered together in the holder above as I joined her by the door.

"What department?" she asked when we got back to the street. Holding her shake, she angled the straw to get the most out of the cup.

"Men's shoes."

She looked down at my feet. "You could use a new pair."

"No, Diana, this is ridiculous."

"Look, you don't have to buy anything. You can browse, can't you? Besides, wouldn't you love to see him at your feet, squeezing on a pair of wingtips?"

"I can't do this." But we were already at O'Farrell, merging with the crowd on their way into the store.

My stomach protested as we passed tables of bargain neckties on our way to the escalator. This time, it certainly wasn't hunger, though that bite of fish hadn't settled well. I tried to ignore the import of what I was doing, to convince myself, and anyone who might see, that I was merely on an innocent shopping spree. A perfectly normal activity for lunch hour. For Diana, though, it was more than that; it was an opportunity for drama. Everything in Diana's life was an opportunity for drama. Each mix-up at the office provided a chance to play a raging Hedda Gabler; each time she described a date, she became a love-lorn Juliet or a vengeful Glenn Close in *Fatal Attraction*. There was no middle ground for Diana.

"Not bad," she said as the escalator deposited us by the shoes, the polished display shelves against the wall, the well-dressed salespeople. "Sure beats housewares."

"Diana, I can't do this."

"Shut up. I'm going to find you the perfect pair of sandals."

"Sandals?"

"Well, you're playing the martyr; you might as well look the part."

"They don't sell sandals here—" But already she was milling about the sale racks, pretending to look for bargains. I followed her into an aisle, keeping my head low.

"Okay," she whispered, pretending to inspect a burgundy loafer, "so which one is he?"

"I don't even know if he's here. I've been keeping my eye on *you*."

"Well, for God's sake, take a look."

I peered through one of the racks, overwhelmed by the smell of leather. A middle-aged woman in a navy suit carried two shoeboxes toward a row of leather chairs and settled them beside a tall man, bent over his stockinged feet. Zach wasn't here; he was probably at lunch, too. We could get away safely.

"He's not here," I said, taking Diana's hand. Her wrist was tiny; my fingers closed easily around it. "Let's go, I'll buy you a frozen yo-gurt." Bribery, that should work.

"Are you sure?" she asked, peering around anxiously.

"Yes, now come on." It was fun to have the tables turned, to lead her somewhere against her will, but somehow it wasn't quite as easy. Her heels clicked against the linoleum as we stepped off the carpet and headed for the escalator.

"Aren't you going to say hello?"

I looked up, into Zach's eyes—nearly translucent in the glaring light of the store—and dropped Diana's hand. "Hi," I said feebly.

"Can I interest you in a pair of white bucks?"

Diana giggled beside me—a high-pitched, effortful sound.

"How are you, Neal?"

"Fine. We were just browsing. It's our lunch hour."

"Oh, I forgot you worked downtown," he said. "Maybe we could have lunch together sometime."

"Sure, that would be nice."

Diana coughed. Even now, she refused to be subtle.

"This is my friend Diana. Diana Chen, Zach—"

"Reddison."

I smiled; his own was contagious. "Reddison."

They shook hands, but Zach kept his eyes on mine. The grumbling in my stomach had passed.

"So," Diana said, "you work in this department?"

"For the time being. They move me around a lot. I figure they're either grooming me for manager or trying to get rid of me." He bounced back on his heels, accentuating his height. Beside Diana's barely five-foot frame, he looked like Coit Tower.

Ignoring the awkward silence, I made a show of looking at my watch. "Listen, we've really got to get back. It was great seeing you again."

"You, too," he said. "And nice meeting you, Diana." He winked, but I wasn't sure at whom.

Diana got on the escalator first, but turned around to wave. "Will you behave?" I grunted, clenching my teeth.

"God, Neal, he's outrageously cute! And he likes you, I can tell."

"Please, Di."

"Yikes, those eyes. They're so—mysterious. I could stare into them all day."

"He might like that. Why don't you go back and try?"

"The truth is," she said, "he only had eyes for you." Still riding backward to face me, she didn't notice her step approaching the bottom, and she stumbled a bit before settling on the floor.

"I say go for it," she said as we emerged back into the sunshine of Stockton Street.

"You always say go for it. It's your motto."

"And what's wrong with that? God, when I think of all those nerds we work with—pathetic, just slogging through the day, poor slobs. No imagination, no *desire*."

"Desire," I echoed.

"What's wrong with desire?"

"Nothing. It just sounds so clinical."

"Okay then, lust."

"Somehow, that doesn't really help."

"Oh come on, you mean you wouldn't like to jump those bones we just saw up there?" She adjusted her purse strap, pulling it in toward her neck.

"Diana, that's not quite the approach I take to relationships."

"Oh," she said, "relationships. Well, now we're in a whole different ballpark. I think you're jumping the gun there, Neal. Try a simple date first."

"Since when was a date ever simple?"

"I've dated several simpletons myself." She hooted out a laugh as we stopped at a red light. "Just keep your options open, Neal. There's a whole world out there."

"Just waiting for me."

"Just waiting for you."

All afternoon, I had trouble concentrating. I stared as disconsolately at Diana's drawing as I had at the wall. All the pieces were there, but I couldn't connect them. So much for interface: I had no idea how anything related to anything else.

I spun around and studied the skyline as the floors of the surrounding buildings vanished one by one behind the thickening fog. I was rehearsing my opening line: *How about dinner Saturday?* No, too forward. *Do you have any dinner plans for Saturday?* No, that was prying; he'd be embarrassed to say no. Maybe I could use my ignorance as leverage, seek his help in getting to know the city. *Know any good restaurants?*

But first I had to get his number. Maybe Martin had it. I began to dial the flower shop, but stopped myself after four digits. I wasn't sure I wanted to tell Martin just yet; already, I could imagine the litany of questions. No, I thought, I'll tell him after the fact. There was no point in blowing the whole thing out of proportion, before anything had even happened. Maybe Zach would turn me down.

But the look in his eyes at the store had suggested otherwise. His eyes had pinned me to the spot, locked with my own. It could have been our hands that touched, or our thighs; it had felt that physical.

I poked my head over the cubicle wall. Diana was gazing intently at her monitor, furiously pressing keys. The rapid click of the keyboard seemed more appropriate for a computer game than whatever she was supposed to be working on.

"Hey," I said, "have you caught Pac-Man yet?"

She abruptly stopped typing and turned toward me, poking the bridge of her glasses to keep them in place. "No," she sighed. "Like all men, he's always one step ahead of me." She leaned back and stretched out her arms, arching her wrists—an exercise she'd developed for preventing carpal tunnel. "And what's up with you?" she asked. "Zach, I hope."

"Do you remember his last name?"

"Sure, it was Red something. Redland? Redbone?"

"Reddison." I slapped the top of the dividing wall. Memos and postcards rippled. Someone on the other side gasped, as if she thought we were having an earthquake.

"Yeah. You gonna call him?"

"Tonight," I said. "Right now, I'll just call information for the number."

"Break a leg."

As I sank back into my cubicle, the insistent clicking resumed on Diana's side of the wall.

I threw my things onto the sofa as soon as I got home and took several deep breaths. If I didn't get this over with right away, I'd never do it, and I was determined not to spend the entire evening rebuilding courage that I had had and lost.

"Here goes," I said aloud, gripping the telephone. There was a light flashing on the machine beside it. I never had messages this early. My family called only on weekends, to save money, and Martin knew my schedule too well to call before the evening. I pressed the button and waited. The tape took several seconds to rewind.

"Hi, Neal. This is Zach, your friendly neighborhood shoe salesman and two-stepper. I hope you don't mind, I asked Martin for your number. I was just wondering if you'd like to have a drink with me sometime." There was a brief pause. "God, I hate machines. Usually. But sometimes they come in handy. I don't generally call virtual strangers for dates. It's a lot easier talking to a machine." He left his number—the one I'd already memorized—and seemed to hesitate again before hanging up. As if he were thinking of a way to erase the message.

I let the phone settle back down and dropped myself onto the sofa. Now, knowing for sure that he'd say yes, I was even more terrified. My stomach howled; I could taste the Filet-O-Fish again, the tang of tartar sauce. I swallowed hard, squirmed around on the sofa, and dialed.

The standing crowd at Café Flore had already spilled into the courtyard, everyone scouring the tables for a vacancy. I ordered a drink and wandered around inside. A couple in jeans and T-shirts got up from a corner table just as I passed by. Sliding in behind them, I laid my cup on the tabletop as though staking a claim, and counted it as a good omen. The table afforded me a view of the courtyard entrance, so I would have no trouble spotting Zach.

I'd spent half of Friday night on the phone. Not with Zach; our conversation had been over in five minutes. His shyness on the machine replaced by a businesslike tone, he had asked if I were free tonight and then we had quickly arranged where and when to meet. Chitchat was inappropriate; near-strangers have little more than chitchat, so we might as well save it for the actual date.

I had barely hung up when Martin called, wanting all the details, none of which even existed yet. I almost laughed aloud at the irony of my short-lived desire to keep it from him. "I felt so strange," he said, "giving him your number without checking first. To tell you the truth, I can't believe I did it. I'd kill someone if they did that to me."

"It's okay, Martin, I haven't put out a hit on you yet. I decided to see how the date went first."

"Well, I see my sarcasm's rubbing off on you. But direct it elsewhere, dear; you don't have enough friends in this town yet to start antagonizing them." He paused for dramatic effect. "Did I hear you say 'date'?" he asked, softly now, almost indifferent.

"Tomorrow night," I told him. "Coffee."

"Coffee is good," he said. "Less of a commitment. If it doesn't work out, you've only invested half an hour and a little caffeine."

"Your optimism is stupefying."

"Hey, what about the Rawhide?" he asked with sudden disappointment.

"Guess I'll have to skip this week's lesson."

"Unless you two end up there after coffee. I could meet you."

"On our first date? Isn't that like taking your mother to the prom?" I twirled the phone cord around my finger, like the knot in a noose.

"Okay then, call me after. I'll be waiting by the phone."

"Martin—"

"Just call."

"You'd think I was going out with Jack the Ripper or something. Should I be home by midnight or do you want to invest in pumpkin seeds?"

"Just call."

"Yes, ma'am." If I'd had a videophone, I'd have saluted.

In the café, I took off my jacket and laid it beside me on the bench. A cool breeze blew through the open doors, but the coffee had already begun to warm me. I was still sensitive to the chill, which apparently went unnoticed by the laughing groups on the other side of the window, lounging at outside tables.

Suddenly, a chair scraped across the floor in front of me. Zach stood before it, one hand clutching the top. "Prime real estate," he said. "You must have got here early." His hair, a halo of lush locks, was windblown and all the better for it. Dark strands spilled out of place around the temples, falling onto chill-pink cheeks, giving him the air of a mischievous boy who'd stayed out playing long after his mother had called him indoors.

I stifled the urge to stand to greet him. "Not long," I said, forcibly relaxing against the stiff bench. "I just got lucky."

He smiled, white dimples slicing the pink like a knife cutting into meat. "Let's hope your luck holds." He squirmed his arms free of his jacket—black calfskin—and draped it over the chair. "Want anything?" he asked.

"No thanks. I'm fine."

He nodded and headed toward the bar. It was still too bright outside for the window to cast back a reflection, but I patted down my hair as best I could. I lifted one arm to hang it over the back of the bench, striving for nonchalance.

Suddenly, the room seemed to have taken on a dreamlike quality, two-dimensional, as if I were watching everything on a screen rather than being a part of it. The laughter in the far corner sounded hollow, monotonous, less a combination of voices than a single one amplified, in harmony only with itself. I stifled a sudden desire to bolt, through the doors, past the happy couples in the courtyard, onto the darkening street, home, home to safety and solitude.

"I'm glad you could make it." Zach sat across the table, his figure lending weight to the room, defining the space. "It's pretty busy here tonight."

"Do you come here a lot?"

"No." He scrunched up his chin dismissively. "Every once in a while, usually in the afternoon, when I'm shopping or something. It's a nice quiet place; you don't get hassled."

I imagined that Zach got "hassled" a lot—by men who couldn't keep their eyes or their hands off him. I looked around the room, searching out envious, competitive glances. "How long have you lived here?" I asked, turning back. I found myself watching his mouth for the answer. It was too hard to look into his eyes; they seemed dangerous.

"A couple of years now."

"After college?" Immediately, the question seemed obvious, a transparent attempt to find out how old he was.

He hesitated, finally smiled. The dimples again. "I never went to college," he said. Something in his tone belied the smile—as if he were afraid I'd judge him. "So, what brought you out here?"

His evasiveness piqued my curiosity. Not going to college seemed more important to him than to me, though it did make him different from the other men I'd known. College defined a period in people's lives; I wanted to know what defined his, what he had done while I was sitting in a library, scanning poetry and practicing chords.

"Wanderlust," I said. I could be mysterious, too.

"There's a lot of that going around." He lifted his glass. I couldn't tell what he was drinking—something bright red, a wedge of lemon bobbing as he sipped.

"You, too?"

He threw his head back and sighed. "I've had my share of bumming around. I hate being tied down. Or I did."

"What changed you?"

"Nothing yet. I just feel like it's time, you know? I'd like to stay put for a while, get my shit together."

"I know the feeling."

We were silent for a while, nursing our drinks, gazing around the room as the light outside dimmed, blending the shadows and murmurs in the courtyard. From time to time, our eyes met and I would be tempted to speak, to break a silence I deemed uncomfortable merely because it was silence. But the way his eyes smiled back at me—probing, oddly expressive—precluded words. He didn't have to answer my questions for me to understand him. I could get to know him simply by looking into his eyes.

"Are you hungry?" he said at last, his drink down to the lemon wedge and slivers of ice.

"Sure."

"There's a nice place across the street. Let's try that."

He led me outside, into the bracing air. We rocked side by side on the curb, waiting for the light to change, trying to keep warm. The coldest winter.

I can't remember what we said to each other over dinner, what remarks we passed on the food, the waitress, the view of Market Street and the determined figures marching past the window. I don't recall how the conversation progressed, from his life to mine and back again. The words seemed insignificant at the time.

When I did manage to focus on his words, I heard about his work, his past, his dreams. Macy's was only temporary, he said. What he really wanted was to help people, maybe become a social worker. He knew he could make a difference, he said, if he set his mind to it.

I believed him. Maybe it was his eyes that I believed; I saw now that they were the same color as the late afternoon San Francisco sky, when the fog begins to steal in and wash away the sun.

He asked me questions—about my own past, my dreams. I made something up each time, some simple, undebatable way to explain myself. I can't recall or imagine now what I might have said, under the spell of those eyes. Probably the same sort of meaningless tripe I'd used a hundred times before, unaware, thinking I was speaking the truth. It wasn't until much later—after Zach, but somehow through him—that I realized the truth, that I was able to see my past as more than a string of unrelated events, my future as more than a nebulous mystery over which I had no control.

He suggested a walk after dinner, to work off the calories. The sky had darkened by then, navy above the neon signs and the palm trees that bisected the street. Same-sex couples strolled by in either direction, holding hands publicly—simply because they could, because here it was safe. It made up for all the other times, the other places where it wasn't safe, where it couldn't even be thought of. At a corner, waiting for the light, I slid toward Zach, to make way for a laughing couple just reaching the curb, oblivious to anything but each other, and my hand grazed his for a moment, knuckles touching. I slid both hands into my pockets as we began to cross the street.

Zach didn't seem to notice. His eyes staring dead ahead, matter-of-factly, he continued, as if he were part of the pavement, the bodies brushing past, the crisp air that once again colored his cheeks—as if it were all his medium, an environment in which he could breathe without thinking, as if he'd been born to it.

At Church Street, the trolley clattered past, the steady light inside cutting a swath through the evening. "You know," he said, stopping on the corner, "we're kind of near my place. Would you like to come up for a drink? It would get us out of this cold."

"Sure," I said. "Lead the way."

In Boston, I might have said no, called it a night right there on the street corner, given him a quick pat on the back, and run for the bus. That was the way you did things in Boston: slowly. But here, the rules were different. I was beginning to learn that the stories I had heard about San Francisco were true.

I'd never wanted to go home with a stranger before. I'd always been looking for love; sex wasn't enough. I'd been afraid, as afraid of the spontaneity of the moment as most men were of the intimacy that came later. While they trembled at the thought of opening their hearts, my heart pounded at the thought of opening my pants.

It was a tiny apartment, a third-floor studio without much of a view. A blue futon sat in a convertible frame, facing the window, a TV, a boombox. Unframed posters adorned the walls, curling up at the edges: a bare-chested young man peering out from a black-and-white landscape that might have been a jeans ad; beside him Madonna, in close-up, pouting for the camera.

Zach tossed his jacket onto the futon and busied himself in the kitchen, which was separated from the main room only by a counter. I headed for the bay window and looked down at the street.

"Soda, or something more interesting?" he asked. I heard bottles clinking together on the counter.

"What constitutes interesting?"

He laughed. "Trust me."

A small bookcase rose to just below the windowsill. The books inside leaned into one another haphazardly, a few turned completely on their sides. I casually scanned the titles—a couple of Stephen Kings, several trendy gay novels, a dictionary. On the bottom shelf, a Mapplethorpe collection leaned disconcertingly against the *Tibetan Book of the Dead.*

In a moment, Zach met me at the window, two frosty glasses in his hands. "What's this?" I asked, taking one. The drink was pale orange, ice cubes climbing like steps inside the glass. It tasted sweet, refreshing. I couldn't trace any alcohol, which always makes me nervous. The easiest things to get drunk on.

"Like it?" he asked.

"Sure. Now are you going to reveal the secret?"

He laughed again. "It's no secret. It's just cranberry and grapefruit juice. With a little soda."

I felt my face flush as I laughed. "Here I was expecting a wallbanger or something."

"No," Zach said, leading me to the couch, "my wallbanger days are over." He set his glass on the coffee table and dashed around the corner. "Have a seat," he said. "I'll be right back."

I sat, sinking into the fold of the futon. Zach's coat slipped off the back, one arm settling limply into my lap. As I lifted it away, my hand lingered on the soft leather, like a baby's skin. It still held the cold from outside, but the lining was warm, heavy with Zach's scent. I folded the coat and laid it neatly over the back of the futon.

"Let me take that," Zach said, reappearing. He pulled the coat away and tossed it onto a chair on the other side of the room, where mine already lay, finally no longer alone.

The futon frame creaked as Zach settled beside me. "It feels good to be home," he said. "I've been running around all day."

"Did you work?"

"Oh yeah. Macy's is having another of their weekly semiannual sales. I barely had time to shower and change before meeting you."

"I'm sorry. We should have made it later."

"Are you kidding?" He tapped my hand, and his fingers, cold from the glass, closed around mine. They warmed each other.

It had been so much simpler with Adam. By the time I touched him, I already knew I was in love. If I didn't touch him, I thought, I would die.

"How long have you known Martin?" Zach asked. His voice startled me. My fingers twitched beneath his, but his heavy hand kept them in place.

"A couple of months."

"Oh," he said, "for some reason I thought you guys had known each other in Boston." Zach leaned forward to return his glass to the coffee table. When he sat back up, he was a few inches closer, his shoulder almost touching mine.

"His sister," I said. "I knew his sister." My throat was dry; the drink had done nothing for my thirst.

"Oh yeah, you mentioned that. Still, you and Martin seem so close, like you've known each other for years. That must be nice," Zach offered, "feeling so close to someone that fast." He was nearly whispering, and when I turned I saw that his gaze had drifted to a point midway across the room, hovering somewhere over the planks of the hardwood floor. His cheeks, having surrendered their pink tone, now looked white and fleshy—I had a sudden image of the Pillsbury dough boy, cherubic and ticklish. I leaned in and pressed my lips softly against his cheek.

He turned, startled. I had caught him off guard; he'd been expecting to make the first move. He smiled a grateful surprise, not quite enough to bring out the dimples, and gently caressed my face. His lips broke against mine, abruptly warm and fresh, his tongue teasing between my teeth, and I found myself falling, Zach holding my back to lower me softly onto the futon, his kisses spreading along my cheek, around my ear, down to the base of my neck, into the hollow of my throat.

We didn't say a word, hardly even a moan of encouragement or direction. His hands explored my body, his lips pressing against my flesh. At one point, when we were still half-dressed, he reached for the light and the room was suddenly swept into darkness, a single streetlamp flickering outside the window. Just enough light for me to see his head moving down my chest, thick hair spilling onto my belly like waves.

In the darkness I moved against him. We slipped off the futon, onto the cool wood of the floor, constantly changing position, grasping at limbs. Our hands entwined—a finger darted into my mouth and I closed my teeth softly around it, shocked to feel the pain myself. Eyes shut, I read his body like Braille, feeling for the grooves where muscle met bone, tracing the prickly hairs that grew thicker toward his crotch. My mind shut off at some point, only my body calling the shots, or Zach's. Beneath his touch, I writhed, transported, as if I had never felt another man's hands, never tasted another man's lips, as if the new world I was discovering really were new. For a moment, in the welcome darkness, I was a pilgrim, reaching out.

I tried sleeping at Zach's place, but I've never been good at sharing a bed with strangers, particularly a bed that small. His arm draped across my chest, Zach had fallen asleep almost instantly, snoring delicately beside my ear. His arm gradually grew heavier and heavier, until it turned into a stone weight, an anchor pulling me down to the sea floor. I focused on that image—being underwater seemed so peaceful, soothing. I let my whole body slip under the waves, feet first, everything going heavy and cold inch by inch—numb, silent. I got all the way up to my shoulders before I accepted the futility of the effort. My eyes had by then grown accustomed to the dark, and I could make out every shape in Zach's apartment—our jackets intertwined on the distant chair, the cereal boxes that lined the top of the refrigerator. And beside me Zach lay, face scrunched into the pillow, eyelashes still against his cheek, as if he were too tired even for dreams. His wide shoulders took up more than half the bed, naked above the sheet that had dropped to his lower back.

I squirmed beside him, finally tried to lift his arm with mine. My left arm, pinned under him, was the only part of me that had managed to fall asleep; it now tingled sharply as I turned.

Zach's breath caught suddenly, but when he spoke his voice betrayed no trace of sleep, as if he were merely continuing a conversation that had ceased over an hour ago. "You okay?" he asked, eyes still closed, though he helped me lift his arm and place it on his side.

"I need to go home," I whispered, as if there were someone asleep in the room, as if this were a dream-Zach who was talking to me.

"Sure," he said, wriggling onto his back. "First-night jitters, I know how it is."

Somehow, I couldn't believe that he really knew how it was. An instant later, before I'd even found my underwear, he was snoring again. If Zach had ever felt this way, he had long since gotten over it.

Finally dressed, I kissed his forehead on the way out, crinkling leather momentarily interrupting the rhythm of his snores. Asleep, his face was calm, precious and innocent as a child's, a little boy without a care in the world, with nothing to keep him awake through the night.

My own bed wasn't much more of a comfort. As I slipped between the sheets, so much cooler than the ones Zach and I had warmed all night, it felt as if this were the foreign world, another environment to get used to. Waiting for sleep, I scanned the room, comparing the shadows to the ones I had memorized earlier. The angles were sharper here, everything more neatly in place, predictable. I lay stiffly, reconstructing the night—the feel of Zach's fingers on my body, the taste of the sweat at the nape of his neck. There were no sounds to remember, no words. We had made love in silence, not even a name to separate us.

And finally, as if recalling each square inch of Zach's body were my equivalent of counting sheep, I drifted off, my own sleep just as undisturbed by dreams.

I waited until morning to play the answering machine, not having noticed the insistently flashing light when I'd stumbled home at nearly two o'clock. By ten, my mind was clear enough to hear the messages, to construct ways to explain myself. Martin had called twice, burning with curiosity.

I called him after a quick breakfast. The word *hello* was barely out of my mouth when he asked, "Feel like going out?" I stumbled for an excuse. "Dress casually," he said. "I'll be right over."

For the past several weeks, Martin had been an irrepressible tour guide, dragging me from one neighborhood to another—to get it over with as quickly as possible, he said, so I could feel like a native. His tour of the city wound up, appropriately enough, at Land's End. From here on, there was only ocean.

"This isn't like me, you know," I said, following him along the rocks. My words were nearly erased by the crashing of the waves beneath us. "I never sleep with people on the first date."

"Never say never, darling. Those things can come back to haunt you." He rounded a corner of the cliff, nimbly hopping from one rock to another. I followed slowly, terrified that one of the rocks would give and send me hurtling to my death. But Martin pressed on, never looking back, seldom looking down, as if he were omnipotent, blessed, as if falling weren't even a possibility.

"Why are we doing this?" I asked, my sneaker scuffing the ground and sending a family of pebbles careening down the cliffside.

"For adventure!" Martin called out, still forging ahead. We were facing into the wind, and his words whipped back as though rejected by the path.

Struggling, I righted myself with the help of a gnarled branch and continued behind him. I decided to stop looking down. Martin's eyes were riveted on where he wanted to go, not on the danger; that was what seemed to keep him safe. The wind, colder with each turn as we got closer to the water, rippled my shirt, my nipples hard against the cotton. I began to long for a sweater.

The landscape finally flattened out, just where the vegetation grew dense. Martin stopped on the edge of the cliff and gazed out at the sea. Breathless, I stood beside him. I was about to speak when a violent gust of wind came off the water and tossed Martin's hair across his face. Still focusing on the distance, he pulled back the hair and I spotted a moistness at the corner of his eye. The wind had brought tears.

"The nude beach is down there," he said, pointing.

Beneath us, large pieces of driftwood cast jagged shadows on the empty gray sand, visually echoing the rocks that broke the waves just off shore. It was too cold today, too overcast, to bring anyone onto the beach. The whole, colorless setting struck me as a still life, an Ansel Adams photograph.

"Were you careful?" he asked, squinting toward the horizon. Sharp lines darted out toward his temple. His skin seemed more fragile in certain spots, brown and worn.

"Of course," I told him. "I'm not crazy." Suddenly, the evening came back to me, as powerful as the waves that struck the rocks beneath us, leaving their dark shadow on the sand as they retreated. I saw Zach's body and mine, moving together, as if from a distance—an observer on the ceiling, behind the bed, crouched on a windowsill, examining every angle. I had never thought much about danger before; Adam had been so undeniably safe, and the others so unimportant. I hadn't given it much thought last night, either, until my mouth drew too close to Zach's cock at the end, until his come dripped off his side and onto the wrinkled sheet. Zach had quickly produced warm towels for our bellies, but the wet spot remained, a stain between us, shockingly cold whenever my leg grazed it during the night.

"So what's he like?"

"Zach?" I paused. I hadn't thought of how to describe him. "You've known him longer than I have."

"Ah, but not as well. I told you, I've hardly ever seen the man outside of the Rawhide. For all I know, he could be four foot six and the rest is just cowboy boots."

"He's closer to six-one," I said.

"Barefoot?"

"We had a very nice time," I said, ignoring his campy wit. "He's interesting."

"For a shoe salesman." Martin sighed melodramatically. "Oh God, Neal, how are you ever going to get ahead? Your mother and I wanted you to marry a lawyer!" He picked up a stone and tossed it out over the cliff. "So onto the important point, how is he in bed?"

"Martin."

"Oh come on, Neal, it's written all over your face. You look like you've just been fucked by the Forty-Niners. All of them."

"It was nice," I said, hoping to kill the subject. "He's a very gentle lover."

Martin sighed. "I never would have guessed. Zach always seemed the brash type to me. Sure of himself."

"What's wrong with that?"

"Nothing. Look, Neal, I told you, I don't know him very well. Just be careful, that's all."

"We were."

"I don't just mean in bed. Men like Zach—well, he's very attractive."

I remembered Zach's profile in the moonlight. "Yes," I said, "he is."

"What's his sexual history?"

"I don't know. We haven't exchanged résumés yet. I'll call his references tomorrow."

Turning away from the cliff, Martin led me along a winding path through overgrown trees and bushes. The notorious drought was clearly over. He pushed a thick branch out of the way and held it for me, to avoid having it fly back and slap me in the face. The air was thicker here, the closest thing to humidity I had yet experienced in San Francisco.

"Where are we going?" I asked.

He turned around and shushed me, his face twisted in disbelief—as though I'd just burped in a theater or used the wrong fork at a state dinner. I'd never thought of silence as de rigueur in the wilderness.

On the other side of a clump of shrubs, a man stood, surveying the area, a khaki baseball cap protecting his head. He had the look of a man who had lost something, a hunter whose prey had suddenly vanished. His eyes passed indifferently over Martin and me, and we moved on, Martin just as indifferent, me self-consciously slinking away. A few feet along, through a narrow hole in the trees, I saw another man perched on a white blanket, his arm resting on a raised knee. He looked out at us, as anxious yet stone-faced as the last one.

"Well," Martin muttered sotto voce, "at least someone's maintaining tradition."

"Just like that?" I asked. "You mean he just sits there all day until someone comes along?"

He nodded. "Looks like it's going to be a long wait, too. God, in the old days you could be in and out of here in fifteen minutes."

I tried to picture Martin sitting on a blanket in the middle of the trees, waiting. Somehow the image wouldn't hold. I kept imagining a picnic basket, champagne, strawberries. Martha Stewart goes cruising.

"No," he said, reading my mind, "I didn't come here often. Usually just to watch. It was entertaining, actually, like a dance. There was someone behind every tree, crouched under every shrub. Like they grew there." He looked around, but we were greeted by only greenery, the wind slipping through the branches.

"Did I ever tell you about Gary?" he asked. He didn't wait for an answer. He knew he had never told me about anyone. "He used to love this place. He should have been a gardener!" Martin laughed, immediately catching himself and stifling the sound to a low grumble. "He died in '85," he said, nearly whispering, and I realized suddenly that the silence wasn't to ensure privacy, but to honor the dead.

Martin led me back to the cliff. It was safer by the edge, where the wind could swallow his words. "Gary was the third one," he said. "I remember that because it was back in the days when I could still count them."

I had no idea what to say, what to do if he suddenly broke. I had never seen Martin like this, so contemplative, so serious. I'd begun to think he wasn't capable of such feelings, that they'd all been buried under the sarcasm, the camp, buried too deep to reach. I stepped closer, close enough to catch him if he fell.

"One after another," he said. "At first. Then it was in twos and threes. You know what they say about celebrities, right, how they die in threes? Well, try fives, sixes. It got so I was afraid to answer the phone. I was afraid to *touch* the phone, as if the virus could travel through the wire."

He laughed again. "I don't know why I'm telling you all this. It's this place, I guess. I shouldn't have brought you here. It's haunted."

"It's beautiful."

He turned to me, dark eyes peering curiously at my innocence, and then he looked around, smiling. "Yes, it's very beautiful," he said, discovery in his voice.

"You don't have to tell me this, Martin."

"Oh, I'm not even sure I'm telling you. Maybe I'm just talking. Maybe I'm delivering a long-delayed eulogy."

On the beach, a flock of seagulls was fighting over something—fish, seaweed, a candy wrapper. Their screeches echoed up the cliffside.

"I used to wonder why I wasn't sick, too. Everyone else was positive, everyone else was dropping like flies, people I'd known for years, people I'd slept with. It didn't make sense that I should be exempt. And it didn't seem fair." He paused. "Maybe this is the punishment," he said. "I get to stand around and watch it all fade away. I get to come back here and be insulted by the beauty."

After a silent moment, I found myself looking around with the same intensity, trying to imagine the sights that Martin could conjure from memory. It was so desolate out here now. Despite all the green that had sprung up, it seemed as dead here, in the cold, as the men who had once prowled among the trees. I fought a desperate urge to run back to the break in the thicket, to see if the man with the blanket was still waiting. I looked around for the other one, to point him the way.

Looking back, I tend to see us in bed—Zach's bed. In the beginning, it was always Zach's bed. He slept on the left, nearer the window, so the morning light would shine directly onto his face and wake him gently. He hated alarm clocks, even radios; it was more natural, he said, to wake with the sun. Life grew stressful enough as the day progressed; there was nothing to be gained by waking up to Bon Jovi.

Actually, we got little sleep in those days, up deep into the night, making love, talking. I never knew what time we finally settled in for sleep; the only clock in the apartment was in the kitchen, its hands invisible in the dark. I'm not even sure I can say that we ever really settled in. After sex, after our bodies and words were spent, Zach would snuggle in, his back against my chest, and I would hold him, measuring each breath, each contraction of his thick stomach muscles. One arm around his middle, the other under his neck, I would pull him against me, stealing his warmth, my cock once again rising and pressing into his flesh. Before long, I would be nibbling his ear as he wriggled beside me. We could go on like this for hours, too tired to do much more than softly play at sex. It was no act of volition that drew us into sleep, but sheer exhaustion, the rhythm of our rolling bodies finally matching the rhythm of dreams.

Zach used his entire body for sex, his cock no more erogenous than the inside of an elbow, the soft webbing between his toes, the tiny scar that ran along his thigh. He welcomed every touch, the slight squirming of his body the only clue I needed for where to go, what to do next. His eyes were always closed, head thrown back, as if he were imagining a different world, a world that was all flesh, all touch. Even when he explored my body, I could never see his eyes. He kept his head down, never turning toward my face, never willing to jeopardize his concentration. Adam's eyes had always been turned pleadingly up to mine, searching out my pleasure, to satisfy himself that he was doing it right. Zach didn't need my approval; when he made love to me, there was only one body in the room—four hands, two cocks, two tongues, but all connected, all one.

"How do you do it?" I asked, whispering into the stillness.

Spent for the third time that night, he lay on his back. He laughed, stretching his arms up into the air. His fingers disappeared into the darkness. "I don't think about it," he said.

"Maybe that's the secret," I confessed. "I can't *stop* thinking about it."

"You think too much," he said, rolling onto his side, facing me at last.

"It's a vicious circle," I told him. "I try not to think, but then I find myself thinking about not thinking. It's not something you can will into action."

"Exactly." He tapped my nose and let his finger fall gently down past my lips, finally swerving away at the chin. I could hear the soft scratch of my beard against his skin; it was my second consecutive night at his place, and I hadn't shaved.

"You need to shut it off," he said. "Stop interpreting everything. Just feel it."

"I don't know how."

"Do you know how to ride a bike?"

"Of course."

"Explain it to me." He arched his back, snuggling closer.

"Well, you . . ."

"Go on."

"You maintain your balance by moving."

"And how do you start moving? Without falling off?"

I was stumped. "You just do."

The comforter shifted noisily as he shrugged beneath it. "Case closed."

I tried to take Zach's advice. Like him, I shut my eyes when he touched me, so that we'd be seeing the same darkness. I let the sensations ripple through me—the brush of skin on my ankle, the wet flick of a tongue tracing my chest. I tried to just feel, but all the while I found myself picturing the scene. There were no simple sensations; they were Zach's fingers that tickled my side, Zach's lips that encircled my earlobe. My body surrendered to his touch, but my mind held on, tenaciously, unwilling to cede control. When the first tremor of orgasm stirred, I pulled instinctively away—not ready yet, not willing. I wanted more. With Zach, I always wanted more.

Those first weeks mesh in memory, like the delicate strands of a spider's web. I can't trace a chronological line through them—this is when we did such and such, this is the first time I said *I love you.* Each attempt at reconstruction veers off suddenly with the arrival of an image, a word, something to thrust me into another time, and eventually beyond those idyllic weeks, into the whirlpool that our lives became only a few months later. I picture Zach in his baseball cap, the almost imperceptible orange merging of the *S* and the *F,* and abruptly, uninvited, another image cuts in—Zach, hair greasy and unkempt, staring off, mute, not even registering my presence.

But in those early days, when our bodies and souls were still new to each other, they couldn't be ignored. On those long nights in bed, the nights that on weekends stretched into mornings, even afternoons, Zach's body defined the world for me. Whatever wasn't me, was him, for there was nothing else. Only us, only the oasis of his bed and the sunlight creeping in and, just as unnoticed, creeping out.

Zach loved breakfast. "It's Kansas," he said, puttering around the kitchen, terry cloth robe flapping behind him as he swerved from refrigerator to counter to stove. "The farmer's life: get up early, fill your stomach with lead, and work in the fields all day."

"You worked on a farm?" I asked, realigning the silverware. He had set the table while I was in the shower, the knife beside the fork, the spoon a poor orphan.

"A little," he said. "I spent the summers at my grandparents' place in the country."

"A real farm?"

He giggled, poking at the bacon strips with a long-handled fork. The grease popped like muffled firecrackers. "Don't I look like a country boy to you?" he asked, each word spilling through an affected drawl. He spun around, rolled up his sleeve, and displayed a thick, rounded bicep.

"You can till my field any day, pardner."

"Why thank ye, ma'am." Letting the sleeve fall back to his wrist, he returned to the bacon.

"I'm just warning you," I said, "anything heavier than Corn Flakes makes me throw up. I'm not a morning person."

"You are now," he sang out, hoisting the skillet off the burner.

I managed to hold down two pieces of French toast and one slice of bacon before pushing the plate away. "Delicious," I said, leaning back in my chair. If I maintained this angle, my belly felt lighter; sitting upright, I would be overwhelmed by the heaviness. I reached for the orange juice, hoping citric acid might burn away the food.

"You eat like a bird," he said, swirling a last piece of toast in a mixture of syrup and bacon grease.

"What can I say? I'm a city boy." I carried the dirty dishes into the kitchen and laid them in the sink. As I waited for the water to get hot,

Zach came up behind me, placed his own dishes atop mine, and reached around me to shut off the spigot.

"Let them wait," he said, burrowing his nose into my neck. His breath smelled of maple, his lips slightly sticky on my skin. Fully clothed, I leaned back against him. His robe was open; I could feel him through my jeans. I spun awkwardly around and kissed him.

"So tell me about Kansas," I said, drawing away for a moment.

"It's flat." He pulled at the collar of my T-shirt, stretching it toward my shoulder to make room for his tongue.

"Do you have a large family?"

"Hundreds." He pulled the shirt out of my jeans, cold fingers stinging my belly.

"Are you the oldest?"

"Older than the world." Now he was working on the belt. I had just come half an hour ago, I wasn't ready for this.

"I'm serious, Zach." I was facing the clock, thick black numbers proclaiming the speed of time that, in bed, had passed so slowly. It was after eleven already. An entire weekend spent below the waist. I leaned against the sink and pulled my shirt back down, fingers entangling with his. "I want to know."

He lifted his head from my neck with a sigh. "Why?" he said, eyes closed again, briefly, as if he were counting to ten. "What does my childhood have to do with anything?"

"I just want to know about you, that's all. I want to know everything."

"This is everything," he said, dropping to his knees. He undid my belt.

His attention to my body was flattering—he made me believe I had the power to make him forget the past, simply by standing there before him. When we were together, all that seemed to matter to Zach was my body, as though flesh were the answer to everything, driving away all the questions.

There were no photographs in the apartment, no mother or father smiling into the lens in front of a rickety farmhouse, no white picket fence, no siblings squabbling in the backseat of a car.

"Why did you come here?" I asked later, lying in his arms, breathing my words onto his chest. Tiny dark hairs fluttered in a circle around his nipple.

"San Francisco? Why does any red-blooded faggot come here?"

"That's rather crude," I said, playfully slapping his chest.

He laughed. "I fell in love with it. The first time I saw the skyline from the bay."

"From Marin?"

"No," he said, "the bay." He squirmed and sat back on his elbows. "I was in the Navy."

I fell onto the mattress as he sat up and reached for a cigarette on the nightstand. "You're kidding."

"How else does a poor boy get out of Kansas?" He bit down on the cigarette and held a pocket lighter to the end. The translucent green plastic revealed a shallow lake of butane sloshing at the bottom.

"How long were you in the Navy?"

"A couple of years. Until they started to figure out I was a little light in the loafers."

"You got kicked out?"

"No." He exhaled a cloud of smoke toward the ceiling. "My term ended just as they were getting suspicious. I would have stayed, but I didn't want to deal with the hassle." He leaned over to tap ashes into the dish at his side. "Or give up sucking dick."

"It must have been a nightmare."

"Hardly," he said. "More like a floating sex club."

I must have blanched. He suddenly stared at me with real concern. "Hey," he said, "don't get scared. I'm negative. Scout's honor." He gave me the salute, wrist thrown back limply. I laughed. "Are you sure you want to hear all this? Let's change the subject."

"No. I told you, I want to know about your life."

"Why on earth would you want to know that?" He blew another burst of smoke toward the wall, into Madonna's face.

Since Adam, I had grown intolerant of secrets. Mystery may have been romantic, but it was too often used as an excuse for lies. If I knew it all, every detail, every moment of Zach's life, there'd be nothing left for him to keep from me. If I knew the past, I could predict the future; I'd be able to read his mind.

"I don't like to think about it," he said. He was sitting rigidly against the wall now, the pale green sheet wrapped around his waist, only the sparse hair on his chest to keep him warm. He moved the still-lit cigarette gently around his improvised ashtray, arranging the ashes in tiny piles. "Besides," he added, "I'll bet your life's a lot more interesting than mine."

"Probably not." I lay on my side, supporting my body on a folded arm. My eyes were level with his chest, the point where his rib cage jutted out firmly, protecting the delicate inner organs.

"Don't be modest, Joe College."

"I'm not. There just isn't anything very interesting to tell you."

"In thirty years?" He stamped out the cigarette and put the dish back on the nightstand. "Well, that's fine with me. I hate thinking about the past. What's done is done." He turned back, caressed my cheek. "I'd rather think about the future. It's much more beautiful."

"Oh yeah? Why? What's it like?" Even as I said it, I realized that I wanted to know if I were part of his vision.

"It's like Halloween and Christmas."

"That's an odd combination."

"They're my favorite holidays."

"Uh-oh. What does that say about you?"

He tickled my sides and we scuffled for a minute, the sheets kicked away and exposing us to the cool air. We lay quietly then, clutching, my head firm against his neck. "No, really," I said, my breath coming back to warm me, "what do you see?"

He was glancing out the window at the fog that hadn't left all weekend. "I see us living in the country," he said, "with three dogs and a horse. Trees everywhere, a big lake to go skinny-dipping in." He squeezed my shoulders. "Our own private place."

His voice had grown heavy, weighted with the image. And for a moment, I saw it myself. Everything was green, new. And it was silent—silent enough to hear your own heartbeat. I bought his vision, seeing myself as part of it, suddenly wanting to be part of it.

In the meantime, there was Zach's scent as my nose lay in the crack between his chest and his arm, the taste of salt on his skin, the dance his fingers performed in my hair.

I fell in love with the baseball cap. I'd hated baseball all my life, from the time my father dragged me to see the Red Sox when I was seven. My little brother, Larry, who wasn't even old enough to hold a mitt, to know what a baseball felt like, was bouncing with excitement on the bleachers. Already, intuitively, he loved the game. Larry would have been a walking advertisement for the male sports and violence gene if I hadn't been there to ruin the family statistics. He started playing with blocks as soon as he crawled out of the cradle. All of his Tonka trucks ended in spectacular crashes. His favorite game was to take any phallic object he could find—wooden mixing spoons were his favorite—and turn them into guns. While Mom was baking a cake, he'd grab her spoon off the counter, clutch the fat end to his chest, both hands gripping the handle, and sway in an arc, all the while punctuating the motion with a trilling tongue for sound effects, to heighten the fantasy of mowing down everyone in sight. Mom was particularly effective at clutching her chest, gripping the countertop, slipping lifelessly—and slowly (play could go only so far before it led to a wrinkled skirt)—down to the linoleum. Most often, I would just walk away. Even at seven, I imagined myself too mature for Larry's antics.

Maturity, of course, meant climbing up to my room to pore through Mom's old magazines behind a closed door. Larry's intuition about violent play was matched by my own instinct to hide my adoration of fashion; without even being told, I knew my parents wouldn't approve of a little boy fantasizing about two-dimensional strangers in tuxedos and evening gowns. Larry's naive imitations of John Wayne were charming, adorable, despite the glow in his eyes as he pictured a string of corpses on the living room floor. By contrast, draping a sheet across my shoulders in imitation of Cheryl Tiegs was completely perverse, justification for a psychiatric intervention, if not reform school. At seven, I knew that. At seven, I began to lock my door.

It was the third week when I fell in love. I remember that because it was Fourth of July weekend, and Zach had made cookies draped in red, white, and blue icing. He presented the platter to me at the door, as I emerged, breathless, having run all the way from the MUNI station, half to work off the frustration of an overcrowded train, half for exactly this, to see his blue-gray eyes, to smell him. The cookies were arranged in a rectangle, most covered in thick red and white stripes, the rest forming a blue corner on the top left, with tiny white dots. Stars, he said, were impossible at that size; he would have needed all night and a pair of tweezers.

Still sweaty from the kitchen (he'd just finished icing the cookies five minutes before I arrived), he was wearing the Giants cap, dark curls spilling around his ears and onto his damp forehead. The glow of achievement was in his eyes—not the achievement of baking the cookies, but of presenting them to me, offering me this silly token. With the hat riding back on his head, he looked like a little boy proudly offering his first bouquet to his mother, and in his innocence, his uncorrupted desire to please, he was irresistible. After a single, astonished glance, I ignored the cookies, concentrating instead on his eyes, the freshness of his gaze, and I felt tears welling in my own. I had an embarrassing habit of crying at the strangest moments. Not just sad moments—that would make sense. I cried more often at beauty, at Barber's *Adagio,* at any scene viewed through Sven Nykvist's lens. In New York, walking nonchalantly through a gallery at the Museum of Modern Art, I had stumbled unexpectedly upon van Gogh's *Starry Night,* and immediately, with the shock of seeing in person what I had loved from afar without ever seriously considering that it actually existed as paint on canvas rather than simply a flat reproduction in a magazine, I had begun to weep. To recover, I ran from my friends, into the next gallery, certain the harshness of Picasso would still the sentimental swell.

"For me?" I asked, reaching for one of the blue cookies. "No," I said, abruptly pulling my hand away, "I couldn't. It would be so unpatriotic, eating an American symbol."

"It's okay," Zach said, nudging my chest with the platter. "I got the recipe from Barbara Bush." His head tipped down toward the cookies, he glanced up at me from beneath the cap's dark bill. That was when it hit me. I had a sudden image of Zach at about eight years old, shy and just a little mischievous, the kind of kid who's loved as much when he misbehaves as when he does everything by the book, whose charm lies in his rebellion. Zach had that charm, that glimmer in his eyes. And although what stood before me was a twenty-seven-year-old man, it was the little boy I fell in love with, the little boy who tugged at my heart.

I didn't need to ask about his past anymore. Despite his best efforts, Zach carried the past with him—in his eyes, in the desperation with which he would suddenly hold me in the middle of the night, clutching me to him as though afraid I might disappear as soon as he fell asleep. His arms would tear me from my half-slumber, arrest me on the way toward dreams, and I would find myself leaning back silently, reveling in the fact that I was needed, that he chose me to cling to.

With the others, I had always been the needy one, the first to reach out, the last to let go of an embrace. They were simply there, all their power vested in the ability to say *no.* David, who just wasn't ready for a commitment, who needed his "space" more than he needed love. Brian, who wanted the world to think he had no needs at all, pasting an indifferent expression on his face no matter what passed before him, no matter what vanished out of his sight. And Adam, who couldn't even commit to a gender, let alone an individual. But Adam, at least, had loved me—as I had defined love at the time. He just didn't have the courage to live out that love.

Zach wasn't interested in my past—at least not its details, its tiny, ugly truths. He knew my life in broad outline—that was all he wanted—and he filled in the rest with fantasy: Joe College Leads His Charmed Life. Whenever I mentioned something from the past—a phrase that had been one of my father's favorites, a film Brian and I had seen together—his face would grow curious, he would encourage me to elaborate, all the while nodding his head as though he were constructing a puzzle, clicking the pieces into place. But otherwise, he seldom asked questions. He seemed to prefer forming the puzzle on his own, letting imagination and osmosis do all the work.

One morning, at my place, on his way back from the shower, he crouched, naked, in front of the bookcase. He pulled a photo album out and began to flip curiously through the pages. "What's this?" he asked, a slight giggle in his voice. He turned and rose to his full height. Through the window, the sun lit his left side, adding a blond tint to his chest hair while the thick book kept his cock in shadow.

He climbed into bed beside me, bent his knees, and supported the album against his thighs. Beneath the black leaves, dark curls of pubic hair peeked forth. I wanted to toss the book aside—to forget the past it contained and throw my head instead into his lap and open my lips around him.

"Just some old pictures," I said as he carefully turned the pages. "*Very* old pictures."

His hands grazed my family on vacation, gathered around a birthday cake, posing at my brother's wedding. I sat naked beside a naked man, my body still sticky with sex, and my childhood stared back at me from his crotch.

"Who's this?" he cried suddenly, smoothing out an eight-by-ten of a toddler, dirty-blond hair falling over his forehead, hands clasped neatly in his lap. He was smiling dutifully for the camera, bright eyes shining out in the glare of the flash. My first thought was: How did Zach get into my family album?

"It's me," I confessed, finally.

"Wow." He turned toward me, comparing. My eyes were darker now. It was Zach who still had the vivid blue: how pale had they been when he was a child? "You were beautiful," he whispered, and leaning forward, he kissed me.

The album fell onto the bed as he pressed against me, lips swirling slowly over mine. He smelled of sex and baby powder.

By the end of July, we were regulars at Café Flore. We would meet there after work, the first to arrive snagging an outside table and saving an extra chair. It was a welcome, easy way to unwind—sipping lattes and watching everyone come back to life after the doldrums of a workday afternoon. Zach didn't care much about the ambience; he was just happy to sit down for the first time since lunch.

Sitting across the table from each other, we seldom said much. Silence was part of the ritual, a quiet transition between work and what I had come to call "real life." Mostly, we looked disinterestedly around the courtyard, at the other customers, the trees whose branches twined intricately above our heads. And sometimes we just looked at each other, linking fingers on the cool tile tabletop.

A busboy walked through the maze of tables, depositing dirty glasses and plates into the gray plastic bin hoisted at his hip. His noisy clatter and the indiscernible multitude of half-heard conversations around us created a kind of wall that insulated us.

Gazing over my shoulder, Zach smiled and nodded almost imperceptibly. I turned in time to see a man emerge from the café. He was a few years older than me, around Zach's height, with bushy eyebrows that nearly met in the furrow above his nose.

"How are you, Zach?" he said, approaching our table. He bent down and kissed Zach, who turned his head just enough to make the man's lips land on his cheek.

"I'm fine. How are you?" Zach's smile was polite, almost formal.

"Great, great." The man let a hand linger on Zach's shoulder. "It's so good to see you."

"This is Neal," Zach said, gesturing toward me.

The man followed Zach's eyes and straightened up rather awkwardly, extending a hand toward me. His palm was clammy and thin, the flesh tight around his knuckles. "Roy," he said. His eyes flickered on my face, dipped subtly to take in more. It seemed halfway between a cruise and a simple attempt to check out the competition.

Apparently satisfied, he turned back to Zach. "So," he asked, "what have you been up to?"

"Shoes," Zach replied. "I'm up to my eyeballs in penny loafers. What about you?"

"Oh, the usual. Work's okay." He looked back at me briefly and explained, "I work at the DMV." The aside over, he returned his gaze to Zach; I suddenly thought of Hamlet delivering his soliloquy downstage and then rushing back to chat with Ophelia. "But the stress is really getting to me. I don't know why, I just can't take it anymore. Must be getting old."

"Well, you look good," Zach said. "It's nice to see you again." There was a finality in Zach's tone. I admired it. Getting rid of people had always been a challenge for me.

"Yeah, you, too." Roy stood still for a moment, nodding, lips sealed in a smile. He seemed to be waiting for the puppet master to lift him off into the wings.

Zach stirred the dregs of his coffee and smiled at me as Roy vanished through the black iron gate onto Noe.

"How do you know him?" I asked.

"We met at the Eagle, I think." He looked back, just checking that Roy hadn't returned to hover by his shoulder. "Poor guy, he's just so clingy."

I didn't bother to ask any more. Somehow, I couldn't picture Zach and Roy together. They had just been friends, I was sure, and from Zach's reaction, even that couldn't have lasted very long.

My latte had grown cold long ago. We picked up our things and left by the Market Street gate. "What do you want to do tonight?" I asked.

Zach sighed, lips pursed pensively. "How about . . ." Suddenly, he pulled me against him. We nearly fell over, into the bushes that lined the café. Zach righted himself, saving us, and kissed me. His lips felt warm against the encroaching chill of evening. The fog was rolling in; I could feel it tingling the hairs on the wrist I had thrown around his neck.

We ended up stopping at the video store a couple of doors down and settling in for the evening. As usual, the video remained largely unwatched, glimpsed casually from time to time as we made love on the open futon. We must have rented two dozen movies that summer, and I can't recall the entire plot of a single one.

Food, for Martin, was more nutritious for the soul than for the body. In the first few weeks I knew him, he took me to more restaurants than I could count, introducing me to ethnic foods I'd never heard of. It was through restaurants that I got to know San Francisco best: North Beach was Little City and the Stinking Rose; the Castro, La Méditerranée; Cole Valley, Zazie. Afterward, we would walk off dinner by exploring whatever neighborhood we happened to be in—window-shopping, admiring the architecture, people-watching. I grew to share Martin's belief that a fine meal was not only conducive to conversation but basic to understanding a culture. Restaurants were one of the most distinctive marks of each neighborhood, a key to the people who lived there.

All the more reason that my curiosity was piqued by the thought of Martin's own cooking. He had invited me to dinner only once, before we knew each other all that well. The next invitation came after Zach and I had been together for a month or so. He'd kept his distance for a while, like a benevolent uncle, longing to look out for me but loath to interfere. When he did call, there was usually a concrete reason—a letter from Natalie, a reminder to watch *Frasier*. Before Zach came along, Martin never felt the need for an excuse. He would call just to say hello, and *hello* would turn into an hour-long conversation that touched on so many subjects I would be at a loss to reconstruct it. Topics flashed between us like synapses in the brain of a schizophrenic, completely natural to us, utterly senseless to any poor soul who might happen to overhear. I was beginning to miss that.

We were only a few minutes late getting to Martin's place, MUNI on our side for once. Climbing the stairs behind Zach, I suddenly felt a queasy sensation—my legs threatening to buckle, my stomach sinking.

It was like bringing him to meet my mother, I thought suddenly. Though they already knew each other, I had separated Zach and Martin into different compartments of my life, compartments that brought out very different sides of myself, as if I were playing different roles with each of them. Now that they were coming together again, I had no idea which part to choose.

Martin had no such problem. He had clearly decided to play the perfect host this evening, putting everyone at ease. He greeted us both with a kiss on the cheek and led us, smiling, into the kitchen. "I just opened a bottle of Chardonnay," he said. "Neal?" He stood at the chopping block, two wine glasses suspended upside-down between his fingers, like church bells.

"Sure." I seldom drank now, because of Zach. But tonight I craved the soothing warmth of the wine.

"And what can I get for you, Zach?" Martin opened the refrigerator to reveal an assortment of juices and soft drinks. Zach gestured toward a bottle of Calistoga, and Martin poured him a glass.

"Cheers," Martin said as we lifted our glasses. "I'll just be a few more minutes in here. You can go sit in the other room if you'd like, or you can watch me mash the potatoes."

"Oh, let's watch," Zach offered. "I bet you're a real wiz in the kitchen."

"Oh yeah, I make a ratatouille that could bring tears to your eyes." He laughed, scrounging for something in a drawer.

It wasn't at all surprising that Martin should choose dinner for our first get-together as a threesome. No matter how awkward things got, the meal would keep us focused; when all else failed, we could talk about the texture of the asparagus. Watching him adroitly squeeze the potatoes through the masher, I realized the greatest advantage: the meal was something Martin could control—his forte, his turf.

Leaning against the counter, Zach watched with a kind of fascination as Martin sprinkled a handful of chives into the potatoes. Except for that one oversized breakfast he'd made me, I had never seen Zach do more in the kitchen than pour out a bowl of cereal. This seemed to be a new world to him, and he watched Martin with the same awe another man might have looking over the shoulder of a painter.

In a few minutes, Martin settled us at the table to wait. A small vase of irises sat at the end of the table, where the fourth place would have been, the center occupied by a pair of ivory candles in crystal holders. Spreading the napkin in my lap, I looked across at Zach, who smiled back more calmly now, as if everything were going according to plan. I was the only one who was still on edge. I took a long sip of wine.

Zach had taken the inside seat, his back to the bay window. Behind him, the buildings across the street seemed closer in the twilight. A little girl stood in one window, gazing up, catching my eye for a moment, her guilt at being caught spying tempered by the knowledge that she had caught me as well.

The warmth of Zach's hand on mine drew my attention back. He squeezed my fingers and smiled. "Great place," he said, glancing around the room.

"Yes," I replied. "Martin has a lot of nice things."

Tucked into the windowed alcove, the dining table afforded a complete view of the living room—an eclectic assortment of furniture, antique and modern, posters from Broadway shows competing for attention with original watercolors. A collection of vases lined the top two shelves of the hutch—crystal, Wedgwood, intricately shaped blown glass. Several of them were from Venice, Martin had told me, a shop just off the Grand Canal where he had watched the glass being made, twirled into shape by burly men in sweaty T-shirts. He'd been fascinated that their brawn could give birth to such beauty.

Martin emerged through the kitchen doorway, carrying a couple of plates. He wore a troubled expression. "You know, I completely forgot to ask. No one's a vegetarian, I hope."

Martin had already seen me carve into most forms of meat known to restaurateurs. *No one,* in this case, clearly meant Zach.

"Are you kidding?" Zach said, scrunching his nose. "We don't grow vegetarians in Kansas."

"Thank God," Martin said, setting steaming plates before us. "I've never been able to do a damn thing with tofu." The potatoes we had watched him make now sat in elegant swirls beside mermaid-shaped salmon steaks and slender stalks of asparagus. He disappeared into the kitchen again and returned with a basket of bread and his own plate, not piled quite as high as ours.

Martin spread a napkin on his lap and lifted his glass. "To new friends and old," he said. Glasses clinked.

Zach had already swallowed a large chunk of salmon before I'd sliced into mine. "This is fantastic," he said, reaching for his water.

Martin tucked his head slightly. "Kansas," he said. "I've never met anyone from Kansas before. What was it like?"

Zach laughed. He was used to this. In San Francisco, the only truly exotic topic was middle America. Tiramisu was a staple; apple pie, a delicacy. "It was wonderful," he said. "Flat, gorgeous. I used to love staying at my grandparents' place, this farm out in the middle of no-where. I'd just wander into the field, far enough out that I couldn't hear a thing from the house. Just the wind, the bees." His face grew soft in the candlelight. "That was my favorite thing as a child, being alone—in the outdoors."

"Grizzly Addams."

Zach laughed. "Peach fuzz at best," he said, stroking his smooth chin.

"Large family?" Martin asked, contemplating his wine.

"There were six of us," Zach replied. His eyes had lit up by now, his face growing more open. He was savoring his new role as storyteller. "I was fourth. By the time I came along, my oldest brother was al-ready in high school. It was wonderful; we all looked after each other. The six musketeers."

In two months, I hadn't gotten Zach to tell me even this much about his childhood. Somehow, he had always squirmed out of the subject, and eventually I'd come to think of it as verboten. Now, as the stories spilled out, I found myself resenting his sudden open-ness—the way he nonchalantly shared with Martin things he'd never said to me even in the safety of a double bed. I tried to control the look of interest on my face, pretending these stories were tediously familiar to me, remnants of age-old pillow talk. But after a while, I just re-laxed and listened. Zach's tone, lyrical yet controlled, inspired a kind of reverence, absolute attention. He had that little-boy quality in his eyes—a sense of wonderment at the things he told us, as if he were reexperiencing them as he spoke, as if everything were just as new and exciting as it had been then, nearly twenty years ago.

He reconstructed his childhood with the details remarkably intact: his grandparents' farmhouse, dark shutters against peeling white paint, the black Lab who limped slightly ever since he'd gotten one step too close to a tractor, the smell of the corn stalks rising above the head of a six-year-old. It was all there, vividly etched in his brain, and it was all beautiful.

I envied his memories—not just their beauty, but their sheer existence. My own childhood was more or less a mystery to me. Except for a few minor incidents, it was all a blur. Zach's past, on the other hand, held some sort of magic. I saw it as a key of sorts, not just a key to him, but to some happy place from which I was barred.

"So you were close to your family?" Martin prodded.

"Oh, yeah," Zach said. He spoke quickly, automatically. "We've always been close."

"Do you visit often?"

He nodded, chewing. "From time to time. Holidays, you know."

"That's good. It's always nice to go home."

Zach returned Martin's smile, lips raised forcefully, but his eyes had suddenly lost their luster. Martin's questions had brought him back to the present, and I couldn't help thinking that—just this once— Zach would have preferred to stay in the past.

I was on my third glass of wine when Martin got around to asking how Zach had ended up in San Francisco. Zach hunched his shoulders sheepishly. "I was in the Navy," he said. "Didn't Neal tell you?"

"Oh, that's right." Martin pushed his plate away, the salmon skin lying alone, an abandoned exoskeleton. "An interesting choice for someone who'd never seen an ocean."

"Only in the movies," Zach said. "Maybe that's why I joined up. I was fascinated by boats. The truth is, the ocean's a lot like the Midwest—all that flat, empty space. If you think the sky's big in Montana, you should see it in the middle of the Pacific."

"No thanks," Martin said, rising to clear. "Just looking out over the Golden Gate Bridge gives me the willies."

Martin brought a pot of herbal tea into the living room and took one of the wingback chairs. Zach and I sat across from him, at opposite ends of the sofa so that we'd each have a side table to lay our cups on.

"So you've lived here forever, haven't you?" Zach asked, swirling a spoon through his tea—more for effect than function; he hadn't even added sugar. "You never really told me what it was like."

"Not forever," Martin corrected, glancing up though his head was still bowed over his cup. He would have needed only bifocals to complete the schoolmarmish expression. "More like twenty years or so."

"Wow. Then you've seen everything."

Martin chuckled. "Yes," he said, "I've seen everything."

"So?" Zach's eyes widened, ready to absorb, ready to draw new pictures for his imagination.

"It's changed a lot, of course. I can't believe how much. When I look back on it, it seems like that time was just a flash. Maybe even a dream."

Now it was Martin's turn to get nostalgic. I'd never had the nerve to ask him so directly about the past. I'd always thought he preferred to keep it *in* the past, where it was safe—where *he* was safe. Whenever it had come up, it had been in counterpoint to the present, each memory an item in a catalog of loss. Martin talked about what was no longer around—bars, restaurants, ambience, people. Instead of re-creating the past for me, his stories had merely pointed out the failings of the present.

"Right on the street," he was saying, just jumping into an anecdote. "I'd just be walking down the street, and some guy would stop me. 'You're hot,' he'd say. 'You want to go somewhere?' Just like that."

"God, that hasn't happened to me in a while," Zach said, throwing his head against the back of the sofa.

"What?" My cup rattled in its saucer. "When?"

Zach laughed and reached for my hand. "Ages ago," he said, casting me what he must have thought was a reassuring smile, eyebrows arched like a clown's. "And it wasn't on the street. At parties, mostly."

"Parties?"

"In my wild days," he said. He leaned closer and lowered his voice in a loud, self-conscious whisper. "When I was drinking." He laughed. "Back when I had an excuse. God, that's the great thing about being a drunk—you always have an excuse."

Martin echoed his laughter. "Oh yeah, we used that one. All the time. Of course in those days, it wasn't just booze. Poppers, pot, speed, acid—whatever was available."

I stayed out of the conversation. I had nothing to add and was somewhat embarrassed by my inexperience. Even in college, I'd smoked pot only once—and that had taken more than a little arm-twisting on my roommate's part. It had had no effect, so I never bothered again. A convenient excuse for what really amounted to simple fear.

They spoke of things that I had known only sketchily—participants in a life that kept me on its periphery. Martin discussed the way the character of a bar completely changed toward closing time, the way people moved closer, changed their minds, lowered their standards. I had always felt uncomfortable in bars, usually dropping in at ten or so, more from a sense of duty than desire, and leaving alone within an hour out of sheer boredom. And fear, of course. Always fear.

Despite the years that separated them, Zach's stories weren't that different from Martin's, at least on the surface. He had wandered into the same sort of world, albeit with a bit less extravagance. On opposite ends of a generational shift, they had both danced the night away, maintaining their energy with drugs and the stimulation of other men's swarthy stares. The only time I had danced with either of them was under the cool light of the Rawhide, counting the steps, anticipating the next turn. But I had no trouble picturing them both in a completely different setting—disco balls shimmering, black light casting a hypnotic glow to T-shirts bathed in sweat. Arms raised as the music peaked, hips swaying, they would become part of the frenzy of a roomful of men, each body moving to the same beat, each pair of eyes scoping out the possibilities. Myself, I pictured on the sidelines—simultaneously dying to dance and dreading an invitation.

"God," Zach was saying, "I really envy you, living through all that."

Martin poured himself another cup of tea. "Everything comes with a price," he said. "I'm not sure the trade-off was worth it."

Zach attempted a smile to cover his faux pas. "Still," he said, "I can't imagine living anywhere else."

"Neither can I," Martin said, "but I did think about leaving San Francisco once. A friend of mine couldn't take it anymore, and he moved to Seattle a few years ago. He called me a couple of months later, told me how wonderful it was. He almost talked me into moving."

"I've always wanted to visit Seattle," I said. At last, a topic I could add my two cents to.

"You've never been there?" Martin seemed to be asking both of us, but Zach had turned away, contemplating the pattern in the rug.

"It's a great town, but I couldn't leave." Martin shrugged, half defeated, half empowered. "I belong here."

"Seattle's dreadful," Zach said, almost in a murmur. "Cold, rainy. Of course, I was just passing through. In my Navy days. Too depressing."

"Well," Martin said, "it's not for everybody." He turned an expectant smile to me.

I asked him about Natalie, whether she'd be visiting soon. She couldn't afford it this year, but he was thinking of flying her out for Christmas. Their parents were both dead; there was no reason to suffer through a New England winter merely for the sake of tradition. While we chatted, Zach turned away, toward the window that had now grown nearly opaque from the outer darkness and the bright lights burning inside. He stared into the glass—as if he saw something there, something he was unable to turn away from.

I'd read too many detective novels as a kid, following Sherlock Holmes or Miss Marple as they sorted through the clues and closed in on the villain. Some people go in for the suspense of those stories—that combination of mystery and fear that propels the hunt to keep the killer from striking again. But it was the logic that attracted me—the intricate interplay of clues and half-hidden facts. On the surface each situation was a complete jumble—a body lying over here, a business deal gone awry over there, a jealous husband drinking too much bourbon in an out-of-the-way bar—all just details that made no real sense together, especially when you knew Ms. Christie's fondness for red herrings. But in retrospect, after the oily M. Poirot explained it all for you, suddenly the underlying order became glaringly clear and you wondered how you could have missed it. Each time I finished a book, once again tricked by the author's sleight of hand, I vowed to pay stricter attention the next time, determined just once to crack the case before the obligatory revelation scene, all the suspects gathered in anticipation of the moment of truth, justice's delayed arrival. I watched for clues—the shade of lipstick on a smoldering cigarette, the lilac smell that clung to a silk scarf taken from the victim's bureau, a minor character's chance encounter with an innocuous stranger on the street. There were always clues: if you looked closely enough, you could figure it all out. If you concentrated, dug down deep, the patterns would emerge with the sudden illumination of neon. There are no mysteries beneath the skin.

Up to now, I'd been pretty successful at solving the minor mysteries of life—how the VCR worked, what my father did on those extralong poker nights, why Adam hadn't loved me enough. It might take me a while, but eventually I figured it out. You don't graduate from Brown by being stupid.

Zach was the first unsolved mystery of my career. Even now I'm not sure all the pieces fit. Just when I think I see it all, there's a tiny corner that's empty, or a seemingly perfect piece for the center that refuses to pop into place. I can't make sense of it. I'm writing this to make sense of it—to understand Zach and what made him what he was. But sometimes I think Zach is really the easy part. The thing I have the hardest time figuring out is where *I* was coming from, why I felt such a need to understand him, why I couldn't just live with the mystery or walk away ignorant.

Zach was silent on the way back from Martin's place, staring out the MUNI window into the indistinct blackness of the tunnel. He caught me watching him in the window once; as if he were a stranger I had to pretend not to notice, I shifted my gaze to the wall behind his head, the confused squiggles of graffiti. There was a language in those fat, caterpillar-like lines—someone's name, a message, a warning to rivals—all conveyed in a tribal code that invited questions but refused to offer answers. Future archaeologists, I thought, would puzzle over these lines and shapes and silhouettes for years, waiting for a post-modern Rosetta Stone to break the code and reveal the secrets of a lost civilization.

Church Street was his stop, of course, where he got off every evening after work, but I had to lead him off the train tonight. Still not watching, he sensed my movement and wobbled to his feet as the train came to a stop. We had long ago moved beyond the stage of invitation: unless otherwise planned, it was now expected that we would spend the night together, so we walked side by side in the chilly air toward Zach's apartment.

Inside, he dropped his keys on the foyer table and kicked his shoes into a corner by the bed. "I'm going to take a bath," he said. "Need the bathroom?" After the long silence, his voice sounded foreign, oddly accented.

"No," I said, "I'm fine."

He nodded, a cursory acknowledgment, and began to unbutton his shirt on the way across the room.

I had left a copy of the *New Yorker* on the coffee table, the subscription my last tangible link to the East Coast. Snatching it up as I passed, I headed for the armchair by the window.

A miniature waterfall echoed through the apartment, Zach's bath running hot into the tub. It was a reassuring sound—a precursor of the peace to come, the silence of lying still in the hot water, steam rising like low-lying fog in the middle of the night. I heard the stream break suddenly—Zach running his hand under the faucet, testing the temperature.

I was just skimming the magazine, catching headlines and photographs, stopping to read the cartoons. I wasn't in the mood for words, the latest sociological theory about the Middle East, yet another short story about working-class ennui. My mind, instead, was busy conjuring up pictures to go with the stories I'd heard tonight—Martin dancing at the Trocadero until the sun came up, Zach dodging passes at secret gay parties off base. It seemed a life I had slept through—always seeking out romance instead, wondering why Prince Charming didn't just gallop up and carry me away.

"Neal?" Zach's voice sounded hollow, constricted by the close walls of the bathroom. Until he repeated my name, I wasn't even sure I had heard it.

I dropped the magazine face-down onto the chair and went to the bathroom. I stopped in the doorway and peered in. The room was lit by votive candles, one on each corner of the free-standing tub, another on the toilet tank. The clear shower curtain was clumped together at the foot of the tub, reflecting the tiny flames on either side.

Zach looked entirely peaceful in the warm light, the steam that rose around him. He was hunkered down so that the water covered his chest, occasionally rippling away to expose part of a nipple. His head fell against the tiled wall, his eyes closed. He was breathing in the steam—evenly, deliberately, like a bronchial patient.

Eyes still closed, he sensed my presence and spoke softly. "Sit with me," he said. "It's lonely in here."

"Sure." I closed the toilet lid and sat, a few inches behind his head, like a psychiatrist out of range of the couch.

"Did I shock you tonight?" he asked. He was sitting perfectly still now, hardly a wave breaking in the grayish water.

"Not really," I said.

"I lied, you know."

"About what?" Something stirred in my chest—fear or excitement, I couldn't tell which.

"A lot. Kansas." He was so still before me, lost, enveloped by the steam. His words might have been coming from a stone.

"The farm?"

He smiled. "I loved the farm. That was where I went to escape. My grandparents took me in."

"Took you in?"

"When my father—" He paused, and a brief splash of water echoed through the room. "He was violent. Really violent."

"He beat you?"

Zach sighed, breath coming out like suppressed laughter. "Beat. Kicked. Punched. Slapped. Anything he could think of. When he was sober enough to think."

"What about your mother?"

"He did it to her, too. He did it to all of us. But mostly to me. That's why I had to escape. He did it to the rest of them for whatever reason he could come up with at the time. But me—he had special reasons for me. His faggy little son—the weakling. 'You have to beat sense into them,' he'd say. 'It'll make a man of him.' He'd yell at me to fight back. But I just froze. All I could do was let him hit me. I deserved it, because everything he said was true."

"Zach—"

"I know," he said. "But I didn't know then. I changed. I hid everything, everything I had inside me, everything I really wanted. I became what *he* wanted. You should have seen how proud he was the day I joined the Navy. He thought he'd finally succeeded, he'd turned me into a man. Of course, the only reason I did it was to get away. To get the hell away from him and all the lying, all the pretending."

He was crying now, and I leaned forward. His tears blended with the steam liquefying on his cheeks. I wanted to touch him, but at that moment his pain seemed sacred. I couldn't interfere.

"I'm sorry, Neal."

"Why?"

"For lying. For what I've done, for what I might still do."

"You haven't done anything."

He lifted a hand out of the water to wipe his face. "I hurt people, Neal. It's like I'm trying to get back at him—or myself, I don't know. I hurt people."

I slid off the seat and knelt beside the tub. "It's okay," I said, stroking his wet hair back. The white tile stung my hand with its cold sleekness. "You haven't done anything."

"But if you knew," he said, "if you knew everything—if you really knew *me*—" He shut his eyes tightly, as though to concentrate on the feel of my hand and let the words spill out of their own accord. "If you really knew who I am, you'd run away. You'd run away so fast."

"I'm right here," I said, my fingers looping a curl behind his ear. "I'm right here."

The tears returned, sliding in steady streams from between his closed lashes. Sobbing, he reached up and took my arm. Warm water soaked through my sleeve. I put the other arm around his wet body and embraced him. The water traveled up toward my collar. We were both in it now, both wet to the bone.

I've been told that I love with a vengeance. Adam threatened to buy a flak jacket once, to protect himself. Sometimes he would cringe as I approached, lips turning gently away as soon as they met mine—*that's enough, one peck is all you get.* But I knew that he really welcomed my advances: I was doing the things he couldn't. Responding to me may have been difficult at times, but it was far less difficult than initiating anything. Making the first move would be too decisive; it would signify to Adam that he was choosing a lifestyle, a decision from which there was no turning back. And Adam was a man who always kept one eye fixed on the past.

Zach was different. At least in those days, he never turned away, never refused me. Most of the time, the first move was his—a foot stroking me on the couch as I tried to read, a kiss on the nape of the neck sending chills down my back, a hand grasping my cock and pulling me out of sleep. I'd never felt needed before. Zach needed me, and need was an aphrodisiac.

We didn't talk about the bath, his tears, the strange intimacy they'd brought. There had been enough talking that night, enough lingering in the past.

On Sunday, we rented a car and drove to Santa Clara. Zach had a craving to ride a roller coaster. The thought nearly terrified me; I could still recall the sensation of my last visit to an amusement park, when I'd left my stomach somewhere near the second turn. "Come on," he coaxed, "I promise I won't toss you out of the car."

"Thanks," I said. "That's truly reassuring."

He cocked an eyebrow, nearly as high as the visor of his cap. "Please?"

We shot the works that day, taking on nearly every ride we saw, pigging out on hot dogs and cotton candy, even playing at the skills booths—games I'd always been convinced were rigged.

Zach wound up, stretched an arm behind him, cocked his leg—a parody of a real pitcher—and let the ball fly toward the pins. He missed entirely the first two times, but the third ball managed to smash through the pins, sending them all tumbling to the floor. Zach lifted both fists in victory, the Red Baron celebrating an enemy plane gone down in flames.

"Congratulations," said the barker, a man in his mid-fifties whose belly, adorned in worn green plaid, hung over his belt like a cake in an undersized pan. "Take your pick." He gestured at a row of prizes—mostly stuffed animals in absurd, unnatural colors.

Zach didn't hesitate. It was as if he'd scanned the shelf before the game began to decide what he wanted. He pointed, and the man passed him the prize.

He held it before me—a tiny blue elephant, trunk extended to reveal a pink stripe underneath and the soft gap of a mouth. Zach wiggled it back and forth, to suggest a lumbering walk. I laughed. It was ridiculous, oddly adorable.

"For you," he said, thrusting the elephant into my hands.

"What on earth am I going to do with this?"

"Add it to your collection."

"I don't have—" The elephant's eyes—wide, lidless—had a cartoon poignance about them, and the fur was extremely soft, like velour. "You're nuts," I said, looking back up into Zach's eyes.

"You got that right," he replied. "Now let's tackle that roller coaster."

"Oh, so this was a bribe, huh?"

He grabbed my wrist and pulled me along—past the families, the suburban couples who'd probably never seen two grown men holding hands before, let alone carrying a baby-blue elephant and running through an amusement park. If nothing else, we were educating people.

Waiting in line for the roller coaster, Zach exuded anticipation. I'd never seen him so excited before—legs trembling, fingers tapping against his thighs. The whole time, he stared up at the roller coaster, the white scaffolding that undergirded the track. His eyes scanned the turns, the alternately wide and sharp twists. Each time the cars sped past, occupants lifting their arms recklessly into the air and screaming in mingled exhilaration and fear, his face glowed—as if the metal cars emitted light—his eyes widening, lips curling into an impatient smile. He followed the cars with his eyes, continuing to watch the track long after they had vanished around a distant curve.

I tried to borrow some of his excitement, but all my mind's eye could envision was a turn taken too sharply, those blood-red cars spilling their cargo into the air, bodies hurled onto the pavement below. All for the sake of a sixty-second rush.

We ended up in the second car (I said a little prayer of gratitude for the teenage girls ahead of us, who had saved me from looking directly into the maw of death). My sneaker skidded on the floor—spilled Coke, I thought, or maybe even vomit from a previous customer—and I plopped into the corner, wishing there were more to hang onto than the bar that slowly sank toward our waists. As the train of cars chugged slowly up the first incline, I turned to Zach—hoping for some comfort, a sign that everything was going to be all right. But he was too busy watching the track—enjoying every clink of the chains beneath us, like the drumroll before a magic trick. I was reminded more of the suspense music in a horror film, just before the nubile and stupid heroine opens the closet door to unwittingly unleash the serial killer.

The first jolt, of course, was the hardest. Thoroughly convinced it was over—life, breathing, pad Thai, everything I'd ever loved—I closed my eyes and clenched the steel bar, the only thing that stood between me and the front page of the *Examiner*. As my stomach sailed up a few inches, I began to regret the cotton candy whose forgotten flavor suddenly returned to my tongue with a sickening sweetness. As we swirled up from the valley of the track, my eyes shot open. With gravity pulling my head back against the seat, all I could see at first was the clear blue emptiness of the sky. I couldn't turn my eyes in either direction—least of all down, God only knew how far down. For all I knew, Zach had plummeted out a moment before; I was afraid to check. It was just me and the sky, and speed, and screams so undefined and constant they had become white noise.

The second fall was surprising—cut short a millisecond or two before I expected, it segued immediately into another turn, sharper even than the first. I found myself getting used to it. I had no choice; for the next few seconds—whose intensity gave them the weight of hours if not months—this was all I knew. This, for now, was life. And by the end, it *was* exhilarating. The last swoop came too quickly—not because it was hard too bear, but because it was the last.

When my heart resumed beating, I released the bar and turned toward Zach. His eyes were already riveted on me.

"What?" The word seemed to scratch my throat on its way out.

"Enjoying yourself?" he asked. Around us, the screams had deteriorated into nervous giggles.

I sighed heavily, just to feel the sensation of air in my lungs again. "Sort of."

He smiled and leaned in for a whisper. "I haven't seen you that excited in *bed!*" he said.

I laughed. "That probably says more about you than it does about me."

He punched my shoulder playfully—lovers' taps transformed into male bonding for public consumption.

My legs wobbled as I followed Zach onto the wooden platform and past the crowd still waiting in line. I couldn't imagine getting back into that line anytime soon, but my whole body tingled with the satisfaction of survival. My shoulders and arms relieved of the tension that had kept me riveted to the protective bar, I felt each muscle come alive. Just a few minutes ago, they'd been taken for granted, but now I had to get used to them all over again.

We sat for a while on a bench near the Ferris wheel, watching the crowd stroll around us. I could feel each rib of the bench pressing into my flesh. I sat still, completely still. Ordinarily, I can't hold the same position for long without wanting to cross my legs or scratch something—but at that moment, my whole body alive, it was enough just to sit.

"There's nothing like a roller coaster," Zach said, looking across the park at the site of our adventure.

"Did you go often as a kid?"

He laughed. "I wish. Truth is, I'd never even been to an amusement park until I was twenty. I've made up for it since."

"I thought the Midwest was full of places like this." That was the way I pictured it, anyway—Ferris wheels towering over endless fields of wheat. There's something inherently middle America about amusement parks; maybe it's just that on the coasts we have other means of escape.

The refreshment stand was directly across from us, a crowd gathered around it in a poor semblance of a line. Off to the side, a little boy, four or five at most, waited with a pale blue balloon floating on a string over his head. In line, his mother turned to check on him every few seconds, her knitted brow of frustration transforming into a reassuring smile each time she met his gaze. He smiled back—an awkward, crooked smile that hid most of his teeth.

Something on the ground caught the boy's attention—a gum wrapper, an insect; I was too far away to tell—and he bent to look at it. Reaching out, he inadvertently released the balloon. The string swirled before him for a second—too fast to register. It had already vanished beyond his grasp by the time he noticed that the tug of the balloon on his finger had gone. He shot back up to his feet now, head tilted toward the sky, and watched the balloon zigzag through the air, trailing the cyclone swirl of its pale string.

At first, he seemed simply fascinated. It may have been his first encounter with the failure of gravity—the first gap in natural law. Or, like me, he may simply have been taken by the beauty of the sight—a release more splendid than the pleasure of captivity. But when he started to cry, I realized that little boys' minds don't register such things; natural and aesthetic principles are lost, and all that matters is sensation.

He cried quietly—no heavy sobs, no stamping of the feet. He didn't even jump into the air, as I might have in his shoes, hoping against hope to bounce myself high enough to reach what I longed for and thereby halt its escape. Instead, he just watched the balloon go, replaced by the tears that spilled, unwiped, along his cheeks.

"Excuse me," Zach said. His arm grazed past my head as he lifted himself from the bench. Wiping the dirt of the bench off his jeans, he headed for the balloon vendor a few feet away.

The little boy was still gazing into the sky when Zach approached him, a huge red balloon bouncing in the air between them. The little boy, dirty blond hair falling over his ears as he brought his head back down to look, opened his eyes wide. It was a day of surprises. Crouching down to bring their eyes level, Zach held the balloon before the boy, offering him the string. His lips moved gently, but I couldn't hear what he was saying. The boy looked quickly back at his mother, who had finally made it to the front of the line and was busy placing her order. The boy would have to make this decision on his own.

He returned his gaze to Zach, and a crooked smile crept up one side of his face as he accepted the string. Zach smiled back, and released the string into the boy's grasp. He set his cap back an inch or so on his head, the bill pointing upward now, allowing more light to wash over his face. They stared at each other for a moment more, the boy more interested in his new friend than his toy. Finally, Zach pressed his hands against his knees and lifted himself up. He now towered over the boy, whose smile remained as he watched Zach walk away.

"Looks like you've made a new friend."

Zach, a few feet in front of me, looked back once more. The boy's mother, passing him a hot dog, did a double-take at the sight of the enormous red balloon. She followed her son's pointing finger and met my gaze. Long blonde hair pulled off her face and into a ribbon behind her head, she was around my age, probably younger—and already she had produced something beautiful, her own bid for immortality. She smiled and nodded curtly—polite gratitude mingled with fear. Today's kind gesture might be tomorrow's threat. Our own parents would have thought nothing of a stranger's kindness; this woman was forced to see perverts everywhere. When you have children, her eyes said to me, you never know whom to trust.

Zach nodded back and turned again to me. "I've always been good with kids," he said, bouncing a couple of times on his heels. "Speaking of which," he added, looking over my head, "there's a ride over there with your name on it."

"Am I tall enough to get on?" I asked. Mother and son had joined hands—the balloon now bobbing between them, just over his head, level with her breast—and walked toward the picnic area on the far side of the square.

"Oh yeah," Zach said. "You're a big boy now." He patted my shoulder and walked around the bench. I had no choice but to follow.

We spent the rest of the afternoon traveling from one ride to another, tossed into the air again and again. I learned to ignore the churning of my stomach as we swung out over the earth. Only the Ferris wheel allowed us the leisure to observe the view, stopping periodically, suspending us for long moments as the next couple boarded an empty car. At the top, when we were completely out of sight, even of our fellow passengers, Zach took my hand—his warm, warmer than the chill air that had crept in with the twilight; my fingers craved its warmth and curled into his palm. Behind his head, the sun was just a golden aura above the earth. Beneath the cap, his brown hair picked up the fading light. It had turned golden at the temples, just where the gray would probably start in a few years—the distinguished gray that men like me, already balding at thirty, long for.

I stroked his hair softly, fingers wading through the gold like January swimmers afraid of the icy water. The color shifted beneath my fingers, refusing to stay on whatever lock of hair I pulled out of place, dropping instead to the next layer and the next. I couldn't capture the gold, only the softness of the strands.

As I lingered just above his ear, Zach leaned forward, our carriage swaying gently with the shift in weight, and pressed his lips against mine. At street level, it might have been a hurried kiss, stolen when he thought no one was looking. But up here, above even the trees, an occasional homeward bird our only witness, he prolonged the kiss, parting his lips slightly and circling my mouth with his own. I pulled at his hair, holding him closer. Our knees touched, the unmistakable rough sound of denim scratching denim. And something moved beside me, spilling along my arm.

I dropped my eyes too late. As I pulled away from Zach and reached down, the cap was already sailing gently through the air, riding a breeze that spun it in swirling arcs toward the ground. Pulling our arms back in to clutch the bar—our sudden movement had given the carriage a disturbing jerk—we watched it go, a black orb spinning, the orange letters on the front invisible in the encroaching darkness.

And suddenly Zach was laughing. Watching the cap vanish from our heavenly station, back to the earth of gravity and dirt, he laughed.

Diana got her big break with a tiny theater company in Berkeley. She called me on a Saturday evening as soon as she got home from the audition, screaming into the phone. I thought she'd wanted 911 and had dialed me by mistake.

It was a small part in an avant-garde retelling of the Orpheus and Eurydice story. Diana played Amor, the god of love who warns Orpheus about his fate. "Look ahead, Orpheus," she said cryptically as he marched upstage, leading Eurydice by the hand. "Never look back."

And when he heard his lover stumble behind him and instinctively turned to check on her, it was Diana who cried out as Eurydice vanished in a sudden flash of dry ice. As Orpheus fell to his knees, bereft, and futilely called her name, the stage went dark. When the lights came back up, dimly, Diana was leading Eurydice slowly toward Pluto's throne.

I didn't know what to make of the play. I was used to the operatic version, with Gluck's gorgeous melodies to humanize a tale that otherwise seemed too fantastic, too sentimental. Without the music, it was just another tragic love story. Without the music, I had no idea what to feel.

As I sat pondering, Zach jumped to his feet in the tiny audience, applauding as wildly as the parents and lovers who so clearly and proudly occupied the first row. His eyes fixed on the stage, his hair flew madly about his head in the draught created by his own applause.

Diana had invited us to the cast party, in an apartment a few doors down from the theater. By the time we arrived, the tiny living room was thick with characters, a few faces memorable from the performance. Eurydice had missed a spot of greasepaint just beneath her ear; up close, it resembled hardened blood. We moved swiftly past her in search of Diana.

Pluto hissed to someone by the bar, "He kept missing his cues all night. The light was never where it was supposed to be; I had to keep squeezing into it. Did anyone notice?"

"No, no," his friend assured him, stirring a drink. "At least I didn't."

We finally located Diana by the fireplace. She was still in costume, though her sleeves were now rolled up to the elbows. Without the bright stage lights, her angelic robe looked pale, faded from gold to a sickly yellow. Her hair, which had been tied in a French twist, now hung free, draped over one shoulder, which gave her a glamorous, asymmetrical quality and accentuated the height of her cheekbones.

Finally spotting us, she called our names and ran over for a communal hug. Zach's shoulder lurched into mine, throwing me off balance. I recovered against Diana's arm, which held tightly to my hip. She was several inches shorter than me, and Zach completely towered over her; together, we must have looked freakish.

"I'm so glad you came," she squealed. "What'd you think?" She pulled away and turned her gaze back and forth between us, as if unsure which one would start, hoping we'd speak in one communal voice.

"You were wonderful," I said. "You can lead me out of hell anytime."

Diana laughed. "I've been trying to do that for months!" She turned expectantly toward Zach, who beamed at her.

"I loved it," he said, leaning in for a whisper. "Especially you."

She giggled and kissed him. Maybe it was the giddiness of being on stage, or the fact that she was already obviously drunk, but Diana seemed very different tonight. It was as if her brassiness was no longer necessary; in the midst of the happiness of the moment, she didn't need her characteristic cynicism. She could just play.

It was the first time she and Zach had seen each other since that day at Macy's, but they acted as if they'd spoken every day for the past two months, as if they were old friends. They were free to dispense with the formality of new acquaintances; I'd already answered all the basic questions for both of them. Without even seeing each other or sharing more than ten words, they were already intimate.

"Originally," she was saying, "I'd auditioned for the role of Eurydice." She looked around. Certain the coast was clear, she leaned in and whispered, "I would have been a lot better than her. Could you believe it? The woman thinks the Method is a form of birth control!"

Eurydice had been particularly stiff—never reacting to the other actors, simply waiting for her cues. She'd seemed almost as bored as I was. I had to wonder why Orpheus would even bother to rescue her.

"But even in regional theater, most people can't see past the face." She splayed each hand out beside her eyes; her drink threatened to spill from the angle. "When you've got these, you're forever stuck in servant roles."

"There's always Joan Chen," I said hopefully.

Zach looked quizzical. "Chen. Any relation?"

Diana laughed. "No. It's like Smith in China."

Pluto suddenly appeared behind her, a tight black leather vest laced up over a white V-neck shirt. A forest of hair spilled out, beady with sweat. "So, Diana, who are your friends?"

"Fans," Zach offered.

"Ooh, groupies!" He still wore Pluto's sinister look, but I realized it was probably just the black eyeliner. Acting reduced to chemistry. His hair, tight curls spun into longish cones, fell in every direction. He surveyed both of us, nodding as Diana introduced us, his dark eyes finally coming to rest on Zach.

"Darren," he said, reluctantly. He was a star, after all; he wanted to believe everyone already knew his name.

"Great show," Zach said.

"Thank you," Darren replied, feigning surprise—as though Zach had been the first person to say it. "It was a good night, I think. A good omen for the rest of the run," he added, turning to bring Diana into his gaze. "The fourth wall just crashed somewhere in the middle of act two. I felt like I was in Berlin." He laughed quietly. I had the feeling he'd used the line many times before, and not just tonight. I had the feeling he had several lines up his sleeve.

"Mind if I smoke?" Darren asked, pulling a pack of cigarettes from his shirt pocket.

"Not at all," Zach said, apparently speaking for all of us.

"My late lover," Darren said, clasping the cigarette between his teeth as he flicked his lighter, "used to smoke cigars. Horrid things."

"Oh, I'm sorry," Zach replied earnestly.

Darren leaned back and blew a puff of smoke toward the ceiling. "Don't be. It was his bad habit, not yours."

"No, I mean I'm sorry he's . . . dead."

Darren laughed. "Oh, he's not dead. I just prefer to think of him that way."

As I watched him watching Zach, Diana snuck an arm around my waist. Her head barely reached my chest as she hugged me close. "I'm really glad you came," she whispered, looking up. "And that you brought Zach."

She apparently wasn't alone in that sentiment. Darren had taken advantage of her gesture to begin a private conversation with Zach, who laughed at an anecdote I couldn't hear. He had turned on the charm again; I hadn't seen that look on his face since the last time we'd been to the Rawhide.

"Not your kind of party, is it?" Diana asked, pinching my waist to redirect my attention.

I arched my eyebrows, a feeble attempt to allay her fears. "It's fine," I said.

She nodded, more at what I hadn't said than what I had. "I know—theater people. We can be real pricks at times." She lowered her voice. "Everyone around here thinks they belong on Broadway. Or Off Broadway, actually; that's more cool."

"Well, you at least should give it a shot."

"God," she said, "I drool for it. San Francisco's a great town, but it's not exactly where it's at for theater. I really have to get my ass in gear and move to LA or New York. Someplace where my looks will be exotic; around here, straight black hair and slanted eyes are a dime a dozen. Maybe I should try London—or Norway! Of course, wherever I go it ain't going to be easy. What's out there for Asian actresses, anyway? They've already filmed *The Joy Luck Club*; that filled the whole quota and then some. From now on all I have to look forward to are endless revivals of *Flower Drum Song*."

Zach was laughing again. He hadn't said more than five words, he was just laughing.

"Don't worry," Diana went on. "He's not going to vanish into thin air."

"What?"

She jerked her head to the left. "Zach. It's safe to let him out of your sight every once in a while, you know."

"What are you talking about? I—"

She pulled my arm. "Come on," she said, "buy me a drink." And louder, yanking Zach and Darren out of their confab: "Can we get you anything?"

I could see the hesitation flicker over Zach's face. He was probably embarrassed to ask for something nonalcoholic in this crowd. "Nothing, thanks." Darren waved his half-full cup at Diana, his eyes still focused on Zach.

At the makeshift bar, a table draped in white plastic and dotted with cracker crumbs and puddles of wine, Diana poured us some punch. "How's it going?" she asked, tipping her plastic cup against mine. Berkeley elegance.

"What?"

"Oh Christ," she said, rolling her eyes. "Zach, you idiot. Jesus, you just saw a play about one of the most romantic couples in history. What the hell are you thinking about, the stock market?"

"It's fine," I said. "It's great."

"Then why are you watching him like a hawk?"

"I am not watching him like a hawk. I just—" I finally, effortfully, tore my eyes away and met Diana's formidable gaze. "Okay, I'm jealous. So sue me."

She laughed. "Wow, an open acknowledgment of emotion. Two points for you."

"Shut up, Diana."

One of the room's twenty-five women dressed in black from head to toe squeezed in between us to reach the table. Her hair was dyed darker than Diana's, which gave her face a tubercular pallor that might have worked for Camille. Awkwardly, Diana and I ceded her the table and found an empty corner.

"Forget about Darren," she said once we were settled. "He's a complete loser. Zach'll see right through him. All flash and no substance." She sighed. "That's the problem around here: they all have the technique, but nobody has any heart. You can't act without heart."

Once again, my eye strayed toward the other end of the room. "Can you do *anything* without heart?" I asked rhetorically.

Orpheus passed before me, stopping suddenly to block my view. A small circle closed around him: more pale, black-haired women listening intently to his every word. Alone among the major cast members, he had changed completely out of costume, wiped the garish makeup off his face. Leaning languidly against the back of the sofa, he looked much more comfortable in his own skin than he had on stage. Despite being the lead, Orpheus—good, faithful Orpheus—was hardly an actor's dream. The villains were always more fun.

We were quiet on BART. Another reason I hated Berkeley: it seemed patently absurd to me that an area so prone to earthquakes would construct a subway under water. From the moment the train left Oakland and burrowed into the bay, until it climbed again into Embarcadero Station, I kept my knees rigidly together, my eyes dead ahead, memorizing the train's emergency instructions in Spanish.

"I'm exhausted," Zach announced as soon as we entered the apartment. He flicked on the light, revealing the sea of clothes and paraphernalia that lay scattered on the floor. He yawned dramatically and stretched, his long arms nearly reaching the ceiling. I glided past him and started to pick things up. They were all his clothes, of course. What few things I kept here were in the closet, snug against the right corner.

I folded a blue shirt and draped it over the desk chair. The desk itself was strewn with unopened bills and unread sections of the *Bay Area Reporter*. I made a pile and placed it on the side, to make room for the clothes.

"What are you doing?" he asked. His voice echoed in the cavern of the open refrigerator.

I folded his black pants, careful to maintain the crease. "Just making room in the jungle."

The door plunked shut and I heard the familiar hiss of club soda. "But I like playing Tarzan," he said. "Can I swing on your vine sometime?"

I folded the socks in pairs, but one of the white ones was missing. "When's the last time you did laundry?"

"Nineteen eighty-six." He sat on the edge of the bed and watched me, the soda still fizzing in his hand. "Aren't you tired?" he asked.

"Second wind, I guess."

"Great. Maybe you can do the windows while you're at it." He placed the glass on the floor and began to unbutton his shirt. "So what the hell's wrong with you?"

"Did you have a good time at the party?"

"Yeah." He scratched the small clump of hair between his nipples. His fingers fanned out and fell slowly toward his navel. "What about you?"

"Diana and I had a nice talk." I'd finished tidying up. Anything else would have required moving furniture. I turned the armchair to face him and sat. "How was what's-his-name, Samantha's husband?"

Zach looked puzzled for a moment. "Oh, Darren! He was really interesting. Can you believe he's a computer programmer?"

"That explains his acting."

"Ooh, the critic speaks."

"You didn't think he was good, did you?"

"He was okay." He peered at me over a mischievous smile. "What's going on? Are you jealous because I talked to him?"

"Not because you talked to him. Because you talked to him *all night.*"

"Neal, I can talk to people without wanting to fuck them."

"You were flirting with him."

"So? I flirt with everybody, you know that. It doesn't mean anything."

"Sure."

He got up, drained his drink, and returned to the kitchen. "Look, you can believe whatever you want. But I won't be questioned like this. If you don't trust me, you can just leave."

I felt something tumble in my stomach, too many nacho chips at the party. "I'm not saying I don't trust you, Zach. I just want you to know it makes me uncomfortable to see that."

"I'm not in the business of making you comfortable or uncomfortable, Neal. Your feelings are your own responsibility."

"Is that more AA garbage?"

"Garbage?" He let out a condescending laugh. "You really don't understand the first thing about it, do you? And you should, you of all people."

"Me of all people?"

He marched toward me. His white shirttails flapped around him like the wings of a seagull struggling to fly. He stopped a few feet away. "You think you're above it all, don't you? That it's just us poor alcoholics who suffer with this shit—or, better still, who whine about it. But you, Neal, you have all the characteristics of an adult child. Tell me, did your parents drink?"

"No." I felt the word reverberate in the back of my throat. Looking down at me, his eyes had grown harsh, self-servingly omniscient.

My parents' liquor cabinet stayed practically untouched from one Christmas to the next, when they poured a little rum into the egg nog, vodka or Scotch into the tumblers of their guests at the only party they had all year. The gin in that cabinet was probably as old as I was.

"I'm sorry," I said. "That was uncalled for."

He smiled and knelt before me. "Look, Neal, if I'm interested in someone else, I'll let you know. We haven't made a commitment yet."

"I know." His eyes, so blue, so bright, were different up close. They'd lost all the anger, all the harshness. I felt a sudden urge to ask for a commitment, to tell him I was ready. If that would keep him with me, if it would keep all the others away.

"And right now," he went on, "all I want is you." He grasped the back of my neck. "I love you." He pulled my head forward, pulled me into a kiss.

I followed him to the bed, our clothes torn off along the way, lying once again in unseen clumps on the floor. He bit into my neck and my nails dug deep circles in his back. His body was hard, a stone I threw myself against, his lips a whirlpool that drowned me. Finally settling down, relaxing into the pillow, I felt the dizziness of too many glasses of punch, my mind reeling back and forth. The images were confused—present, past, imagination, all blended into the darkness of the moment, the flesh that pressed against me, the moans that sang into my ear. Finally, if only for a moment, I forgot. Finally, my body was all there was.

Reading in bed was a habit I hadn't been able to break since childhood. Torn away from the TV at nine o'clock and tucked in tight as a pupa, I waited for my mother's footsteps to fade away down the hall before flicking on the bedside lamp. Larry would already be sound asleep in the next bed, but he could sleep with a mushroom cloud bursting in his face; a sixty-watt bulb was no threat to his dreams. Propping the pillow against the headboard, I would sit up and reach for a book on the nightstand.

Zach, I soon discovered, was a sound sleeper, too. After sex, he would nod gradually off beside me, as naturally, I thought, as a baby, as comfortably as if I weren't even there. But I had never given myself freely to the night. I fought it with lightbulbs and words.

I crept out of bed and, wrapped in Zach's blue robe, curled into the armchair by the window. The floor lamp beside it had a dimmer switch, so I could keep the light just bright enough for my eyes but too dim to reach the bed. I always brought a book with me, in my briefcase if I'd come from work, tucked into a deep inner pocket of my denim jacket if I'd gone home first.

"It must be awfully good to pull you out of a warm bed." Zach was leaning over the chair, breathing the words into my hair. Engrossed in the book, I hadn't heard him get up and cross the room. He stretched his arms down and spread open the robe, his hands cold upon my chest. "Is it sexy?" he asked.

I laughed, closing the book around my finger to hold the place. "Not compared to this." I arched my neck and waited for his lips to press down upon mine. My nose grazed the stubble on his chin. "Did I wake you?" I asked, pulling a leg under my body as I squirmed to get a better look at him.

His forearms lay comfortably along the chair back, one wrist draped in front of the other. The spotlight of the floor lamp highlighted the dark freckles on his bare shoulders. "No," he said. "I do this sometimes, wake up in the middle of the night. I like it—it's so peaceful." He gestured out at the empty street.

I followed his eyes toward the window, the deep blue light that coated the street like film. The fog was thick tonight, the kind of mist that sinks into your skin unnoticed, until you get indoors again and suddenly find yourself soaking wet. Already it clung to the windowpanes, the few silhouettes I could make out on the street as fractured as figures in Seurat.

"So what do you do when you wake up in the middle of the night?" I asked, still watching the street. The longer I looked, the more distinct the shapes became. Even still and asleep, the night was alive.

"Nothing," he said. "I just watch, listen to the silence."

I reached a hand into the air behind my back, a blind man grasping for contact. And though Zach, too, I knew, was looking beyond, into the night, his hand met mine, the two drawn together effortlessly, as naturally as the loose chemicals beneath an ancient sea, waiting for each other to create life. I gripped harder, binding the atoms together.

It was my idea for us to move in together. In two months, we'd slept apart a total of ten times. After a while, when Zach's futon had grown too small, too lumpy for entwined bodies to find comfort, we started spending most of our nights at my place. The queen mattress afforded us more room—both for our characteristically acrobatic sex and for the cool satisfaction of sleeping untouched. In the wee hours, after someone's arm grew tingly from the weight of the other's head, we would roll apart, backs to each other, hands curled up around separate pillows. Occasionally, a cold foot grazed my leg, a warm cheek pressed against my back—as if Zach were simply reminding me that he was there, that I was not alone.

But Zach needed time alone, and every few evenings he would keep to his own apartment, to stretch out in his own bed and be surrounded by his own things, the familiar shadows in the dark. I never made a fuss about it, the evenings when he went straight home after work. Most often, I was just as glad to be alone—to putter around the house, catch up on my reading, rent an old Bette Davis movie I'd always wanted to see. It was only later, when I got into bed, that I felt Zach's absence. More than once, I woke with a start, having rolled onto the other side of the bed and been shocked by the coldness of the sheets.

I'd grown used to Zach, to the weight his body lent the other side of the bed. After all this time (back then, two months seemed like a very long time), I began to take for granted his inevitable place in my life. It never occurred to me that he could be temporary, like the others. I didn't think in terms of temporary or permanent; Zach was simply there. That was all there was to it. He was real to me in a way that no

other man had ever been—in a physical sense, as inexorable and undeniable as a mountain range or a sea. Before, I had made fantasies of
my lovers, loved them for the most abstract of reasons—the creamy
notes of longing that wept from Adam's cello, the swirl of ideas that
excited me whenever Brian opened his mouth—but Zach was different. Unique among them, Zach struck me primarily as a physical,
tangible presence—flesh, bone, blood. He was a tousled head of
chestnut hair, unkempt on the pillow beside me in the morning when
I woke early and waited for his eyes to open. He was a hardness between my thighs, hot white bursts of semen forming streams and
puddles on my chest. He was a broad pair of shoulders to rest my
hands on when we kissed, a thick, knotted back I kneaded smooth
with fingers that had never felt more alive.

"There's plenty of room," I said, gesturing into the space around
the bed. The apartment, in fact, was still pretty spartan; I hadn't had
time or money to buy much furniture.

He looked away, toward the window, the white curtains luminous
in the morning light. His head resting on my shoulder, he lay perfectly still. "I'm just not sure we're ready," he said. "It's kind of soon
to be talking about this."

I was too hooked on romance to think about timetables. "What's
too soon?" I asked. "Some people move in together after two weeks,
some take a year. You just do it when it feels right."

"You've sure changed," he said, finally rolling away to look up at
me. "What happened to Little Miss Logic? I thought you had your life
planned out to the last second."

"I did," I answered, smiling. "But I left that in Boston."

"So now you're the spontaneous Californian? Why do I find that
hard to believe?"

I pinched his nipple—harder than he liked. "Stop avoiding the subject," I said. "Do you want to move in with me or not?"

He stuck out his lower lip, a parody of pensiveness. As he squinted
at me, a smile appeared on his face. "Of course I do," he said.

I suddenly became aware of my heart beating. "When?" I asked.

He laughed. "My lease is up next month."

"Great. That'll give me time to rearrange things for you—make room in the closet. And where are we going to put your furniture?" I sat up in bed and scanned the room.

"Hold on," he said, settling a warm hand on my shoulder. "Let's take it slow."

I let him pull me back down to the bed. In a moment, he was above me, his smile growing. It was the way you might look at an excited child on Christmas morning. "What?" I asked.

He shook his head. "Shut up," he said, and covered my mouth with his.

Diana swore she wouldn't have taken the job if she'd known it was on the thirteenth floor. "They tricked me," she said. "The elevator button may say twelve, but this place has thirteen written all over it."

"It's just the European system," I reassured her. "They don't count the ground floor."

"And how was I supposed to know that? Do I look European?" She cocked her head, straight black hair falling over one shoulder, dark defiant eyes still not losing their narrow almond shape. A clump of sprouts fell from her sandwich and plopped onto the paper wrapper unfolded in her lap. She looked up at the building behind us, as if the sprouts had been dropped from there—the thirteenth floor, no doubt.

"You're just making excuses, Diana," I said to the back of her head. We were sitting side by side in the tiny garden between the building and the noonday traffic of Market Street.

"Excuses?" she repeated, turning fast enough this time to send a pickle plummeting from the sandwich. "That place is cursed. The company mascot is probably a black cat. I never stood a chance."

"You never *wanted* to stand a chance."

She finally took a bite. "Can you blame me? I was meant for better things."

Diana had always been a little high-strung. Actresses usually are, she assured me, though it remained an open question as to whether the career choice or the emotional state came first. Today, though, she had an excuse. Just before lunch, she had finally given her notice. Diana had been threatening to quit since the day I started; I'd eventually just added *disgruntled* to my mental list of her personality traits. But this morning she'd surprised me with her rationality. "Today's the day," she'd said with a smile as she stopped by my cubicle. "Two weeks from now, I'm history."

She'd decided last night. There was no point in waiting any longer. "It's now or never," she told me. "Dreams don't wait." She'd spent half the morning booking a flight to LA, arranging to stay with a friend in West Hollywood, finding a place to store her furniture.

"So," she said now, abandoning the recalcitrant sandwich in favor of a bag of Doritos, "I'm finally going to do it. Julia Roberts, look out."

"LA will never be the same," I said, toasting her soda with my iced tea. "And neither will San Francisco."

Psychologically, Diana had had her bags packed for months. All she needed, she said, was a boost. "Sure I'm scared," she admitted. "Don't think I'm not completely terrified by the whole process. LA's a scary place: if the casting directors don't get me, the drive-by shooters will. But I don't have much of a choice. What's that line from *A Chorus Line?*—'God, I'm a dancer. A dancer dances.'"

I shifted position on the bench; the sun was in my eyes.

"What about you?" she asked suddenly, tossing an orange chip onto my sandwich. "You shouldn't be writing copy for a living, either. You're selling yourself short."

"Who isn't? It's the nineties." I popped the chip into my mouth, the indistinct cheese taste assaulting my tongue.

"No, really, Neal. What the hell are you doing here, anyway?"

I laughed. "Paying the rent."

She sighed, rolled her eyes toward the sky. The sun was unusually strong today; her skin seemed the color of paper. "What do you want to do, Neal? What's your *dream?*"

Dreams. I turned toward the intersection, hordes of people crossing in every direction—business suits, uniforms, torn jeans. Some wore a purposeful gaze, others the shaky look of terror. One man stood impatiently at the light, glancing at his watch, rocking on his heels at the edge of the curb. Which of them, I thought, had dreams?

"I have lots of dreams," I said, turning back with a snap of the neck. "They just take time."

Diana pouted, incredulous. "Well, mine's going to take a bunch of eight-by-ten glossies and a handful of sore knuckles from knocking on doors." A smile crept onto her face. She looked like a child who'd just cajoled her parents into revealing her Christmas present. "And I'm going to love every minute of it."

She was in the flush of excitement after making her decision. I couldn't crush that mood by bringing her abruptly down to earth with statistics. LA was full of actors, I wanted to tell her—as the song says, all "parking cars and pumping gas." Diana's plan was like leaping out a window and just hoping there was a mattress on the ground to catch you. She couldn't be sure; even looking down as she crept onto the ledge would be considered cheating. All she could do was close her eyes and jump. And on the way down she'd be thinking of the cushiony comfort of the mattress. I, on the other hand, would imagine only the shape of the chalk outline on the pavement. That was the difference between us.

"You took the plunge in coming out here," she said. "That must have been just as scary."

"Not quite," I told her. "My expectations weren't so high. I just wanted to escape, and everyone says San Francisco's the perfect place for that."

"Too perfect, I'd say." She gestured at the crowd milling past. "It's amazing how much people are willing to sacrifice for a view."

"Now you're picking on your hometown?"

"No. I love it here, but really. This town is full of people stuck in the most boring jobs—they'd all rather be doing something else, but God forbid they should leave Paradise."

"It is tempting." Already I couldn't imagine living anywhere else. Of course, the last thing I needed was another shake-up in my life. One per year is more than enough, thank you.

"Anyway," Diana went on, "I can't afford to think about what I'm leaving behind. It's what I'm heading for that counts."

I lifted my iced tea into the sunshine. "Then here's to the future."
She smiled and knocked her can against mine. "To dreams," she
said.

If, as Diana lamented, I hadn't been lucky with my job, I had certainly struck pay dirt on the home front. Considering my rent, the
apartment was huge for San Francisco: a large bedroom, a spacious
living room/kitchen area, complete with breakfast nook, and—if you
craned your neck sharply out the bay window—a view of one tiny corner of the Golden Gate Bridge. The view, of course, was available only
at the expense of climbing four flights of stairs—stairs so steep and
creaky that it was probably the only building in town where the first-
floor apartment was the most expensive. The apartment had needed a
lot of work when I moved in. I'd done some of it already—painting
over the dirty ivory walls, scrubbing the hard-water stains from the
tub. Other things, like the chips and scuffs in the hardwood floor, I'd
simply hidden with strategically placed furniture. The place now had
a distinctly homey atmosphere—a great comfort after a hard day.

In the beginning, I'd thought of the apartment as a hideaway, protection from the strangeness of a new city. Inside, surrounded by familiar objects—my favorite movie posters, the ancient metronome
my grandfather had given me when his fingers grew too twisted to
play the piano—I could feel safe. Everything between these walls was
within my control. As long as I avoided the windows, I could pretend
I was back in Boston, back where the world held no surprises.

After only a few months, though, the view had become my favorite
thing about the apartment. I liked reminding myself that I was in a
new city. Whenever I found myself feeling homesick, I would stroll
through Pacific Heights, where every corner offers another view of the
city—the bay on one side, hills rolling elegantly downtown on the
other. That sight was all I needed to feel the magic of San Francisco
again, the conviction that my definition of *home* had irrevocably
changed.

Diana's news had only exacerbated the usual stress of the day. In an office of isolated cubicles, she was really my only friend. When she'd gone, it would be like starting over—feeling out of place once more, searching for someone to connect with.

I hurried out of my dress clothes and reached into the closet for jeans and a T-shirt. I had to push a few hangers aside to make room for my slacks on the rack. Behind them, leaning into the corner, my cello case caught the fading light from the window. I saw it every day, barely registering. But Diana's prodding about dreams today made me stop and notice it. I pulled it out, its neck jostling the shirts that hung from the rack. It was lighter than I'd remembered. Sitting so stiffly in the closet, it had looked like an immovable boulder.

The latch gave way easily, revealing the red velvet lining, the still gleaming wood of the cello. I stroked it, tracing the grain, swirling my finger over the knot just below the neck. I hadn't played in months, hadn't even looked at the thing. I'd moved it into the apartment just like any other piece of furniture or kitchen utensil. Its place had been unquestioned—the back of the closet, out of sight. I had no need of it now. It was a piece of the past. I shut the case quickly and returned it to its spot, behind everything else. It still wasn't time.

The living room got most of the evening light, everything nearly golden as the sun fell out of sight. I looked out, but the bridge was already shrouded in mist.

It took a few minutes to find the disc I wanted. Arranging my CDs on the shelves was one thing I had never gotten around to doing; the Dvořák was standing uncomfortably between Sondheim and Madonna. I'd always prided myself on being eclectic.

The cello, Adam had said, was the instrument closest to the human voice—something about its range, or perhaps the plaintive sounds it made in the right hands. Listening now, lying back on the couch in the dying light, I thought I heard tears in the music, cries of refusal. Adam had tried to teach me this piece—only after weeks of practice, of course. When I started studying with him, I hadn't touched the cello for years, since my brief stint in the college orchestra. My fumbling had given my father a headache, and the frustration had only exacerbated my impatience. I'd given up. Music was an absurd dream, I'd told myself. Of the millions who try, how many succeed?

Adam had watched me carefully, nodding in time to the music, his eyes telling me when to speed up or slow down. During the sticky patches, he would come up beside me and place my fingers delicately on the strings, his own gently twisting them into place. That was when I first felt it—something in the warmth of his shadow as he stood behind me, enclosing me in arms that reached around from either side. The air changed suddenly, full of his scent and pulsing with his heat. As he leaned closer, I imagined that I could hear his heart beating in my ear. Listening for it, I barely registered the notes he made my hands play on the strings.

Until that point, it had never even crossed my mind that Adam might be gay. Although I'd found him attractive, I'd always had a rule that straight men were off limits, even for fantasy: my heart had been broken enough already, there was no reason to set myself up for another fall. But as he lingered, counting the beats in my ear, his breath washing over my shoulder, I began to wonder. And when he pulled away and his eyes met mine, I knew. He looked at me differently—not as a student, but as a man. The way other men looked at me, in bars, on South End streets.

We didn't talk about it then. In a moment, the feeling was gone, driven underground by the music. But I spent the next day thinking about him, waiting for our next lesson, wondering what he would teach me this time.

As it turned out, I was the one who had to teach him. He gave me another of those looks as soon as I walked through the door, and that was all I needed. I leaned my cello against the wall and walked toward him, and kissed him. He seemed stunned at first, momentarily frozen, but soon his lips pressed back against mine, and we embraced. He hadn't been with many men before. That showed in the awkwardness of his movements, his hesitation to touch me, as if he were afraid I was too fragile.

It was a week before he told me that he considered himself bisexual. "You're kidding," I said, staring down at him, head supported on my hand, elbow boring into the mattress. I'd never met a bisexual before, at least no one who'd admitted it. They were like ghosts or angels to me; I refused to believe in their existence until I'd seen one with my own eyes.

"I date women," he said. "Usually women, as a matter of fact."

"Are you seeing one now?" I asked. I was hardly the most sexually experienced man in town, but I'd already heard every conceivable excuse for not getting involved—men who lived with their parents, had lovers, wanted to sow their wild oats, were too obsessed with their careers, needed "space." A woman waiting in the wings was a new one on me.

"No," he said. He seemed almost ashamed to admit it. He looked down the length of the mattress, at our feet entangled above the crumpled sheets.

"Do you want to?"

He laughed. "Not at this moment, no."

"Good." I tilted myself forward and kissed him.

When the session at Tanglewood was over and we both returned to Boston, the lessons stopped—but we continued to see each other. And I soon learned that he had "not quite lied" about not dating a woman at the moment—"not quite" was his phrase. Adam parsed his words as skillfully as he negotiated the intricacies of Dvorák.

The rest, as they say, is history, and I'd come 3,000 miles to escape history. I stopped the disc now, in the middle of the second movement, the mournful adagio. Silence was more fitting.

Even the phone, screeching abruptly, seemed to belong to a different place. I answered it before the second ring, just to stop the noise.

"Yo." Zach and I had grown monosyllabic on the phone, primitive grunts replacing language. We enjoyed the fantasy that words were unnecessary in our lives; we nurtured the idea that we instinctively understood each other.

"Whenever," I said, continuing the game. His volley.

"Half an hour. I'll wear leather so you'll know me."

"What makes you think you're the only leather queen to knock on my door on a Thursday night?"

"Intuition. Common sense."

"Wishful thinking."

He laughed. "Later," he said, and once again there was silence.

No two men have ever been more different. With Adam, every date was dissected days before it happened, activities planned to the minute. It was as if he carried an internal metronome to keep himself forever aware of the tempo—never too slow, never too fast.

And Adam had felt safe in language. We'd spend hours talking—in bed or out, lights on or off. He told me, I thought, everything there was to know about himself—his past, his thoughts, his plans. Unlike me, he didn't seem to compose his ideas as he spoke, but rather spat them out, like a prepared script—perfect, no holes. He would have found Zach's comparative reticence unbearable. Zach told me more with his eyes and his body than he did with words. His feelings for me were clear in his touch, as electric as the synapses in my brain, and just as communicative.

I'd had enough of words for now, too. When Zach came through the door tonight, I would clamp his mouth shut with my lips. I would hold him against me all night and not even let him speak. We would be only bodies tonight—as instinctive as two figures on a dance floor, spinning in an elegant circle around the room. Quick quick, slow slow. That simple, that sure.

You always think the major events in your life are going to be introduced by a thunderclap—Moses descending from the mountain with the tablets, Dorothy whisked into the eye of the tornado. Turning points deserve such attention—a buildup of some sort, a drumroll, something to let you know that you're about to enter a new and dramatically different chapter. But even when those thunderclaps do rend the silence, we don't really notice: Oh, thunder, we say, I guess it's going to rain. We never really expect the torrential downpour; we never gather the animals two by two and load them into the ark for protection. Instead we look back after the waters have receded and ask ourselves, What was the first sign? Could I have predicted this? And when we do remember the thunderclap, the eerie stillness in the air just before the first drops began to fall, we have to wonder if we're only imagining it, constructing an explanation after the fact in a feeble attempt to deny our helplessness, our profound lack of prescience.

Zach had been acting strangely for a while—irritable, moody—I realize that now. At the time, I'm not sure what I thought. I was so wrapped up in readying things for him, I probably failed to notice what was really going on. In my happiness, I couldn't see beyond the idealized future I'd created for us.

I started with the closet. He'd need a place for his clothes, all those beautiful shirts and pants he wore to work every day. Zach made sure to iron out every wrinkle in a shirt before he'd put it on: every crease in the sleeves had to be perfect. If a wrinkle appeared once he was already dressed, that was just the price of movement—it would be natural, willed by the way he bent to tie his shoes, the turn of his arm as he lifted a coffee cup to his lips. Once the shirt was on, he was done with worrying; before that, only perfection was acceptable.

I picked out the things I wouldn't need for a while—all the winter clothes I'd brought from Boston. They were useless unless I traveled back east, and that didn't seem very likely, at least until Christmas. I stuffed all of it into the cedar chest I kept at the foot of the bed; I had to sit on the lid to get it to close properly. What I had left still took up more than half the closet, so I weeded through, picking out the things I hadn't worn in a year, the things I couldn't imagine wearing again. I'd been a pack rat for too long; it was time to get rid of the pieces I no longer had any use for. The pastels that Martin had warned me against—so outré in San Francisco—still hung together in the corner, untouched since I'd arrived in town. They would be the first to go.

I rented a storage closet in the basement and carried down the cello, a few boxes, an end table that no longer seemed suitable. I already imagined Zach's armchair in its place, under the floor lamp. He could sit there and read the paper while I fixed dinner. Dinner for two. I would no longer have to choose between half-recipes and leftovers.

I asked Zach's opinion about everything—which side of the medicine cabinet he wanted, how we should organize the kitchen—but he always deferred. "Whatever you want," he said more than once. "Don't change everything because of me; I'm flexible."

"This is going to be your place, too," I told him. "If there's anything you don't like, just tell me."

"It's all fine," he said. "I wouldn't change a thing."

But I would. I was changing everything. Every day I would come home and find something else to hate—the Picasso print over the fireplace, the prayer plant in the foyer, leaves browning at the tip. Talking to Zach on the phone one night, I'd ask who his favorite painter was, seeking out a fitting replacement for the soon-to-be-departed Pablo. "I don't have one," he said. "Why?"

"No reason." I was sitting on the sofa, studying the Picasso—half faces staring at each other from a variety of angles, colors too bright, lines too bold. I was trying to remember what I'd ever seen in cubism, trying to decide whether Monet might be more suitable to Zach's temperament, maybe even Turner. When he next came over, I grilled him about the Picasso. "It's fine," he said. "I like the colors. What are you getting at?" He looked at me as if I were crazy. "It's just a painting."

The move was set for Labor Day weekend. That would give us a couple of days to get used to the situation before we had to go back to work, before routine took over our lives. He had planned to borrow a friend's van to transport his things; it would take two trips at most, he thought. He was going to call me when the van arrived, so I could grab the bus to his apartment and help with the packing. We would drive to my place together—*our place*. The phrase still brought an automatic smile to my lips. In my fantastic imagination, I regretted that the place wasn't equally new to us both: some crazy part of me wanted Zach to carry me over the threshold.

Up even earlier than usual, I decided to rearrange the bedroom for the third time that week. Suddenly remembering how tall Zach's dresser was, I cleared a space on the opposite wall, where its height wouldn't block access to the window. I was carrying a chair across the room when the phone rang.

Zach sounded like he'd only just woken up. His *hello* was garbled, half-swallowed by a yawn.

"Did you get the van yet?" I asked. I slapped a gray smear of dust off my knee, thankful I'd worn the grubbiest clothes I could find. A reminder not to throw away *everything* that crowded the closet.

"What van?"

I laughed and plopped onto the bed. "*What van.* Gordon's van, you knucklehead. Is he going to help us pack?"

Zach paused. "I'm not coming," he said.

"You didn't get the van." I frowned. I'd never met Gordon, but from what Zach had told me, he didn't seem like the most reliable person. "Is he held up or something?" I asked. "What time is he coming over?"

"He's not," Zach said. "I canceled it."

"You canceled it?" I wanted to laugh again—he was full of jokes today. But usually a nervous tone would give his jokes away; it was a rare occasion when he could really manage to pull my leg. That tone wasn't there now, but I still held on, hoping he'd just improved his technique. Afraid to laugh, I simply remained confused.

"I'm really tired," he said. "Can I call you back later?"

"No," I said, bounding off the bed. The phone rattled on the nightstand, the black cord twisted around itself like strands of DNA. "What's going on, Zach? We've been planning this for weeks."

His tone remained languid, despite the now stinging words. "No, Neal, *you've* been planning it for weeks. *Months,* for all I know. I'm just not ready for this yet. I'm not going to let you smother me just because you're feeling lonely."

"Lonely? I'm not doing this because I'm lonely. I'm doing it because I love you."

"In your case, Neal, I think that amounts to the same thing."

The receiver had grown warm against my ear, the dangling cord finally still in the crook of my arm. I was staring at the space I'd just cleared across the room, the dust bunnies clinging to the floor molding. A slight draught swirled beneath them, giving them a leisurely sway, but still they hung on, as if afraid of a mere two-inch drop.

"What brought this on?" I asked. I was amazed to hear my voice as quiet, as peaceful as his.

"I've been thinking about it for a while. It just doesn't feel right, that's all."

"But everything's ready. I—you were supposed to be here to-night."

"I can't."

"Won't."

"Okay, won't."

I took a deep breath, feeling something tremble upward from my chest to my eyes, a tremor caught just in time. I wouldn't cry. That would only backfire. "We have to talk about this," I said.

"I'm so tired, Neal—"

"Why? Haven't you slept?"

"I don't sleep very well these days. Too much on my mind."

"What? Me?"

He sighed again, loudly, as if he were finally waking up. "Not everything is about you, Neal."

"I didn't say it was. I just don't want to—"

"Be a burden?" He laughed. "That's what my grandmother used to say. 'I don't want to be a burden. When I can't take care of myself, go ahead and put me in a home.'"

"This isn't about your grandmother, Zach, it's about us. I can't let it go like this. We have to talk."

"I'm not saying it's over, Neal. I just don't want to live with you. What's to talk about?"

"You can't just make a promise and then renege. What kind of a relationship do we have if you can hold back your feelings like that?"

"I don't know. What kind of relationship *do* we have?"

"That's what I want to talk about." Images were flashing through my head. I was trying to reconstruct his body from head to toe, remember every freckle. "What are you doing today?"

"Sleeping."

"After that."

"I have no idea."

"Lunch."

"What time?"

"Now?"

He sneered. "It's nine-thirty. How about twelve?"

"Flore?"

"Why not? We'll go back to the scene of the crime."

"Is that what we're calling it now?"

"Jesus, Neal, lighten up."

"I don't see anything funny at the moment."

"That's your problem. For someone who's always telling jokes, you just don't know when to laugh."

I sat back on the bed, the spring squeaking beneath me. "I love you."

"I'll see you at noon."

"Okay." I held the receiver even tighter against my ear after the click. I couldn't let go.

I waited at an outside table. I hadn't eaten all morning, but I still wasn't hungry. My stomach churned at the thought of food, so I had just gotten a Calistoga and carried it into the sunlight.

The café was a riot of color and noise, excited voices raised with increasingly outrageous anecdotes—the top-this style of conversation, Martin called it. The sunlight drew people out as the water at Lourdes draws pilgrims, as a wound draws blood cells. After the incessant fog of summer, San Franciscans were grateful for any trace of sun—basking in it, short pants and tank tops pulled anxiously out of the closet lest they languish for yet another season. Finally, the ubiquitous trendy black had given way to brightness, as if for just this once it was okay to be less than subtle, to stop feigning indifference.

Zach arrived fifteen minutes late, staggering past the tables at the front, his head nearly bumping against a Cinzano umbrella. He was looking around carefully, so I didn't need to wave. A simple nod was enough to pull him toward me.

He sat in the chair opposite with a decided plump, shoulders rounding beneath his white T-shirt, legs spread in a languid V, the knees of his red jeans poking out beneath either side of the table. His hair was unkempt, but that might have just been the wind. It was his eyes that disturbed me—dark rings beneath them, like days' worth of makeup a drag queen had forgotten to wash off. The lids drooped halfway, as if he had no control over them. He seemed to be squinting at me, but the sun was behind him.

"Thirsty?" I asked.

"No," he said. "I'm fine."

"You don't look fine."

He shrugged, tilting his head to one side, as if pointing to something just over his shoulder.

"So what's wrong?"

"I'm so tired of hearing that question, Neal." His voice had the same dreamy monotone I had heard on the phone—lifeless, drained.

"Well, maybe if I got a good answer, I'd stop asking it."

He let his eyelids fall all the way down, tongue twisted up to rest on the sharp edge of a tooth. He seemed to be thinking, or at least imagining something—wishing this moment away. "Look," he said after a pause, "maybe this isn't going to work. You seem to want something that I'm just not ready to give. I'm going through—something—a rough time right now. I can't—I don't have the energy to deal with this." His eyes darted open suddenly, belying his last words.

"Can I help you?"

He threw his head back and spoke to the billboard that hovered over the building. "No. That's not your job."

The emptiness in my stomach was spreading, eating up everything inside, leaving only space. "I don't understand."

"Maybe we should just stop seeing each other," he said.

I swallowed hard. "Why?"

He smiled. "Because you ask too many questions." His face softened as he looked me in the eye for the first time. "Look, Neal, I'm not good enough for you. You're smart. You're well educated. You have so much going for you. You're *normal*. Believe me, you don't want the kind of shit that I have to deal with every day of my life. You don't want it. Just count your blessings that you could get out of this when you could. You're better off."

I reached for his hand, the fingers curling nervously against the tile tabletop, but he pulled it away as soon as my palm grazed the hair on his knuckle. "What are you talking about? I know you."

"You think you know me. Nobody knows anybody, Neal. Not really. If they did, nobody would ever get involved."

His pale cheeks were mottled with stubble, at least a couple of days' growth. His beard came in patchily, thin just beneath the sideburns, thicker toward the chin; only the mustache looked even. "So what do you want?" I asked.

"I don't know."

"That's it? It's just over—because you don't know?"

He bit his lip. "What do *you* want?"

Bright blue eyes stared back at me, the whites cracked by red, like veins in marble. "You," I said.

"You know something? I think I believe you."

A space closed inside, solidity returning for an instant. "I never lie," I said.

"That'll change."

A busboy came by. He reached for my bottle, pulled away when he saw it was still half full. I picked it up, took a long sip. "So what do we do now?" I asked.

"Go back to the way it was," he said. "Casual."

"It was never casual, Zach."

"Okay, then we at least slow it down a little. You have to give me space. I think we both need space."

I'd had enough of space, distance threatening to overwhelm me. Three thousand miles between me and everything I knew, everything I'd cared about for thirty years. It wasn't space I was looking for, but if space was the way to connect to Zach, then I'd give it a try. I'd never run away from paradox.

"Okay," I said. "Just let me know when I'm being—too much."

"Oh, you'll know. Believe me, you'll know."

The umbrella beside us rattled in the wind and one of the men be-

neath it wound it closed. The sun poured more openly onto the courtyard now, making everything glow.

Zach visibly flinched when I touched him now. Sitting beside him
on the couch, watching TV, I would instinctively let my hand fall
onto his leg, only to feel it flex suddenly, as if a doctor's hammer had
tapped his knee. Greeting him at the door, I would move my lips toward him and meet the stubble of a quickly raised chin. I learned to
hold back every gesture. I had never before realized how many there
were—how many times a day I had automatically reached for him,
curled his hair in my fingers, kissed his forehead, caressed his butt,
blew into his ear, settled my foot atop his under the dinner table.
Only by holding back did I learn all that my body craved, all the
things it had done as if without my knowledge. Keeping it in check, I
observed myself now as carefully as I did Zach—as if he and my own
body were equally strangers, to me and to each other.

Despite his avowed need for space, we spent nearly as much time as
ever together, though now it was less event oriented. Hours would
pass with him on the couch at my place or the futon at his, watching
Star Trek or *Cheers* reruns, while I read in a chair off to the side, away
from the brightly flashing images, imagining the book's words recited
loudly in my brain to block out the dialogue and the laugh track.

He seemed to want me there, if not for company then at least for a
sort of balance—to even out the room, him on one side and me on the
other, like weights on a scale. Occasionally, when the commercials
came on, I would catch his eye over the spine of my book and see a
smile curling onto his lips. He was checking that I was still there, that
I hadn't vanished while the Klingons were attacking the Enterprise.

I held back even in bed, waiting for Zach to take his place beside
me. Lying on his side, facing the wall, he would scoot backward, toward me, until my legs were snug in the crook of his knees. He would
arch his back into my chest, his signal that I should bring my arm

around to cradle him. Zach preferred to be in front now; lying behind me made him claustrophobic, he said, as if my back would cut off his air.

Most nights, we would just lie like that, until my arm got tired or until he decided to turn onto his stomach. (Apparently, I thought, rolling over, his air isn't cut off when he's face-down in a pillow.) He was tired almost constantly, falling asleep within minutes of settling his head on the pillow. I'd never been such an easy sleeper; it would usually take close to an hour for my mind to stop swirling around the events of the day and plans and anxieties about tomorrow.

I spent that hour now with an extra thought—wondering if and when Zach's arm would find itself on my side of the bed, reaching out to caress a nipple or stroke the hair on my chest, signaling that he wanted more than sleep. On those nights, waiting for him to touch me, I felt more alone than I did when he wasn't even in the room, more alone than I could remember.

I hardly ever had erotic dreams, at least remembered ones. My sleep was usually filled with the other half of the standard gamut— missed trains, elevators stuck between floors, arriving for a meeting naked or otherwise unprepared. When visions of penises, let alone tingly sensations, interrupted my sleep, it was news.

This one was so real, it woke me up. And when the feeling didn't stop, I thought I had simply moved into another dream, as if there were layers and I would never get out into the light of day. I looked down to see a moving lump under the sheets between my legs. I fell back again, letting the sensation continue, the wet warmth of Zach's mouth pulling me in, his fingernails gently scratching my inner thigh.

I'd always been a noisy lover, the kind the neighbors complain about, but in the middle of the night, awakened from sleep, the moans seemed locked in my throat. Sound would spoil the dream quality of the moment; the most I could let out was fractured breathing as my neck arched away from the pillow. I had no idea how long he'd been doing it, but after only a brief wakeful moment, I felt myself coming. I tried to pull away, into the mattress, but his hands gripped my ass firmly and pulled it toward him. "Stop," I hissed, "I'm coming. Stop!" But he wouldn't. If anything, he sucked harder, as if my reluctance were a challenge, an incentive. His fingers pressed into me, searing scratches in my skin, while his lips burrowed into my crotch. I squirmed beneath him, half struggling against him, half letting go.

And I came. With a sudden shock, moans finally giving way to a muffled screech, I felt my entire body tremble, my cock still rigid in Zach's mouth, shooting against the back of his throat. He sealed his lips around me and sucked firmly at the last drops before finally pulling away.

I was heaving, eyes closed, when he swam up beside me. He traced a line along my cheek and I looked up at him, saw the mischievous smile, a look he seldom wore these days. "You shouldn't have done that," I said. "You know you shouldn't have done that."

"You can't hurt me," he said. "You'd never hurt me."

His eyes were soft, a child's eyes illogically sketched above the lascivious lips of a man. "No," I said, "I wouldn't."

He dropped his head onto my shoulder and reached an arm across my chest, pulling me toward him like flotsam from a sinking ship.

In the beginning, it had been easy to pigeonhole Zach. He was a dependable smile, a blend of childlike mischief and innocence that served as the perfect antidote for my disordered life. In those first few months, I was still floundering, reaching for something to buoy me in an unfamiliar environment, and I willingly granted Zach that role. He anchored me.

But now the only predictable thing about him was his unpredictability. His moods shifted so quickly, to such extremes, I had trouble keeping up. I found myself looking for signs, clues that his joy would soon swerve into dull silence, that his enveloping affection would give way to icy indifference. I looked for evidence in his eyes, hoping their color would fade or brighten like a mood ring. I watched him from across the room, the force with which his fingers manipulated the remote—pressing the buttons violently, or merely skimming the channels as if he didn't really care what he found. I studied his touch, the relative warmth or cold of his hand, the pressure his leg exerted on me in bed—whether he pulled it away when I accidentally strayed into his territory or wrapped it invitingly around mine. I became an expert on his moods, memorizing his behavior with the same attention that I had once addressed to his face—the tiny scar beside his left eye, the slight asymmetry of his nose. I learned the way he poured cereal—shaking the box at an acute angle to the bowl rather than letting the cereal spill directly from a height. I knew the twist of an eyebrow that signified he didn't understand something, the subtle trembling of his chin that indicated reined-in anger. I learned to read him—like a book, I might say, if the cliché weren't so ridiculously inappropriate. If Zach was a book, it was a postmodern novel, the kind that zig-zagged past logic, always a step ahead of the reader, perhaps even the author. Just when I thought I had him figured out, there'd be a new twist, something I'd never expected, some detail that refused to fit into the neat picture I was busy drawing.

I stopped asking what was wrong. The only answer I ever got was that the question was the culprit: everything would be fine if only I'd stop asking what was wrong. So I let him stare at the TV. I let him sleep until noon on Sundays. I let him go for the long walks alone that he said would help him think, even though he always returned with the same blank expression, the same silent indifference.

We spent the night together only a few times a week now. He was on his own on weekdays. Somehow, he managed to get himself up in the morning and go to work. I stopped by to see him on my lunch hour once—to spy on him, really, confirm that he was okay.

At the end of my first week in kindergarten, I had glanced away from my crayons and seen a familiar face behind the wired glass in the classroom door—my mother, watching me. She jumped out of sight as soon as our eyes met, caught in her anxious vigilance. I never asked her about it—must have assumed I'd imagined it, mistaken the face of a custodian or another teacher for hers. It wasn't until I was leaving for college—the next time she had to confront a radical change in our relationship—that she admitted being there. Not just that day, but the entire week, she had visited at the school for a few minutes, just to observe, just to assure herself that I was okay, that I could really survive without her.

I slid off the escalator and peered around the corner, past the racks of shoes. It was like that first day, when Diana had dragged me here, to spy with a completely different motive. Then, I could just say that I needed a pair of shoes; this time, there was no credible excuse.

He was with a customer, on the far side of the floor. The man waited patiently as Zach pulled a pair of loafers from a box, tearing out the tissue paper stuffed into the toes. He was smiling, and he passed the man one shoe at a time. I noticed that his cheeks were as pink as ever, his eyes as bright. There was no sign of the moodiness he turned to me as soon as he walked through my door or I through his. Here, where charm was required, he had no trouble pretending.

When we were together, that sense of joy was reserved for the bedroom. Zach seemed most alive when making love, as if it were the one thing he felt sure of, the one thing he knew he did well.

I had been fucked only a few times before Zach, without much enthusiasm or satisfaction. Adam had been afraid to do it—afraid of hurting me, he said, though I think it was more himself that he was worried about. Fucking was the ultimate taboo, an admission that homosexuality was more than an experiment. Needless to say, he never allowed me to fuck him.

But I welcomed Zach. From the beginning, I had wanted him inside me. Having him inside, moving inside me, seemed the most intimate thing we could do, the most special gift I could offer. After the first few weeks, it became a regular part of our sex life.

It had been awhile, though. Since Labor Day, our sex had been relatively tame—quick and uncomplicated. So when he offered at last a few weeks later, I was more than willing.

He started gently, probing me with one finger for a while before finally offering another, working his way up to three, not pushing too far in but simply circling around, preparing me. I'd been nervous at first because his cock was larger than most, but I was surprised to find that it was actually less painful than the others. My body shaped itself around him more easily. Within minutes, he was pushing in all the way, and I felt nothing but pleasure. I stopped stroking my own cock; I didn't need the distraction, and the sensation couldn't compete with the feel of him inside me. His cock rubbed against my prostate and I thought I would come spontaneously. He slowed down with my cry and carefully pulled out. "Roll over," he said.

I rolled onto my belly. Zach got off the bed and pulled me around so that my legs were hanging over the side. I looked over my shoulder to see him positioning himself, crouching on the floor, pulling my ass against him, finally plunging in. Not gently this time; the tenderness wasn't necessary anymore. He pushed violently into me, his crotch smacking noisily against my ass. He slapped me a few times; the sting rippled along my spine. Sweat was building up, spilling from my back, from his chest, and each time our bodies met they clung for a split second, wet and hot. He bent over, his whole body leaning over mine, and suddenly a tiny cold bottle was under my nose. He held one nostril closed and I inhaled. The acrid smell burned into me, pressure building, a rich warmth spreading through my body. I squeezed his cock between my cheeks, pushed and pulled along with him, my own cock growing hard again upon the mattress.

I cried out, but Zach remained silent. Only the hardness of his breathing indicated his pleasure. I became absorbed in the silence, concentrating on the sensation, the rest of the world fading away, beyond my comprehension. I wanted it to go on forever. I wanted him inside me forever.

He stopped moving suddenly; I was writhing alone. And just as suddenly, he pulled out, a cold draught rushing into me, and the abrupt sting of emptiness. I looked around. His head was thrown back, his body drenched. I followed the sweat down to his crotch, where his hand held his now limp, glistening cock.

It took a moment to register. "You came?" I said. And with the word, I felt the wetness seeping between my thighs—stickier, warmer than sweat. I flipped over and sat up. His cock was dripping, and my ass felt sticky. "You came." I looked down, dumbfounded, watching the puddle on the sheet as if it were some foreign substance I'd never seen before. I hadn't even noticed that he hadn't put on a condom—

after the first time, I hadn't had to ask. He'd been spontaneous this time, and reckless.

I ran past him and into the bathroom.

When I came out, he was curled fetally on my side of the bed, the sheets still in a twisted pile at his feet. His broad back blocked most of the light coming from the lamp. He was gazing at the lampshade, the orange T-shirt he had slung over it for mood lighting. I circled around the bed. The sweat had dried on his chest, its only vestige the tufts of hair that stuck together in tiny curls.

I sat beside him and caught one of the curls, twisted it gently between my fingers. Oblivious to my touch, he continued to stare at the light with the fascination of a child. My panic suddenly gave way to a sense of peace. This moment was real, not the fears that had raced through my mind in the bathroom, the terror I'd seen in my eyes in the mirror above the sink. This was Zach, half-asleep at my side, quiet, gentle. I couldn't possibly be harmed by this. I remembered him a few nights before, swallowing my own come, indifferent to the danger, certain that there was none—trusting, believing that we were both somehow protected, if only by love. Looking at him now—his smooth pale skin glowing sepia like an old photograph—I felt that same sense of safety. I felt it concretely, as firm as a suit of armor: as long as we loved, nothing could harm us.

Then there were the days when he wouldn't leave the house. He called me at the office in the morning, groggy, to tell me he'd called in sick to work. Nothing specific, he said, he just didn't feel like getting out of bed. There was no reason to get out of bed.

We all take stress differently, I thought. God knows there had been plenty of days when I'd longed to stay in bed, and several when I'd called in sick for precisely that reason. There was no shame in it. I called them mental health days. Bad moods were as valid as the flu or a broken ankle; we were all entitled to our share.

It was when the feelings lingered that I began to worry. He took to bed one Tuesday and was out of work three days in a row. I visited on Friday evening, complete with a bagful of groceries—chicken soup, Pepperidge Farm cookies, the usual comfort food. But he wouldn't take even a spoonful.

"I'm just tired," he said. "Maybe I have mono."

"Have you called a doctor?"

"No," he mumbled. "I'll be fine if I just get some sleep."

"Zach, you've been sleeping for three days straight. Any more and you'd be comatose."

"Well, that would end my problems. I could just sleep through the next fifty years."

"Don't make jokes, I'm worried."

He rolled his eyes. "I'll be fine," he said. "Why don't you take yourself out to the movies? Go to a bar—find someone with a little more energy."

"Jesus Christ, Zach, what is it with you?" I left the bedside and held the curtain open, looked down at Church Street. "That's not my scene, I've told you. I'm not interested."

He laughed—a harsh, guttural sound. "I just like to see your reaction," he said. "Such passion."

The trolley across Market Street spilled out another batch of commuters, men in business suits and bold ties clutching briefcases as they headed for home. They would emerge a few hours later in jeans and leather, transformed, unrecognizable.

"Call the doctor, will you? This could be anything."

"What are you worried about, Neal? Think I have dementia?"

I stared back at him, his head propped up by throw pillows. "Just call the doctor."

What bothered me most was the way Zach had given in to whatever was wrong with him. Unwilling to fight it, he had no curiosity even to identify his enemy. He seemed to welcome it, as if there were some tangible pleasure in escaping from the world, escaping into this tiny apartment, which grew smaller by the day with the accumulation of dirty clothes and the other objects he left lying around, too tired to pick them up—escaping further still, into the circumscribed world of his own mind, where I couldn't follow.

I stood by the window for a long while, watching him. Back stiff against the pillow, he didn't fidget. Only his eyes moved—away from me, across the floor, back to the futon, studying the blue folds of his blanket. The room acquired a funereal stillness, both of us silent as if in respect for something that had died.

"Call me," I said, finally giving up. I kissed his forehead and gathered my jacket off the armchair. "If you need anything. Or if you want to talk."

He looked up at me—shocked, confused—a vulnerable little boy. For the first time, I saw something akin to fear in his eyes. But it was too late. I was already on my way out the door.

"It's not working out," he said. His voice was slightly muffled, as though the receiver had dropped, the mouthpiece hanging under his chin. He had a habit of holding the phone like that; I'd seen him do it more than once—talking to an empty room rather than to the person who clung on the other end of the line.

"What isn't?"

"This," he said, and paused. "Us."

I sighed. "Zach, I thought we'd gotten over that. We're taking it easy, right? No strings."

Silence. I rose from the couch and carried the cordless phone to the window. The fog was creeping in; the buildings on the other side of the Panhandle had lost their top stories.

"So that's what this has all been about?" I asked. "Your moodiness—it's because of me?"

"Not you, Neal. Us."

"Uh-huh."

"It always has to be about you, doesn't it? Look, I'm just not happy with . . . us."

"And I'm not supposed to take it personally."

"Right." I listened to his breathing as I clutched the curtain, still gazing out the window. "Besides, all I'm asking for is a time-out."

"A time-out? What is this, a football game? You get to call time when your shoe's untied?"

"Chill out, Neal. There are more important things in the world. Children are starving in Africa."

"Children are *always* starving in Africa." I let the curtain fall closed. The grayish fabric matched the fog; it might as well have stayed open.

"Look, I just can't deal with the extra stress right now."

"I'm a burden to you? Look, instead of shutting me out, why don't you let me help? Tell me what's wrong."

He lost patience. "At the moment, Neal, you *are* what's wrong. This conversation is a case in point."

I moved to the bedroom doorway. The blue elephant from the amusement park stared at me from the bed, its trunk curled in a derisive salute. "I see."

"Look, I'll call you."

"Don't go out of your way." I'd been dumped before. I knew all the clichés.

"I know how you feel," Martin said. "Believe me, I've been there." Forearms flat on the table, he leaned in and hunched his shoulders, as though to draw a protective circle around the drink before him. "But, to be perfectly honest, I think this may be for the best. I always wondered what you two had in common, anyway."

I laughed. Martin's idea of common ground was cocktail conversation—Nietzsche, Sondheim, the federal deficit. "We don't *need* to have anything in common," I said, reaching for my own drink, the lime bobbing against the side of the glass. "We have chemistry."

Martin sat back in his chair, his ghostly shadow dancing on the plate-glass window behind him. Fillmore Street was quiet this late at night, the bar the only thing left open besides the movie theater a few doors down. "I just wish you'd take it easy for now. Give it time."

"That wouldn't be so difficult if I believed him." I stabbed the lime wedge with my swizzle stick, drowning it in gin. "I just think there's something else wrong."

"And it's your job to fix it." He studied me, tongue curled ruminatively against the roof of his mouth.

"Why does that sound like an accusation, coming from you?"

Martin sighed, a forced gentleness suffusing his features. "I just think you've already done as much as you can."

"Well, obviously not. I mean—look at him." I turned around in my chair, searching for a waiter. The crowd was thick at the bar, a very different group than you'd find in other neighborhoods. Up here, on the Heights, it seemed more like a country club than a pick-up joint—as if these men, with their impeccable hairstyles and their Perry Ellis sweaters, were searching for a golf partner rather than someone to spend the night with.

"You act like he's your special project. Like your role in life is to put all the pieces back together."

I gave up looking for the waiter and swung back around to face Martin. "Look, I love him. Isn't that what you do for the people you love—try to help them through their problems?"

"Not if they don't want you to."

I took a final gulp of the drink. It was tart at the bottom, thick with lime juice. "How do you know he doesn't want me to?"

"He's told you! Or don't you speak English anymore?"

"Maybe he's like you, Martin. Maybe he just doesn't want me to get hurt." The waiter, a tall blond, finally passed by. I held up my empty glass and waved it gently back and forth. He nodded on his way back to the bar.

We were silent for a long moment. I kept my back to Martin, eyes following the waiter on his circuit around the room. I felt like a desert straggler in an old black-and-white movie, his thirst all the greater from the tantalizing sight of an oasis that might or might not be a mirage.

Martin sat patiently through my next drink (at least my third of the evening), but caught my arm before I could wave the waiter down for another refill. "Let me take you home," he whispered.

"Have I had enough?" I asked. "I've always wanted somebody to tell me I've had enough."

He met my gaze, his eyes as firm as the fingers that gripped my wrist. "You've had enough."

"Good." I pulled my hand away and sat back. "I've never had enough before."

We got up, our chairs screeching across the floor, and Martin led me down the steps to the exit. A cool wind met us at the door and I felt myself staggering over the threshold, Martin righting me with a controlled grip on my arm.

"I've never had enough of anything."

Martin drove with the windows halfway open. The wind carried the mist with it, beading my face like the cold hand towel I used to seal my pores after shaving. My head began to pound as we bounced over various hills on the way downtown. The pain was focused behind my eyes, but slowly began to spread across my brow and down to my temples, as if to complete a mask. I dropped my head into one hand, the wind blowing around my ears, and concentrated on breathing.

"One too many drinks?" Martin asked.

"Yes," I said, "just one."

"Which one? The first?"

We pulled up in front of my building sooner than I'd expected. I'd been half-hoping he would just drive all night, so I wouldn't have to face the prospect of shifting position, let alone walking up stairs. "I'll help you in," Martin said. He turned off the engine and walked around to the passenger side.

He opened the door with the polite grace of a valet, holding it for me as I stumbled my feet to the curb. "I'm okay," I said, waving away the hand that reached toward me. "Just give me a minute." I had to keep my gaze down. The pain in my head was like a ball rolling around at the whim of gravity, and I had to take care to keep it in place.

"Do you have your keys?"

"Of course I have my keys," I snapped, feeling my pocket for the familiar bulky outline. I pulled out the key chain, the brass G clef that anchored the keys on a ring. Adam had given it to me—so I'd always have music in my pocket, he said. I fumbled through the keys and found the long, square-headed one that fit the front door.

Martin walked to the entrance with me and stood on the stoop as I pushed the door in. The vestibule was warm, its two-tiered rows of mailboxes shining in the too-bright overhead light. "Can you get upstairs okay?"

I was already regretting my earlier tone, so I tried to be more civil now. "Thanks, Martin. I'll be fine. You just go home, it's late."

"Are you sure?"

"I'm a big boy," I told him, waving him away with the key chain. The G clef felt solid in my palm, the keys rattling a delicate arpeggio against my knuckles.

"Call me if you need anything."

"Mm-hmm." I turned away and started up the stairs. I heard the door close when I was nearly at the first landing.

The hallway upstairs was darker than the main entrance, so it took a moment longer to locate the right key. Finally, I twisted the door open and fell against it as it gave way. I flicked on a lamp and began to shed my clothes. I would clean up tomorrow. For now, it hardly mattered where anything landed—coat on the couch, shoes dropped one by one in the living room, shirt hanging from the bedroom doorknob.

A red light flashed on the answering machine. Someone had called, I thought. Someone had thought about me. Someone had been disappointed when I wasn't there to answer.

The tape rewound through two unusually brief messages. The machine abruptly shifted forward, and I heard silence, followed by a sudden click, a receiver clattering to its cradle. And again, this time muffled breathing and another click. Wrong number, probably. They'd tried it a second time, thinking they'd just transposed a digit. Once or twice, I'd done that myself, too embarrassed to leave an apologetic message. I'd even hung up on real people when I'd realized the voice was wrong.

I didn't have the energy to brush my teeth, but I headed for the bathroom, just to get some aspirin. At least three, I thought, shaking four into my palm. I swallowed them all and caught my reflection in the mirror. "Not a pretty sight," I told myself. "Not pretty at all."

And then it hit me. As though triggered by my own drunken ugliness, something rattled in my belly, the queasiness shifting as though caught by an undertow, and I found myself crouched over the toilet, clutching the cold porcelain sides with the panicked grip I might have granted a life preserver. Vomiting had terrified me since childhood—the violent control it wrenched over my body, its complete unpredictability. It was simply the body's way of rejecting the foreign, the unhealthy, but it was always hard to remember that. I always felt that I was the one under attack, that my body was rebelling against me.

The aspirin, of course, was gone, but I didn't bother to take any more. I simply rinsed with some mouthwash and trudged into the bedroom. My head had stopped pounding, the sensation giving way to a dull ache, but I was so tired, even that couldn't keep me up. Naked, I threw back the covers and crawled in.

At first I thought it was the alarm clock, and I cursed myself for setting it on a Saturday night. But, rolling my nose into the pillow and reaching for the clock, I gradually recognized the sound, the insistent ringing. I sat up quickly, suddenly sober at the thought of bad news. Good news never came after midnight.

"Did I wake you?"

I felt oddly relieved at the sound of Zach's voice. At least it wasn't someone calling to tell me that someone else had died. Zach and I had no one in common but Martin, and I'd just seen him. "No," I said, shutting my eyes again and falling back onto the pillow. "I mean, I don't think so. I just got to bed."

"Where were you?"

"Out with Martin," I told him.

"How is he?"

The pounding had started again—like a tiny ball insistently bouncing against my left temple. I massaged it as my other hand cradled the phone. "Why are you calling?"

He hesitated. "What's the matter? Aren't you alone?"

It took me a few seconds to realize why he sounded so panicked. "Of course. It's just late, Zach. Are you all right?"

"Sure. I just wanted to see how you were."

"At two o'clock in the morning? Generally, I'm *asleep* at two o'clock in the morning."

I heard him breathing gently through the wire. "I just thought you might like to talk."

"About what?" I was shocked by my own impatience. Maybe it was the headache, or maybe I was just still angry.

"I don't know, I—Never mind, you're tired." A rustling came through the wire, as if he were preparing to hang up.

"No, that's okay," I said hurriedly. "What have you been up to tonight?"

"Nothing much. I didn't even leave the house today."

"What'd you do?"

"Nothing."

I wondered if he meant it literally. I couldn't imagine actually doing *nothing*. It seemed at once tempting and terrifying.

"So how's Martin?"

I cleared my throat and the ball in my head rolled around as if in a pinball machine. "Martin's fine," I whispered, careful not to make the ball angry. "He's a very good friend."

"Well, you know what they say: new friends are silver, old friends are gold."

The saying had lost its poetry in the translation, I thought, but he was right. "Martin's not exactly an old friend."

"Well, you've known him longer than me."

I laughed. The ball didn't like laughter. It didn't like laughter at all. "By about two months," I said.

I wished I could see his stance, his gestures, something to explain the silence. I was sure that right now, halfway across town, his body language was speaking volumes.

"Well, I just wanted to check in," he said after a very long pause.

"Okay."

"We're still friends, right?"

I was in a foreign country, hearing idioms I'd never been taught in school. "Of course."

"Good night, Neal."

The line went dead before I could respond. Without rising from my back, I dropped the phone into its cradle and tried to decode the conversation. It was Zach who had left those hang-ups. He'd probably been calling all night, regularly. That was how he knew I'd only just gotten home, why he thought he wouldn't wake me even at this hour. He was alone. He was lonely.

Fortunately, I was too tired to think about it, my head pounding too hard to roll over and pick up the phone again, my mind racing with too many thoughts to bring his pain back in. I let my body go limp, my head sink into the pillow. It was nearly noon before I opened my eyes again.

The calls became routine—usually late at night, just as I was heading for bed. On nights when I was especially tired, I hesitated crawling into bed too early, afraid I'd sleep through the call. Zach sounded so sad most of the time, so unstable, I felt a need to be there for him— even if it was solely on his terms, terms that he was never willing to spell out.

I called him a couple of times, attempting to circumvent the expected, but his tone was impatient then, resentful—as if he thought I was checking up on him. When I reached out, he asserted his independence. Only when I feigned indifference would he reach for me. So after a while, I learned patience.

Even though the calls were his, I ended up doing most of the talking. His answers to my questions were cryptic—monosyllabic grunts masquerading as English. He wanted to hear me talk—and not, I soon divined, about anything in particular. At times I combated the silence with mere babble—office gossip, the MUNI Metro breaking down in rush hour when I was already late for a meeting, the density of the fog in late summer. All things were equal to Zach—just sounds crackling through a wire. Connection.

I kept a picture of Zach on the wall of my cubicle—a 3 × 5 photo snapped at Great America just after we emerged, wobbly legged, from the second of three roller-coaster rides. I had hung the picture at Diana's insistence—humiliating pressure might be a more accurate term. "The rest of these bozos have pictures of *their* significant others all over the place," she'd said. "Not to mention their squealing brats. At least Zach's nice to look at."

Sometimes I forgot how attractive Zach was, so accustomed had I grown to the pale blue eyes, the steep cheekbones, the dimples that carved out homes in his face when he laughed. I hadn't seen the dimples for weeks. In the photo, he looked back at me with wide childlike eyes, his smile brighter than the sunshine that spilled over the bill of his cap and cast a dim shadow over his brow. The roller coaster stood in a haze far behind him, lending a three-dimensionality to the picture—as if at any moment Zach might step out of the frame and do a cartwheel on my desk.

I turned away from the photo in favor of my monitor, the cursor flashing insistently on an otherwise blank screen. Writer's block was my greatest occupational hazard, as real as carpal tunnel syndrome, if less well understood. And no wrist guard or ergonomically designed keyboard could cure it. The solution, if it came at all, would fall unbidden from the sky, like hail in July, or Mary's archangel.

I rolled my chair out from under the desk. Staring at the screen wouldn't help. My inspiration was as likely to come in front of the vending machine down the hall. Besides, chocolate couldn't hurt.

Before heading off, I peeked into the cubicle next door. Fred, Diana's replacement, was busily typing away. He seemed to be on a roll, so I decided not to disturb him. Fred didn't strike me as the chocolate-run type, anyway. Diana, on the other hand, had poked her head over the wall at exactly 3:00 every day with raised eyebrows that nearly spelled "M & Ms." Later, spilling the bag into her palm, she would sift through the colorful pile, searching out the green shells for their legendary aphrodisiac qualities. A superstition held over from adolescence, she said. "Silly, I know, but with the state of my love life, I need all the help I can get."

The phone stopped me on the way past Fred—the double ring of an outside call. Most of my outside calls were personal—such is the life of the lonely copywriter. I ran back to my desk to answer it.

"Are you busy?" Zach asked.

I was still standing, one hand splayed on the desktop for support as I leaned forward. He hadn't called me at work in weeks, not since this whole thing started—the forced silence, broken by those odd late-night conversations. In fact, we had just spoken a couple of nights ago. I'd even managed to convince him to have dinner with me. A platonic dinner, of course. It was to be a kind of time-out from our time-out.

"Neal?"

"No," I said, dropping into my chair and scooting my knees under the desk. I whispered, uncomfortably aware of Fred. "No, this is a good time."

"How are you?" I heard voices in the background, the familiar bell of a department store code. He was at work today; that was a good sign. I was afraid he'd lose his job, he'd taken so many days off lately.

"I'm fine," I said. I didn't return the question anymore. Even when I meant it only in disinterested politeness, he took offense. Of course he was fine. He was always fine.

"My cousin's coming into town tonight," he said. "I'm sorry, but I'll have to break our date for tomorrow."

"Your cousin?"

"Liam. He lives in Australia. He's going to start school in New York next week, and he's stopping in San Francisco for a couple of days. I haven't seen him since we were kids."

I sat mesmerized by the winged toasters flying through space on my monitor, chased by burnt pieces of toast. "I didn't know you had any relatives in Australia."

"My mother's brother moved there in the sixties," he said. "He met my Aunt Margaret when they were both on vacation in New York. She refused to leave her family in Melbourne, so he had to move. Anyway, Liam decided to go to NYU for college. Personally, I think he just wanted to get as far away from Australia as he could."

It seemed an awfully elaborate lie just to get out of a dinner engagement. But then again, I thought, only lies *need* to be elaborate.

"I would invite you to meet him, but I don't think he'd be too comfortable having dinner with a couple of poofters. That's what they call fags in Australia." He laughed.

"Doesn't he know you're gay?"

"Well, yeah, but . . . knowing it and seeing it are two different things."

"Seeing is believing," I said. As long as we were on platitudes.

"I'm really sorry," Zach said. "I hope this doesn't fuck up your plans for the weekend."

"Don't worry," I told him. "I'll keep myself busy."

"Well, he's leaving early Sunday morning. Maybe we can reschedule."

"Don't worry about it," I said. "Have a good time." As I hung up the phone, I gave my mouse a furious spin, knocking the toasters into oblivion for another five minutes. I left the cubicle and nearly ran down the hall to the vending machine. I'd decided on one thing at least: no green M & Ms.

There's nothing more pathetic, I decided, than a TV dinner when you'd rather be on a date. So that Saturday night I made an elaborate meal for myself. I cooked to the accompaniment of Puccini—chopping vegetables as Tosca flirted with Mario in the church, turning veal medallions in a bath of olive oil and garlic as she negotiated with Scarpia, lifting the cover off the steaming rice at the precise moment that she stabbed him. And as I settled myself at the table, sipping the wine, evaluating the play of sweet red peppers against the veal, I listened to Tosca's growing delusions—her naive belief that she had saved her lover's life, the startling moment of revelation when she realized that she had failed.

After dinner, I planned to spend the rest of the evening with a book. I'd been avoiding *Wuthering Heights* for years, despite constant protest from Natalie that it was the greatest novel ever written. Now seemed as good a time as any to test her theory.

The phone rang in the middle of Lockwood's dream, the wrist torn and bloody, rubbed viciously across broken glass. I was jolted by the ring, but grateful to be relieved of the horrid image.

"Hi." His tone was matter-of-fact, almost breezy.

"Zach?"

"What are you doing?" There was a stillness in the background, almost an echo, so different from the hubbub of the last time we'd spoken.

"Reading. What about you? Is Liam there?"

"Uh-huh. He's taking a shower. I had to call. I'm sorry about tonight."

"That's okay," I told him. "I understand." I let my finger slip out of the book, losing my place.

He hesitated. I pictured him looking over his shoulder to see if Liam had entered the room. "I miss you."

"How's Liam?" I asked.

"Fine. We went to Alcatraz today. Scary place."

"I love it," I admitted. Alcatraz had been one of the first stops on Martin's tour of the city. I'd been utterly fascinated by it—the ghostly quality of those empty cells, the tangible traces of history in the dilapidated stone. The island was another world, the prison all the more terrifying for having that painfully tantalizing view of paradise.

"So did Liam. But he's from Australia; the place was *founded* by convicts." He paused. "I told him about you."

"Oh? What'd you tell him?"

"Everything."

"What's everything?" I asked.

"I told him that we were dating."

Are we dating? I wanted to ask. During the winter hiatus, are the Giants playing ball?

"Is he okay with that?"

"Yeah, he's fine." I heard movement on the other end of the line—a door closing, perhaps, a rustle on the bed. "Do you want to talk to him?"

It was a test, I thought suddenly. Liam was a test, but I couldn't be sure of what. Either Zach had made him up, or he wasn't really Zach's cousin at all: he was my rival, and Zach just wanted to see if I was smart enough to catch on.

I didn't have time to respond. Another rustle, and the phone suddenly came alive with a new voice. "G'day," it said in an accent not quite as strong as I'd expected.

"Hi," I said.

"Sorry I stole Zach here for the evening. I told him he was silly not to have mentioned you before."

I decided to change the subject as quickly as possible. "How do you like San Francisco?"

"It's a beautiful town," he said. "Reminds me of Sydney. I told Zach he should come visit us next summer, when I get out of school."

He meant next winter, I thought; either that, or he had already acclimated himself to a new hemisphere. "Look," he went on, "we're just getting ready to go out for some dinner. Care to join us?"

"No, thanks," I said. "I've already eaten." I looked at the clock across the room. It was already past nine.

"Ah, too bad, mate. And I'm leaving in the morning."

"Maybe next time," I offered.

"No worries. Well, look, I'll put Zach back on. You take care."

"Thanks." I leaned back in the chair and closed my eyes.

"Neal?"

The phone felt cold on my ear, remnants perhaps of the Australian winter. "Yeah."

"I'll call you tomorrow, okay?" I realized now how thoroughly American Zach's voice was—that Midwestern plainness, no twang, no dropped letters, no drawl. Walter Cronkite's English.

"Good night," I said, straining to hear another voice in the background. I wanted Liam to get on another extension, to hear them both say good-bye at once, a chorus of good-byes. But Zach hung up with a sterile clatter, and I held onto the receiver for a moment longer. The wires were dead now; they couldn't tell me a thing.

I was almost glad when the phone calls stopped. I had nothing to say to Zach, nothing to talk about besides work and the books I pored over through the night. The interesting stuff had always happened when we were together.

Still, the silence terrified me. After Liam, I came home to one or two more hang-ups on the machine, but never Zach's voice, never an actual message. The hang-ups were oddly reassuring: at least he was still around, at least he was thinking about me. I laughed at myself for thinking that, for reading an excuse for hope into the situation. Like Noah looking out a rain-soaked porthole for the thirty-ninth consecutive day and smiling because the grass would be green if the deluge ever stopped.

Martin thought the movies would be distracting. But when we stepped out of the theater, into the brilliant October sunshine, the celluloid images disappeared, disintegrating in my memory as irrevocably as if the film itself had burst into flames inside the projector. Instantly, Zach reentered my mind. I wondered what he was doing as Martin and I strolled around the upper level of the Embarcadero, wandered into the quiet garden tucked away behind the theater like a secret world.

"Something's wrong, Martin. I know it. I haven't heard from him in three weeks."

Martin stopped on the steps leading up to the trim, rectangular lawn. "I thought no news was good news," he said, attempting a smile.

"No. No news just means I worry."

He hoisted up his jeans at the knee and sat down. "Maybe you should call him."

"I can't."

"Well, what are you worried about?"

"I don't know." The stone was warm beneath me, the sunlight revealing flecks of color throughout it.

"Well, you could always hang up when he answers the phone. I mean, if you're just worried about him being okay."

"He'd know it was me."

Martin leaned forward. "He asked for space, didn't he? Maybe you should just let him have it. Trust him."

"I don't *dis*trust him, I just—"

"Don't think he can take care of himself?"

I plucked a blade of grass and twirled it between my fingers. It was translucent in the light, lime green. "I'm just afraid."

"If Zach falls down in the middle of the forest and Neal isn't there to pick him up, does he make a sound?"

The grass splintered from the friction, bleeding green on my fingers. "You're a real help, Martin, you know that? I ask for Joyce Brothers and you give me Carl Sagan."

He sat back, stretched his arms out onto the grass, and was silent for a moment. He closed his eyes and arched his neck, presenting his face to the sun. Finally, he looked directly at me. Fine lines radiated around his eyes, splintered across his cheeks. "Do you feel responsible for Zach?"

"I want to help him."

"Whether or not he wants your help."

I looked away, toward the office building that towered over the garden. We were in an oasis, a tiny patch of green surrounded by concrete and glass. "I'm not sure he's capable of making that decision right now."

"So you *are* responsible for him."

"No." I swiveled my head back to his. "I don't know. What is this, a quiz?"

He smiled, surrendering. "No. To tell you the truth, I don't know any better than you do how to handle this. And if I did, I couldn't tell you. You're the only one who knows how you feel. I can only tell you what I see, what I think this is doing to you."

I asked his eyes, afraid to invite too much in words.

"Just have patience, Neal. Sometimes that's the hardest thing in the world to hold on to."

I tried to smile. But right now, I just wanted the lecture to end. I wanted to go home and escape into the stereo, the TV, whatever noise I could find to drown out the noise in my head.

Martin could walk home from here. I left him on Battery Street and headed toward the subway. The skyscrapers cast long shadows across the street, creating a tunnel that belied the abundant sunshine in the distance. I walked quickly to minimize the chill.

I finally found sunlight on Market Street, just in time for me to stomp my way into the subway. The Haight bus would have been more convenient, but I wanted the longer walk from the trolley stop. Getting off the train just outside the tunnel, I relished the sunshine and the odd assortment of characters milling about the street, sitting at tiny tables outside the creperie, inspecting the houseplants on display outside the hardware store. I walked slowly down Cole, the yuppie element quickly giving way to the bohemian as Haight Street emerged at the foot of the hill. Thirty years after the Summer of Love, and tie-dye still hadn't disappeared. The only difference was that it now covered indifferent bodies, children rebelling because they were supposed to rebel, rejecting the status quo without the first idea of what to replace it with.

I turned and walked through the sauntering, self-consciously hip crowd, the purple hair and pierced faces, the clothing that had been bought with the fashionable tears already in it. And I turned again on Ashbury, the Ben & Jerry's that now crowned the most famous corner in counterculture history.

Sanity revived on Oak—traffic whizzing past, families returning from weekend excursions to Marin. A young woman on the Panhandle held loosely to her dog's leash, her other hand gloved by a plastic bag, waiting patiently as the spaniel squatted beside a tree.

I didn't notice him at first. There was always someone sitting on a stoop out here, watching the traffic go by. He was leaning forward, the sleeves of his bright white shirt supported casually on the knees of dark jeans. I didn't recognize him until he lifted his head, the chestnut hair falling back to reveal his eyes, the sharp curve of his nose.

He sprang up as he saw me and stood on the concrete step he'd been perched on for god knows how long. "Hi," he said. The smile was back, the charming broad smile he'd flashed that first night, parading around a dance floor.

"Hi." I felt a little unstable, swaying out over the steps as if I might tumble back onto the street. "What are you doing here?"

"I have great news," he said. "Well," he added, shrugging, pouting self-deprecatingly, "good news and bad news, actually."

I found myself staring at him, taking in everything as if we'd only just been introduced. He looked the same, every element was exactly the same—his eyes, his hair, his voice, the color of his skin, the shape of his ears—but something seemed off. Taken together, it didn't fit. My gut told me this wasn't Zach. It was an optical illusion. I was still in that desert, and this was indeed a mirage.

"I finally took your advice and went to the doctor. There's nothing physically wrong with me."

"That's the good news."

"Bingo." He pointed a finger playfully toward my nose. I flinched but quickly regained my balance. "The bad news is, he sent me to a shrink."

"A shrink?" I had always been skeptical of therapy. Spilling your guts to an absolute stranger who sits there calmly nodding his head while you dredge up every unseemly event of your life, reliving the pain to no purpose other than padding his bank account.

"But that's not all bad news, either. You see," he said, leaning in for a whisper, "I'm not crazy. I'm just depressed." He stood back again, shoulders straight. He didn't look depressed at all. "Just a little chemical thing. Not enough serotonin or whatever they call it." He stretched the word out carefully, as though struggling to remember each syllable. "Or maybe too much, I can't remember. Anyway, he gave me some pills and here's the result—a new me."

"Just like that?"

"Just like that." He smiled, like a car salesman. "Prozac. Can you believe that? It's like they named it after me. If I ran for president, that could be my campaign slogan: *Pro-Zach!*"

"What is it?"

"Oh, sweetheart, where have you been? It's the wonder drug of the nineties—sort of like LSD, only legal. Everybody's doing it."

"And that's all there is to it?" I found myself glancing around, scouting for neighbors.

"Look, I have a chemical imbalance in my brain. It's very common. Shift the chemicals around a bit, and I'm just like everyone else. Everything was out of whack before, so all I wanted to do was sleep."

"And now?" I peered at him, looking for signs; perhaps the chemicals had affected the color of his eyes.

"Now all I want to do is fuck. Are you busy tonight?"

I laughed. His eyes were dancing, as they had that day at the park, when he'd dragged me from one ride to another, unable to get enough of the excitement.

"Come in," I said. "We'll talk."

He followed me to the door. As I fumbled nervously with the key, he slapped my ass, his hand resting firmly on one cheek, as if he were testing a melon.

Once inside, I avoided looking back at him as we climbed the stairs, half-afraid that he would vanish behind me, that the mirage would reveal itself as just that—a mirage.

"Can I get you anything?" I asked when we got inside the apartment. I dropped my jacket over the back of the couch.

"Just some Calistoga, maybe."

"I'll see if I have any." I headed for the kitchen. I twisted open a new bottle, the gas bursting toward its mouth. I released the cap carefully and poured. I poured brandy into another glass, for myself.

He was still there, on the couch. He'd folded my jacket and draped it over the armchair. He smiled as I passed him the glass and gestured toward the empty cushion beside him.

I sat toward the end of the couch and took a sip of brandy. It tasted odd this early in the day, too warm, even bitter. There was something about brandy, I thought, something that demanded darkness and a crackling fire.

"It's good to see you," he said. He shifted position slightly. When he set his glass down on the coffee table, he was an inch or two closer.

"Are you really feeling better?"

"Neal, I haven't felt this good in years."

"Just because of the pills?"

He laughed. "I wish it was that simple. No, I have to see the doctor a couple of times a week. There's all the other shit to deal with. The pills only help the symptoms."

"I don't understand. If it's just a chemical thing, then why do you need therapy?"

"It's complicated."

"I'm sure it is." Another sip. It was beginning to taste better now.

"I'm sorry," he said. He laid a hand across the back of the couch and caressed the nape of my neck. "I'm sorry for shutting you out. I just couldn't deal with anything. It wasn't you."

I nodded, biting a corner of my lip. There was a Monet print directly across from the couch—my replacement for the Picasso—a rainbow of colors swirling, merging to approximate water. On the surface, the water lilies looked like islands, sparkling wholes floating on a mosaic chaos.

"You . . . you helped, you know?"

"What do you mean?"

His hand fell to my shoulder. "You gave me something to shoot for. Without you I probably would have given up." He stroked my cheek and moved closer. He kissed me, turning my head gently by the chin until our lips met. His eyes were directly in front of me now, and I closed mine as his hands reached around to my back.

He drew away and settled himself lengthwise on the couch, his head in my lap. I stroked his hair as he talked. "It's so weird," he said. "I feel like Rip Van Winkle, just waking up. I'm still getting used to being happy."

"When did it start?"

"Oh, I started taking the pills a few weeks ago." Around the time Liam was in town, I thought. "They take a while to kick in, so I've only really noticed this feeling for the past few days. The first sign was how easy it was to get up in the morning. I didn't have to drag myself out of bed. The first day, I was already shaving before I even realized anything had changed. That's the most amazing part: everything feels so normal. It's only when I think back on how I used to feel that it seems strange."

I almost envied him. Was there a pill for everything? I wondered. Was there a pill for me?

"It's not all easy," he said. "There are still ups and downs. But it's going to be okay, I'm sure of that. Dr. Porter thinks so. We still have to work our way through Kansas."

"You make it sound like a cross-country trip." His hair felt cool in my fingers. His shoulder lay gently on my crotch, massaging it innocently with each breath.

"It is kind of like that," he said. "As soon as I get Kansas behind me, I'll be fine."

"Well," I said, "if it's any consolation, I don't think Dorothy liked it much, either."

He laughed and reached up, his fingers coming to rest again on my cheek. "Thanks," he said. His hand dropped silently into his lap and he closed his eyes. I held him gently, cradling him, ignoring the bulge growing in my pants. He needed to be held. And I needed to hold him.

Martin was skeptical. He couldn't have survived this long, he said, without being skeptical.

He peered at me across a cobblestone walkway at the Japanese Tea Garden, the red pagoda rising behind him like a stealthy dragon. "Back to normal?" he said. "Just like that?"

I shrugged. "More or less."

"Are you sure that's all it is—depression?"

"That's what the doctor said."

"Or so he told you." With his blue eyes and his height, Martin looked completely out of place in these surroundings—as out of place as the sympathetic look on his face, which seemed utterly disconnected from the judgmental tone of his words.

"It seems obvious to me," I said, glancing away from his probing eyes. "He's been so down."

"Well, he's also been up a lot, don't you think? I wonder if he might be bipolar."

"Manic depressive?" I caught his gaze again, seeking ballast—ballast anywhere.

He nodded. "I've known other people like that. It's very different. It ain't just the blues."

"Well, I'm sure the doctor knows what he's doing."

"I'm sure he does."

Martin walked on, leaving the pagoda exposed in the distance. I followed, breaking past a gaggle of German tourists—cameras hanging bulkily at their breasts; round, incomprehensible syllables strung between them like twine in a child's game of telephone.

"Everything's going to be fine now," I added, catching up at last. My Topsiders slid on the gray tile.

"Just like before?" He stopped and looked past the wooden rail of the bridge. He might have been speaking to the dwarfed branches in the bonsai garden beneath us.

"Of course it's different," I said, following him into the shadow of a pine. "But what's wrong with that? Every relationship has to go through changes. Otherwise, what's the point?"

Martin leaned back against the rail, crossed his arms casually before his chest. "What's the point?" He sighed. "The point is, Neal, that what Zach's going through right now is a lot to handle. And if you're going to promise to stick by him, you'd better be sure you're prepared. That's only fair."

"Fair?"

"To Zach. And to yourself. I mean, are you ready for this? Are you sure it's worth it?"

"Of course it's worth it."

He paused. When he finally spoke again, it was in a near-whisper. "What do you get?"

"That's not the issue," I said. I moved closer, to allow a young couple to pass. The man had his arm around the woman's waist, guiding her, protecting her from the branches that spilled over the rail. "Zach needs me."

"So that's the issue. Being needed."

"Well—maybe it is. I've never been needed before. It feels pretty good to have someone depend on you. It makes the whole thing seem more real. Like it's moved beyond romance, you know, beyond that crazy, visceral thing."

"Love, you mean."

"Jesus, Martin. Aren't you even listening? This *is* love. I'm with Zach because I want to be, not because he buys me flowers or whatever else you do when you're in that romantic stage. This is the real thing. I'd have thought you of all people would understand that."

He turned around, facing away from me, his hands now clutching the rail. If he'd hefted himself up, he might have split the bamboo in half. "Oh, I understand. I *have* been in love, you know. And I've watched the people that I love—" He took a deep breath. I could hear the leaves rustling around him. "I've taken care of them. I've watched them slip away. I've buried them, Neal."

I watched his profile, but his expression was blank, cold. "You don't regret it, do you?"

"God, no." He bit his lip. "It was probably the most important thing I've ever done. But I didn't choose to do it. It just happened. I'm talking about people I spent years loving before I had to spend months watching them die. The balance was in my favor."

"Zach's not dying, Martin."

He gripped the rail, knuckles white, looking out as if there were something there, some moment from the past that I was blind to. He was getting it all confused, confusing my life with his, confusing Zach with the others. But there was no comparison. I had never intended there to be a comparison.

"It takes something out of you, Neal. Watching that—shoring up against something that refuses to yield. It saps your energy, and then it wins, anyway."

"Zach's not dying," I repeated.

Finally, he turned to me, half of his face still shaded beneath the tree. "We're all dying, Neal. All the time. And we can't spare a minute."

The capsules rolled along Zach's palm, cresting just beneath his fingers and then sliding back down, green and ivory stripes resting atop his lifeline. He scooped the extras up with the mouth of the brown plastic bottle, which he placed back on the counter. He tossed the remaining capsule into his mouth, fingers creating a slight pop as they grazed his lips, and washed it down with juice.

I wasn't supposed to be watching. I was busy at the other side of the tiny kitchen, pouring hot water into the teapot. We had started having formal breakfasts on the weekend, so Zach would have something in his stomach to keep the pill down. During the week he waited until he got downtown, where he would stop for a muffin, but when we had more time, I would make eggs or pancakes, whatever he was in the mood for.

He turned now and beamed at me, eyebrows arching almost as sharply as his smile. "It's show time," he said brightly.

"Is that really all you have to take? One little pill?" The kettle hissed as I placed it onto a hot burner.

"For now. Dr. Porter says we may need to make some adjustments. We just have to wait and see what happens."

"Careful," I muttered, "you could become addicted."

He laughed. "Oh, I already am. I couldn't live without the stuff."

I was still amazed by the power of that innocent-looking capsule. It seemed to have transformed Zach, completely dispelling the morose figure I'd been struggling with for weeks and replacing him with a personality whose perkiness was just as foreign, just as one-dimensional. Zach's eyes contained the same effervescent joy that had always attracted me, but the sadness that gave them character and complexity had disappeared. He wasn't quite as real now. Or maybe I was still romanticizing sadness. Maybe it was joy that made me uncomfortable.

Zach set the table while I put the finishing touches on breakfast—folding the omelets at just the right moment of golden brown, sliding them carefully out of the pan, dressing the plate up with parsley, a slice of orange. Works of art, Adam had called them, looking over my shoulder as I'd made him breakfast for the first time. It's all in the details, I'd told him. God is in the details.

"What do you want to do today?" I asked, dipping two tea bags into the pot, watching the water turn a rich crimson. Satisfied, I set the dripping bags in the sink and carried the pot to the table.

Zach was already carving into his omelet. "Just relax," he said. "Maybe we could take a walk later."

Zach loved taking walks now, though he seldom ventured more than a few blocks from the house. He wanted to stay on the flat, he said; the hills were getting to be too much.

"I thought we might go to a movie," I said, pouring the tea. One of the mugs was chipped just above the handle; I set it beside my plate.

"Oh, I don't really feel like it." He drained his refilled juice glass. "But you go if you want; you haven't been to the movies in weeks."

We stayed at his place most of the time now. Zach's new confidence was clearly fragile, and I didn't want to risk it by disrupting his routine too much. He liked the comfort of being surrounded by his own things—knowing where everything was, having no surprises. He was much more willing to share his own space than mine; it was safer that way. I'd gotten used to the cramped quarters; it wasn't much of a sacrifice, and just being with Zach made up for it. Though technically we lived miles apart, we were together nearly every night, and I still got to play at domesticity—making him breakfast, shopping for him, tidying up the apartment at night if only to give myself a place to sit. He didn't mind my taking over with the details of living; his grateful smiles encouraged it.

The only evenings I didn't see him were Mondays and Thursdays, when he had therapy. He liked to be alone after that, to process what he'd talked about with the doctor. He never discussed it with me, no more than to say whether it had been a productive or a difficult session. Zach held greedily on to those visits, like a miser with his hoard of gold. After a few weeks, I found myself envying his psychiatrist, wondering if he got to see the real Zach, the one in pain, the one who had existed before those tiny capsules had intervened.

All he was willing to talk to me about was the drug—as if that were all that mattered, as if there were nothing to his problems now but chemicals. Prozac was to him what religion is to a new convert—a miraculous salvation, a lifeline in turbulent water. Again and again, when gazing out the window or walking down the street, he would get a look of wonder in his eyes—as if the visible world were all new to him, its clarity suddenly revealed and with it a sense of meaning and connection that he had never known. "I feel like a new me," he would say. "For the first time in my life, I'm really myself."

I wondered what that meant—wondered how Zach could be so sure that for twenty-seven years he had been living a lie, and that only now was the truth available to him, wondered whether I had ever known Zach's real self or had fallen in love with an imposter. An imposter who had now run away, superseded by an unfamiliar original.

He wasn't always up, of course, and less so as the weeks went on. The doctor, he said, was considering other medications, adjusting his dosage, attempting to hit just the right balance. In the meantime, he would remain subject to mood swings, only now the drugs were partly responsible—too much and he'd be bouncing off the walls, too little and he could barely manage to hit the remote control buttons. It would take time, only time.

I decided against the movie. I'd brought *Wuthering Heights* along; the book had become my albatross, but I refused to start anything else until I'd finished it. I'd seldom had such trouble giving in to a story, but it was impossible to sympathize with these characters. It was obvious to me that Cathy and Heathcliff were both mad, causing much more pain for each other than pleasure. I couldn't begin to understand why they didn't just murder each other and get it over with.

Zach flipped quickly through the pages of a magazine. He seldom stopped for more than a few seconds—skimming headlines, I assumed, occasionally poring over a Calvin Klein jeans ad.

In quiet moments like this, Adam and I would sit reading at opposite ends of the sofa, our stockinged feet gently touching. We exchanged books freely, introducing each other to our favorites. I'd tried that with Zach—his bookshelf was littered now with the titles I'd given him over the past few months, but I'd never seen him actually pick one up. While E. M. Forster and Charlotte Brontë (who, I was now convinced, bore no resemblance whatsoever to her passionately disturbed sister) languished in a toppling pile, Zach sat across the room, snapping the pages of *GQ*.

It seemed odd to me that he should be imbued with such enthusiasm but none of the focus to put it to work. He was honestly happy, I thought, but it was an entirely internal happiness—disconnected from the world. It was as if he'd decided he didn't need the world to be happy; it was enough to simply *be*. Perhaps I'd been hanging around Martin too long; I, too, was becoming skeptical.

I'd been reading for only half an hour when Zach's magazine snapped against the back of my chair. The draft of its falling to the floor ruffled my hair. "What's going on?" I asked, leaning over the chair arm and turning to look at Zach. My legs were thrown over the other side of the chair, so I now hung like a fainted heroine in the arms of her lover.

"It's time for that walk," he said, slapping his thighs and rising.

I wanted to at least finish the chapter before leaving, to have some sense of progress, but I couldn't deny being grateful for the distraction. I simply replaced my bookmark and followed.

Zach led the way down Church Street. The more picturesque route would have been west on Market, but he was avoiding the Castro these days. Too much stimulation, perhaps; his doctor had told him to take it easy. It wasn't hard for me to keep up; Zach's usually quick pace had slackened, and I could easily compete with his longer, stronger legs.

He hadn't shaved today; the stubble clung in patches along his jaw. Now that we were in the sunlight, I also noticed the dark rings beneath his eyes. He hadn't been sleeping well lately. The nervous tapping of his leg against the mattress would often wake me in the middle of the night, and I would turn to find him lying on his back, eyes wide to the ceiling—as if he were waiting for sleep to descend like an angel. His lips were inevitably pursed, arms folded atop the sheet—the disapproving stance a preparation to scold the angel for being late.

He was remarkably out of shape, comparatively speaking. We walked along the edge of Dolores Park, Zach breathing heavily just halfway up the hill. Now I understood why we hadn't been to the Rawhide lately: a few circles around the dance floor would probably wind him.

We stopped at the top of the park and sat on the grass. In the distance, we could see the downtown skyline, the Bay Bridge arching behind it. We sat quietly for a long moment, both facing the view.

Zach's arms planted behind him for support, he said, "Dr. Porter says I should be more open with you."

"What does that mean?"

"I should discuss my feelings with you."

I looked off at the buildings in the distance. The sky was pale over the city, indifferent. "Do you want to?"

"I don't know. I don't know how you'll react."

I hesitated. "Trust me," I said.

He sighed, threw his head back and gazed into the sky. "I'm scared," he said at last. "I'm always scared these days."

"You don't act like it," I said. "Not since you started seeing the doctor."

"That's the weird part. The feeling's still there. It just doesn't control me, you know?"

"That's good, isn't it?"

"Maybe."

Even now, a nervousness spilling through his words, Zach maintained the look of calm he'd been wearing ever since the medication had kicked in. The expression didn't change as I listened to his story—as though he were now completely separated from the pain he was relating, his skin numb to anything but joy. I watched him carefully, distrustful of the flat look in his eyes, the even turn of the lips, searching out a crack in his polished veneer. Surely, I thought, such peace and strength couldn't be true, or at least not lasting.

"I never told you the real reason I went to the doctor."

"You were tired. I saw that. I'm the one who told you to go."

"No, Neal." He bit his upper lip. "One night, I had this really vivid dream. I was rummaging through the kitchen, looking for a sharp knife. None of them was sharp enough. Whatever it was I wanted to cut, I needed a really sharp blade. I pulled everything out of the drawers—cleavers, steak knives, scissors. I even ran into the bathroom for razor blades. Anything sharp."

The sun was almost directly overhead, bearing down on us. I looked down at Zach's hands, wide fingers clenched in the grass.

"And just at the end of the dream, as the pile was getting so big things were falling off the table, I realized what I had to cut. It was me. I was going to cut my throat. I don't know why; I just knew I had to do it. And I wanted to do it right, so . . ."

His hand was rigid, stiff as wood, as rigor mortis.

"I woke up in the morning, feeling just as usual—a little tired, whatever, but I didn't remember the dream." He paused, throwing his head back farther. "Until I looked over at the nightstand. And there it was. Every knife in the house was on the table. Waiting for me."

His tone was so dry, he might have been speaking in the third person—telling someone else's story, living someone else's life. There was no hint in his voice of the terror the moment must have caused. But as he spoke, a shiver crawled up my back and burst slowly along my shoulders, denying the power of the sun. I walked my fingers toward his and interlocked them, resting my palm in the grass. He squeezed his fingers together, trapping mine, holding them firmly, as if without them he would tumble headlong onto the ground.

I kept it all to myself now. No one, not even Martin, could understand. I didn't want to hear the so-called voice of reason. I didn't want to see the pity in his eyes, the sense that he knew better than I. Zach was wearing me down, that's what he would have said. I couldn't bear Martin's scorn, sympathetic as it might have been. I couldn't handle his feelings. Zach's were enough.

The roller coaster finally dipped in early November, at the tail end of San Francisco's delayed summer. For whole days at a time, Zach would be quiet—staying home from work, once even forgetting to call in. He routinely canceled our plans, said he just needed to be alone. And I gave him the space, the quiet time. I'd learned the consequences of interfering.

Then, within a couple of days, the other Zach would return— vibrant, apologetic, making excuses for his slump, alternately blaming and praising the wonders of the latest medication. The pills now were responsible for everything. The pills made him happy or sad, awake or asleep. The pills determined whether he would love me or push me away. I was dispensable, but the pills stayed.

Martin called a few times a week, and I steered the conversation as far away from Zach as I could. I distracted him with old jokes, relived scenes from our favorite movies. We quoted *Auntie Mame* to each other until we laughed ourselves silly, re-creating entire scenes, him as Mame, me an especially acerbic Vera Charles. We found laughter in their slapstick lives, a parallel universe where a sense of humor would get you through any crisis, where life really was a banquet.

And when I hung up the phone and wiped the tears of laughter from my eyes, people were starving to death. I began rating Zach's days on a scale of one to five, almost dreading too many fives, knowing a one was sure to appear soon enough to even the score. Ordinary illnesses, I thought, were linear: you get progressively worse, the fever breaks, you climb steadily back up. This was different—like a cancer gone wild, punctuated by tiny, teasing remissions, as if the tumors just couldn't make up their minds.

Even on good days, I was afraid to get too close. The roller coaster was making *him* dizzy, too. He grew defensive. It was as if he were afraid I might jostle him and redistribute the chemicals in his brain. Or perhaps he just thought that too much happiness would provoke another episode. Happiness had its price, and Zach was growing frugal.

I poured myself into my work. Somehow, I came up with especially strong copy in those weeks. I briefly became the toast of the office, praised for one or two particularly witty campaigns. I savored the attention. It saved me.

I got more and more difficult assignments. Fred, the new guy, was more than happy to let me tackle them. He was still struggling just to get up to speed. My cubicle, meanwhile, was awash in paper, ideas scratched on scraps of envelopes and pinned to the walls. I typed furiously, hardly thinking. I'll fix it later, I thought. For now, just let it flow.

I was in the middle of a particularly mad rush when the phone rang. I'm not sure I even heard it until the third ring.

"So how's my replacement?" The voice sounded different long-distance, but the sarcastic tone was unmistakable.

"Diana! How are you?"

"Irreplaceable, of course. Please tell me that whoever it is, she can't hold a candle to me."

"He. And no, he can't."

"Well, is he at least cute?"

I lowered my voice. Not that Fred was likely to be eavesdropping; he was the most focused person I'd ever met, his eyes never leaving the computer screen except for bathroom breaks. "If you like nerds. Straight ones, that is."

"Is there any other kind?"

"So how's LA?"

She sighed dramatically. "Dreadfully pretentious. . . . I love it."

"Any luck yet?"

"Darling, it's been barely two months. I haven't even found the casting couch yet. I am, however, calling you from the lovely Paramount Studios."

"What?"

"Temp job, hon. Reception." I heard a buzz in the background. "Speaking of which—hold on, would you?"

Diana's voice was suddenly replaced by a Muzak version of "Achy Breaky Heart."

"I think that was Dustin Hoffman," she said, finally coming back on the line. "Or Rich Little."

"Sounds like you're having a great time."

"Oh sure. I already have calluses where I didn't even know I had skin. I think I've hit every agency in town; next, I'm thinking of putting my picture up in the post office—right next to the latest ax murderer. It couldn't hurt. Casting directors need something to look at when they're waiting in line for a stamp."

I tried to hold back the laughter. Suddenly, I missed her terribly.

"So how's that hunk of yours?" Diana asked. "Weren't you going to move in together?"

I'd forgotten how long it had been since we last spoke. "He's fine," I said quickly. "But we decided to wait a little while. No need to rush into anything. What about you?"

"Who has time for love?" she said. Another line buzzed in the background and she put me on hold again. This time it was k. d. lang homogenized for the elevator set.

"Why don't you just call me tonight?" I asked when she got back. "When you have more time."

"What—and give my money to MCI instead?" The hold button clicked once more. I drummed a pencil against my desktop. Experimenting, I let it fall eraser-side-down and calculated the bounce.

The music died suddenly, in the middle of an old Elton John number that sounded like it was being played on 16 ½. After a momentary silence, the dial tone rang loudly in my ear. Clearly, she was still new at this. I hung up and turned back to my monitor, hoping I hadn't completely lost my powers of concentration. Maybe Diana would call back when she was less busy, so we could lob more than two sentences over the net before another interruption.

I hardly had time to get back to work before the phone rang again. "Don't tell me," I said. "Kevin Costner."

The line was silent, and a queasy feeling bubbled up to my throat. All I needed was to mistake my boss—or, god forbid, the company president—for Diana.

"No, but close." It was Zach, his voice muffled and rather hoarse.

"Hi. What's up?"

He sighed deeply, the sound that reverberated in the bedroom on his insomniac nights. "How are you?" He spoke slowly, even monosyllables drawn out as if the sounds were hard to form.

"What's the matter, Zach? Where are you?"

"I'm home," he said. "Called in sick."

It was Friday. We hadn't seen each other or even spoken last night—the sanctity of therapy. I glanced instinctively at the photo on the wall, green thumb tack poking the top of the roller coaster. "Are you okay?"

His breathing was loud and slow enough to count. One one thousand, two . . . "Just tired."

"Did you take your pill today?"

He giggled. "Oh, I took 'em."

I clutched the phone, imagining it his arm. "Zach—listen to me. How many pills did you take?"

"All kinds. The little white ones, the green ones . . ." He paused, and I was suddenly aware of the thunderous pounding of my heart. "I think there are even a couple of pink ones here somewhere."

He must have been hoarding them, leftovers from the constantly changing prescriptions. No wonder the pills weren't working with any predictability—he wasn't taking them. "Zach. How many did you take?"

"A few."

"Hang up, Zach. I'm going to call an ambulance for you. You'll be fine."

"No!" He was roused finally, as though wakened from a nightmare. "No," he repeated a few seconds later—calmer now. "It's just a few pills, for Christ's sake. I couldn't sleep."

"Zach—"

"Don't call the ambulance," he pleaded. "Just come over. All I need is some company."

"But Zach, you could hurt yourself."

"No great loss," he said, almost a whisper. I couldn't be sure whether he intended for me to hear it.

"Okay," I said, "I'll be right there. Can you do me a favor, Zach? Are you in bed?"

He laughed. "What kind of favor did you have in mind?"

"Get up, Zach. Walk around the room, make some coffee, turn on the TV—anything. Just don't fall asleep, okay? I'll be there in a few minutes. Just don't fall asleep."

"Neal?"

"What?"

"I love you," he said sheepishly, as if for the first time.

"I know, Zach. Wait for me."

The phone started to ring again as I made my way through the maze of cubicles. Whoever it was could wait.

At ten, I ran away from home—if setting off with lunch, a favorite book, and the meager contents of a piggy bank counts as running away. It wasn't a Tom Sawyerish episode, little Neal angry at the world and seeking adventure in the great outdoors. In retrospect, twenty years later, I see it as simply an opportunity to clear my head, little different from the rituals of adulthood—a long run after a hard day at work; an evening spent in silence on the sofa, no music, no television, no human contact. When my sandwich was gone, when I had grown hungry and tired and had sufficiently memorized the back roads of my suburban neighborhood, I trudged back home, hours late for dinner, prepared for a lecture—eager for the attention, however earned. And after my mother's frantic complaints and my father's stoic indifference ("Boys will be boys, Helen," he'd said, looking proudly over her shoulder, cigar dangling from the corner of his mouth), each of them brought me in for a hug, as if only touching could confirm that I had come back from the dead—doubting Thomas caressing the wound in Jesus' side.

And now, as I let myself into Zach's musty apartment, my only thought was the feel of his hair, the sound of his breath.

He was sitting up, the futon miraculously folded back into a couch, sheets and pillows stacked neatly beside him. Turning as I approached, he attempted a smile.

I stopped abruptly, my breath short, hollow. Aside from the vague, unfocused look in his eyes there was no sign of concern in Zach's appearance or demeanor. "Hi," he said, the word sharp and breathy as a seduction. He tried to rise, but stumbled, plummeting back onto the futon.

I sat beside him and held an arm across his back for support. "Are you all right?" I asked.

"I'm fine," he said defensively.

Two pill bottles stood on the coffee table, their lids askew like jaunty sailor hats. I picked one up and peered inside. The familiar capsules—at least a dozen—spilled over one another. The label was dated a week ago and made out for twenty, one per day. No problem. I put the bottle back and reached for the next.

"What are you doing?" Zach said, tearing the bottle from my hand.

"I want to see how many you've taken."

"I'm not a drug addict, Neal. You don't have to spy on me." Suspicion injected a sliver of life into his eyes. "Did my doctor tell you to spy on me?"

"For God's sake, Zach, I've never even met your doctor. I just—"

"Good. Because it's none of his business." He returned the bottle to my palm. I didn't recognize the name of the drug, but I was more concerned with how many he had taken. Again, I checked the date and dosage, then spilled the remaining pills into my hand—only one or two off, by my count.

"Are there any others?" I asked. "Any other bottles?" I felt like a narc, a naive mother who finds her teenager sniffing glue.

Zach stared dumbly at me, and his face slowly hardened into something disturbingly akin to hatred.

"Well, don't take any more today, okay?"

"Aye-aye, sir." He gave me a mock salute, degenerating into a limp-wristed slap to the knee. "I don't like them anyway," he said, shaking his head. "They make me feel funny."

"Zach, for the past month, they've made you feel great."

"Yeah, well, not anymore. I—I don't like them." He kicked the table lightly, and the bottles wobbled.

"Let's call the doctor," I said. I swerved around to reach the phone.

"No." Zach encircled my neck and, pushing me back against the arm of the futon frame, he kissed me. His lips missed mine, falling sloppily onto my cheek. He adjusted and drew one hand down along my side. I pushed at him, but Zach had always been stronger than me, and in his present state rejection was probably more than he could handle. I gave him my dead lips and held him close.

His thick hair spilled through my fingers, chestnut giving way to mahogany in the light. I circled the back of his head with one hand, and he gave with the gentle pressure, his face falling against my shoulder. His breath was warm on my shirt, blowing softly through the collar opening. My other hand stroked his back, tracing the breath up from the diaphragm, echoing its rhythm.

"I'll call the doctor in the morning," he whispered at my ear. "I promise. I just want you tonight, Neal. I need you tonight."

A mustiness was clinging to everything, but Zach refused to let me open a window. I was the only thing he would allow in from the outside world. Not even air.

He hadn't eaten all day. Whatever effect the pills had, that in itself couldn't be good. I ordered a few things from the Szechuan restaurant down the street and set the table while Zach waited on the futon.

When the food arrived, he played at eating, poking things with his chopsticks, pushing the rice into clumps on the side of his plate. Months ago, I had taught him to use chopsticks; he'd never bothered before, automatically picked up a fork to save himself the embarrassment of the learning curve. He had enjoyed it then, making fun of his own fumbling gestures. But tonight, long an expert, he used the chopsticks mechanically, reducing them to the impersonal instruments they were intended to be.

"Thank you," he said finally, in the middle of a long silence. He moved a spare rib from one side of his plate to the other.

"For what?" I asked. "I didn't cook it. I just picked up the phone."

"No," he said, ignoring my joke. "Thank you. For being here. For not asking any questions."

I thought I had done nothing *but* ask questions, but perhaps they had all been asked of myself. I knew that Zach was in no state to provide answers. I'd gotten used to his silence, the wall he had built around himself, all the bricks tightly packed so that not even a chink remained for me to peer through uninvited. I'd made up my own theories, always second-guessing what was going through his mind. When I was feeling good, his pensive expression became merely an indicator of his impatience with the drugs. When I was more insecure, it became a sign that he had tired of me, that I had lost whatever quality it was that had attracted him to me in the first place.

I never did have a good sense of that, of why Zach claimed to love me. We shared no common interests, only a brief history together—people we knew, places we'd visited. When I'd told him about my own past, the life I'd lived before he came along, he had hardly commented—as if none of it mattered anymore. All that mattered to Zach, it seemed, was the moment we were in—the feel of his skin against mine, the peace that came as our breath converged, sharing at last a rhythm. I may not have taught him a thing about music or literature, or any of the other things that had possessed me for so long and pretended to constitute a life, but he had taught me that. He had taught me the intensity of a single breath.

He gave up pretending to eat, and I gave up pretending not to notice. "I'm going to take a bath," he said, folding his napkin on the table.

I nodded and concentrated on my dinner, careful not to let him think that anything seemed out of place to me. As he passed my side of the table, he stopped and placed a hand on my shoulder. "Thanks," he said, bending forward.

He kissed me—a gentle, almost brotherly kiss, if brothers dared to kiss on the lips.

While the water ran in the bathroom, pounding into the tub like bullets, I cleaned up in the kitchen. I found a Tupperware container for Zach's dinner, thinking he might find himself hungry in the middle of the night, as he often did, particularly since he'd started taking the medication. The bath water had stopped running by the time the dishes were done, and through the closed door I heard Zach settling into the tub. He liked the water extremely hot, so it always took several tries before he could get himself to sit in it: a series of quick splashes indicated that he was still adjusting to the temperature, drawing his body in and out until the sensation got more comfortable, or his skin grew numb from the heat.

As the splashing finally subsided, I retrieved *Wuthering Heights* from my briefcase and took to the armchair again. Over the past sev-

eral weeks, I had gotten more reading done in this chair than anywhere else. The worn fabric had come to seem irrevocably connected
with books, even its dust suggesting the scent of the dark, musty
stacks in a library, the ones deep in the bowels of the building where
only the most intrepid of scholars dare to go. Turning the chair to face
the window, I settled, legs curled under me, toes scrunched against
the chair arm. I opened the book without looking, just feeling the
spot left by the bookmark. I'd become lost in the convolutions of the
plot, unable to recall what had happened from one sitting to the next.

And, looking out at the November night, I realized suddenly that I
didn't even care. The characters were alive only on the page, held in
their positions like dummies in a wax museum: no matter when I
chose to return to them, they would still be there, waiting, perhaps in
midsentence, not minding that I'd been away, that I'd been ignoring
them, that other, more pressing demands had stolen my attention.
They would forgive my absence—better still, they wouldn't acknowledge it, wouldn't even be aware of it. When I returned, reading at my
own pace, they would simply go through their preordained motions,
as if no interruption had occurred, as if my presence were at once inevitable and unnecessary. A tree that falls alone in the forest makes no
sound, because there's no ear to catch it.

If I could only get through this night, I thought, watching the
lights come up on Church Street, commuters home and preparing
dinner in kitchens all over town. If I could get us both through the
night, everything would be all right in the morning. He'd be more
reasonable in the morning, the drugs washed out of his system, sleep
replenishing his energy, my night-long embrace lending him strength.
He would see the doctor, and all of this would be cleared up once and
for all.

I had already resigned myself to passing a sleepless night. It was
Zach that mattered. As he slept, I knew I'd be thinking about the
pills, hoping he wouldn't get up in the middle of the night to look for
them. I would have to hide them somewhere, somewhere he wouldn't
think to look—behind a book on the shelf, tucked into the flour canister on the kitchen counter. Tonight, he had accused me of being a
spy, and now I was thinking like one.

Staring out the window, I watched a woman across the street make dinner—settling grocery bags on the table, still wrapped in her coat; returning to the kitchen in jeans, laying ingredients out beside the stove; leaving something to simmer on the burner while she set the table. A neat ritual, enacted with the serenity of habit—as if she prepared the same meal every night, without thought, without worry. She knew exactly how many grinds of pepper to use, the perfect wine to match, how long it would take to cool the food for that first bite.

In the apartment, the splashing had ceased long ago, though it was hard to tell with the bathroom door closed. I had no idea how long Zach had been in there. Long enough to turn his skin prunelike, I assumed, long enough to sweat off in the steam a day's supply of water.

I dropped my unread book onto the chair cushion and walked quietly down the hall. "Zach?" I called, ear against the door. "Are you okay?"

Nothing, not even a splash of water as he raised himself at the sound of my voice. He might have fallen asleep. Drugged as he was, his head could have fallen under the water, too tired to lift up. Babies, I'd heard, could drown in an inch of water if they slid over the wrong way, unable to turn their tiny bodies around. How many mothers had lived through nine months of expectation only to walk into a bathroom just weeks later, after stepping out to answer the phone or take a whistling kettle off the stove, and find their babies ass up in a pool that didn't seem deep enough to drown a fly?

I knocked, quietly at first, then steadily louder as panic set in. I tried the knob, but it twisted defiantly in my hand, refusing to give. "Zach!" I called. "Zach!"

My father had a trick for getting in the house when he'd forgotten his keys. He'd gotten so used to it that he would often do it even when the keys were still in his pocket; it was easier than digging them out, finding the right one, turning it in the lock. I had never tried it myself—never forgetful or curious enough. But now I remembered. Now, there was no other way.

I pressed my back against the hinges and lifted one leg until my heel was against the door frame. Hand on the knob, I pushed my foot against the jamb, prying it away, and threw my weight into the door. It gave easily, sliding into the room, pulling me behind.

I stumbled down, suddenly inundated by the steam of the bath— thick and gray as the fog that would coat the city in the morning. As it dissipated before my eyes, I headed for the tub. Zach's hair shone dark through the clouds, falling over the face that bobbed down, as if searching out ripples in the still water. My body trembled despite the heat as I saw his arms submerged, angled as if his hands lay folded in his lap. He had the stillness of a yogi, meditating, awaiting enlightenment. Only when I got right up beside the tub did I realize that the water was pink, that the glint on the ceramic tile shelf came from a pair of manicure scissors, stained red to the hinge.

part two

entropy

Entropy is the second law of thermodynamics. I don't remember the first one; I guess it didn't leave as much of an impression. Entropy, though, was something I could relate to.

Simply stated, the law of entropy holds that all things in the universe tend toward disorder. Molecules jostle one another endlessly, causing mini-explosions everywhere. The planets spin around the sun in wider and more erratic orbits. And all around us, at every moment, everything deteriorates just a tiny bit more. You walk into a room that hasn't been touched in days, and there's a layer of dust on every object—powdery evidence of decomposition, the never-ending process of death.

Most of the time we don't notice. We vacuum the dust away, never asking where it came from, how much lighter our prized possessions have grown, how many skin cells have flaked off our bodies, how much hair has been slurped down the bathtub drain. The deterioration is too gradual to notice, but it's still happening. It's always happening. And one day you do start to notice. One day the grains of sand slipping through your fingers reach a critical mass that can no longer be ignored.

He called her Bertha. I thought it was her real name, until he explained how she moaned her heart out every night. "Bertha *Mason*," I responded, nodding. It was Zach's one and only literary allusion—

Chemistry
Published by The Haworth Press, Inc., 2006. All rights reserved.
doi:10.1300/5501_02

which I took as a personal triumph, having given him a copy of *Jane Eyre* months ago. Before this, I hadn't realized he'd ever read it.

Bertha shuffled along the corridor, clutching one side of her head, gray hair in complete disarray. Her flowered housecoat was ragged and stained, scuffed at the hem, where her pink slippers occasionally caught it as she slid slowly across the checkered linoleum. She'd been pacing out there since I'd arrived, her gaze flat, indifferent to her surroundings.

We were in the day room. All the patients—*inmates,* Zach called them—filtered in and out at some point, most settling just long enough to fetch a magazine or finish a cigarette. I still hadn't gotten used to the atmosphere—the lack of privacy, the blank faces lifelessly staring—but eventually I realized that this was home for them—some had probably been here for months already, if not years. I was the intruder, the one who was free to leave. To them, I was the freak.

There was a long table at one end of the room where art therapy was in full swing, Laura bent over her sketch pad, surreptitiously stealing pastels from the communal box and hoarding them at her side. Harold—in his midforties and grossly overweight—sat across from her, absorbed by his own masterpiece, mouth hanging open to signal his concentration. Several other patients ringed the table, lost in separate worlds, quiet for now. Bonnie, the nurse, sat at the head, doling out words of encouragement to each, *ooh*ing and *ah*ing in turn. After years with schizophrenics, she had adopted their characteristic monotone.

Zach and I sat apart, in two of the maroon armchairs that lined the wall. The large window behind us overlooked the hospital grounds. Zach had been promised a walk on the grounds with a staff member tomorrow—if he behaved himself.

From what I could see, he was behaving very well. He smiled, distancing himself from the others, even venturing an occasional joke at their expense. *"They're* sick," he whispered to me, laughter hiding in his throat. I heard the unspoken message—the ridiculous comparison. Next to these people, Zach was as sane as Einstein. He was doing just fine. Even the scars on his wrists had healed beautifully.

Bonnie was his favorite nurse. She was the only one he ever told me about, during those evening phone calls, when visiting hours were over and everything was quiet on the ward. Bonnie talked to him, he said, like he was a real person. And, as she held out a Bic to light his cigarette, her eyes told him that he was different. Leaning into the blue flame, he looked up and saw approval in her eyes. Her eyes told him that he wasn't like the others. He was just going through a hard time. He would be out soon, good as new.

Now, in the day room, he was focusing on her, his island of stability. She was sitting directly beneath the clock—oversized numbers and a minute hand that fell with a thud on a schedule of its own devising. The clock, I thought, glancing up at its large round face every so often, must have been calibrated for dog years: each minute passed like seven.

Bonnie got up and glided through the day room on silent white shoes, her smile unflinching—painted, but somehow sincere. She lingered over a patient's shoulder, admiring the drawing he'd been compulsively working on all afternoon. In her eyes, he might have been Michelangelo, coaxing perfect form from implacable stone.

Coming around the table, she finally passed by Zach and me. She turned the same smile to both of us. I worried for a moment that she wasn't sure which of us was the patient. I would have to show my driver's license on the way out or risk being locked up with the others.

I'd been coming here every day for two weeks now, since they started allowing Zach visitors. He spent the first day sleeping, recovering from the loss of blood, the trauma of discovering himself alive. Birth is a frightening, painful experience—that's why we repress the memory. Watching Zach sitting in cold silence on my first visit, bandages still wrapped around his wrists, I imagined how much more horrifying it must be to be reborn into a world you already know and chose to leave.

We didn't say much in the day room. (Zach seemed to think everyone was watching, listening. Mental hospitals, I decided, breed paranoia as much as they attempt to treat it.) Instead, we would simply sit side by side—like this, as the others milled silently around us. Each day, I searched his face for signs—clues to the past, to explain what he was doing here; portents of the future, when this nightmare would end.

We had never talked about what happened, never acknowledged how he'd gotten here. He called the hospital a prison, a trap that suddenly and without cause snapped shut around his unsuspecting foot. He talked only about getting out, as if the hospital were merely an arbitrary obstacle, just another episode to be got through.

Like most hospitals, it was always warm, at least ten degrees hotter than outside. Except when I came directly from work, I'd taken to wearing just a T-shirt under my jacket, to keep as cool as possible once I got inside.

Zach didn't seem to notice the heat. He'd gotten used to it. He leaned out over the chair, elbows perched on his knees, and discreetly flicked ashes onto the floor. He seemed used to everything now. As much as he longed to leave, he looked remarkably at home here. He had had to give in to it, just to survive. If he rebelled too much, I thought, if he dwelled on it too much, he'd go crazy.

"I've had enough of this circus," he announced suddenly, leading me out of the day room. The teenage girl beside Bonnie threw us a knowing smirk. She'd been eyeing Zach the whole time, but now she looked away in mild disgust.

"I told them you were my brother," he said when we were out of earshot. "I'm not sure they believe it."

I followed him slowly past the nurses' station, where a tall young man was getting a light from an orderly. He leaned his lanky body over the counter, cigarette angled up toward the lighter like a snorkel.

The hallway led to a large space with armchairs arranged in a semi-circle around the TV. At the Ping-Pong table against the far wall, a teenage boy was playing with an older man. They had established a rhythm, the ball landing in the same spot each time, lobbing back with the same force—a Philip Glass arpeggio, monotonously repeated. They'd turned the game into art, music—the form dominant, the competitive purpose forgotten.

Zach's room was off of this one, near the corner. It was usually a little quieter at this end of the ward, so we spent most of our time here when I visited, except when he wanted to smoke.

Inside, he kicked off his slippers and settled cross-legged on the narrow bed, facing me while I sat on the edge of a hard plastic chair. "Have you seen the doctor today?" I asked. It was a standard question, part of the routine.

"Yes." His answers were often monosyllabic when the conversation turned to himself. He was chatty only about other people.

"What did he say?"

"He said I'll probably be here for a while. They have to keep an eye on how the medication's working."

"How *is* it working?"

"It's too soon to say."

"How do you feel?"

"Fine."

I flashed him a skeptical look. He knew better than to try to pull that on me.

"How do you think I am, Neal? I'm locked up in a mental institution." He grabbed the pillow from behind him. He cradled it in his arms and then began to squeeze it fiercely. "Stop the nurse routine, okay? I get enough of that from people who get paid for it."

I told myself that anger was an improvement. They say it's the opposite of depression, which is anger turned inward. Apparently, it's healthier to vent your spleen on *other* people.

"You have no idea what this place is like," he said, staring at the carpeted wall. The room was decorated in various shades of brown, soothing colors that seemed to close in on you if you looked too long. "I'm not crazy, Neal, you know that. But it's no wonder people *go* crazy in a place like this. Listen to them out there!"

Down the hall a woman was loudly sobbing, her cries arching higher as though to compete with the insistent tap of the Ping-Pong. Zach was right: I didn't think I'd last more than a day in this place.

"Is there anything else I can bring you?" I asked. "Magazines? Crossword puzzles? Anything?"

"No," he said softly. "I still can't concentrate—not with this racket. Just bring cigarettes." He reached into the drawer of the nightstand and pulled out a five-dollar bill. "Here."

"No," I told him. "Keep it; you might need it for something else later." He hesitated and then returned the bill to the drawer, tucking it between the pages of the paperback I had brought him the first day. (Several of the patients were known to steal things.) The spine of the book was uncracked, the corners still smooth.

Patty, the perky nurse, rapped at the door now, her face floating in the tiny meshed window. She pushed the door open and stuck her head inside. "Dinnertime, Zach."

"Thank you." When she turned away, nonchalantly leaving the door ajar, Zach added, a copy of her smile painted on his face, "Bitch."

"What's wrong with her?"

"She treats me like a fucking child. 'Dinnertime, Zach.' Any minute now she'll be asking if I've done number two today."

I could barely remember the last time he'd laughed. It was nice to hear him laugh.

"Well," I said, rising stiffly from the chair, "I guess I should be going so you can have your dinner."

"Yum," he said, groaning his way off the bed. "It's probably something dee-licious, like franks and beans."

"Not exactly Chez Panisse, is it?"

"Not exactly." He put his slippers back on. "I'll walk you to the door."

We had to stop at the nurses' station so that one of them would get the key to let me out. Zach and I parted midway down the hall; he wasn't allowed to come too close to the door. "See you tomorrow?" he asked. His voice was suddenly childlike, his features softened and pale.

"Of course." I reached out, and he took my hand, held it between cold palms.

"Good night," he said, slowly pulling away. And then he turned abruptly, as if afraid to watch me go, and headed back to the day room. Dinner was waiting.

Patty led me to the heavy steel door. The bolt clicked loudly as she turned the key. She pushed the door open just enough to let me pass through and smiled cheerfully. She was in her early forties, gray just starting at her temples, brown eyes dull, unrevealing. I was struck suddenly by the paradox of her job: spending all day trying to get other people in touch with their emotions, she'd been forced to bury her own. "Good night," she sang out, like a hostess. I supposed I should have said, *Thanks, I had a lovely time.*

I stopped on the threshold, her hand still on the knob, ready to pull the door shut. "How's he doing?" I asked. "Really."

Her smile refused to fade. "Just fine," she said. "It takes time, that's all."

"What can I do?" I was whispering, one eye peeled for the day room. It was like spying, or tattling to the teacher. "I never know what to say to him."

"Just act normally," she said. "Say whatever you would say if the two of you were out to dinner. Sometimes the best medicine is to be reminded of what he's missing." I searched her face for irony, but all I got was the smile. It was a faithless smile, I saw now—a smile of resignation, not hope. She was just going through the motions. What is he here for, I wanted to ask her. What's the point if there's nothing you can do, if exposure to the outside world is all he needs?

I went to his apartment first, the morning after they'd checked him in—or, as Zach preferred to say (for accuracy), locked him up. I'd pulled his gym bag out of the closet and hurriedly packed everything he'd asked for into it. Not reading more than one item ahead, I ran dizzily back and forth from one room to the other, checking things off my list—toothbrush, underwear, comb, socks. Rigid adherence to the list kept my mind off why I was there, why he needed all this stuff. I went through his apartment with a singular purpose, opening drawers and cabinets like a robot, sifting through his things solely to find what I needed. I didn't stop to read the notes that lay in piles on the desk, to examine photographs tucked inside drawers. I didn't have time to be nosy, and perhaps I was a little afraid of what I might find. I had a job to do. He needed me. That was enough.

Zach was right about Bonnie. I remembered her from that first day, when she went through the bag I'd so hastily packed. She reminded me of a customs agent, though she was more matter-of-fact, less eager to discover contraband. Her smile was tender, her eyes full of an I'm-just-doing-my-job reluctance as she made two piles—the things Zach could keep, the things I would have to take back. Sweatpants were forbidden, she said; the drawstring was too dangerous. And the hairbrush—Zach spent ten minutes before the mirror each morning, trying to get each strand just so—its handle came to a sharp point; I'd have to find him another one, something softer, rounded at the end. The shirts and underwear were fine, the slippers. He was most insistent about the slippers when he'd called me the night before. It was impossible, he said, walking around in his sneakers with the laces pulled out.

Finished with her sorting, Bonnie locked up the forbidden items ("You can pick them up on your way out," she said, turning the key) and led me through the public area to Zach's room. "This is where we do group," she said, gesturing toward the semicircle of heavily cushioned chairs. "Every morning, to see how everyone is, to share." I nodded, attempted to match her smile. I wanted to know how long she'd worked here, how long it took before you could look at this place and not be shocked—how long before you could no longer hear the mumbling of that man in the corner, rocking himself in clenched arms, no longer notice the smell of urine beneath the disinfectant.

But instead, I smiled again as she plopped Zach's things onto the bed. "We'll let him put everything away," she said. "Sometimes they're very particular about where things go." She indicated the chair by the window. "He won't be much longer," she said. "You can wait here."

I nodded, still staring at the mound on the bed. A white sock hung over the edge, its elastic worn and outgrown. I should have been more careful in choosing.

The room was narrow, barely twice as wide as the bed. Perhaps the cramped quarters were meant to discourage patients from keeping to themselves. After a few minutes in this constricted space, you'd probably forget how to breathe, I thought. Instinctively, I went to the window. There was no sash, no hinge, just a narrow, immovable pane of glass.

In a moment, the door clicked shut and I turned around. Zach's smile was broader than ever. He looked fine, perfectly normal. For a second, I almost forgot where we were, and I completely forgot why. He crept toward me, like a child sneaking out of a room, hoping his parents wouldn't notice, and kissed me—softly, his lips puckered out in an exaggerated fashion. A parody of a kiss. A kiss that said *I love you, thanks for coming,* not *I want you.* I allowed my own lips to pucker just as severely in response, so that our faces were that much farther apart. I was grateful for the lack of sexuality.

"I'm supposed to keep the door open," he said, "especially when I have company."

"Then open it."

He scowled. "Screw 'em," he said. "I don't want to share you with the rest of them." He stared at me, scanning my face as you might a painting in a museum, to force the memory.

"My stuff!" he said, suddenly distracted by the pile on the bed. He began rifling through it, tossing aside the shirts and socks. "Where's my Walkman?" he asked. He was sifting through the pile like a forty-niner panning for gold.

I hesitated, didn't reply until he had sat on the edge of the bed and looked up at me. "They won't let you have it," I confessed. I scrunched my nose; it was the best I could do to try to convey my own disapproval of bureaucracy. "The cord."

He rolled his eyes. "It's not long enough to hang a mouse," he said. "What am I going to do with it—strangle my pinky?"

I shrugged. "Rules," I said.

"Yeah, rules."

That was nearly two weeks ago; Zach was used to the rules by now. He knew which ones he was breaking; he was selective.

I never knew what I would find, from one day to the next. This was one of the bad days. He was sitting in a chair at the foot of the bed when I arrived, staring out the window at an orange sky. He hadn't taken a shower today; his hair was stiff, full of cowlicks on one side. He didn't turn to acknowledge me, so I stood in front of the window. If the mountain wouldn't come to Mohammed . . .

"What do you want?" he mumbled. He hadn't looked up, but still he knew it was me.

"How are you?"

"I asked you first. What do you want?"

"I just came to say hello, see how you are. Like every day."

"Every day?" His jaw was set, the veins in his neck bulging above the collar of his red sweatshirt. "You haven't been here in ages."

"Zach, I saw you last night."

He hesitated, then his voice softened, the rigidity giving way at last. "You did?"

"Yes. Don't you remember? I brought those flowers."

He laughed and turned to the bouquet on the bedside table. "Yeah. I guess I forgot. I lose track of time. There's no clock in my room."

"Did you take your walk today—outside?"

"They wouldn't let me go." He was looking at my belt buckle now, not yet willing to lift his head.

"Why not?"

"Never mind." He turned to the window again, that dull indifferent look reasserting control over his face.

"Well, do you want to go to the day room?"

"No," he said quickly. "They're all crazy out there. They ask too many questions." He straightened himself in the chair and finally looked up at me. His beard was getting full: he looked older, more distinguished. "Remember Carla—that teenager, the one who never stops smoking? She asked me today if I was queer. Just like that, I'm sitting there, having a cigarette, minding my own business, and she asks me that."

"What'd you tell her?"

"I told her she was ugly. She just wanted to know why I wasn't interested in her, that's all. Now she has a reason." He laughed again, a child's mischievous pride in his eyes.

It was getting dark out, but Zach hadn't turned on the light. Instinctively, I reached for the switch, but then thought better of it. He enjoyed the dimness, the silence, the wilting warmth. It was like a co-coon in here, a waiting room where time had stopped. It reminded me of our first few weeks together, when we'd practically lived between the sheets—gathering food and magazines around us, the remote control our only connection to the outside world. Weekends, from Friday evening to Monday morning, that now lived in my mind as im-ages of flesh on flesh and the sound of his moans in my ear.

At home, I put away my briefcase and changed quickly into a pair of jeans and a sweatshirt. It was nearly 7:00 already, and Martin was never late.

I was chopping vegetables when the doorbell rang. When in doubt—or a hurry—throw a few things into a wok and call it Chi-nese.

Martin smiled broadly in the doorway, holding aloft a bottle of Merlot. "I would say 'sweets for the sweet,' but in your case I thought something dry was in order."

"Thanks," I said, leaning in to kiss his cheek. His five-o'clock shadow was especially rough, scraping my chin. I led him into the kitchen and dug through the silverware drawer for a corkscrew. "Would you do the honors?" I asked, passing it to him. "I'm dying for a drink."

"Rough day?"

I turned away and pinned a red pepper to the cutting board. "What do *you* think?" I said, chopping it in half. I bent over the wastebasket to scoop out the seeds and ribs. The meat was lighter on the inside, like fresh blood.

"How is he?"

"Better, I guess. I don't know how to judge. I mean, someone goes into the hospital for appendicitis, they slice him open, they pull the damn thing out, they sew him back up. A few days of rest and he's back to normal. The body heals that way. I'm not so sure about the mind."

"Well, he's talking, right? That's good."

"It depends on what he talks *about*, Martin. I'm not exactly getting the Gettysburg Address."

"You never did."

I dropped the pepper slices into a bowlful of other chopped vegetables by the stove. "No, you're right. I didn't choose Zach for his mind. Why should I care if he loses it?" It never took me long to start making up sick jokes; I excused myself by calling them a defense mechanism. I was becoming well versed in psychobabble.

"So how are you holding up?" Martin asked, handing me a glass of wine.

"Fine." I gulped a large mouthful, hoping for an instant buzz. "I go to work. I go to the hospital. I come home. I manage."

Martin's deep blue eyes were wide, pondering. "Do you have to go every day?"

"Who else is going to visit him?"

"What does that have to do with it?"

I pulled the diced chicken out of the refrigerator and set a high flame under the wok. "Martin, he's my lover. I owe it to him."

I dribbled oil into the wok and swirled it around before dropping in the ginger and meat. The chicken sizzled as I stirred it, the pink fading quickly from each piece.

"You've known him for—what, five or six months?"

"So?" Some of the chicken was sticking to the pan; I hadn't put in enough oil.

"You obviously didn't know everything there was to know about him. You're not under any obligation."

"You make him sound like a defective appliance. Do you think the hospital will give me my money back?" I lowered the heat and tossed in the vegetables. The aroma from the onions wafted toward me in the steam, and I regretted not wearing my glasses. "God, Martin, if the man had cancer, or AIDS, would you say that?"

"It's not the same, Neal."

"Yes it is. He's sick. He's not crazy, Martin—as if *that* would make a difference. He has a chemical imbalance."

"And what does that mean?" He had moved beside the stove now, facing me.

"He's only in the hospital until they can find the right drug and dosage. It's like diabetes, for god's sake."

"Neal." I felt his eyes on me, but, still concentrating on the wok, all I could see of him was the bottom of the glass cradled in his hand. "You know it's not that simple."

The vegetables were beginning to wilt. I stirred the sauce quickly and poured it into the wok. Everything settled down immediately. Everything except the onions; they were still searing my eyes.

"I can't take it, Martin. You should see that place. The patients, they're—"

"Crazy?"

"It's terrifying to see what can happen to people. I look at some of the other patients and I think, they probably used to be normal, functioning human beings—like Zach, like me. And now they're babbling to themselves and making papier-mâché puppets."

"And Zach?"

I turned off the heat and checked the rice on the next burner. Everything was done. "Zach. I don't know. Sometimes he seems like himself, and other times he's just—absent. Like I'm talking to someone else and *he's* not there anymore."

"Maybe he *is* there, Neal. Maybe that *is* Zach."

"What do you mean? You mean the man I fell in love with was a fraud?" I turned away, scooping the rice into a large bowl. It had grown thick and lumpy, clinging to the spoon.

"No, not a fraud. He just wasn't the whole picture."

"And this *is?*"

"Well, another piece of it at least."

"And where does that leave me?" I asked. I could feel my back growing rigid.

"That's up to you."

We began dinner in silence. Martin stared at me half the time, practically ignoring his food. A more sensitive chef would have been offended.

"Okay," I challenged him, "say it." I tested my chopsticks, opening and closing them over the plate like a narrow set of jaws coming in for the kill.

"I worry about you," he said.

"Well, don't, okay? I'm fine." I closed the chopsticks around a cube of chicken.

Martin was more practical, or more stubborn. He stabbed his food with a fork. "I hate to see you wearing yourself down like this. You need to take care of *yourself* for a change. You need to get on with your life."

"I haven't stopped living, Martin."

"You're in storage, Neal." He gestured toward the bookcase crammed into the corner beside the table. I'd moved it from the bedroom to make room for Zach's favorite chair, the same day I emptied half the closet into a trunk.

"That's only temporary. We'll get a bigger place soon."

"*We?* Neal, you don't even live together *now* and you're talking about moving to a bigger place?"

"I have to think about the future."

Martin laughed and swirled his wine glass. "You know what your problem is, Neal? You *live* in the future. *Fantasy Island.*"

Suddenly, Zach wasn't the only stranger in my life. "I expected support from you, Martin, not sarcasm."

"I'm sorry. I just don't see an answer, and it kills me to see you destroying yourself to find one. Or worse, pretending you don't need one."

"You act as if it's easy to just give up. You saw us together in the beginning. For Christ's sake, you introduced us."

"I didn't know about any of this."

"That's not the point. I'm *glad* you introduced us. Zach was great for me. You have no idea what it did for my ego to have someone like him paying attention to me."

"And look what he did to you."

"Stop it!" I felt the trembling now; it started in my legs, where he couldn't see it. "Zach hasn't done anything to me. This is my choice."

"Like Adam, right?"

"What does he have to do with it?"

"Maybe nothing, maybe everything. But he did take a year of your life, didn't he—stringing you along?"

"That was a completely different situation."

"Granted. But the two do have one thing in common. You."

I pushed the plate away. One of the candle flames wobbled wildly. I wasn't hungry, anyway. "What are you saying, Martin? Should *I* go to a shrink next? The family that pops psychotropic meds together, weds together?"

Martin set down his fork and laid his elbows on the table. "You're under a great deal of stress, Neal. Maybe this is an opportunity to . . . look at your life."

What life? I wanted to ask, but I knew that was precisely the kind of question he was waiting for—his chance to pounce on me. *Codependence,* that's what he would have said. Nineties code for *love.*

I said nothing. We both said nothing, as the plates grew cold between us.

When he appeared in the day room, he looked as healthy as the night we met, swirling across the dance floor, wearing a smile that seemed indelibly tattooed on his face. I was so pleased to see him at all—alive and smiling—that at first I didn't notice the shadows under his eyes, the pallor everywhere else. How odd, I thought, that my mind should flash back that far so unexpectedly, imagining the Zach I fell in love with rather than the morose stranger he'd been for the past couple of months. And I remembered my grandfather. In his eighties, he could recall every detail of his sixth Christmas, what my grandmother had been wearing on their first date, but he couldn't tell you what he'd just watched on TV, couldn't remember my name.

I'm not sure how much of all this I can remember, that's why I have to write it down. Before it slips away. If there's one thing Zach taught me, it's the importance of holding on to memory, feelings. I watched him lose them, one by one, like the air escaping from a balloon, leaving it limp and parched. If I write it all down now, while it's fresh, I'll remember how it felt. I can't afford to forget.

I was amazed at how quickly you can get used to things. Already this daily journey had taken on the air of ritual. I boarded the bus to the hospital with the same detachment as the bus I took every morning to work; it was part of my commute now, like stopping at the grocery store to pick up ingredients for dinner.

Brick buildings are rare in San Francisco. They're incapable of swaying; in a strong earthquake, the mortar between the bricks would liquefy, and the building would crumble to dust. A hospital was the last place you would expect to find made from such vulnerable material, but this one had been built on bedrock and was therefore allegedly immune to the random trembling of the earth below. If the land did rumble again, the building might lose a few scattered rectangles of brick but would, it was hoped, remain standing.

The facility had seemed out of place to me the first time—fire-red in a neighborhood of subdued pastels. The grounds were neatly landscaped, though none of the tree branches reached too close to the building, none of the bushes was wide enough to conceal a human figure. It was open greenery that they were after here, a simpler and safer beauty. Passing through the ten-foot wrought-iron gate and onto the concrete path that bisected the lawn, I had the sense of entering a new, radically different world—Dorothy opening the door onto a sinister version of Oz.

The first floor housed the reception area, administrative offices, and some of the outpatient services. The wards were upstairs, but the signs gave no indication of how they were arrayed. I imagined a system determined by increasing disorder—the higher the floor, the more serious the case: posttraumatic stress on 2, depressives on 3, schizophrenics on 4, the criminally insane on 5. I had an incorrigible habit of seeking out order, even hoping for a method in this, very real, madness.

On the third floor, just off the staircase, I stood before the steel door and rang the bell. A moment later, Wanda peered through the mesh window and let me in. I'd learned the names of all the nurses on this shift, and one or two who worked weekends. They'd even begun to take on personalities—something beyond the white uniform that was probably all the patients could see. Wanda was the one with the saddest smile, the martyr's smile. She was clearly devoted to her job, but I saw a hopelessness in her eyes: the same strain I'd seen in photos of relief workers, doling out food on a barren African plain; each time she looked up from her work, the crowd got larger, and by the time she'd fed the last, the first was hungry again.

"Zach had a good day," she told me as I signed in at the desk.

I looked eagerly into her eyes, waiting for details, hoping for a breakthrough. But Wanda's definition of a good day was probably leagues away from mine.

He was playing solitaire at his desk when I entered the room, slapping the cards down each time he found a match, shuffling impatiently when he didn't. Absorbed in the game, he didn't notice me until my shadow fell over the cards, nearly obliterating the Jack of Hearts. He looked up then, ready to scold an unwelcome companion, but the anger in his eyes softened when he saw me, and he tossed the cards onto the table, disfiguring the neat rows.

"Hi," he said, a full-toothed smile breaking through for the first time in weeks. His enthusiasm took me aback, and I just stared at him for a moment before speaking. "I've been waiting for you," he continued. "How are you?"

"Okay." I wasn't used to him asking the questions. I laid my leather jacket on the bed and sat on the edge as Zach turned his own chair around to face me.

"I won the Ping-Pong tournament," he announced, half proud, half ironic.

"Congratulations."

He rolled his eyes. "Don't get your hopes up; I'm not going to be in the Olympics. The only competition was that old man who talks to himself all day and a couple of schizos down the hall."

"Still." *Rome wasn't built in a day,* I thought, in my mother's voice.

"Dr. Porter thinks I'm doing really well. I bet I'll be out of here by next week."

"Is that what he said?"

Zach jerked his head to one side. "Not in so many words." He affected a portentous baritone. "'You're making progress, young man.' That sort of crap. But I feel great."

"Good."

"And I've been thinking." He leaned forward now, elbows on his thighs. "About when I get out. First thing is I'm going to get a new job. I've been a salesman long enough; I'm going to try to get a job as a buyer. That's where the money is. And God knows I know all there is to know about shoes."

I couldn't tell anymore. I couldn't tell the difference between the illness and the cure. Was this excitement, this mania, a consequence of the drug or a symptom of the disease? I stared into his eyes, the blue nearly obliterated by the encroaching black of the pupils. Another of my mother's clichés popped into my head: windows to the soul. But I couldn't see in; it was too dark.

We finished up our visit in the day room, Zach smoking two cigarettes in a row. He was playing a game with the ash, seeing how long he could let it grow before it fell off. He quit after half an inch, not content to waste the entire cigarette, and tapped the ash into the plastic tray between us, pale green teeth rising on either side to hold the stubs. "It's going to be great," he whispered. "And I'm going to do it."

"What?"

He took a long drag. "If there's one thing this place has taught me, it's that I never want to come back."

"You won't," I told him. And finally, through the smoke, it felt like our smiles matched, his determination at last equal to mine. I wanted to take his hand, kiss the raw, bitten cuticles, warm the fingers that were always so cold when he reached out to me in bed. I would hold them cupped between my own, and breathe into them, as you blow on a fire that's starting to flicker.

Life is full of rituals. Maybe that's what keeps us sane. At the hospital, they were very strict about making the patients adhere to a schedule. Deviation—or what the rest of us call freedom—might have sent them over the edge.

I'd developed a whole set of rituals of my own—reading the paper on the couch after dinner, laying out the next day's outfit before bed, writing in my journal every day—all to balance the ritual I couldn't control: boarding that bus to the hospital every night, preparing myself for the unexpected.

An occasional beer helped serve the same purpose. One of my favorite spots was the corner beside the back pool table at Badlands. It was a little quieter back there, not so many bodies squeezing past one another, less chance of getting a drink spilled on you.

I pulled myself up onto the bench, smooth wooden slats, knots untraceable in the dim light, and settled the beer bottle in the space between my thighs.

I observed mostly—the impromptu dance, the smiles that went unreturned, eager glances unmet. A young man slid through the crowd, hand brushing delicately against a series of shoulders like a swimmer breaking the waves. No one turned to acknowledge the touch or reject it—their shoulders numb, inured to the indifferent gesture.

I sipped the beer and looked up at the stained glass light fixture, so incongruous amid the cattle skulls and license plates that adorned the paneled walls. Georgia O'Keeffe meets John Wayne.

A thirtyish man in a flannel shirt and jeans stood beside the cigarette machine, cradling a Miller and gazing absently at the crowd. Another man, somewhat older, his leather jacket zipped halfway over a white T-shirt, moved toward him and settled just a few inches away, looking nonchalantly in the opposite direction. Every once in a while, one of them turned his head slightly to check the other out. They were discreet about it, watching peripherally to make sure their eyes never met. They stood together like that for several minutes, gradually moving closer as the crowd thickened around them or jostled past. They never spoke and finally, perhaps giving up hope, the older man swallowed the dregs of his beer and left, cutting through the men's room to avoid the crush by the bar. The other looked back briefly, then indifferently returned his gaze to the room. He was still there, alone, ten minutes later, when I hopped off the bench and made my way out the door. It was nearly midnight; the last bus was due at any minute.

Whereas Zach would barely speak when he first entered the hospital, now I could hardly get him to shut up. Every time I visited, he told me more, reconstructing his life episode by episode, as if believing that the accumulation of detail might one day reveal some great truth—as if by telling, he could make it all make sense. He seemed to have found a freedom in talking about his past—reveling in the lessons he'd learned. He would have gone on all night if we weren't limited by visiting hours. Perhaps these diatribes were inspired by therapy, leftover information that his doctor didn't have time to hear. And perhaps that explained why they sounded so empty to me—as if a core were missing. He told me the stories, but they came out in an almost clinical recitation, a mere series of actions, like a novel without a theme. Dry, emotionless, the stories might just as easily have been about someone else, someone Zach had never actually met. I had to add the meaning myself.

The first time he ran away from home, he told me, at twelve, he hitchhiked and got as far as the Nebraska border. The truckdriver, who was at least thirty, had wanted to dump him out when he noticed how young he was, but Zach was an inventive kid. He convinced the driver that he was older by mere braggadocio, and sealed the argument by giving him a blow job right there in the cab, traveling sixty miles an hour on the interstate. He looked up every few seconds, to gauge the driver's expression, and saw the wheat fields passing by more and more swiftly, until they became a yellow blur, a Van Gogh burst of formless color.

At a diner on the border, while the truckdriver was in the men's room, Zach was spotted by a friend of his father's, and that was the end of his first adventure. Mr. Hicks called the house and got permission to bring Zach home; he was on his way back from a tractor show in Lincoln. His father was waiting at the farmhouse when they pulled up, and while Mr. Hicks and Zach's grandmother silently watched, he gave Zach the worst beating he'd ever had. The last beating, Zach decided, as his father's work boot kicked him into the porch railing. The next time he ran away, he wouldn't be so unprepared. He'd save money; he'd have a plan. He'd behave himself until then, to throw them off. The next time he'd make it, he'd be gone for good and never look back.

It took the Navy to get him out. Six more years of playing the good son. Only his grandmother ever knew about his deceptions—the drunken nights with his friends in the barn, driving wildly through the countryside in beat-up cars in the wee hours of the morning, smoking pot behind the house. She was too old and naive to recognize the smell; she thought they were just European cigarettes. But she kept Zach's secrets. She, too, didn't want to see any more beatings.

On those drunken nights, he began to give blow jobs to his friends, too—for money, cigarettes, whatever they were willing to offer. He pretended to do it because he was drunk, because he needed their meager gifts to compensate for the pathetic allowance his grandmother could barely afford; they pretended to let him because it was meaningless, because a boy's mouth was as good as a girl's as long as you kept your eyes closed, because none of the girls in school would do it—except Cathy Hooper, and she always had cold sores. Every once in a while, though, glancing up, Zach would catch one of them watching him. Once, Bobby Peterson even put his hand on Zach's head, guiding him to go deeper. Zach savored the pressure of the hand; it was more sensual than the taste of the cock in his mouth, the Ivory-soap smell of Bobby's virginal crotch.

In the barn, they would stand in a circle, with Zach on his knees in the middle—moving clockwise from one to the next. That was how he learned all the various sizes and shapes of cocks—Bobby's long thin dick, which curved slightly to the right just below the head; Curt's fat, stubby one, which had made him gag until he learned how to breathe through his nose; and of course, Jake's uncut miracle. He was fascinated by Jake's cock, the sheath of skin that gathered like a tight fire hose at the end and opened wide as the head got harder. He played with it, pulling the skin down, running his tongue into the crevice between foreskin and shaft. He had to be careful not to spend too much time on Jake. He had to treat them all equally, lest they think he was really enjoying this. Similarly, he had to be quiet, stifle the moans of pleasure he longed to emit; and he had to crouch carefully in the darkness, to hide the hard-on that jutted so boldly against his jeans. He wanted to whip out his own dick as he sucked, to stroke himself and pretend his own hand belonged to each of these oblivious boys. But he controlled himself. He waited until each of them had come, shooting into his mouth or onto the bitter dirt of the barn, until they silently lifted their pants from their ankles, disbanded, and went home—marching in single file out through the barn doors, not acknowledging what had happened, not even acknowledging that they were together. He waited until the sound of their footsteps had died in the darkness. And, still in the middle of the circle, now stained by the scuff marks of their boots and the dark spots on the ground where their come had moistened the dirt, he released his own cock. He came within seconds; he hardly had to touch it. All he needed was the memory, the still-lingering smell of their sweat and semen in the musty building.

These stories baffled me—less for their content than for the context in which he relayed them, in a quiet corner of his hospital room, or outside, walking under the arbor—sites that seemed so foreign to sex, or at least the kind of sex he was describing. I tried to get him to stop, to wave the stories away. "I don't need to hear this, Zach," I said. What I meant was, there was no need for confession. Whatever he'd done in the past, however many men he'd slept with—none of that had any bearing on our relationship or how I felt about him.

"Does it disgust you?" he asked. The wind parted his hair on the wrong side, a lock flopping into his eyes.

"No. I just—you don't have to relive it for me."

"I'm not doing it for *you*," he said. "I'm doing it for me."

The anecdotes jumped back and forth in time. He wasn't telling me his life story so much as tossing pieces of it in the air, hoping they'd fall into some recognizable pattern. I remembered a game I'd played as a child—peeling an apple in one long, curly strand and tossing it over my shoulder. Someone had told me it would land in the shape of a letter—the first letter of your future spouse's name. I couldn't even remember now which letter I got.

Zach's first "husband" was another sailor, when they were stationed in Puget Sound. They shared an apartment off base; everyone had roommates, so there was nothing suspicious about living together. George was about ten years older—a career man, with ambitions of commanding his own ship. As if to compensate for being gay, he wore his machismo like a badge—or a disguise. He was the toughest guy on base, Zach said. And Zach had the bruises to prove it.

George liked his sex rough. He encouraged Zach to resist, to fight his advances as he threw him onto the bed, rolled him over, slapped his ass. He liked to hear Zach's grunts, as long as they weren't loud enough to travel through the wall.

Zach had two commanding officers in those days—one on base and one at home. While the first would yell if his collar was askew, George would rage at dirty dishes in the sink or a shirt left dangling from a doorknob. But the marks he left were always conveniently under Zach's uniform—nothing for show-and-tell on base. And afterward, he was gentle. Those were the only times George was gentle, the only times he cradled Zach in his arms. After a while, Zach came to crave the beatings, even encourage them, knowing the reward of tenderness that would follow.

George's career ambitions finally took him away. Posted to a ship in the South Pacific, he sailed away from Washington, away from Zach. Zach contented himself with a string of other men then, nights spent in dark bars, drinking until his memory and his discrimination faded to nothing, waking up beside strangers and dashing onto base bleary-eyed. He missed George more than he was willing to admit. He told himself that he enjoyed the freedom, that he was glad to be out from under George's thumb. But the nights became more and more oblivious, and the mornings later and more frantic. People started to notice, and Zach found himself losing control, not caring, slipping into lethargy.

He roamed the streets now, picking up men while still in uniform. He knew he was being watched. The Navy had spies everywhere; they were paranoid about what went on at night. They had an image to uphold, and it had nothing to do with cocksucking.

Zach didn't care anymore. He'd never loved the Navy the way George did; it had just been a ticket out of Kansas. And now that George was gone, he had nothing to lose.

By the time his commanding officer called him into the office, he felt as if he'd already said good-bye to the Navy. "You've been a good sailor," the commander said. "We don't want to have to give you a dishonorable discharge. Just resign now and no one will be the wiser."

And he did. It was that simple. The simplest thing he'd ever done, Zach thought. Leaving the base for the last time, he hardly felt any different at all. His step was a little lighter, perhaps, but that might just have been from abandoning the stiffness of his uniform. He was the same man, just not dressed in white.

"Wasn't it a difficult adjustment," I asked, "getting used to the outside world?"

He shrugged. "No. You know me, I just go with the flow."

That seemed to be the main difference between Zach and me—his ability to "go with the flow." I envied his talent for walking through life without questioning, without grasping for the unreachable. Zach lived in the moment. But ambitions, expectations, were all I could think about. I'd always had it all mapped out—where I was supposed to be a month from now, a year, a decade. And I always lamented where I was at the moment. For me, it seemed that only the future had substance—only there would my feet have weight.

Bonnie said it was a good sign.

He was sick of wearing the same clothes. Although everything got laundered once a week, he had only two shirts, which he alternated daily. At first, he didn't care; he would wear the same shirt day after day, even sleep in it and keep it on right through the next day. His hair had grown greasy and tangled, his cheeks lush with the light brown fuzz of a developing beard. But now, suddenly, he was down-right persnickety. He had even become obsessive about showers, complaining that they allowed him only one a day, and he insisted that Bonnie trim his beard twice a week.

It was a good sign, Bonnie said, that he had started to care about his appearance. It indicated a sense of pride coming back—a positive self-image. Even though the only people who saw him were staff and the other patients, he wanted to look his best.

I hadn't been back to Zach's apartment in over a month, not since that first day, when I'd fetched his things and cleaned up the bath-room. This time, I made sure to pee before I left my own place, just so I wouldn't have to go into that room again. I'd left it shining, cleaner than it had ever been, glistening like a layout in *Architectural Digest*— but still I couldn't bear the thought of going back in.

Martin had offered to come with me this time. He didn't want me carrying a suitcase on the bus, he said, when his car was hardly ever used. He said he was just saving my back, but I thought it was my mind he was worried about. After all, one of his friends had already lost his; it could become an epidemic.

He entered without comment, just gazing around like a tourist in a foreign shrine—silent out of respect for other people's beliefs. He headed straight for the window and looked out at the street, as if he'd come here simply for the view.

The apartment reeked of the mustiness of being shut up for so long, unlived in. I slid past Martin and pulled open the window, hoping for a breeze. But it was nearly winter in San Francisco, the air still and lifeless. We would have to wait for summer to get the cleansing cold wind. The curtains barely rippled.

"I'll just be a minute," I said, leaving him at the window. I had a list of the things Zach had asked for—his favorite polo shirt, the red one that gripped his biceps so tightly; a couple of other shirts, he didn't care which, but long-sleeved; his black cardigan, because black goes with everything; the framed photo of us at Great America, which he kept on the nightstand. I would be in and out of here in five minutes, tops.

I opened a dresser drawer, overwhelmed for a moment by the scent of cedar. Zach's balled socks, a rainbow, bounced against one another, vying for attention. Except for the whites, none of the socks was ordinary—they came in a variety of shocking colors and subtle patterns. But then, a shoe salesman would be a little more concerned with footwear than the rest of us.

I squeaked the drawer closed and moved on to the next one. The red polo lay under a neat pile of T-shirts, one of which came unfolded as I slipped out its neighbor. Gently, I replaced the creases and patted the pile into place. I then laid the polo shirt on the futon, its blood-red cotton warring with the blue duvet. I returned to the hallway; the long-sleeved shirts were in the closet.

Martin coughed softly behind me. He was still standing by the window, arms folded across his chest. He looked like an indifferent sentry, watching over his post without any concern for the particular value of what he was guarding. His folded arms said it was none of his business, what I found significant in this tiny space, the hours I'd spent here. He was quite consciously reserving judgment, refusing to acknowledge the temptation.

"How is he paying for this place?" Martin asked. "Out of work all this time."

I pulled out the first two clean and pressed shirts I found—a white flannel, and a plaid shirt Zach had worn more than once to the Rawhide. I suspected it was one of his favorites, he looked so good in it. That shade of blue brought out something in his eyes, something I hadn't seen in weeks.

"Disability insurance," I said. "It pays about sixty percent—just enough for the rent."

Martin sighed sympathetically. "Thank God it's a small place."

As the pile on the futon grew, I allowed myself to look around, wondering what else I could bring, some trinket that Zach had forgotten to ask for, something to remind him of home, something to give him hope that he'd be back here soon. I'd never before noticed how small the apartment was, how the walls met one another with such a determination to enclose. I wasn't claustrophobic, hadn't even been worried when I was trapped inside the elevator at work one day. But now I understood the cliché of walls closing in. I sat for a moment, the pile of shirts and sweaters spilling toward me, and closed my eyes, leaning forward to rest my head in my palms.

Martin's warm hand settled firmly on my shoulder. I hadn't even heard him approach. He remained as silent as before, only his grip revealing the slightest emotion—comfort, reassurance, balance. I took a deep breath, willing that warmth through my shoulder, along my spine, through each limb, the digits I now flexed to bring them back to life.

"Thank you," I said, lifting my head after what felt like half an hour, though it could hardly have been a minute. "I don't know what—"

Martin squeezed my shoulder, his grip at once soft and prodding. Telling me to buck up, but letting me know he'd still catch me if I fell. "What else is on the list?" he asked, reaching down to pull the crumpled paper from my hands.

"A Bible?" he said incredulously, squinting at the paper as if to decipher hieroglyphs.

"He said it's in the desk drawer. His grandmother gave it to him. He probably wants it more for the sentiment than for what it says."

"We can only hope," Martin said, yanking open the drawer. He shuffled through some loose papers. "How big is it?" he asked. "They come in all shapes and sizes, you know. Like penises."

"I have no idea."

Martin pulled the drawer out farther, so that it dangled over the desk chair. Torn pages from a looseleaf notebook, jagged edges frayed like peeling skin, spilled from the drawer, along with credit card receipts and colorful postcards. "What is all this stuff?" Martin said. "It looks like he never throws anything away."

"Zach's a lot more sentimental than he looks," I said, coming over to help. I picked up a pile of papers from the floor—newspaper clippings, an assortment of the tiny flyers they shove into your hands on Castro Street to advertise dance parties, half-naked bodies decapitated by the margins of the card, writhing against a psychedelic background. The looseleaf paper was full of meaningless notes—phone numbers, appointments ("Neal, 7:00/Café Flore"). I tapped the pile against the desktop, smoothing the edges.

Finally, Martin found the Bible and handed it to me. No more than an inch thick, it was printed on paper so thin that the text of each page bled through. I had to lift each sheet and place my hand behind to make it legible.

"Who's Jenny?" Martin asked, pulling another loose sheet of paper from the drawer.

"His sister, I think." I crossed the room and laid the Bible on the pile of shirts. "What are you doing?" I asked. He held the paper up, catching the light spilling in from the window.

"You should read this, Neal."

"A letter from his sister? I'm not going to read that. It's private." I tried to pull the paper from his hand, but he turned away, toward the window. "Martin."

"It's not *from* his sister," he said. "It's *to* her." He twisted his back to keep me from peering over his shoulder. "Dear Jenny," he read. "At times like this, I really miss what we had as kids. I always felt like I could talk to you, you always understood me when no one else even tried. I'm sorry things changed. I wish we were still together, to share everything—the good and the bad."

"Martin, stop it. You can't do this." I pulled at his shoulders, but he wouldn't budge.

"I wish you could meet my new lover. You'd like him, Jenny, you'd understand why he makes me so happy. He's different from the others. I know you never approved. I know you never understood. But if you could meet Neal, Jenny, you'd see. He's so good to me. Better than I deserve. And the thought of losing him terrifies me. I shouldn't love so much, Jenny. That's my problem. I love so much, I'm afraid that if I have to let go, I'll die."

My hands slid off Martin's shoulders and rested against his back, catching only fluffy pills from his dark sweater. I pulled away and sat in the armchair. His voice went on over my head.

"And I think I'm going to lose him now. He wants me to live with him. You know I've lived with men before, but it was different then. *They* were different. They deserved me. We deserved each other. But I can't do that to Neal. I can't let him see who I really am. I'd hurt him, I know that. Inside of a week, I'd break his heart. I can't let him see me—not the way I really am, the part I hate so much myself. I don't know what to do, Jenny. I wish you were here to tell me. I wish I could call you up and ask. I wish I had the guts to mail this letter. I wish I really deserved love—yours or his. I wish—"

He stopped. "What?" I asked. "What does he wish?"

The paper crackled as Martin turned it over. "It ends there," he said. "He never finished it."

"What's the date?"

"There isn't one."

"All this time," I said, clutching the arms of the chair, "I thought he didn't love me enough. But he loves me too much."

"You can't love too much," Martin said.

"Oh yes you can." I threw my head back against the chair and took a deep breath. Beneath the dust and the damp, I could smell Zach's scent—the musky odor he emitted after sex, sweat dripping from his brow, his chest hair knotted in wet curls.

A warm pressure on my knee pulled me back, opened my eyes. Martin was crouching before me, his hand lightly settled on my jeans. His sympathy seemed natural, unrehearsed, as though drawn forth by a single note. I remembered now the hours he had spent beside deathbeds.

Our eyes met for a long, silent moment, his the color of an evening sky—steady, hinting at permanence. Pale rings hung below them, tiny lines fractured out toward his temples. Even his cheeks had sunken in the past minutes, fleshy now, and limp. Martin and I looked nothing alike, but at this instant I had the sensation of looking into a mirror and seeing what I should be feeling.

He waited for me to break the connection. My breath came deeper after a while, and I blinked, hands falling to my knees as I lifted myself out of the chair. His own hand slipped away and he rose to his feet. We must have looked like dancers, choreographing a simultaneous movement. I marched to the closet, pulled out Zach's Navy duffel bag, and began to pack the things I'd laid out.

"We'd better get going," I said, refolding a shirt whose sleeve had fallen out of place as I'd started to put it in the bag. "They're pretty strict about visiting hours over there."

Martin walked to the door first, leaving me to turn, the duffel bag suspended from my shoulder, and check that we hadn't forgotten anything. I joined him in the hall and made sure the door was securely locked. The contents of the bag shifted as I moved down the steps, and something pinched my back. It must have been the picture frame—the two of us posing before the roller coaster, Zach trying to force-feed me cotton candy, the gooey pink fiberglass clinging to our fingers.

"You don't have to come every day, you know."

Zach blew smoke through his teeth, two thin gray streams curling around his head, and turned back to the window. He was in one of his quiet moods today—not silent, not obviously depressed, but unusually sensitive. Commonplace sounds—a door creaking down the hall, Bertha's slippers scuffing across the floor—made him cringe. He was appalled when I told him I couldn't hear Laura's crayons scratching against her drawing pad; she was, after all, curled into an armchair at least twenty feet away, hoping not to be seen. "God," he said, "either you're deaf or I've turned into a dog."

"I like coming," I said. "I want to see you." There was no reason, of course, no explanation. All I knew was that I needed to be here, even if only to watch Zach blow smoke rings toward the ceiling light. Even if only to lean in close and be reminded of the scent I used to inhale all night long. Every week, stripping the bed, I would draw the sheet up to my nose to capture that final remnant, the only part of Zach that remained on Monday morning.

"Well," he said, the words swallowed by a sigh, "there's not much to see these days." His beard, full now, added a few years; he could easily have passed for thirty, perhaps even be mistaken for the older of us. Visiting every day, I'd had time to get used to it, watching him age before my eyes.

"How's Martin?" he asked. Every day we went through the same round of questions, me seeking details on his progress, prognoses from the doctors, and he getting the lowdown on the outside world.

"He's doing okay," I told him. "You know Martin."

"Does he hate me?"

"What?"

"Martin. Does he hate me?"

I forced a hasty chuckle. "Don't be ridiculous. Why would anyone hate you?"

Zach continued to stare out the window. A blue-gray light had settled over the neighborhood, bare branches silhouetted against the sky, piercing the just-risen moon. "Martin's got a lot going for him. He's smart, successful. You know, that's the kind of guy you should be with, Neal. Somebody like Martin."

"I'm not in love with Martin."

"No." He paused, lips still pursed from forming the word. "But somebody like him. Somebody you can talk to about . . . whatever it is you guys talk about. Somebody who's got his shit together."

"I love *you,* Zach."

He turned his head farther, diminishing my view of his profile. "Maybe you just think you do."

"Zach, where is this coming from? After all this time, how can you doubt how I feel about you?"

With all that hair, his eyes withheld from me, it was hard to read his expression. "What's love, Neal? Think about it. Do you really have the first idea?"

He dropped his cigarette into a styrofoam cup on the windowsill. The ash sizzled as it met the cold remains of someone's discarded coffee. "It's hell in here," he whispered. "This place. This constant . . . feeling. I know I should be happy, Neal. I have you. I have so much. But I can't." He turned slightly, his gaze still riveted on the moon, and I could see a tear starting to form, hanging heavily at the bottom of his eye. "I'm just so miserable all the time. That's the hell. It's like I carry it with me."

"No, Zach." I laid my hand on his forearm. I no longer cared whether anyone saw. "No. I'm right here. I'll take you out of that hell. We'll leave it together."

Finally he turned to me, his eyes full of tears, but masking something else, what I wanted to believe was a faint glimmer of hope. It was as if I were looking through the depression, like the bars of a prison, to the real, whole man trapped inside.

The room had no windows, no evidence of the outside world. All I saw were strangers, feigning intimacy.

"My name is Janice," she said, the woman at the far end of the oblong room. She had been coming here for weeks, I guessed, maybe months; the cold concrete walls didn't seem to bother her at all. I suspected that she liked them. She liked not having the distraction of a window. It was safer in here, between lifeless slabs of concrete. The outside world was a threat, and she wasn't the kind of person who could handle threats.

"Hi, Janice!" A staggered chorus of voices erupted, so that three simple syllables took ten seconds to finish echoing through the chamber. The voices were cheery, as though greeting a long-lost friend, someone they'd known for years—not a poor soul they'd never met before, whose face would be as absent from their consciousness an hour from now as it had been an hour ago.

Janice strained to smile, her lips rising uncomfortably for a moment before halting in a slightly curled line. She was in her forties, or so I assumed by the lines around her eyes, the gray swirling its way through her hair.

I couldn't imagine what I could possibly have in common with this woman. I couldn't imagine what I was doing here, pretending that I did.

She started in a low voice that gradually grew stronger. The silence of the others seemed to encourage her, as if she equated it with attention. But instead of listening, I found my mind wandering—studying her hands rather than her words: thin, gnarled fingers that toyed ceaselessly with a rubber band she had taken out of her hair before beginning to speak. She stretched the band between her index fingers, twirled it around one, released it, snapped it onto her wrist, plucked at it like a guitar string. And all the while she droned on, her voice an odd accompaniment to the finger dance.

I caught only snippets as I watched her hands or gazed around the room, studying the faces that feigned interest, the eyes that claimed an understanding of a language that was still foreign to me. "My father was an alcoholic," she said. "Same old story." Titters of recognition from the audience drove her on. "He was never really there for me. If he was home, he was either drinking or drunk—abusing my mother, yelling at the top of his lungs, or falling on his face on the living room floor. That's the way I thought life was supposed to be, I guess. I never knew anything else."

Directly across from me, an incongruously muscular man of about thirty hunkered in his chair, arms folded across his chest. His legs were spread wide in faded jeans, workboots planted firmly on the floor, pointing out at a right angle. He was looking down at the linoleum—listening, or perhaps just counting the squares.

"So when Marcia started seeing other women, I didn't say a thing. I knew she was doing it; she didn't hide it from me. She didn't even care what I thought. The truth is, she knew that no matter what she did, I wouldn't leave. She could get away with anything, and I'd still be there to pick up the pieces."

I fidgeted. The chairs were hard, brightly colored metal—like the ones soldered onto desks in elementary school classrooms. Mine was a peach color, the paint chipped here and there, an occasional pair of initials scratched in ballpoint.

Martin had suggested that I come here. He had known a lot of people who'd been helped by such groups—talking out their problems with people they'd never met. "Therapy," he told me, "is like sex used to be—safer with strangers. You don't have to worry what they'll think, you don't have to worry that it'll change your relationship, because you don't *have* a relationship. But still you have someone to listen to you. Try it, Neal. Just go and see what it's like."

I saw what it was like the minute I walked in the door. I'd felt more comfortable at twenty-one, entering a gay bar for the first time. At least then I'd known I had something in common with the people I confronted, the eyes that evaluated me as I entered the room. Here, I felt like an intruder slipping into a private club I wasn't even sure I wanted to join.

"I confronted her last week," Janice said. Her voice hadn't lost its monotone. She might as well have been reciting the Pledge of Allegiance or the phone book. "I said if she wanted to continue our relationship, we'd have to change the ground rules. She just stared at me, like I was speaking French or something."

She'd moved on to twirling her hair—long, twisted locks that hung around her shoulders. Her fingers moved dexterously through the strands, as if they'd memorized the gesture—like typing, or the piano. "But I felt like I'd accomplished something. Even if she didn't understand, I had expressed *my* feelings for once. I had done something for *me*. And I owe it to these meetings. Without these meetings, and my Higher Power, I wouldn't have had the strength."

All evening, people had been talking about this Higher Power. The very term made me cringe. Since ninth grade, when I had had a temper tantrum on the way to church and finally admitted to my parents that I no longer believed in God, I'd been skeptical of anything that smacked of religion. I wanted no part of the church I was raised in—a church that told me I was evil and condemned, while its own priests raped little boys—and no part of a God who would condone it. And even though every person in this room was similarly condemned, they embraced at least some form of spirituality. Just desperate, I thought, afraid to take responsibility for their own lives.

Finally, Janice finished, with a simple "Thanks for listening," and the room erupted in a cacophonous "Thanks, Janice." The sound pulled my head up in time to see a surprisingly broad smile crack awkwardly across Janice's face.

The meeting leader called for a break and chairs squeaked across the floor as people got up to stretch. I followed a group out to the street. The air was bracing—on another night I would have been shivering, but tonight I welcomed the chill. It woke me up, gave life to my skin.

"You want to leave, don't you?"

I turned, feigning curiosity, though I had no doubt that the words were directed at me. A woman I hadn't noticed inside, midthirties, stood beside me at the curb, her red hair impeccably cut, framing a firm but expressive face. She looked like a business executive—all the confidence I saw on those determined faces marching through the financial district, not a doubt in their minds about the world or their place in it. I couldn't imagine what she was doing here, in the land of the broken.

"Everyone feels that way the first time," she said, ignoring my silence. "You should have seen me when I first walked in here. CoDA, I thought to myself—sounds like a poisonous snake; what on earth can it do for me?" She pulled a pack of cigarettes from her pocket. "Do you mind?" she asked, gesturing with the pack. I shook my head, and she pulled out a stick. She held the pack toward me, offering, but I shook my head again, and she put it back in her pocket.

"My last remaining addiction," she said, after blowing out the first puff. She laughed. "Well, not really. That's why I keep coming to meetings."

"How long have you been coming?"

"To this one? About a year. I'll get my chip next month." She arched her foot against the fire hydrant, stretching. "But I've been going to AA for six years now. And not a drop since I started."

I smiled. It was the thing to do. "Congratulations."

"I say that to myself in the mirror every night. 'Congratulations, Annie, you made it through another day.' "

"Is it very different?" I asked. "CoDA and AA, I mean."

"Not at all," she said. "An addiction is an addiction."

"That's the thing I don't really get," I said. "I don't see how you can be addicted to a person. I mean, what one person calls codependence, somebody else would just call love."

"It depends on who's doing the defining," she said. "In my book, if two people do that sort of thing for each other—caring, affection, opening up—then yes, it's love. But if only one of you does it. . . .

Well, love isn't supposed to hurt, you know. And if you're co-dependent, you don't see that distinction. I used to think it wasn't love *unless* it hurt. No pain, no gain. Only in my case, it was all pain."

"But what if the person you're involved with has his own problems—things that keep him from being there for you, through no fault of his own? Like sickness."

She sighed. Smoke wafted from between her fingers; thinking, she seemed to have forgotten the cigarette altogether. "But," she said at last, "it's not really about him, is it? If your identity depends upon another person, no matter the circumstances—if you define yourself through relation with somebody else—that's codependence."

Something in her tone, or her face, made me talk. Inside that sterile room, I couldn't have said a word. "I just think this is incredibly self-indulgent. I mean, here I am acting like *I'm* the one who has a problem. Poor little Neal, he's anxious and angst-ridden. Meanwhile, my boyfriend's in a hospital bed and could be losing his mind."

"It's okay to worry about yourself."

"He needs me," I said. The words came out slowly, and as they did, each syllable caught in my throat. In another moment, I would be crying.

"And what do you need? What good are you to him if you don't get your own needs met first?"

I glanced away, at the palm trees on the Market Street divide, their fronds swaying gently in the evening breeze. "I don't have the luxury of thinking about my own needs. I don't have time right now."

Behind us, I heard people shuffling back inside. "Make time," Annie said. I turned to meet her eyes again. She wasn't smiling.

"Let's go in," she said, twisting her cigarette out with the pointed black toe of her shoe. She winked, nodding toward the door, and I followed her inside.

I hadn't been to the hospital for three days, but still my feet carried me steadily, automatically, up the sixty-two steps to Ward F. I had tried to shut my mind off on the bus, thoughts of the day spilling back onto the street with the exhaust fumes. By the time I started up these stairs, my head was a tabula rasa—unshockable, immune to surprise. Even Bertha's screams didn't get to me now; like everything else, they had become just a fact of life, background noise.

Zach was waiting impatiently in the day room, fingernails tapping a disjointed rhythm on the tabletop. His lips were set, parallel pink lines of annoyance. They stood out all the more because he'd shaved off his beard—or, more likely, had had one of the nurses shave it for him. The last thing they were likely to put in Zach's hands was a razor.

"I hardly recognized you," I said, sliding into the chair across from him. We had the table to ourselves, except for Laura, drawing on her pad at the other end. Her tongue poked out, curled around her upper lip, she was lost in her drawing; our conversation was safe. "It looks good."

"I shaved it yesterday," he said sarcastically. The real message was that if I'd been here yesterday, I'd have known that.

"You didn't say anything on the phone last night."

He glared at me—a challenge. "I had other things on my mind."

"How's it going?"

"What? The food still sucks."

"No. Therapy."

"Oh, that. Pain and Suffering 101." He folded his hands on the tabletop, but his thumbs escaped and drummed rapidly against each other. His nails were so long, I wondered why the nurses bothered to worry about razor blades. "They're still trying to get me to cry. It ain't happened yet."

If they wanted tears, I thought, they should just follow me home. I kept a box of Kleenex on Zach's side of the bed these days; it saved me the trouble of reaching up to the nightstand. "Any news on when you might get out?"

"Same old shit," he said, shaking his head. "Next week. Until next week comes, and then they say, 'Next week.' So, I guess I'm getting out next week."

I felt obliged to say something, to explain away the absurdity. "They just want to be sure you're ready. It's a big adjustment."

He sighed and rolled his eyes. "I'm ready. I've never been more ready in my life. I could tear the roof off of this fucking place, I want out so bad." His nervous energy was palpable. Even his shoulders seemed to be trembling, as if he couldn't keep any part of himself still. Like the leg that had kept twitching in bed when he'd started on the Prozac.

"So what have you been doing with yourself lately?" he asked.

"Working, the usual. Nothing exciting."

"Maybe we should trade places," he said. "Sounds like you'd fit right in here."

I laughed and scanned the room. Even the armchairs by the window were empty, but it didn't take long to figure out why. A TV was blaring in the distance, the sharp ding of letters lighting up on *Wheel of Fortune.* Zach said it was the favorite show on the ward, but he couldn't stand it. They had run out of normal words long ago, and now resorted to contrived phrases that no one would ever really use: "*Rock Hudson Hawk*—what the hell does that mean?"

"Why don't you let me talk to the doctor?" I asked. "Maybe I could get something more definite out of him."

"No," he said quickly. "It wouldn't make any difference."

On the first day, I had asked Bonnie for details about Zach's case, but she had said she wasn't allowed to tell me anything, and I couldn't even speak to the doctor. Only family, unless Zach okayed it first. So it was all still a mystery to me, except for the bits and pieces Zach slipped me when he was feeling generous—items I had to piece together later, looking for patterns, weeding out the parts that simply didn't make any sense. First it was depression, then bipolar. One day the doctor said it was all chemicals, the right level of serotonin and he'd be fine; the next, the word *psychosis* popped into the conversation. That was hardly reassuring, considering that it was the potential psychotic who was telling me all this.

I'd learned to read the truth in Zach's eyes. When he spoke, it was his eyes I paid attention to, more than the words. When they darted nervously around the room, I knew he was lying. Only when they were steady, with the old tenderness, could I trust what he was saying. Right now, he kept them focused on the table, not daring to look at me.

"It's all bullshit, anyway," he said. "They don't know what they're doing. There's no magic pill. I'm not going to wake up tomorrow morning and be happy. Jesus, if I did, then I'd *know* I was crazy!"

"You've been happy, haven't you?"

"Sure. When I was drunk or high or fucking my brains out." He poked one fingernail along the underside of its mate, driving out the dirt.

"You don't give yourself enough credit, you know."

He looked up suddenly, that challenge back in his eyes. "Like you do." His eyes were hard, angry. "When was the last time *you* were happy, Neal?"

I hesitated. A communal cry went up in the next room; someone had solved the puzzle. "I was happy with you."

He smiled matter-of-factly, as if he'd predicted my response and didn't believe a word of it. "Like I said: drunk or high or fucking your brains out."

What about the other times, I wanted to ask—laughing at a movie together, holding hands as we walked through the Castro, looking into each other's eyes over the dinner table as our food got cold. Hadn't that been happiness? Didn't that prove there was more to us than what happened between the sheets? But there was no point in arguing. I couldn't argue what I couldn't understand.

"I'm sorry," he said at last. He blinked and his eyes grew suddenly softer. "I'm just in a really bitchy mood tonight. I've been climbing the walls lately. You can't imagine what it's like—to see all that sunshine and not be able to walk out into it. To talk to you and know that the world goes on, and I'm trapped here, watching it through chicken wire. It sucks, Neal. It's killing me." He folded his arms now, that forced constriction the only way to keep himself still, keep himself safe. I reached for his forearm and squeezed it through the worn red sweatshirt. The muscle was hard, ready to spring in self-defense, but he sat still at last and held on, let me continue to hold on.

On the bus home, I cocooned myself behind dark glasses, between tiny headphones that sat nearly weightless in my ears. Alanis Morissette screeched at some midpoint in my head, replacing the echoes, shunting aside Zach's pain, my sympathetic terror. "It's like ten thousand spoons when all you need is a knife . . ."

We were at Mission when I felt his eyes on me. The bus had grown unusually crowded somewhere along the way, the woman beside me balancing a shopping bag half in her lap and half in mine as standees hovered over the seats. He was standing in the aisle, one row ahead of me, one hand closed firmly around the steel bar above his head. Shorn of shades, his gaze was open and unmistakable. He was concentrating too much, as though memorizing each line of my face. Something rose in my gut—part excitement, part fear. From time to time, I'd caught the casual cruiser's glance, but it had always been fleeting—flattering but not serious, seldom an actual invitation. I turned to the window and gently increased the volume.

A prolonged rustle beside me, a muttered and accented "excuse me" announced the departure of my seatmate. I watched her fight against the tide toward the back door, an overburdened salmon asserting its incomprehensible right to spawn and die. The crowd shifted around her, maneuvering for a steady position. With surprising, determined agility, the man slid around the others and lowered himself into place beside me. His leg jostled against mine with a credible inevitability, but he didn't pull it away. I looked resolutely ahead.

Our knees met, flesh touching through denim like a mirrored image. I glanced to the side, into the natural light of the bus. He was younger than me—early twenties, at once proud and terrified of his boldness. Now that we were beside each other, he had stopped staring, focusing instead on the long frizzy red hair of the woman in front of him. His nose was sharp, sloping gradually down to a clean-shaven upper lip.

The bus turned onto 18th, bearing my leg against his. He pushed back, both of us straining as if in an arm-wrestle. I pressed the stop button on my Walkman and let my hand drop to my knee. Looking down, I saw his own fingers—lithe but strong—dance along his jeans until our pinkies lay only millimeters apart. I froze for a moment, breathed, and flexed my finger so that it barely grazed his skin.

He needed no further encouragement. In a moment, our fingers were intertwined, swirling together. His fingertips teasingly caressed my downturned palm.

By now, past Castro, the crowd had dispersed. There was no one to see his hand move up my leg, his palm flatten forcefully against my crotch. I thought of Zach staring at a carpeted wall across town, given over to a world that—here and now—no longer existed. At the moment, there was only here and now, a stranger's hand urging.

In the sudden safety of the emptying bus, we turned to face each other. He smiled, sharing a secret. "What's your name?" he asked quietly, slowly. He had an accent I couldn't identify on the basis of so few words.

"Neal," I said, too quickly. "And yours?"

"Uri," he said, again flashing an innocent, expectant smile. I saw now just how young he was, how young I must have looked in college.

"Where's your stop, Uri?"

"Diamond," he said.

"That was five or six blocks ago."

He smiled again, this time like a mischievous child glad to be caught. "Where do *you* live?"

"Oak," I said, "near Ashbury." The bus was just assaying the sharp turn off Market. On our right, the downtown skyline fought against encroaching fog.

We got off together, and he followed me to the apartment. The etiquette was new to me. I didn't know how much conversation was appropriate: Should I treat him like a dinner guest? If a neighbor passes us on the stairs do I introduce them? I led him upstairs silently and closed the door behind us.

I didn't need to know the rules. Uri took care of that with a kiss, pushing me up against the closed door, pressing his lips against mine, splaying his hands across my body. By the time he pulled his lips away, I was no longer thinking at all. I took his hand and led him into the bedroom.

He was from Russia, he said, pulling a purple T-shirt off over his head. His biceps ballooned out, then deflated as he straightened and lowered his arms. His chest was less well-defined, hairless except for two rings of pale brown strands around his nipples and a thicker line that began at his navel and disappeared into his jeans.

His kisses were warm. It had been weeks since I'd felt more than the most perfunctory peck on my lips, since another tongue had dared to find its way past my teeth. I sank against him, still dressed, the buttons of my shirt scraping his bare skin. His hands made circles on my back, rustling the fabric on their way to the front. Under the spell of his kiss, I felt each button give way, a draught of cool air floating between us to shock my chest. He pulled my shirt open, finally, and slipped it off my shoulders. His fingers kneaded my skin, dropped soothingly into the hollow above my collarbone, at last began to flutter over my nipples.

Sitting up against the headboard only a moment later, I looked down at the crown of his head, blond waves swirling in all directions, and savored the gentle warmth of his mouth on my chest, lips closing softly around a nipple, tongue flitting against it, teeth finally teasing it to erection. I arched my back as his hand made its way along my chest, my belly, and began to unbuckle my belt.

All I knew was his name, the rest mere conjecture. It was as if we were both afloat somewhere beyond history. His accent, in the few words he muttered in my ear, enhanced the air of unreality: we were beyond language, as well. He was skin, a smile, a musky odor that lingered in the hairs I pulled at with carnivorous teeth. He was a chest, a cock, a tongue that teased and probed and soothed. He was here, and now. And that, for once, was all I wanted.

Later, lying back on the pillows, the bedclothes wrinkled but still tucked around the mattress, he cradled me in his arms. His odor, strong but somehow comforting now, pervaded the air. And he began to talk, his sharply accented voice oddly musical, its rhythm eloquent enough to compensate for the broken words.

He had come to America just last year, hoping eventually to become a citizen, though even a green card was still months away, if not years. Life in Russia, he said, was even harder since the fall of communism. A cousin who'd left years ago invited him to share his apartment in San Francisco, and Uri had jumped at the chance. America was a fantasy to him—a fairyland. To him, the whole *country* was Oz.

I'd never done anything remotely like this before, lying on a bed, sharing the intimate thoughts of a man who had been a complete stranger little more than an hour before. I'd always felt supremely out of sync with the gay world: I never tricked; I dated. By comparison with some of my friends, I might as well have been Wally Cleaver. And now here I was. It was as if I'd crossed a line and finally joined my tribe.

But the shock that I felt—if it was indeed shock that lay queasily under the euphoria of a just-released orgasm—had nothing to do with that. I wasn't surprised that I'd finally taken this step—or been taken by it. I was surprised only by how easy it had been, and how truly unextraordinary it felt.

It was the first time he'd been outdoors in weeks. "It's amazing what you start to look forward to," he told me as we passed through the doors behind the nurse and a couple of other patients. He stopped on the walkway that encircled the hospital and took a deep breath. "Fresh air," he said. "I've been looking forward to fresh air. We can't even open the windows up there." He laughed suddenly, looking around, spreading his arms to embrace the air.

Bonnie looked at us over her shoulder—just checking that everyone was together. She was trying not to be obvious. Allowing them out at all was a vote of confidence; to play mother hen would only have alienated them. I started walking behind her, hoping Zach would follow.

"I think it's working," he said suddenly, a crooked smile playing on his lips.

"What is?"

"The medication," he said. "Or being here, I don't know. I just—suddenly, I feel strong again, you know? Like I can do anything."

Dubious, I stepped toward him. I needed a closer look, I needed to see his eyes. He opened them wide, welcoming my examination, perhaps, expecting me to shine a light at his pupils for diagnosis. The blue seemed brighter; the life had returned.

"When did this start?" I asked.

"I don't know. It's been pretty gradual, I guess. But I woke up yesterday morning, and it was like someone had opened a door, you know?"

"Dorothy," I said.

"Yeah." He laughed. "And everything's in Technicolor."

Despite myself, I smiled back. I couldn't yet trust Technicolor. It had devolved to black-and-white before.

It was a beautiful day for December. It had rained a lot lately, and everything was turning a luscious green. The grass at our feet was thick, the color of cooked spinach.

Zach and I found an empty bench across the yard, facing the cold brick of the hospital. Gingerly, he walked his fingers toward my leg and settled them on my thigh. "I'm sorry," he said.

"For what?"

"What I've put you through. You've been wonderful, standing by me like this."

Across the grounds, Harold reached into a tree, pulled a branch down to smell the buds. Bonnie called to him to rejoin the group. "Well, you're worth it."

"Am I?"

I turned toward him, the still-dancing eyes. "Of course you are."

He squeezed my thigh, thumb tucked fiercely under my jeans. "It'll be different now, when I get out of here."

"Of course."

"I mean, I—" He bit his lip, looked around the grounds. "I'm ready now," he said finally.

A hollowness gripped my heart, my breath caught.

"I want us—I want to be there for you the way you've been there for me."

"You are."

"No," he said, looking back at me. "I mean really—literally, *be there*."

"Move in?"

He nodded. "I love you."

I felt a wink creep into my eye. I never wink. "Let's get through this, okay? One day at a time, isn't that what they say?"

"Yeah." He blushed slightly, and I realized how hard it was for him—saying that, making himself vulnerable. I reached down and held his hand in mine, squeezing his long fingers together.

I looked to the left, where the hospital grounds ended and the hill sloped downward. Far in the distance, I could just make out the bay, the pale sky blending into the deeper blue of the water. The horizon seemed infinite, light-years away. And so much unexplored land lay before it.

Besides my own, the first erect penis I ever saw belonged to Wally Doner. Every Monday and Thursday morning, after gym class, Wally Doner would turn his back in the shower and then rush into the locker room ahead of everyone else, hands cupped in front of his crotch, though not enough to hide the pubescent erection that had become his habitual mark of shame. We never knew whether it was homosexual urges, the hot water, or just really bad timing, but Wally's hard-ons were as regular as clockwork. He became the butt of jokes after the first week—jokes ironically reinforced by a name cruelly susceptible to puns. Wally Boner, we called him; like most adolescent viciousness, it was crude but irresistible.

It was a long way from a Boston junior high gym to a San Francisco sex club, but that was all I could think of as I stripped off my clothes in the locker room. Other men moved back and forth behind me, some undressing, others languidly rebuttoning shirts, their skin a bit more alive though their eyes were glazed, as though tired of ogling and wanting now to be unseeing as well as unseen.

Nearly naked, I wrapped a white towel around my waist before stripping off my underwear. I tucked everything into the locker, but the hooks weren't large enough to hold it all and my shirt slid into a clump on the bottom. I slipped the lock onto the handle and snapped it into place. The key they'd given me at the front desk was attached to an elastic armband that fit snugly around my biceps. I wondered if it would leave a mark, a red badge as evidence of where I'd been.

I wasn't sure what to expect. I'd never even spoken to anyone about these places. I couldn't help wondering if, venturing through the rooms, I would run into someone I knew. Somehow, I'd always assumed that people like me just didn't come to places like this. I believed that mercenary sex was the province only of the truly desperate, men who were too far gone for dating and relationships.

My excuse was impatience. With Zach so inaccessible, I just wanted sex—no courtship, as little conversation as possible. I wanted a man's arms around me, shared lust without any of the complications that other venues entailed. I didn't want to stand in the back of a bar, watching, wondering whether anyone was watching *me*. I didn't want to make small talk with someone, all the while wondering whether he was just killing time with me until someone better came along. And I didn't want the awkwardness of the aftermoments, that endless goodbye with Uri at my apartment door as I'd debated with myself over whether to exchange phone numbers. I didn't *want* to exchange phone numbers. I didn't particularly want to exchange names.

The playrooms were upstairs. I tightened the towel around my waist, afraid it would come undone in the climb up the stairs. It was a short towel, with only a couple of inches of excess to tuck in and hold it in place: the idea, I supposed, was easy access. I turned the corner on the first landing and saw a line of men filing along a hallway on the second floor. Their keys jangled, bouncing against the tags imprinted with their locker numbers, glinting against their upper arms. They reminded me of Marley's Ghost, drifting silently except for the constant reminders of his past that trailed noisily behind.

The first room, on the right at the top of the stairs, wasn't as dark as I'd imagined, mostly because of the video screens in the back, glowing images from porno movies. A series of thin walls, composed of a motley arrangement of two-by-fours and twisted metal, created a kind of maze, giving the illusion of private space where everything was unmistakably public.

Men in towels like mine posed against the walls, like shy boys at a high school dance, waiting to get up the nerve. They all glanced as I walked by, some turning their eyes immediately away, others lingering, taking in the entire picture. I slipped past them, bare feet shuffling on cold linoleum. Some of the men were wearing socks, even the occasional pair of hiking boots, and I felt a sudden panic, wondering what I might accidentally step in, hoping there were no cuts on the soles of my feet.

The men paraded through slowly, nonchalantly, with an air of ease that I'd seldom seen in bars. It seemed that they'd left their attitude, as well as their clothing, downstairs. They couldn't afford inhibitions up here, and any form of pretension was impossible, as transparent as the slits in their towels as they walked. Up here, in the dim light, what you saw was precisely what you got.

The next room, larger, less foreboding, was bathed in a rich red light. The immediate corner was dominated by a raised platform with two or three men poised atop it, their backs to me, while others stood before them at floor level. A video lounge lay at the far end of the room, and in the middle several bunk beds stood at odd angles to one another. I passed silently by. The noises of sex—the squeaking of the beds, an occasional moan or murmur—were softened by the music that pounded harshly from large speakers suspended from the ceiling. As I made my way through the room, the faces grew familiar—the same men, making the same circular path, always looking for something new.

I wiped sweat from my forehead, suddenly conscious of the heat. The air was thick, the pounding music somehow meshing with it, until I felt that I was walking in a kind of dreamscape. The outside world faded away and with it any sense of—or even desire for—escape. Continuing in the endless circle, I might have lingered here through eternity.

I'd lost count of my laps by the time I noticed him—a handsome balding man leaning against one of the bunk beds. He was only a few years older than me, thirty-five at most, and about the same height and weight. Dark hair coated his chest and belly, disappearing into the towel draped low on his hips. He smiled coyly, almost invisibly, his features muted by the red light.

I stopped directly across from him, and his eyes made their way slowly from my face to my feet. Glancing up again, noting that my eyes willingly met his, he crossed the few feet of space that separated us and stood at my side. He looked around the room then, as though to suggest that he'd come beside me merely for the view. And as I turned my head, toward the audience so rapt by the video screens, I felt a finger softly fluttering against my nipple.

I looked back and caught his eye again. His smile grew broader and he leaned down, clamped his mouth against the nipple and sucked. I gasped as his teeth closed gently around it, capturing its erect plume like a painless bear trap. His hand caressed my belly, meandering up toward my free nipple, and he raised his head. Gently, he led me toward the bunk bed. The bottom one was free, and we climbed onto the mattress together, the dark vinyl squeaking beneath our bodies.

We did everything without words. A simple moan, a coaxing hand, was enough to direct us. Tucked into the shadow of the bottom bunk, we were locked together like twins in a womb, sharing everything, uncertain whose limbs were whose. It didn't matter. We didn't need to know, because everything felt good as if by instinct. We simply knew what to do to give us pleasure. Giving and getting seemed somehow the same in this primitive world.

I was hardly oblivious to the figures that glided past, the heads that ducked under the bunk to gawk, as though we—this nameless stranger and I—were in a porno movie they'd rented, as though we were there for their pleasure as well. But that didn't matter, either; there was only pleasure—nonspecific, nonindividual pleasure. I suddenly thought of all those *National Geographic* specials my father had coerced me to watch as a child, studying a family of lions sitting in a circle, sharing the kill. Nature in the raw, free of judgment or morality. Simple, unaccommodated nature.

We came almost simultaneously, and the man grabbed his own towel from the foot of the bed to dab at my belly, his touch as gentle as a nurse's. "You're a lot of fun," he whispered in a soft baritone. He had an engagingly crooked smile, his teeth lined up off center. I noticed that one of them, just past the canine, was missing—obviously pulled when he was still a child, the others having shifted to compensate.

"Thanks," I said, laughing. "So are you."

He finished cleaning me up and tossed the towel back toward the foot of the bed. He sidled up beside me, one arm supported on an elbow, and swirled the thin line of hair that bisected my torso. "I'll bet you don't come to these places often, do you?"

"Was I that bad?"

"No. You were that good." Up close, his eyes were green, sparkling. "Most of the guys here are so jaded they can't quite get into it, you know, can't release themselves."

"Well, I don't know about that. Letting go has never been my strong point."

"You learn something new every day." He kissed me—quickly, no more than a peck. Despite the intimacy we'd just shared, it was the first time our lips had touched. "I'm James," he whispered. The name came out more quietly than his other words, as if it was the only thing worth keeping secret.

"David," I replied, automatically reverting to my middle name. At least that way it wasn't technically a lie.

"Glad to meet you, David," he said, rubbing my shoulder briskly. "Are you new in town?"

Our legs had entwined, his toe caressing my calf and evoking a rhythmic tingle. "Not exactly," I said. "But it's my first time here."

"And what brings you here?" I could tell that he was trying to sound cavalier, but a sincerity—almost a vulnerability—resonated through his tone. His loquaciousness shocked me; I expected a silent parting after sex, as abrupt and definite as the obligatory hang-up after you come with a stranger on the phone.

"Curiosity," I said. "I wanted to see how uncomplicated sex can be."

He laughed again. "Oh, it can be as uncomplicated as you like," he said. And suddenly his eyes darkened and he glanced out, beyond our toes, toward the red light in the corner. "Too uncomplicated sometimes."

"So why are *you* here?"

He looked back at me, the rigidity of his expression restored. "Sometimes I get bored," he said. "Dating can be . . . difficult."

Lying there against him, I suddenly realized that I was completely relaxed. It was as if my orgasm had taken away with it every worry, every site of tension in my body. Every muscle felt alive but torpid, finished with its work and now rewarding itself with the luxury of complete exhaustion. "Story of my life these days."

"Boyfriend trouble?"

"You could say that."

I looked across the room, at another couple entangled on a mattress like ours, bodies writhing in the red light.

"So tell me about him."

"My boyfriend? Why do you want to know?"

"Call me a busybody. I like to know what makes a guy like you tick."

"A guy like me? What are you, a shrink?"

"No," he said, "a writer."

"So am I going to see my story splashed across the front page of the *Chronicle* tomorrow morning?"

"Please," he said, "I'm not that famous. Yet." He kissed me again, longer this time, his lips opening and closing against mine. Pulling away at last, he said, "So? Tell me about him."

"There's nothing much to tell. He's . . . unavailable these days."

James stroked my hair, wiped the sweat from my brow. "Literally or just emotionally?"

I closed my eyes and tried to concentrate on his touch, the warmth of his fingers on my skin, the delicate smell drifting from beneath his arm. "Both, I guess."

"How long have you been together?"

"About six months."

"Are you in love?"

"Of course." His hand froze on my forehead, suddenly clammy, as I turned to look him in the eyes. "Why do you ask?"

"I'm sorry," he said. "It's just the writer in me—looking for drama."

"Oh, I can give you plenty of that."

We were silent for a moment. The warmth of his caress returned and I settled back into the darkness.

"So what do you love about him?"

Eyes closed, I felt peaceful, anonymous. I had nothing to hide, no reason not to tell the truth. "I don't know," I told him. "I mean, I never thought of it in terms of reasons. He just does something to me, when I look at him."

"Chemistry."

"I guess."

"Chemistry is sex, David. *We* have chemistry." His hand swooped swiftly along my torso, flicked gently at my limp cock.

I opened my eyes and smiled at him. "Hey, don't knock it."

"I'm not. In this place, chemistry is what you dream of. But out there—" he pointed toward a window, its black shade drawn and taped down—"it's not enough."

"Shouldn't it be?" I asked. "Enough?"

Our faces were only a couple of inches apart, his eyes probing mine. "You don't really mean that, do you?"

I shook my head, entranced. It was one thing to share my body with this stranger, who hadn't even existed half an hour ago, like some character I'd conjured up in a daydream. But now he was asking for another kind of intimacy, something deeper than flesh and fluids.

"I'm sorry," he said. "It's none of my business." He shifted on the mattress, straightened up against the plastic sheeting that separated us from the adjoining bunk.

"No, it's not that." I touched his shoulder, the slight pressure all it took to hold him in place. "I just don't know what to say. Zach—Sam—and I, we don't really have that much in common, I suppose. I mean, if we weren't lovers—"

"You probably wouldn't be friends?"

"I never thought of it that way before."

James settled back down on the mattress and took my hand. Our fingers played, interlocking in a complicated series of combinations, like dancers at a ball, changing partners with each turn. "And what about you?" he asked. "Aside from your relationship. Who *is* David?"

"What do you mean?"

"Well, what are your aspirations? What do you want from life?"

I laughed. "Besides ten million dollars and Antonio Banderas?"

"Yes."

"I don't know."

"Well, what do you do?"

"I'm a copywriter."

"Oh, right up my alley."

"So, what do you write?" I asked.

He sighed. "Well, when I can squeeze in the time—when I'm not cavorting in dens of iniquity—I write fiction. Novels, the occasional short story."

"Wow. Maybe I've read something of yours."

He laughed self-deprecatingly. "Oh no, you haven't."

"So what's your day job?"

"I'm an editor. That way I get to take out my frustration on other people." His voice grew even deeper, a parody of Karloff.

"I have no talent for that," I said. "I'd love to be a *real* writer, but . . ."

"Really?" His eyes probed mine dubiously.

"Well, if I had my druthers, I'd be a musician."

"Do you play?"

"I used to play the cello. I was pretty good."

"What happened?"

"The usual. Too much competition, too few opportunities. I just didn't think it would ever go anywhere."

His hand pressed tighter against mine as our fingers continued to twist around each other. It felt oddly familiar, and suddenly I remembered Adam's hand, riding atop mine at the cello's neck, placing each finger on the strings, creating chords. "Dreams don't have to go anywhere, David. They just *are*." He peered at me, seeking something, perhaps. "I've barely made a dime by writing, but I still call myself a writer. Because that's what I do. There's no other word I can use to describe myself as truthfully. I am a writer. And even if I didn't do it, even if I never put pen to paper again, I'd still be a writer."

"Well, I guess you have a passion."

"Of course," he said. "You have to have a passion." He leaned forward and kissed me again, his lips warm and full.

Drawing his lips away, he tightened his grip around my shoulders. "What's your passion, David? What would you give up everything else for?"

I didn't answer. Staring up at the bunk above our heads, I could think of nothing to say.

We lay in silence for a long moment. James sat up and brought my head to rest against his chest, my ear tickled by the hairs around his nipple as I listened to the soft pounding of his heart. The steady rhythm was insistent, implacable, and even after I'd gone home, pressed my head against a soft pillow, spread my body across the full width of the mattress, I couldn't get it out of my ears.

It was easy to picture him as a child: all I needed to do was look into his eyes. Despite what they'd seen, there was an innocence in their soft gaze—none of the hardness most of us acquire as the years go on. It was as if Zach had been immune to the emotional effects of age: if he had retreated from the world, it was only to return to the comforts of childhood—the simple solitude that only children are allowed. He knew the world, that was certain—he knew it, I think, better than I—but Zach always had a place inside to escape to, somewhere he felt safe, somewhere that was his alone.

I imagined him in the middle of the field he so often talked about—the one behind his grandmother's house, where the tall grass could hide a little boy, where his own footsteps flattening out the blades created the path that would lead him home at the end of play: He breaks off the green tip of a blade, twirls it between baby-fat fingers, slides it through the gap in his teeth, imagines himself a modern-day Huckleberry Finn, scanning the horizon for an invisible Mississippi.

It was that image I always came back to, when I felt the need to explain what had happened to him, how that perfect little child had become the deeply injured man I had fallen in love with. It was the one hurdle I still couldn't get past. I couldn't comprehend the pain he had lived through then, I couldn't imagine why anyone would put a child through it. Beside that image in the field, so clear in my mind in the burst of noonday sunlight, I juxtaposed another, dark and hazy still: The same child, the same fine angelic hair, cowering in a corner, forehead resting on folded arms, knees bent to pull his body into a tight, fierce little ball. He's crying, holding his breath to avoid being heard, dreading each footstep in the hall—worse, the silence when the footsteps stop outside his door.

Zach had been in the hospital for several weeks before he told me about the beatings, his father's alcoholic rages. Even then, he didn't go into much detail. The horror of the stories lay in their very sketchiness. Zach described each incident with the clinical detachment I had come to identify with this new side of him, and I realized now that it must have helped him. The only way he could re-create the beatings—the bruises, the sharp slap of a belt, the terror of his father's angry voice—was to see them as stories about someone else, not the Zach who sat before me, but the little boy he used to be. In a movie, the roles would be played by two actors; Zach seemed to take comfort in seeing the characters as separate, too.

Most of his childhood stories, though, focused on his grandmother, whom he now saw as a savior. That white clapboard house in the middle of nowhere was the safest spot he knew then. Its silence, the gentle whisper of the grass, was his music. Every afternoon he would run out into the field, deep into the tall grass, far enough that nothing else could be heard—not the slamming of the screen door on the porch, not the traffic passing on the road half a mile away, not even his grandmother's frail calls. He would spin around in that spot, his arms outspread to catch the wind. He swayed in the breeze like one of those leaves of grass, slowly lowering himself to sit on the cool ground, making a bed of green upon which to lay his head. And, lying at his full length, arms listlessly at his sides, he would look up at the sky, the sun off to one side at this time of day, busy warming the kitchen window where his grandmother would be preparing dinner. He would play with the shapes of clouds, if there were any, reading in them things he'd never seen, as if they represented magic kingdoms he would one day come to know.

But on most days, warm summer days when clouds were scarce, he would merely study the color of the sky—the near white of noon that faded through pale blue, to azure, drifting toward the mistiness of dusk, the color of his own eyes. He would tell me, each time he narrated this story, that he believed he'd borrowed that color from the sky, that in the hours he spent gazing up into it the sky had imprinted its shade upon him, as the sun burns, then tans the skin.

He barely remembered his mother. She'd run off before Zach had even started school—swept away by a soldier, his father screamed when he'd had a few too many. Just like that—never mind the kids, her husband, never mind responsibility. There was an army base twenty miles away, just outside Topeka, and the new recruits would come out to the country to do their carousing, out where their officers couldn't find them and see what a disgrace they were to the uniform. And Zach's mother, according to his father, had never been able to resist a man in uniform. He'd seen it with his own eyes, he said, the way she flirted with every one of them who came through the door of the club where they used to go on Saturday nights. Out for a night on the town with friends, and her eyes would be scanning the room the whole time, looking for better prospects.

Her behavior had caused its share of arguments. Zach heard them through the wall, voices raised at two in the morning, accusations flying back and forth—*If you treated me better, I wouldn't have to*—*If you acted more like a wife, you'd get treated like one*—and the other sounds— the sharp slap of skin upon skin. And glass shattering, clothes tearing, fists pummeling against a chest. That was when Zach learned to cower, to cover his ears and blot out the sounds, to rock back and forth in his corner, creating a rhythm, a pattern that the sounds couldn't shatter.

His grandmother said it wasn't a soldier at all. Or if it was, it was no wonder. Poor Elizabeth would have done anything to leave that house, should have left it long ago. The sin was in leaving her children. That was the one thing Zach's grandmother couldn't forgive. Taking care of the children was her penance as well as her joy, taking upon herself the sins of her daughter.

Blame wasn't something that entered Zach's mind in those days. It was a concept his therapists introduced. All he knew at the time was the world he'd inherited, and that, to him, was normal.

There were six siblings altogether, but it was only Jenny that he talked about. Two years older, she was the one who'd told him most of the stories about their mother—how pretty she was, how lively. She never looked lively in the pictures Zach had seen, their father's arm swooped around her shoulders, pulling her close so that her own arm got lost between them. To him, she always had the frightened, wiry look of a bluejay, cautiously approaching the birdseed he'd laid out in a paper plate in the backyard, but ready to flee at the first sign of danger.

On my first visit, I had been startled by the breadth of the grounds—all that open space just two blocks from the bus stop. It reminded me of a college campus—isolated, self-sufficient. It must have been beautiful in the spring, when the trees were fuller, greener. Now, with Zach, I zipped up my leather jacket and clenched my fists in the pockets. Zach strode beside me, his long coat hanging open, welcoming the cold.

We walked in silence—Bonnie and her charges, a lopsided pentagon of figures. Zach slowed the pace, lagging behind the others. "You don't have to come every day, Neal. I know you have other things to do—especially on a Saturday."

I stared up at him. His cheeks were pink, jarringly alive. "Zach, I come here because I want to. If you weren't in the hospital, I'd be spending my weekends with you anyway, wouldn't I?"

"Yeah, well—" He pulled a pack of cigarettes from his coat pocket. "You don't have to."

He placed the cigarette between his lips and bent toward me for a light. Bonnie had given me permission to do this for him, but only when we were outside. "Zach, I want to come. I like to see you."

"Well, maybe you shouldn't bother anymore." He held the cigarette between his fingers and blew out a puff of smoke. "You don't have to keep your life on hold on my account."

"My life is not 'on hold.' And besides, you'll be home soon."

He laughed and took another drag. Ahead of us, the others had settled around one of the picnic benches in a corner of the grounds. Bonnie was trying to engage the patients in conversation, pointing toward a bird on the tree above them. Zach sat on top of the other table, far enough away that they wouldn't hear us if we talked quietly.

"All right," he said, looking toward the tree as well. "I just want you to know that whatever you want to do is okay with me."

I didn't answer. There was no point when he was in one of these moods. I just stood before him, hands still buried in my pockets. He had already smoked nearly down to the filter; he now gripped the cigarette tightly between thumb and index finger—like Sam Spade.

I had tried to get him to quit months ago. I didn't have any ashtrays in my apartment; most people took that as a hint. But Zach would just flick the ashes onto dinner plates or into potted plants, so eventually I gave in and bought a cheap plastic ashtray that I brought out only when he came over.

He was silent for a long moment, casting a frozen gaze across the lawn. Only his arm moved every few seconds, drawing the cigarette to his lips. As he sucked in the smoke, the flame burned brightly, the ash growing quickly, quickly destroying itself.

"They've got me in therapy three times a day now," he said, tossing the burnt-out stub into the dead leaves. "My shrink, the group, whatever else they can come up with. These people don't know what they're talking about."

"Maybe it's just complicated, Zach."

"Oh, so you think I'm crazy, too?" He stared defiantly, challenging me to respond. His eyes were dilated; the sunlight must have been killing him. Not waiting for an answer, he dug into his pocket and placed another cigarette between his lips.

Dutifully, I leaned forward and lit it for him. A chill ran through me, as though his sucking on the cigarette were pulling the warmth from me as much as the match. When he drew away at last, I drove my hands deep into the wool-lined pockets of my coat.

"I hate this," he said. "The way they make me feel. I was better off without the damn pills."

"You'd rather be depressed?"

"Some people have natural highs. I have natural lows. Big deal."

"That's not the way I see it. That's not how you felt the night before you came here."

"When was that?"

"Don't you remember? The apartment?"

"No. I came here from my doctor's office."

"Zach, you came here from the hospital. They brought you there from your apartment—in an ambulance."

"*You're* crazy. I should ask them if they have a spare room in here."

"You really don't remember?"

"No. I don't remember." He wouldn't look me in the eye now; he was focusing on the cigarette.

I didn't know whether I should tell him. Maybe it would make things worse. Maybe some memories are better left in the dark. "Look at your wrists, Zach. How did that happen?"

He flipped one wrist casually, the cigarette now pointing downward so that the smoke rose between his fingers. He stared at the scar for a long moment, as if he had never seen it before.

He began to rock slightly, still staring at the scar. I couldn't see his eyes, just a lock of dark hair falling before his face.

"Zach?"

His voice emerged quietly, like a child's. "I'm sorry, Neal. It's all a blank. What did I do?" He was whimpering now, a sound I hadn't heard since that night.

I remained silent. I couldn't describe it to him, not now anyway, and I knew he didn't really want me to. He remembered. I didn't need to say a word. Instead, I moved closer and placed a hand upon his shoulder, let it sink into the rough wool of his coat. Finally, I turned around and sat on the bench, my head now a foot or two below his.

The blood had made a ring around the tub, and when the red water splashed as I lifted him out, it stained the grout between the white floor tiles. I had had to use a toothbrush to get it out.

As soon as we got back inside the ward, Zach nearly ran toward his room, his cheeks still pink from the cold. I followed behind, unzipping my jacket as I went.

He tossed his coat on the bed and sat cross-legged on top of it. His legs began to move, the denim scratching out a dull rhythm. He looked around at the dim carpeted walls, as if measuring the room.

"It must have felt nice to be outside for a change," I said, smiling. I could still feel the cold in my ears, though the rest of me was burning up. Sweat had gathered uncomfortably under my turtleneck.

"Great," he said flatly. "And now it's back to normal."

"But Bonnie said you can probably go for a walk every day now. That'll be a nice change."

He cast me the look that said *Don't treat me like a child.*

I got up from the chair and made a show of looking at my watch. "It's nearly your dinnertime. I'd better get going."

He stared straight ahead, toward the single narrow window at the far end of the room. "Okay."

"I'll see you tomorrow."

He nodded, the movement echoing the steady beating of his legs. I reached out a hand to touch his shoulder, but he shrugged and my hand fell into dead air. I remembered the first day I'd visited—the surreptitious way he had crept into the room, looking around first for witnesses before kissing me lightly on the lips.

I shut the door quietly behind me and walked through the ward. In the day room, several patients were gathered around the table, color-

ing books open before them, crayons spread haphazardly on the tabletop. Bonnie was at the head of the table, supervising their work.
"That's beautiful, Colleen," she said to the old woman at her side:
Bertha had a real name, after all. "I like those colors. Ooh, but watch
out there. You want to stay between the lines, don't you? Stay between the lines or the picture gets all blurred."

Slowly, I approached the nurses' desk. I had learned by now that a
simple nod was enough to signal that I was ready to leave. Dwight,
one of the orderlies, led me to the door and pulled a heavy set of keys
from his pocket.

"Good night," he said, holding the door open for me.

"Thank you. Good night." I passed quickly through and heard the
door clang shut once more. I couldn't wait to get outside again, into
the cold.

I had changed my reading habits. It was no longer novels that kept
me up past midnight—one more chapter leading to another and another. Now I found myself devouring a range of nonfiction titles—
self-help books, psychological studies, monographs on psychotropic
medication. Zach wouldn't give me anything concrete, and he refused
to let me talk to his doctor, so this was all I had—a burgeoning library
of books I only half understood.

The only thing this research had taught me so far was that Zach
was probably right about one thing: the doctors didn't know anything for certain. A hundred years after Freud, psychology was still an
inexact science.

The latest trend, of course, was to reduce everything to genetics. If
you blamed DNA, then you could let everyone off the hook for their
behavior—even parents no longer had to feel guilty, unless they
wanted to beat themselves up for having bothered to reproduce in the
first place and pass on defective genes.

But even chemistry couldn't explain it all. "It's the chicken or the
egg," I told Martin, gesturing with the hefty paperback he had

caught me reading when he unexpectedly dropped by. Martin had never just dropped by before. He must have been worried about me. That plastic smile—that studied nonchalance—was another undeniable clue.

"The chicken or the egg?" He plopped onto the couch and draped one leg over the other.

"Well, it seems that a chemical imbalance can cause all sorts of weird behavior. *But*—" I put the book down, feeling suddenly and uncomfortably like a college professor. "That chemical shake-up can in turn be caused by trauma."

"What do you mean?"

"Well, he wasn't necessarily born with this condition. It could be that all the shit he went through as a kid created chemical reactions in his brain."

Martin leaned back, exasperated. "What good does it do you to know all this, Neal?"

"It helps me understand," I said. "Understand what we're dealing with here."

He sighed. "It sounds to me like he's more fucked up than you thought. There's no magic pill, Neal. It goes much deeper than pills."

Our eyes met—Martin's tired, drained. "I know."

I didn't tell him how much I knew, how much deeper it really went.

After leaving the Navy, Zach told me, he had settled in Seattle. He had no education to speak of, no skills outside what he'd learned on a ship. He taught himself to type and began doing temp jobs here and there, never making much more than his minimum expenses. And then he met Wayne.

Wayne was older, nearly fifty. He was a banker, with a condominium on the twentieth floor of a high-rise—a view of the Space Needle and even, on those rare clear days in Seattle, the ocean.

Zach moved in after a week. He'd been sharing a tiny walk-up apartment with two other people, strangers, and the lack of space was beginning to get on his nerves. He'd been raised on a farm, with the great outdoors as his backyard. He couldn't spend all his days in a ten-by-twelve room.

He didn't love Wayne. He knew that from the beginning. But love wasn't the only reason to move in with someone. Wayne was attentive. He gave Zach whatever he needed. He listened. He told Zach he was beautiful. No one had ever done that before.

"I used him," he told me, admitting it like a dark secret. "He bought me things, and I took them. All I had to do was be nice to him—fuck when he wanted to fuck, pretend that I loved him. He knew the truth. He knew I was just pretending. But that didn't matter to him. Any more than it mattered to me. He loved me for my body. I loved him *because* he loved my body. That was enough."

They were fine alone, in that high-rise haven above the world. It was in public where the flaws showed. Wayne brought him along to the opera, to dinner with his rich friends, showing him off—the beautiful young man with glittering eyes and pecs that strained the Armani shirts Wayne buttoned him into. In public, though, he was no longer affectionate, no longer admiring of Zach's beauty. Instead, he focused on other things—patting Zach's hand when he said something wrong, pointing out his lack of education, his newness to all things cultural. In the silks and gold that Wayne bought him, Zach knew he was little more than a trophy, on display for others to envy. But he accepted all that for the sake of the quiet times—after the parties, the theaters, the dinners—when they were alone, lying naked by the plate-glass windows and looking out at the skyline, their limbs entwined. On those evenings, he felt that the romance he had always longed for had finally entered his life. Lying close to the window, he looked up at the blackening sky, bursting with stars, and he felt as he had on those evenings in Kansas when he'd escaped into the field. With the entire universe open before him, he felt free, invincible. All his needs were met, all his dreams fulfilled.

They drank together, he and Wayne. At those fancy dinner parties, bottle after bottle of wine was handed around, no glass left empty long enough for anyone to notice. By the time they got home, he would have no idea how much he had drunk. After a while, he lost the ability to notice what it did to him. And after a while, it took longer for it to work, more drinks for him to feel that pleasant numbing he called happiness.

But alcohol didn't seem to have the same effect on Wayne. Instead of calming him down, it roused him, made him louder, more jittery. His memory would grow sharper, and as they rode the elevator up to the condo, he would enumerate each of Zach's missteps throughout the evening—each mispronounced word, each missed reference, each misused fork. The evenings became a test, and Zach inevitably would be lucky to pass with a D.

He wasn't violent. After George, the one thing Zach had learned not to tolerate was violence. Wayne's preferred means of punishment was simple withdrawal. He would ignore Zach, stop taking him out, barely talk to him, not even touch him in bed. He liked to hear Zach beg. He liked to refuse.

Zach learned to drink on his own. With nothing to go home for, he would linger at bars until the early hours, staring into a glass. He would seldom be alone for long. There was always someone to sit beside him at the bar, offer to refill his glass. They were usually older— not as old as Wayne, perhaps, but still, older. They wanted to take care of him. They could see that he needed to be taken care of.

He never told Wayne about his escapades. He preferred to slink wordlessly into the house early in the morning—making just enough noise to wake Wayne, cause him to look at the clock—then crawl into bed and fall asleep. Wayne would let it go most of the time. He would cough and roll over, yank the covers off Zach's side of the bed. Only once did he confront him directly.

"I can smell it on you," he said, lying on his side and facing away.

"Smell what?" Zach drew the covers up over his naked chest, to his chin.

"Sex."

Zach patted the blanket around him, creating a cocoon, a wall between him and Wayne's skin. "I'm surprised you can remember what it smells like," he said quietly.

"You son of a bitch." The tone, soft, matter-of-fact, was so disconnected from the words, Zach thought he must have misheard. "I'm working late tomorrow," Wayne went on. "I'll be home around eight. I want you and all of your things out of here by then." He was breathing shallowly, as if something were caught in his throat. "And get it all," he said, "because you won't be coming back."

With no time to find an apartment, and not much inclination to start over, Zach packed a bag and moved into a residential hotel downtown. He stopped calling the temp agency for work. He spent his evenings in the bars, stumbling home late at night or early in the morning, if he'd gotten lucky; during the day he slept or drank at home, a hair of the dog.

The doctors now called that a depressive episode, but most of it was just blackness to Zach, so he didn't know what to call it. The memory existed only in images—cockroaches, real or DT hallucinations, marching along the windowsill; empty bottles piling up around him as if at a recycling center; unknown, unremarkable bodies flailing above him. There weren't enough images, though, not enough to explain the weeks that had vanished from his life.

What he remembered most clearly were the thoughts of suicide— the first he'd had since childhood, when he'd longed to escape his father's anger through death, fantasized about stealing his grandfather's shotgun. One evening, just outside one of the noisiest bars in town, when he hadn't even had that much to drink, he ran into the street—completely aware of the traffic, the cars bearing down upon him. Someone—a complete stranger—pulled him onto the sidewalk, seconds before a truck passed, horn blaring. They tumbled together onto the pavement and Zach screamed, "Let me go! Let me die!" and began to sob uncontrollably. He struggled free of the samaritan, brushing off the arms that reached out as he regained his footing. He ran. He remembered running, running what seemed like halfway across town but could really have been only a few blocks. He ran to a bridge and—quickly, he knew he had to do it quickly, before fear had a chance to stand in his way—he stepped over the railing, where a cold wind rushed up from the water.

"I didn't really want to die," he told me, looking down at his hands as he related the story. "If you really want to die, you don't do it in front of two hundred people in downtown Seattle."

"Or one person in a studio apartment in San Francisco?"

He almost laughed then, catching one corner of his lip with a sharp tooth as he tilted his head to peer up at me. I could see him holding back the laughter, yet savoring the absurdity—as if he were starting to look at himself from the outside, to recognize the bizarreness of his behavior. It was as if he were discovering himself.

He must have stood on the bridge for a long time, contemplating the water, barely visible in the darkness, wondering how far down it was, if it was far enough to kill him instantly or would merely break a few bones, paralyze him, and make his life even more miserable. He was there long enough for the police to arrive, long enough to hear one of them whispering behind him, as if directly into his ear.

"That was the first time they locked me up," he said. "I never told you. I wanted to forget it. If I told you, that would mean it really happened, and I wouldn't be *able* to forget it. So when things started again, when I started to feel trapped again, I had to pretend it wasn't happening. Because I knew what it meant. I knew it meant I'd end up here."

They'd put him on medication that first time, too, when nothing else would work. And after a couple of months he was fine again, and they released him. Rejuvenated, even optimistic, he got a full-time job and an apartment. He was happy—perhaps for the first time, truly happy. He rebuilt his life and finally began to plan for the future.

Everything was fine, as long as he kept taking the medication. But he hated the side effects. He had trouble sleeping, lost his sex drive, and often felt nauseated after taking a pill. It was only memories of the hospital that gave him the strength to continue with it. He felt sometimes that he'd be willing to give up everything else, everything except his freedom.

After a year, he felt he'd beaten it. He'd been happy for so long—or at least not depressed—that he didn't need the pills. He stopped, cold turkey, as an experiment. And he was fine—no depression, not even any unusual tiredness. He was cured.

Six months later, still clean, he decided to move to San Francisco. He needed a change of scenery. Seattle held too many memories.

Every day there were more stories, more details than I needed to hear. I left him with memories like slides projected onto the wall. Lying back in the chair, eyes dully open, he seemed to focus on the nubby ridges of the wall carpeting—the fabric intended to buffer pounding heads. His stories emerged with the monotone of a newscaster—as if they were someone else's stories, event without sensation. He narrated his past as if it were simply that—a closed chapter with nothing spilling off the page, nothing left to influence the present.

None of this was a Zach I knew or even suspected. Sitting on the edge of the bed, watching his profile as he addressed the blank wall, I realized that until now my image of Zach had consisted solely of what he'd given me. In my mind, he had been what he'd wanted to be—beautiful, happy, uncomplicated. I had accepted that, as content as he to believe the fantasy. It came with sparkling eyes and an affectionate caress. It would have been pointless to question that.

With Zach in the hospital, I didn't feel comfortable going back to Boston for Christmas. I told my parents I couldn't get the time off. Someone had to be at the office on the days surrounding Christmas, and I was low man on the totem pole. My mother nearly cried, and of course my father gave me an unsolicited strategy for getting what I wanted—something about marching into my boss's office with a mixture of charm and assertiveness; after all, he was sure I was the most valuable employee in the place, and I deserved special treatment. My father's advice was always filtered semantically—"if it was me, I'd do such and such"—the implication, of course, being that "if it was me" really translated to "the only possible way to handle the situation." I thanked him for the advice, and a few days later, lied, told him I'd done exactly what he'd suggested, but to no avail. The laboratory for my father's hypotheses basically extended a few feet around his armchair, so he didn't exactly have evidence to disprove my assertion. His response, quite simply, was that I must have gone about it all wrong. He grumbled into the phone, "You can't send a boy to do a man's job."

It was conversations like that that helped me feel better about not going home for Christmas.

It had been more than nine months since I'd last seen Natalie, at an outdoor café on a warm spring evening in Boston, my last night in town. We got pretty drunk—she from the sadness of losing me, me from the sheer terror of change. After I'd settled in San Francisco, we spoke on the phone fairly regularly, but our interaction tapered off once Zach entered my life. All connections to the past grew a little shaky then.

Walking up the stairs to Martin's apartment that Christmas afternoon, I suddenly felt an odd jolt in my stomach. Natalie was one of my closest friends in the world, and I was more nervous about seeing her again than I would have been if she were a complete stranger. As long as she remained 3,000 miles away, I could pretend that nothing had really changed between us, but up close I was terrified of discovering that it had, that we were now very different people who would barely recognize each other.

I had hardly finished my knock when the door flew open and Natalie was standing before me, her smile wide enough to fall into. With only a sigh as greeting, she drew me into her embrace. She was warm from the kitchen and smelt vaguely of nutmeg. "I've missed you," she whispered in my ear and hugged me harder.

We drew apart and stood gazing at each other for a moment. Her hair was pulled back and tied in a red bandanna, blonde wisps falling over her cheeks. She hadn't changed at all, and I realized how short nine months is in most people's lives. I couldn't imagine what changes she must have seen in me.

Martin's voice resounded from the kitchen, echoing the deep insistence of Hattie McDaniel. "Land sakes, chile, let 'im in! Time's a-wastin'!"

Natalie and I burst into laughter and shut the door behind us. Arms around each other's waists, we marched into the kitchen.

Martin was bent over the open oven door, basting the turkey. "I sure hope you haven't been impregnating any lesbians with that thing lately," I said.

He stood up and held the baster aloft, waving it at us admonishingly. "You'll never know how many of my little bastards are running around Bernal Heights even as we speak."

"Well, keep it away from me," Natalie said, pulling wine glasses from the cupboard. "My clock may be ticking, but I'm not *that* desperate!" She grabbed a bottle of Chardonnay from the refrigerator and began to uncork it.

In a minute, we all had our drinks, and Martin closed the oven door with a clatter. "Another hour," he announced. "Time for yours truly to put his feet up." He led us into the living room and settled with a deep sigh into an armchair. "I'm not as young as I used to be," he said melodramatically.

"No arguments here," Natalie said. She sat on the ottoman before him, leaning forward, elbows on her knees. "As long as I have you around, I know there's always somebody older than me."

"Little sisters are so charming, aren't they?" Martin said. "You know, in India, they used to drown little girls as soon as they were born."

With the obligatory needling out of the way, we made chitchat for a while, Natalie and I reliving Boston memories and comparing notes on Martin. "I warned you about him," she said. "His sarcasm is merciless. Just be grateful you've been subjected to it for only a few months. I've had it for thirty years. The way I figure it, he owes me about thirty thousand dollars in therapy bills."

Over her shoulder, Martin caught my eye and affected a placating smile.

"Oh, I'm sorry," Natalie said, interpreting the silence. "There I go, sticking my foot in my mouth again."

"Another nasty habit she got from her older brother," Martin added, rubbing her shoulder.

"It's okay," I said. "I'm planning to visit Zach tonight. It can't be much of a Christmas for him."

"No," Natalie agreed, her brow furrowed. She wore the look of concern that had once been so familiar to me—and so dreaded. It was the look that pitied my pain and tried so earnestly to comprehend why I tolerated it. But she never offered a solution: probably knowing I wouldn't accept it, she simply listened to the pain.

"So," I said, abruptly changing the subject, "have you sold any paintings lately?"

"Didn't Martin tell you?" she asked. "I've just been offered my first show."

"You're kidding! That's fabulous."

"Don't get too excited. It's this tiny, unheard-of gallery in the North End. I'll be lucky if three people show up, even luckier if any of them has a bank account."

"Still. Your own show. Now *that's* impressive. Can I touch you?" I reached over and grazed her arm.

"Jesus," she said, "you *have* been hanging around Martin, haven't you?"

"Oh, yes, Natalie," Martin said, "I've been giving him bitch lessons every Thursday night. He's a straight-A student."

We caught up over dinner, passing steaming bowls of mashed potatoes and broccoli across the table. The initial discomfort was over. Once again, it was as if we were in Natalie's apartment on Beacon Hill, having tea by the window on a rainy Sunday afternoon. Our conversation, rapid as a tennis match, was full of in-jokes, anecdotes we could recall for each other with merely a word or two. Natalie and I joked once that our stories were so familiar, we should simply treat them like a Chinese menu: number 12 was the time she got her heel caught in an escalator at Neiman Marcus; number 76 was my disastrous date with Lenny the physicist. We could simply spout numbers at each other all night and still be in hysterics.

When the plates were clean, Martin put an abrupt stop to it. "Attention," he said, clapping his hands, "Memory Lane is now officially

closed, due to flooding. Everyone please adjourn to the Yellow Brick
Road for coffee, dessert, and a return to the present day." He gestured
toward the living room, arms just waiting for semaphores to make
them complete.

Natalie, still laughing at the last anecdote, an awkward contre-
temps with a musician on the Harvard Square subway platform, rose
from the table and began to gather plates.

"No, no, dear," Martin said, rising beside her. "I'm the hostess; you
go sit down and entertain the troops."

She slid bones from one plate to another. "Oh, big brother, fear
not. I'm not doing this because I'm a girl. I just want to behave so
you'll bring out the good sherry later." She stacked the plates and disappeared into the kitchen.

Martin led me back into the living room and we resumed our seats.
He rested his feet on the ottoman.

"So, what have you been doing with yourself lately?" he asked.

I looked up, feeling a pang of guilt, the sudden, irrational sense
that he knew something I should be ashamed of.

"Nothing," I said. "The usual."

"How's Zach?"

Martin always asked, but his tone was merely polite, as devoid of
emotion as a priest reciting the communion blessing, a store clerk
thanking a customer for a purchase.

"Up and down," I told him. "Mostly up these days. I think I can finally see steady progress."

"That's good. It's been what, two months now?"

"Almost." I leaned back into the safety of the sofa cushions.

"Wow. Most *relationships* don't even last that long."

"Well, we've been together since June."

"I know," he said. "I meant—your sticking with him through all of
this, it's—" His voice trailed off and he turned his head toward the
kitchen door.

"What?"

Natalie appeared, pushing the door open with her back. She was
carrying a tray and settled it down on the coffee table between us.
Coffee cups and a white porcelain pot formed a ring around an apple

pie, juice congealed around its domed crust like lava frozen on its way down the slopes of a volcano. "Who wants it à la mode?" she asked. Then, into the silence, "Just kidding. I already checked—can you believe this guy? The fridge is completely devoid of ice cream. I may have to make a run to the store before breakfast."

"Ice cream for breakfast?" Martin said, laughing. "What would our sainted mother say?"

Natalie joined me on the sofa and sat forward, gazing eagerly at Martin. "She'd probably tell you to shut up and slice the damn pie."

"Yes," Martin said. He leaned over the table and picked up the knife.

"You didn't answer my question," I said.

The knife hovered over the pie as Martin searched for the perfect place to begin. I might as well have been attending a bris. "What question?" he asked, finally settling on a spot. The crust sank as he sliced, the dome caving in and crumbling.

"What did you mean about my 'sticking with' Zach?"

He was on the hardest part now, scooping that first slice onto a plate. The crust toppled over, leaving a gooey mass of still intact apple slices. "Nothing, Neal." He set the messy plate aside and carved another slice. "I just know it must be very hard for you. Going to that place all the time, not knowing if he's going to get out." He distributed pie to each of us as Natalie began pouring the coffee.

"*When* he's going to get out," I said. I balanced the plate on my knee, my stomach suddenly churning.

Martin settled his pie and coffee on the small table beside him. "Of course," he said.

"When *is* he going to get out?" Natalie asked, stirring her coffee.

"What is this, an intervention?" I clutched the fork and noticed that my hand was trembling. "Time to confront Neal about how he's throwing his life away?"

"What are you talking about?" Martin asked.

"No, Neal, of course not." Natalie's words overlapped his in perfect counterpoint.

"I know you don't approve. Natalie, Martin's probably told you all the worst about Zach. But there's so much more. This is just a bump we have to get over."

She met my gaze earnestly. "We don't disapprove, Neal. I don't even know Zach. How can I disapprove?"

Martin's cup clattered back onto its saucer. "What do you think I told her, Neal?"

"Well, that's just it," I said. "I don't think you know all his good qualities, the things that I know."

"Then why haven't *you* told me, Neal?" Natalie's fingers, perfectly shaped nails, lingered upon the delicate edges of the china plate, the pie still untouched.

"Haven't I?"

"Neal, I haven't gotten a letter from you since June."

"I've been . . ." I glanced down at my own plate again. An arc of apple, golden brown and dotted with cinnamon, had fallen from between the layers of crust. "Busy."

Gold tinsel garlands hung in gentle arcs on the walls of the ward, dotted here and there with plastic sprigs of holly. The windows in the day room were lined with strings of tiny white Christmas bulbs that shone steadily, lighting up their own reflection in the darkened glass. Visiting hours were nearly over, and a peaceful calm had settled over the ward. Scraps of gift wrap lay here and there on the table, one red-and-green wad idling beside the couch. I imagined that the nurses had had to stand guard as each patient unwrapped a family present, scooping the ribbon away lest it be saved to form a noose, inspecting the tissue paper for sharp objects or electrical cords. But now, everything had been put safely away, and all the guests had gone home, content that they'd done their duty, that they'd brought a sufficient slice of Christmas spirit to this place, this stable in the desert.

Carrying Zach's Christmas present, I walked softly through the common room, afraid to disturb the almost sacred silence. Carla, the teenager, was curled up on a chair near the Ping-Pong table, intently examining a Santa Claus doll little bigger than her palm.

I tapped on Zach's open door, but he remained frozen in the chair, his back to me, looking out at the hospital grounds. As I approached and peered over his shoulder, I saw that the street-lit bench was visible from the window, the bench where I had just sat, building up the courage to come inside. He might have been watching me. I had never thought of that before, never imagined how Zach saw the outside world from this isolated vantage point. It was as if, in my mind, the hospital had no windows at all.

Before I could speak, he turned slowly around in his chair. Only when he was directly facing me did I notice the broad smile on his face. "Hi," he said, looking up.

"How are you doing?"

He scrunched his chin pensively, distorting the smile into almost farcical proportions. "I'm just fine," he said cryptically.

The face he turned to me now wore a quality I had trouble recognizing—the skin faintly pink and smooth, the eyes deep and clear. I hadn't seen that degree of calm for a long time. I wasn't completely sure I'd ever seen it before, not in Zach.

"You look great," I told him, and I wondered if he could read the sincerity in my own face—if, therefore, he knew that I'd been lying all this time.

"Thanks." He gestured for me to sit on the bed. It was neatly made, clear of the magazines and clothing that usually littered the covers. The mattress sprang slightly beneath me, and I reached out an arm to settle it.

As soon as I was comfortable, Zach got up and pushed the chair back. "I have news," he said, looking down at me. "Great news."

A drop of sweat ran cold along my neck, dripped into the collar of my shirt.

"They're releasing me on Monday." His smile burst open, revealing teeth whiter than I remembered.

"That's wonderful," I said. My hand clutched the blanket. I'd never touched it before, never realized the coarse fabric he'd been covering himself with every night. "What did they say?"

He took a deep breath, as though preparing a speech. "Well, it's finally working, I guess. I've been really stable for the past couple of weeks. As long as I keep taking the medication, there's no reason for me to be here anymore."

"Are you sure? I mean, in here you're kind of . . . protected, you know?"

He smiled again. "You mean, can I handle the big, bad world? Yeah, I'm not worried about that."

"What about the doctor?"

"They're not just sending me out to the lions, Neal. He still wants to see me once or twice a week, to make sure everything's okay." He moved closer, laid a hand on my shoulder. "But it *will* be okay." His face—pink, clean, healthy—was inches from my own. "I have you, right?"

I smiled, wondering if mine was as broad, as alive as his. "Of course."

"Merry Christmas!" Zach stood back and tilted his head toward the ceiling. He bounced on his feet, unable to contain his excitement. He looked so tall now, towering. I'd never seen him this happy before. The thought of freedom, of escaping from these walls, had invested him with enviable energy. All I could compare it to was college graduation, the excitement of leaving the safety of the known world for something larger: the potential rewards seem worth the risks, even if you have no idea what either might be.

I clutched the tiny box in my hands, played with the gold ribbon. My gift seemed so much smaller than his.

"Merry Christmas," I said.

part three

half-life

Zach was all packed by the time I arrived, his bulging duffel bag lying atop a freshly made bed. He stood by the window, looking out at the world that would be his in a few minutes. It seemed he was always peering out the window when I arrived, and I imagined that he spent most of his days in just that pose, as if by merely focusing on the outside world he could will himself to rejoin it.

"Ready?"

He bounced on his toes as he turned to face me. "I've been ready for weeks," he said, smiling. Enthusiasm colored his voice; the monotone I had grown used to was completely gone. I wondered suddenly if I would have to get to know him all over again.

"I've checked with Bonnie. She says you're all set."

His eyes widened in anticipation. "Great," he said, drawing out the word like Tony the Tiger. He pulled the duffel bag off the bed and hoisted it onto his shoulder.

He stopped at the nurses' station to say good-bye. Smiling broadly, he hugged Bonnie and shook Dwight's hand, his gestures no more formal than if he were saying good night to his hosts at a dinner party. "Thank you," he said. "For everything."

Dwight came with us and unlocked the door. "Take care of yourself," he said. His ragged teeth lent a sincerity to his smile. I imagined that he didn't experience this situation often enough, saying good-bye and believing it was for the last time.

We walked slowly along the corridor, down the stairs, seeking sunlight. I wasn't used to making this journey with anyone else in tow. I

Chemistry
Published by The Haworth Press, Inc., 2006. All rights reserved.
doi:10.1300/5501_03

had to turn around every few steps, to check that Zach was still behind me.

On the first floor, we turned a corner. Sunlight at last. It poured
through the glass doors at the end of the long hall. We could see the
grounds, the hedge that ran along the side, the trees that towered
over the gate. "It's nice and warm out today," I said. "You'd never
know it was winter."

I stopped, my hand on the cold metal handle of the door. Despite
the warmth outside, the glass held in an icy chill. "Are you okay?" I
asked, searching Zach's face.

His expression had tightened. "Yeah," he said quickly, as if I'd just
woken him from a daydream. "Onward and upward."

I pushed the door out and stood on the walkway, holding the door
open with my back. Zach passed before me, bracing himself for something I couldn't feel. And then he smiled again. "It's so simple," he
said, looking down the walkway to the street. "All you have to do is
walk out the door."

I had borrowed Martin's Toyota for the occasion, an ancient red se-
dan that he hardly ever used. It wasn't worth taking it out, he said,
because finding a parking space in North Beach could take half the
night.

I led Zach across the grounds, to the lot that lay tucked behind a
row of trees. We threw his things into the back and headed home.

"You okay?" I asked, turning at the end of the street.

"I'm fine," he replied, singsong masking his irritation. "Will you
please stop asking me that?"

We drove across town in silence, Zach looking absently out the
window through neighborhood after neighborhood. His expression
suggested less reacquaintance than an odd skepticism—as if he didn't
quite believe that this was all real, that anything actually existed on
the other side of the glass.

By the time we reached the Castro, I sensed that reality had begun
to settle in. He cracked the window to feel the breeze.

Miraculously, I found a spot on Church, just in front of his building. Zach bounded out of the car before I had even turned off the en-

gine. When I came around to the sidewalk, he was already leaning into the back seat to pull out his bag.

"Home sweet home," I said, locking the door.

"Beautiful, isn't it?" he replied, looking up at the building.

Several shingles stripped bare from sun and rain, a broken window on the first floor—*beautiful* wasn't the first word that came to mind. I jumped ahead to unlock the metal grate on the front door, but Zach, fishing in his pocket, pushed past me. "Let me," he said.

His fingers fidgeted through the key chain—finally restored to him today by Bonnie, along with his belt (which seemed tighter on his waist now, his gut bulging slightly over it) and the shoelaces he'd been wearing that first day. I had no idea what all those keys were for, but almost instantly, Zach found the one he needed. He led the way inside, up the creaky staircase. I had been by to check on the apartment just yesterday, to make sure everything was in order for Zach's return. I dusted a little, restocked the bathroom with soap and toilet paper, put fresh milk in the fridge. I wanted to make everything easy for him. Stress was the last thing he needed.

Entering the apartment at last, he didn't bother to look around. Instead, he simply brushed through the hallway and around the corner to the futon, where he immediately began to unpack. He bore the demeanor of a man who had been gone for an overnight business trip, not someone who hadn't seen his home in two months. Adjusting the duffel bag, he hesitated, as if suddenly caught by a thought or an emotion. I saw then that the matter-of-factness was just a facade: the more nonchalant he acted, the more nonchalant he would feel. He didn't want this to be a huge homecoming, with banners and party hats and hugs all around. Any attention paid to his return would actually be attention paid to the reason for being away, and he preferred to forget that.

"Hungry?" I asked. Pushing the curtain open with one hand, I saw that I'd forgotten to clean the windowsill. It was filthy, and the curtain's movement caused a tiny tornado of dust that assaulted my nose.

"A little." Behind me, he rummaged through the bag.

"Let's go out."

He was silent for a moment. I turned and saw him making piles on the futon—underwear on the left, jeans on the right, toiletries on the nightstand. "I just got home, Neal."

"Just for lunch," I said. "Let's go out for lunch. The weather's nice enough, we could sit outside. And it's Monday, so we'll actually be able to get a table."

He spoke to his sweatshirts, whose pile leaned precariously against the jeans. "I'd rather just take it slowly. One step at a time."

"Okay." I resisted the urge to come by his side and help sort the piles, carry things to the dresser. He needed independence, today of all days.

He carefully refolded everything before placing it in the drawers. Before, he would have thrown it all in haphazardly. Given the startling lack of organization in this apartment, I'd always marveled at his ability to find anything. Settling things in place now, he opened and closed the drawers quietly, as if afraid of disturbing the neighbors.

"You know, I *am* hungry," he said at last, when everything was finished. "If you really want, we can go out."

He was putting it on me; my hunger was easier to deal with. "Sure. That'd be great."

"Just let me run to the bathroom."

I felt the click of the bathroom door inside my chest. The last time he'd gone in there—I shook the image out of my head and turned back to the window. There was a new palm tree on the Market Street divide, its fronds tied up in a bouffant, unlike its neighbors, whose leaves flowed free.

My chest relaxed when the door reopened. Zach stood in the hall, lips pursed in expectation. I smiled and joined him at the front door.

The café was more crowded than I'd expected. Fortunately, we arrived in time to grab the last free table in the courtyard. While Zach waited, sunglasses planted firmly on his nose despite the shade of the umbrella, I went inside to place our orders.

I came back with a couple of iced teas. Zach was still in the same position, shoulders arched, staring straight ahead. The noise around him—crackling conversation, peals of laughter—went unnoticed. In his polo shirt and dark glasses, he looked suddenly like a tourist, separated from his surroundings by their very foreignness, the incomprehensibility of an unknown tongue, unfamiliar customs.

"Beautiful day, isn't it?" I asked, setting the glass before him.

"Yes. Did you get any Sweet 'n' Low?" He stirred the tea absently with a straw.

"It's in there," I said. "I know how you like it."

He sipped, testing the tea. And me. "It's fine."

I had always abhorred silence. A lack of words, I thought, connotes a lack of agreement or understanding. Two people just sitting together without words must be angry. At least that had been my parents' preferred method for expressing anger. The silent treatment was their way of punishing each other. They had grown capable of going for a week at a time without speaking, signaling to each other in more subtle ways. They were experts. On TV, the mother would say to her child, "Tell your father to pass the potatoes." But my parents had learned to go beyond that transparent subterfuge; they didn't need a go-between. A simple look and my father would pass the bowl down to her end of the table. Predicting each other's moods and desires may have taken more effort, but it was safer than talking.

I struggled now for small talk, but all I really wanted to say were the most forbidden things: *Are you all right? Isn't it great to be back? I missed you.* I knew Zach didn't want to hear any of that. He probably didn't want to hear anything at all.

"Bertha's been screaming again," he said suddenly. "Two in the morning, I wake up to hear this bellowing. Like she was being stabbed or something."

"That's terrible. I thought she was getting better."

He used his straw to push the ice cubes toward the bottom of the glass. Insolent, they kept floating back up. "Apparently not."

"Has she been there a long time?"

"Forever, I think. Or she will be."

Our salads arrived, and the waiter took away the numbered sign that had signaled him to the table. Methodically, Zach unwrapped his silverware from the napkin. The knife gleamed in the sunlight on the edge of the table.

He picked at the salad, avoiding the olives and tomatoes, idly stabbing the occasional lettuce leaf. "They brought a new boy in last night. He OD'd on something; I don't know what."

"Suicide?"

"Must have been. They don't lock you up for accidents." He sliced a purple onion and wedded it to some lettuce. "Kind of cute, too. Except for the bags under his eyes. Mental illness, Neal, is not pretty."

I smiled. His first joke. He'd be fine, I thought. He just needed time. Being out here, so suddenly and completely in the middle of the real world, had to be overwhelming. He just needed time.

I was finished with my salad before he'd gotten halfway through his. "I'm not very hungry after all," he said, still playing, rearranging the elements on his plate.

I'd stayed with him through dinner a few times at the hospital. He would eat ravenously, moving from one slot on the tray to the next— meat first, then potatoes, then vegetables—until it was empty, almost clean.

"Ready?" I asked.

He sucked the last of his tea through the straw, the scraping sound of emptiness echoing in the bottom of the glass. He nodded, and I led him back onto the street. He kept close to the buildings on the way back, out of the sun. In front of Tower Records, I brushed my hand against his, but he pulled it away rather abruptly and draped it into his jeans pocket, thumb hanging loosely for a moment before sliding into a belt loop. I pulled a few inches away, into the sunlight.

We stopped on the street in front of his building. "I really need to be alone for a while, Neal," he said. "Do you mind?"

We hadn't been together for nearly two months—alone together, without a nurse watching over us or a patient crying in the near distance. The last time I'd held him, truly held him, his body had been cold and wet, limp in a pool of pink water.

"Sure," I said. "Whatever you need."

He smiled gratefully.

"You can come over for dinner, though. We'll get takeout." He giggled. "I'm not sure what I have in the house." He stepped forward and kissed me. I leaned in, draped my arms lightly across his back, and kissed him harder, longer. His lips were firmly closed beneath mine, and dry. The drugs dehydrated him, he said; he was always drinking.

"I could bring stuff," I said, "and cook."

He smiled and patted his stomach. "I don't know. That hospital food, you know; they spoiled me."

"I'll make Jell-O."

"Deal."

I watched him go inside. The door rattled behind him, its peeling paint the color of an overcast sky. I turned and got back into the car.

I hadn't driven in a long time—so long that today, before picking up the car, I'd worried about forgetting how. Even back in Boston, I'd never had my own car, and I'd hardly ever borrowed anyone else's. You didn't need a car in Boston; public transportation was perfectly adequate, except for those rare times when you wanted to leave the city. Cities were what really counted to me; the country was simply what lay in between, what you had to get through before once again finding the security of steel and glass.

I had let Zach drive that day at the amusement park. My relative lack of experience behind the wheel wasn't something I readily admitted to my California friends. This, after all, was the land of the automobile, where cities weren't located in relation to each other (south of Mendocino, west of Sacramento), but by freeway intersections (where 101 meets 380). San Francisco, of course, was the one haven from this insanity, the one city in the West where automobiles weren't absolutely necessary—where they were often, in fact, more burden than advantage.

Fortunately, Martin's car was like the proverbial bicycle: within a block or so, I had begun to feel comfortable behind the wheel. It was the oddness of San Francisco streets I had to get used to—the preponderance of one-way signs, all pointing exactly where I did *not* want to go.

By the time I left Zach at his door, I'd completely forgotten my nervousness. I roared across Market Street, heading north with no clear sense of purpose. I just felt driven toward the water, driven to get away from anything recognizable.

He wanted to be alone. I could understand that. After two months with virtually no privacy, I would want precisely the same thing: a few hours, even days, by myself—no conversation, no obligations, no pressure. He needed to get his bearings again.

I could understand all of that, and I was afraid for him. I'd seen the fear in his face, I knew how overwhelming it all felt to him—the sudden enveloping burden of the once familiar. What if it was too much for him? What if he snapped? What if—right now, as I bounded over the crest of Pacific Heights, as the peaceful blue of the bay came into view in the distance—what if right now, he was cowering in a corner, far from the window, blocking out the great world that terrified him as much as it would a baby screeching for the familiar blankness of the womb?

I understood his fear. I'd seen it before, heard it in his voice that night when he finally began talking about his life, behind the scrim of steam in the bath. I'd felt his fear in the clammy cold of his skin weeks later, when I lifted his body out of that same tub, the pink water splashing onto the floor, my shoes.

I still had his extra set of keys. If need be, I could use them. I could save him.

As the car swooped down the hill, tires bouncing speedily, I pressed gently against the brake. The hill was so steep at this point, I was afraid of losing control, hurtling into the intersection below. A jogger stopped, breathless, at the corner, pumping her legs in place, an armband Walkman plugged into her ears. She glanced matter-of-factly toward me as the Toyota came to a rest six feet before the stop line, and crossed. Her afternoon ritual continued, unimpeded.

Zach didn't want me to save him right now. Maybe he saw this time alone as a test. Having me there would be cheating.

I understood. I understood all that. But still my foot held firm upon the accelerator as I wound my way toward the bridge, still my eyes burned with something close to anger. I didn't want to be angry. made no sense to be angry. I drove to chase the anger away, to leave scattered behind me, dispersed in the rush of wind left in the car's wake.

I killed the afternoon in Marin—walking through forests dense with redwoods, smelling the freshness that never quite makes it across the Golden Gate. In the shade of the trees, so tall the sky seemed no more than a backdrop, the air was cool, a gentle breeze swimming across the paths. I followed the narrower, zigzagging paths less frequented by tourists, where the silence was deeper.

Beyond the barriers that lined the path, the woods were untouched. Trees that had fallen in last winter's storms still lay like beached whales atop the bracken, overgrown now with leaves and vines that twisted through the splintered, rotting wood. One tree, wide as the path on which I stood, had snapped neatly about six feet from the ground, the body now forming a right angle with the trunk, whose jagged edges pointed accusingly up at the sky. The break was clean, sharp, the tree as resigned to its fate as a broken promise, or a dream.

In life, the redwoods were majestic, proudly dwarfing all around them. In death, they lost little of their glamour, but gained in mystery—the mystery of how something so grand could ever grow vulnerable enough to fall.

I stopped at Safeway on the way back, to pick up ingredients for dinner and enough staples to replenish what must have gone bad while Zach was in the hospital. I decided to use my key rather than ring the doorbell and risk waking him. In the hospital, I knew, he'd gotten into the habit of taking afternoon naps.

Bounding through the door with the groceries, I heard a clatter from the kitchen.

"Zach?" Clutching the bags to my chest, I ran down the hall.

"Hi!" He was smiling behind the counter, a butcher knife in one hand. "Wow—groceries!" He laid the knife on the cutting board, beside a carrot, half of which was already chopped into neat slices little thicker than a nickel. He took one of the bags from my arms and settled it on the counter.

His smile grew rather sheepish and he shrugged innocently. "I decided to surprise you," he said, tossing his head toward the stove, where steam wafted from a covered rice pot. "Chicken Kiev. Do you like it?"

I tried to wipe the shock from my face. "Yeah. I didn't know you—"

"I don't," he said, biting his lip and picking up a fat book from beside the flour canister. "But Julia Child does."

I laid the remaining bag on the counter and began to unload.

"So, what did you do all day?" he asked, turning his attention back to the carrots. I imagined the knife in a pile beside his bed, that horrifying nondream he'd described to me not so long ago.

The refrigerator light flickered as I opened the door. The shelves were mostly empty, so I had little trouble storing what I'd brought. "Nothing much," I said, pausing over a jar of pickles. "I went to Muir Woods."

"Oh," he replied longingly, "I've always wanted to go there."

"I'm sorry," I said. "If I'd known, I would have waited until the weekend."

"That's okay," he said, spilling the sliced carrots into a steamer. "We can go some other time."

I'd bought a couple of steaks for dinner. "Shall I freeze these?" I asked, holding up the package for inspection.

"Wow," he said. "You'll spoil me."

I found a freezer bag and transferred the steaks. Drops of blood dotted my hands; I came beside Zach to wash in the sink.

Dinner was ready in a few minutes, the table already set and lit by tall white candles in crystal holders I'd never noticed before.

"To the future," Zach said, toasting with sparkling cider.

I mirrored the gesture and turned to my plate. Zach had never cooked anything more elaborate than spaghetti for me before, and that had been served with bottled sauce. Now, the chicken lay rolled in a golden-brown sheath of bread crumbs, beside a mound of wild rice, the carrots piled together, some spilling into the butter that leaked from the meat.

"This is wonderful," I said between bites.

"Thanks." He cocked an eyebrow. "Hidden talents."

Surely, I thought, they haven't discovered a drug to turn people into master chefs. Zach was matter-of-fact about it all—as if he cooked meals like this every day, as if he were always this happy, always in complete control.

"So what should we do about Christmas?" he asked.

"What do you mean? Christmas was last week."

"I know," he said, stabbing a triad of carrots. "I'm not completely delusional." He laughed. "Nevertheless, we need to celebrate. I have to smother you in riches."

"No, you don't."

He waved the fork comically at me, the carrots slipping along the tines. "Don't tell me what I have to do. How about New Year's? We'll do it then. After all," he added, "it's time for a new beginning."

We left the dishes in the sink and watched TV for a while before bed. Zach was already settled when I came out of the bathroom. Naked, I slipped in beside him and shut off the light. He was on his side, and I pressed myself against him, ready to spoon. He felt warm, his soft, hairless back alive in contrast to the chilly air outside the covers. I traced the ridges of his vertebrae, the hard muscles that gave weight to his flesh—soft, warm flesh I hadn't seen or touched in what seemed like years. He wriggled a bit, straightening his legs until our feet touched. I reached an arm around his chest to pull him closer, and my hand explored the familiar curves of his pecs, the feathery clump of hair that nestled between his nipples.

My cock grew hard, the tip reaching gently toward his shorts. Slowly, he rolled onto his back, and I propped myself up on an elbow to look down at him. "What do you eat for Christmas?" he asked.

I laughed. "Planning the menu already?"

"Why not? I like looking forward to it; it's half the fun."

"Too much anticipation can spoil the experience," I said, smiling. "Fantasy beats reality every time."

"All the more reason to indulge in fantasy," he said. He pursed his lips, thinking. "How about ham?" he asked. "Turkey's so cliché." Of course, I thought, Zach had spent Thanksgiving in the hospital. He probably couldn't bear to see another turkey ever again.

"Whatever you want," I said. I bent down and kissed him. His lips gave easily, instinctively, then flattened out. I lifted my head.

"Ham," he said. "Ham it is." He paused, looking up into the darkness. "I'll make out the rest of the menu tomorrow."

"Are you cooking?"

"Of course. You can wash up."

"Ah. A woman's work is never done."

"Good night," he said. The smile still sat on his lips, just as broad as before, his teeth nearly glowing in the dark. He rolled back onto his side and pulled the comforter up around him, his legs curling into a fetal ball.

I fell back onto the mattress. We never said *good night* to each other, not when we were sleeping in the same bed. *Good night* implied some kind of parting; it was meant to be said on the street, at the door, on the phone. Not when your bodies would lie side by side, lending each other warmth all night long. *Good night* was closure. When we'd first met, lying together in the dark had been a beginning.

He fell asleep within minutes, and I watched him. As my eyes grew accustomed to the dim light, I traced the freckles on his skin, searching for patterns.

I woke early to find Zach curled beside me, his nose burrowed against my armpit. I shifted gently away to get a better look. His features had grown soft in the night, as though some long-forgotten god of sleep had cast peace over him at last. In sleep, in dreams, he returned to innocence, his fetal posture more than just a comfortable pose. My own sleep had been disturbed by a dream I could barely remember. All that remained was a foreboding feeling, as if I'd been chased by something that was gradually catching up to me. I remembered running, but being afraid to look back, afraid to confront my pursuer and acknowledge how close he was.

It was barely 7:00, but I didn't bother trying to get back to sleep. Quietly, I slipped out of bed and into my robe and headed for the kitchen to make a pot of coffee.

I was watching the last drops fall into the glass pot when Zach appeared in the doorway. He was naked, his hair tossed to one side with the sharp angle of a ski slope. He held onto the counter with one hand, the wall with the other, and swung back and forth gently.

"Did you sleep well?" I asked, pouring coffee into a mug.

"Oh, yeah."

I fetched milk from the refrigerator. "Aren't you cold?" I asked.

"No." He had a partial hard-on, his cock long and thick against his thigh. "You abandoned me," he said. His cock fluttered as he swung back and forth, rising gradually.

"Only for coffee," I said, gesturing with the cup. "Want some?" He thrust forward, his cock finally reaching full erection. "Coffee?"

He leered at me. Dutifully, I set the cup back on the counter and moved toward him. Keeping my robe closed, I dropped to my knees and took his cock in my mouth. I felt his back arch as I began, and the swaying continued, his cock thrusting gently in and out of my mouth, teasing toward the back of my throat. I held onto his ass to regulate the rhythm, my fingernails biting into his skin.

He refused to come, pulling away just as the familiar tremor rippled through his legs. I looked up to see him leaning back in the doorway, eyes closed, head tossed toward one shoulder, arms still outstretched. Letting go, I remained on my knees, sweat now beading up on my brow, and watched him. His expression wore a different kind of release now—not the sudden exhaustion of orgasm, but something deeper, lingering. It looked like he was savoring something, as if a delicious relief had settled over him, leaving him willingly, thankfully paralyzed.

A moment later, silently, he let his arms fall to his sides, his head droop forward, and opened his eyes. Smiling slightly, as silent acknowledgment, he left the room. In another moment, I heard the shower running. I took my coffee and settled into the armchair to watch the city come to life.

Zach spent New Year's Eve at my place. The apartment looked like Santa's Village, at least compared to its usually spartan appearance. The Christmas tree commanded the living room. I'd never had my own tree before, and I was proud of it. It was barely five feet tall, and a little thin, but still it smelled like Christmas. I'd draped tinsel on its pale branches and hung various baubles I'd found in the arts and crafts shops on Haight Street. Most of them had to be suspended from the middle of the branches, which would droop precipitously if anything heavy were hung too close to the edge.

Zach clambered into the apartment like Santa Claus, a shopping bag in each hand, brightly wrapped presents protruding toward the handles. "Merry Christmas!" he said, hefting the bags in the air in a shopper's toast.

"Merry Christmas." I kissed him, his lips still cold and slightly chapped from being outside. He placed the bags on the floor and headed for the tree. "It's beautiful," he said. He towered over the branches, embraced by the reflective halo of tiny white lights in the dark window.

As Zach arranged the presents under the tree, I poured egg nog—unspiked, of course. I looked back with trepidation, afraid his presents for me would overwhelm my own for him. Scurrying around the tree, mixing the gifts in a configuration of his own design, he struck me once again as an overgrown child, in love with the holiday, completely sold on every commercial and legendary detail.

"It looks like you cleaned out Macy's," I said, standing before him with both glasses in my hands. He was crouched on the floor, reaching around to place a large box behind the tree. He crawled out backward, laughing.

"Not really," he said. He pulled himself up and took the glass. "I just like to see a lot of presents under the tree."

"Oh. So most of those boxes are empty."

"Yeah." He bit his lip as though to contain a smile that would otherwise explode. We clinked glasses.

"Merry Christmas, Zach."

"Merry Christmas."

I felt a shopping bag crunching beneath my feet as he kissed me. I was startled and stumbled backward, toward the couch. He took the glass from my hand and settled it beside his own on a side table. And he kissed me again, his lips warmer now, opening around mine, his tongue floating in between my teeth, darting up toward the roof of my mouth. I felt myself fading away, swallowed. His passion had come from nowhere. I'd forgotten what Zach's passion was like, how easy it was to lose myself within its folds.

He pulled me into the bedroom and suddenly we were swimming together on the bed, tossing pieces of clothing to the floor indifferently, as thoughtlessly as someone who jumps into the water to save another from drowning abandons his shoes, his pants, to increase the speed, the lightness of his stroke.

The bedroom was dark, the only light coming through the half-closed door from the Christmas tree, still glimmering against the blackness of the window. Zach's hair glowed in that light, falling over his eyes, grazing my forehead as he kissed me. My body bucked beneath him, pressing against him with each provocative touch. I moved instinctively with him, each caress pressing a button whose electrical connections escaped me. No one else had ever had the power to do that, to make my body disengage so completely from my mind. Even with my eyes open, I felt that I was observing someone else, as people describe watching from above as doctors try to resuscitate their temporarily dead bodies. Only my body was the most alive part of me now; it was my mind that was in temporary suspension—the mind that planned, weighed consequences, questioned every gesture, sought motivation and meaning in every caress. The mind that had waited for this moment, prayed and begged for it, was denied its pleasure. Zach's attentions were given solely to my body—the skin that sizzled and writhed beneath his touch, the blood that flowed hot through every limb. Once again, I'd been split in half by his love, and the separation seemed inevitable and right. Every sensation, even the teasing pauses between, was inevitable and right.

As a child, I'd always had trouble sleeping on Christmas Eve. Visions of sugarplums or whatever you want to call it—the anticipation was too great for me to surrender to sleep. When I did eventually succumb—after hours of turning, speculating on what lay in wait for me beneath the tree, imagining I could hear a sleigh landing on the roof, the gentle clatter of reindeer hooves above my head—I slept fitfully and inevitably woke before the sun. I would turn to the clock and wonder if 5:00 were too early to wake everyone else and run down to the tree. Thinking better of it, I would try to sleep. At 6:00, I would wonder again. Finally, by 7:00, I could wait no longer and would immediately toss the bedcovers aside and run into every room, announcing the morning with the annoying inevitability of a rooster. My brother would toss a pillow at me and bury his head under the covers. My mother would smile and pull on her robe while my father yawned loudly and stretched his arms over his head.

By the time I was a teenager, with the fantasy of Santa Claus and various other miracles long dead, my mother would have to wake me on Christmas morning.

Now it was Zach's turn. Barely past dawn, he nudged me awake. "Merry Christmas," he said, leaning in for a kiss.

"Happy New Year." I stretched every limb as Zach bounded out of bed and into the shower.

When I was finally dressed, he was already in the living room, pouring coffee. I sat on the couch and took the proffered cup. Zach kissed me again and settled himself in front of the tree. He became Santa's elf, passing me presents one by one. He was insistent about the order; it was as if he had numbered them.

The first few were trivial, even laughable—a spongy thumb-size Bart Simpson doll, huge eyes bulging in cynical confusion; a bottle of our favorite lubricant. Meanwhile, he gushed over everything I'd gotten him, though my choices were far less creative—the latest Madonna CD; a polo shirt whose blue reminded me of Zach's eyes.

I opened two presents for every one of his. After a while, I began to feel like the youngest child in the family, spoiled rotten with toys of every stripe while the adults politely *ooh* and *ah* over socks and handkerchiefs. According to family legend, I had once interrupted the Christmas revelry by bawling in the middle of a pile of gifts that I was tired of opening presents. "No more, no more!" I'd screamed as my mother handed me box after colorful box.

Twenty-five years later, I wasn't much more comfortable being the center of attention. "Here," Zach said, digging toward the back of the tree and finally pulling out a tiny box adorned with an oversized red bow. He dropped it into my hand, light as the paper it was wrapped in.

It was an inexpensive ring, a faux silver band, the kind you could find at a street fair anywhere in the city. A series of interlocking circles ran all the way around it, no beginning or end. I spilled it into my hand and held it up to the light, palm cupped as though to accept a communion wafer. The ring had been polished, the silver gleaming.

"Do you like it?" Zach asked. He was sitting back on his heels, his hands pressed anxiously between his knees.

I nodded silently, speechless for a moment. I didn't know what to say. I didn't know what the ring meant. "Yes," I said at last. "Yes, it's beautiful."

"Well?" He stared at my hands. I couldn't tell which one.

"You do it," I said.

He rolled his eyes and took the ring from me. He pulled my left hand toward him; I felt it trembling, tried to steady it so he wouldn't notice. Finally, he slipped the ring on my middle finger.

"I can't believe I got the right size," he said. "I figured it would be just a little smaller than mine, so I had her measure me first and subtract one."

I opened my eyes and looked down. It was beautiful, glittering in the light reflected from the tree. I glanced up over my hand and saw Zach, his head still bowed, mesmerized by the ring, the finger that quivered in its grip.

He needed only a few days to readjust to the world. By the end of
the first week, he seemed completely acclimated, at ease with his surroundings. More at ease than before, even. He walked blithely
through life now, as if nothing could touch him, not even the air.

After New Year's, we spent the whole weekend together, then evenings for the week that followed, falling into bed together as though
that was where we belonged. When I touched him in the darkness, his
body twitched beneath my fingers, as though relearning the sensation, the way a muscle in training is built up by being torn down first.
I stroked him gently, tentatively. I think I was afraid he might crack
beneath my pressure, or recoil like a worm tapped gently by a pencil.
In the past few months, I had come to see him as fragile, delicate as
glass. So I restrained the passion bubbling inside me, resisted the urge
to clamp him tightly to my chest, to turn my soft caressing kisses into
hungry bites. Instead, I ran my fingers gently over his skin, cupped
him in my hand, drank him in like a long-cherished wine, to be
savored, not drained.

His reactions were tentative, less directive than before. He didn't
take the initiative, placing my mouth where he wanted it, reaching
down to control the pace of my hand. And when he reciprocated,
when he reached out to me, I had the feeling he was reaching toward
uncharted territory, as though afraid he'd forgotten how. He treated
me with the same distanced tenderness—as if we were both made of
glass, as if one false move could leave us both in shards.

But outside, in the world, Zach had a new confidence, a sense of
ease that permeated everything he did. Suddenly, I felt I was the one
who was unbalanced, each of my neuroses highlighted by contrast to
his mysteriously even keel. Crowds on the street, drivers cutting us off
in the crosswalk, long lines at brunch—nothing bothered him.

He went back to Macy's a week after getting home. Of course, he'd
been replaced on the floor, but they found work for him in the stockroom—cataloging shipments, replenishing the shelves. I suspected
they were just afraid to let him deal directly with customers again. His

supervisor knew where he'd been but none of the details. For all she knew, he might have been locked up for shooting from a watchtower or diddling little boys. She wanted a chance to judge for herself before setting him loose.

Zach didn't seem to mind his new assignment. In fact, I think he was grateful for the relative quiet it afforded him. When we met in the evenings, he wore a carefree smile and seemed imbued with energy. Maybe it was just the drugs, but I could hardly complain. Even if his mood were completely artificial, at least he was happy. Besides, I thought, everyone's mood is hostage to hormones, anyway. His were just directed. Maybe I could learn something.

He talked about the future as if it were a tangible entity, as clear before his eyes as the palm trees lining the street outside his window. It was all planned, to the last detail.

"I bought a study guide for the SATs," he told me over dinner one night. Hungry for soup, I'd persuaded him to go to our favorite Thai restaurant, just a few blocks from his apartment. He'd insisted on a curry dish, which he now scooped onto his plate in dripping spoonfuls. "I've been craving spicy food lately," he said. "Everything else tastes so bland."

For my part, I craved a beer, but decided to abstain on Zach's account. I hated flaunting before him things he couldn't have. Even at the hospital, I'd found myself downplaying the value of being able to come and go as I pleased.

"SATs?" I asked, thinking I must have misheard him. I warmed my hands around the soup bowl and dug in. The tangy blend of coconut milk and lime juice fizzed on my tongue.

"Yeah." He poked at the curry, finally spearing a piece of meat with his fork. "It's time to plan college—at least part-time, anyway. I'm not going to sell shoes all my life."

Zach had always been self-conscious about his education. He would clam up whenever Martin and I fell into one of our inevitable intellectual conversations. He'd seldom ask what I was reading, as though afraid to admit he hadn't read it himself. I had barely noticed the gradual weaning away of my own intellectual interests: At a party, when someone else alluded to Shakespeare or Mahler, I would automatically change the subject, subconsciously trying to protect Zach from embarrassment. I stopped going to concerts, so as not to shut him out. The language of music, I knew, would be completely foreign to him, and he refused to learn because that was tantamount to admitting his ignorance.

All of which made the current decision something of a mystery. I couldn't quite picture Zach taking notes in a lecture hall, writing papers until the wee hours of the morning, arguing at a dinner table about Foucault.

But that was my Ivy League view of education. Zach's approach was more practical. He wasn't going to college to satisfy intellectual curiosity or to please his parents; he simply wanted to better himself, to lay the groundwork for a more prosperous life.

"I know I'd be great at social work," he said. "You know, guiding people through their problems, figuring out where they should go for help, checking that they're getting what they need."

I nodded, scooping a large mushroom out of my soup and setting it aside on my plate.

He had already ordered catalogs from several colleges in the area. Going to school part-time, he could still get his degree in six years. Then, if he needed it, a master's. After that, he said, "the world is my oyster."

I laughed. It was one of my father's favorite expressions, the one he'd used when I got into Brown. *The world is your oyster, Neal,* he said before leaving me that first day for the drive back to Boston. *Look for the pearl.*

"I can't believe it's January already," Zach said. "Time flies when you're locked up." He smiled, holding his water glass up in a mock toast. "It's going to be a great year. The best." He sighed delightedly, elbows on the table, eyes glowing.

Still, my pessimism, my fatalism—or perhaps a darker side of my father's voice—kept reminding me that everything comes with a price. And I kept my eyes open for the tag.

Zach cooked for me several times a week now, mostly things he concocted by blending recipes from a variety of cookbooks. Some meals were virtual masterpieces, others unmitigated disasters. More than once, he would take a single forkful of some failed combination—a little heavy on the turmeric, sour from a few teaspoons too much lemon juice—and immediately march to the phone to order a pizza. He would return to the table, silently retrieve both plates—mine out from under me, fork still heavy with dripping meat—and promptly dump their contents into the disposal.

He never got upset about his failures. The charred pork chops and ruined vegetables were mere facts of life to him, no more frustrating than traffic on the street or a cloud that stubbornly blocked the sun most of the day. Rather than deter him, the mistakes seemed to goad him on. The next night, he would tackle an even more complicated recipe, always trying to surpass the cookbook by adding a special "secret" ingredient or omitting an unneeded flavor. He was re-creating the world, meal by meal.

I thought sometimes that it was a front—his security, the matter-of-fact way he approached the bad as well as the good. But only occasionally did any streaks of light show through his opaque facade. The first came just a few days into the new year; he was still a bit nervous, I thought, still unsteady on his feet. We'd gone to a late movie and got back to my place at around midnight. He was tired, and the film had been disturbing—yet another dysfunctional family drama. As soon as we got inside, he strode past me, into the living room. I closed the door and dropped my keys onto the side table. Zach stood stock-still before the darkened tree, the globes and angels on its branches mere silhouettes before the closed curtains.

"Christmas!" he whispered dismissively, folding his arms before his chest. "God, I used to hate Christmas when I was a kid. Every year, all the other kids would get so excited, come running back to school to brag about all their presents and how big their dinner was, how much candy was in their stockings." I moved closer, drawn by his tone. His eyes seemed blank, lost in the thin branches of the tree. "And I just had to sit there. What was I going to say? How my father drank his way through the evening, how the one toy I got ended up broken by the end of the day when he tore it out of my hands because I was making too much noise? God, I hated it. We always pretended. Every year, we acted like it was going to be different. For one day of the year, we'd be a family. One day."

Tears brimmed at the corners of his eyes. I moved behind him and reached around his waist, clasping my hands against his stomach. I felt his breathing slow, a warm tremor spread along his back. His hands rested gently on mine and, secure that I was unable to see, he wept. One tear—just one—dropped onto my hand.

At first, I shrugged off his sudden emotion: It was late at night, the medication was wearing off. But after a couple of weeks of Zach's almost unabated energy, it was oddly refreshing—nostalgic, almost—an instance of pure feeling, rare in the chemical days.

Most of the time, he was on the run—working, cooking, dragging me out to dinner. After that night, he never expressed interest in movies; I suspected it was because he couldn't bear to sit still for two hours. At the theater that night, I'd noticed his leg shaking, as if he were ready any moment to spring. At least when we watched a video at home, he could thumb through a magazine during the dull parts or go to the kitchen to fix a late-night snack.

The weekends were especially demanding. Zach always expected an adventure—a trip to the wine country (though he couldn't drink), an afternoon at the beach (though it was too cold to take off your clothes, let alone swim in the choppy winter surf). On Saturdays, we would take long walks—a different neighborhood each week. These excursions were oddly reminiscent of my travelogue with Martin when I'd first arrived in San Francisco, but touched now with a strange sense of desperation. Zach sped past things that Martin and I would have lingered over—blazingly colorful paintings in gallery windows, out-of-the-way cafés where writers sat clicking away at laptops, a screechy but somehow endearing street singer wearing a Valkyrie helmet and accompanying herself on the accordion. Zach missed it all—the cacophonous, outrageous variety of urban life, the clash of cultures and types that is San Francisco.

I blamed everything on the drugs. They became my scapegoat. Zach was in a bad mood—it must have been the drugs. Zach was in a *good* mood—it must have been the drugs. His moods now were as unpredictable as the weather I'd grown up with in Boston. At least before, when he was consistently depressed, I knew what to expect from one day to the next. But now, his body a battleground for the drugs and his own natural chemistry, anything was possible.

The first real casualty—the first thing that surrendered in the battle—was sex. Despite a few ravenous moments—that New Year's morning in the kitchen, once or twice since—Zach soon settled down to a sexual routine predicated more on duty than desire. He attacked sex as if it were as essential and flavorless as water. But most nights, a chaste kiss and a stiff-turned back were my signals to drown my desire in silence or control it with a good dose of patience. Unfortunately, doctors don't give out prescriptions for that.

One morning in February, I awoke on my stomach with my head tucked under Zach's arm, which lay outstretched on the mattress, my own hanging softly over his chest. I breathed in his sweat and lay quietly, wondering if he were awake. My erection lay hard against the mattress, and every time I stretched, it sent a shiver through my lower back. I ducked my head down and out and opened my eyes. Zach was still asleep, his breathing soft and even.

As I arched my back, the sheet fell and settled at Zach's knees. His cock lay limp but long against his thigh. I stroked it with one finger, watching it flicker with signs of life. Quietly, I bent down and licked the head. I lifted the shaft with two fingers and placed his cock in my mouth—softly, as if it were an egg I might crack by biting down too hard. I sucked him gently, slowly. As he had once done for me, I wanted him to wake gradually. I wanted him to imagine that this was a dream, to open his eyes still in the dream, and only after a few minutes realize the reality.

His cock grew in my mouth, giving in to the soft strokes of my tongue, the gentle pressure of my cheeks pulsating around it. The head pressed back, scraping the roof of my mouth, and I changed the angle until it began to thrust toward the back of my throat. I was now twisted down, facing his feet, the better to get more of him in me.

I heard a quiet moan behind me, and Zach's body suddenly shifted, his hips swiveling a bit against the mattress. I began to suck harder, to hold him in place.

He squirmed beneath me. "What are you doing?" His voice was hoarse, full of the phlegm of morning. He coughed to clear his throat, and I pushed my head deeper into his crotch, my chin tickled by pubic hairs.

"What are you doing?" He was fully awake now, and suddenly he pulled in his hips and pushed at my shoulder. I fell against the mattress, his cock slipping from my mouth and flopping against his belly as he rolled over. "God," he cried, "it's like rape!"

"Forgive me," I said, struggling to maintain a sarcastic tone while wiping drool from my lip. "I thought you'd enjoy it."

"No," he said, turning just his head toward me. "You thought *you'd* enjoy it. Look, if you're not getting enough from me, you have my permission to go elsewhere. It's only sex, for Christ's sake."

"What is wrong, Zach? Have you told your doctor about this?"

"Please!" He pulled the sheet up around himself, leaving me naked on my side of the bed. "I'm not in the mood when you feel like pouncing, and you assume I should be locked up."

"I didn't say that. I just think there might be a problem."

He rolled over and sat up. His lips compressed into a sneer, he glared at me, blue eyes glowing. "The problem, Neal, is that sex is supposed to be fun, not a goddamn crisis. It's such a big deal for you all the time. You can never just relax, just let your body do the work. No, you're always thinking—every step of the way, you're thinking: 'Why did he do that? Doesn't he love me anymore?' I'm not your goddamn shrink, Neal, and sex isn't therapy."

I felt suddenly cold, exposed, but the sheet was wrapped tightly around Zach. I couldn't reach it. "Where's all this coming from?" I asked.

"You're too needy, Neal. There's nothing less attractive than some-one who begs for it."

I laughed nervously. "So if I didn't ask, I'd get what I want?"

His tongue pressed tentatively against his upper lip. "Maybe."

"I see." I got up on my knees. My side of the bed was against the wall; I had no choice but to crawl over Zach. I lifted one leg over him and climbed out onto the cold wooden floor.

"Where are you going?"

I didn't turn around on my way to the bathroom. "To take a shower," I said.

He didn't call me back. There was no sound behind me of him slouching back down or pounding a pillow in frustration. Just silence, calm.

I ran the water as hot as I could take it and stood in the surrounding steam, the water pounding against my chest, splashing up toward my face. I ducked my head into the flow and spat out the excess that drib-bled into my mouth.

I wondered if the water was loud enough to cover the scream I longed to emit. Resisting, I stood quietly and breathed in the steam. After a few seconds, the rage drifted toward my feet, finally washing down the drain with the sheets of water pouring off my shins. I was needy! The man who sucked every ounce of energy from me was call-ing *me* needy.

I threw my head back and drank the hot water, felt it beating against my throat. Cleansing. Rejuvenating, but somehow numbing all the same.

My skin felt refreshed when I finally turned off the water, every pore open, tingling. Nerves frayed by the heat, I couldn't feel any-thing else. I pulled back the curtain and reached for a towel behind the toilet. Holding it against my chest, I stepped over the rim of the tub and out onto the tiny blue rug—an island in the sea of white tile.

There hadn't been a rug that night, three months ago now. Noth-ing to absorb the bloody water, nothing but the grout.

Golden Gate Park had become part of our Sunday routine, after Saturday nights at my place.

I could barely keep up with Zach now. He moved as quickly through the park as the rollerbladers skating along the drive, his speed compensating for their occasional graceful spins. There was no point in asking him to slow down. Every time I tried, he would just nod matter-of-factly, as though I were commenting on the weather rather than puffing desperately beside him. He kept his head erect, eyes focused on something far in the distance—a destination, perhaps, a destination with an inexorable deadline.

Lagging behind, I attempted my own brand of indifference. When I thought about my feet, they began to ache, each step another thorn. I made music fill my mind instead—Bach's first cello suite, the one I'd been listening to this morning while washing the breakfast dishes. The alternating melodies of the first movement had always fascinated me—like a dialogue that begins quietly and then erupts into an argument. The voices so distinct, it seemed impossible that they were played by a single instrument. Only when I'd watched Adam at a recital did I finally believe there weren't two separate cellists on my recording. I'd never gotten through the first few bars myself; in my less experienced hands, the dialogue became a dull monologue, the monologue of a schizophrenic who can't figure out which voice is his.

"Who died?" Zach had asked, emerging from the bedroom. His hair still wet from the shower, he'd changed into jeans and a black jersey.

"What do you mean?" I rinsed the frying pan and laid it gently atop the dishes in the strainer before shutting off the water.

"This music," he said, shaking his head as though to knock the water from his ears.

The fourth movement, the moody saraband, the cello moaning out its lower notes. "It's Bach," I told him.

"Well, it certainly isn't Nirvana."

I'd always thought *Inferno* would be a more appropriate name.

I was still wiping my hands on the dish towel when Zach grabbed my arm. "Let's go out," he said. "It's a beautiful day. A day to be alive, not listening to a dirge."

He'd never complained about music in the beginning. Neither of us had. Classical at my place, pop at his, it was always just background. I'd even learned to make love to Smashing Pumpkins. But lately he'd become sensitive to sights and sounds he craved or hated—as if his senses were overstimulated.

Out here, though, in the sunshine, he had no trouble maintaining focus. Out here, everything else slipped away. He was untethered, beyond reach.

Somewhere in the South Pacific section of the Arboretum, Zach said, "God, I love it out here. Maybe I should move to New Zealand."

"That would certainly be a change." We passed a large willowlike tree, branches drooping gently over the pavement. I pushed one out of the way, shocked suddenly by the rough texture of the leaves—a different species altogether, merely masquerading as the familiar.

"You don't like change very much, do you?"

"Well, not when it comes out of thin air."

"But it always does, Neal." He stopped in a grove of even more exotic trees, leaves as large as his head. "I just feel totally different these days. It's like I'm a new person."

"Different from before the hospital?"

He smiled. "Very. I hardly know myself." I sensed a slight tremor in his voice, a sudden flickering of his smile, despite how quickly he moved to catch it.

"Must be scary."

"No." He touched one of the leaves, fondled its round edges. "It's like an adventure."

Perhaps, I thought, Zach was the type who could march into the unknown with just a bag lunch and a smile. I would have a compass, a map, food for a week, and a cell phone—just in case.

"I guess I never really knew who I was, anyway," he said. "That was part of the problem. But now I have a chance to find out. I just don't really know how to *not* be depressed." His face was half in shadow, the sun casting a jagged line across his features. "Who am I if I'm not a mess?"

I let the silence sit for a while, the birds flitting above our heads, the wind beating gently through the trees. "I just want to help you, Zach."

"You *think* you want to help me. But maybe you're the one who's in pain."

I sighed loudly, eyes turned toward the roof of the trees. "Will you stop with the psychobabble, please? Every time I reach out to you, you throw it back on me. Like I'm the needy one, like *I'm* the one who's burdening *you*."

"Am I a burden to you now? Is that how you think of me?"

"I didn't mean that."

"Of course not," he spat. "Jesus, when we're at dinner, I see you resisting the urge to cut my meat for me!" He crossed the path and looked into the trees. "Neal, this is way beyond you. I don't know what's happening, and here you are, expecting to 'help' me, expecting me to be 'better.' Well, it's not that easy. I can't just break out of this trap and have all the answers. And you can't give them to me." He paused and, finally, his voice grew softer. "Jesus," he said, "I don't even know the questions."

His back was toward me. I reached up, fingers inches from his shoulder, hovering for a long moment. At last, I pulled my hand down to my side and crossed the path. On this side, the bank sloped down into a lush canyon of green. More unidentifiable plants, species far from home.

When the drugs did work, late at night, when the twitching had subsided and he was able to let go, Zach slept peacefully. Before that, I would lie next to him, on my side, my face half-submerged in the pillow, feeling every wave of the mattress as he tossed, the echo of every sigh deep within my own chest. And finally, when his side of the bed had grown quiet, his breathing light and rhythmic, I would turn onto my back and face the darkness alone. Zach's tension had vanished, defeated by sleep, but mine was just beginning.

Each day was different, bringing its own set of problems, its own deceptions. Zach's nocturnal peace was the only constant. It anchored me, watching him sleep. Looking down at him, I would study every line of his face, though the angle and the darkness pulled most of them away. I memorized the shape of his hairline, the curve sloping gradually from his ear to the top of his forehead, the small hints of recession at the rounded corners of his face. At twenty-seven, he still had a full head of hair, but I could imagine how it would look in another ten years—swooping in on either side, a tufted widow's peak in the middle. In my imagination, the style flattered him, calling even more attention to his eyes, lengthening his chin.

First thing out of the hospital, Zach had insisted on getting his hair cut. He'd wanted it much shorter than usual. Every time the stylist stood back to show his work, Zach would wave a hand vaguely around his head, the polyester smock squeaking, and make him go just a little shorter. He wasn't pleased until the sides were little more than a quarter-inch long; he let the top stay fuller, just enough to fall over his brow and give him something to comb back in the wind. The sideburns were now nearly even with the top curve of his ears, revealing a tiny birthmark beside his right ear, a perfect pear shape I'd never seen before. Peeking at it in the handheld mirror, he'd said over his shoulder, "Now I know how Gorbachev felt when he started losing his hair."

When he first got out of the hospital, he made jokes like that all the time—casual, witty remarks that were, to me, signs that he was able to appreciate life again, to stop taking it so seriously. I listened for more jokes as the weeks passed, always ready for encouraging laughter, even when the humor was questionable.

The jokes fizzled after a while, like a showerhead after the water's been turned off—the sudden rush devolving to an awkward stream, heavy drops falling one by one as they lose the ability to cling to the surface. Zach's wit went gradually dry, replaced by a sternness, a hypersensitivity that saw all things as urgent. He became vigilant about the passage of time, longing to fill every moment, as if there were a finite number left, as if time were already as scarce as laughter had become.

His coffee table was full of college catalogs, which he was poring over every time I walked in. "Look at this," he said, pointing to a course circled in pencil—everything from microbiology to Russian literature to graphic design. It all interested him; he wanted to do it all.

"What happened to social work?" I asked, clearing a space on the futon. I sat on something hard, raised myself to reveal a pencil.

"Oh, that's for later," he said. "I can get a master's in that." He flipped through another catalog. "You know, what I really should major in is psychology. I mean, who better than a nutcase to understand other nutcases, right? They say even Freud was a real wacko."

Something had changed. Before, Zach had always run away from such challenges, but now he seemed to be embracing them. He wanted to learn, and he was asking my advice for how to go about it—tossing terminology and requirements and application forms around the room, struggling to rein it all in, to make some sense of it and find a way to use it to his advantage. He was adrift in an unfamiliar sea, but he was determined to learn how to swim.

He was always busy now, rushing me off the phone when I called, ignoring me in favor of catalogs when I stopped by. He was obsessed with his plans, studying every piece of paper like a scientist or a sleuth, certain that a longed-for, simple answer lay somewhere in the rubble before him, convinced that only diligence and concentration were required to find it. Still, he would call me late at night, usually to ask a perfunctory question about the SATs or class offerings. But it was always questions, never answers or decisions. Every time I asked, he hadn't yet registered for the test, hadn't decided which schools to apply to or who to ask for letters of recommendation. He was a whirlwind of activity, a tornado spinning quickly around itself but never getting anywhere.

He usually called around midnight, when I was reading in bed and just about to turn out the light.

"Do you think I should take a Kaplan course?" he asked one night. Holding the receiver between ear and shoulder, I slipped a bookmark into the latest Tim O'Brien.

"It might not be a bad idea," I said, "especially if you're not used to standardized tests."

"Yeah, that's what I thought."

Something rustled on his end of the line, probably more catalogs spilling off the table. I laid my own book on the nightstand and sat back against the pillows. I waited for Zach to carry the conversation.

"What are you doing?" he asked. His tone mingled curiosity, lascivious suggestion, and suspicion into one lukewarm brew.

"Reading," I said.

"Oh. Anything good?"

"Yes. It's a novel about a Vietnam veteran."

"Is he crazy? You know what they say, they're all crazy."

"No, but he has his problems."

The electronic hum of the phone line played like a backbeat to Zach's silence. I imagined him sitting on the bed with a blanket pulled up to his shoulders, clutching the phone like life-support.

"I'm sorry I've been so busy lately," he whispered.

"That's okay."

"I have a lot of things on my mind. A lot of changes, you know. I have to get my life in order."

"Sure." I turned out the lamp, the glowing numbers on the phone pad now the only source of light in the room.

"Well . . . I'll call you tomorrow."

"Good night, Zach."

"Yeah." The phone clattered into place on the other end of the line, as if he were about to change his mind and pick it up again. I waited until the line died, screaming out its steady groan of disconnection.

Martin had his secrets. From the beginning, I had seen him as a puzzle, a recluse of sorts—Magwitch to my Pip, the Wizard to my Dorothy, proclaiming his powers but always keeping himself hidden behind a curtain. Somewhere along the way, he had detached from the world and now just watched it pass by. In my mind's eye, I always saw him at work, surrounded by flowers, peering through the lacy fronds of a fern, safe from the hubbub on the street outside. If he took an interest in the present at all, it was *my* present, not his. His life lay somewhere in the past, in a time when he was still connected, when the streets were like veins carrying him through the body of the city. The prehistoric days, he called it, before a virus began creeping through the same streets and the corpses started piling up.

When he talked about the past, he sounded like a historian, more observer than participant, though I knew that couldn't be true. He spoke of "*the* life," never "*my* life." I had heard of his ambitions, his path to disillusionment, a few of the personal bumps along the way, but still it was all narrated, never felt. And his eyes were no more revealing than the words.

He told me to let go of my own past, pushed me to embrace the present, the life he attempted to give me. And under that spell—the newness of everything, the tremendous power of self-indulgence—I did forget my past, or at least its details. And I failed to consider that Martin had one, too.

The past has a way of charging back when it's least welcome, like a rash, like an old guilt. It bit me every time I heard the almost human moan of a cello beneath the flightier woodwinds in a symphony, every time a fresh breeze off the bay brought me floating back to Provincetown. For Martin, it came in more tangible form—in flesh, in ashes.

Much later, he excused his reticence by saying he hadn't wanted to bother me—not while I was new to the city, still recovering from Adam, not in the midst of the drama that was Zach.

In the middle of February, he disappeared. There was a message on my machine when I got home from work one day, Martin telling me that he was going out of town, asking if I'd come over in a couple of days and water the plants, take in the mail. No mention of where he was going or why, not even anything I could capture in his voice—the frenzy brought on by a family crisis, the quiet sadness of an expected disaster. He could as easily have been calling to tell me about a sale at Nordstrom or to invite me to lunch. Only the timing was unusual, the fact that he had chosen to call at home when he knew I would be at work. This time he had preferred to tell my machine, to announce his plans to an empty room.

That weekend, I watered his plants. They were, of course, all over the apartment—a pair of Dracaena trees in the living room, a philodendron hanging over the kitchen sink, a prayer plant by the bed, an African violet on the toilet tank.

The apartment felt unusually still without Martin, and I realized I'd never been there before without music—Patsy Cline, Dvořák, Sondheim, whatever happened to fit the mood of the moment. The shelves by the front door were full of CDs, arranged by genre. The bottom shelf, taller than its upstairs neighbors, contained LPs, relics of nearly two decades ago. I ran my hand along the cardboard spines, my finger rattling across them like a little boy's stick against a picket fence in some dreamworld suburbia, even older than the music these packages contained.

Martin had replaced his classical and folk collections with CDs— Mozart, Beethoven, Joni Mitchell, Dylan, all in tiny plastic boxes on the upper shelves, though the music itself was recorded in the '60s or '70s. Most of the remaining LPs were disco titles—Donna Summer, the Village People. I pulled at the ratty cardboard, but the records were packed tightly, as if they'd expanded on the shelf. With more effort, and two hands, I was able to dislodge a short stack. Dust spilled off the shelf in cloudy puffs. So much for Magwitch, I thought; more like Miss Havisham. Laying the records out on the floor, I flipped through them.

Each album cover was garishly designed, full of colors seldom seen together outside of a rainbow. The singers, usually in close-up, all had full, pouty lips, too much hair, too much makeup. Divas, I thought. Disco divas. Even then, they must have known it was camp. Patti LaBelle herself couldn't have taken it seriously.

That was the point, of course, or so Martin had told me. It wasn't serious. Nothing was serious. The only thing anyone was serious about in those days was having fun. Failure to have fun, to appreciate the moment, was the one thing that couldn't be tolerated.

Standing, I pulled one of the albums from its sleeve and set it on the turntable. The record began with a familiar scratchiness, comforting somehow in its imperfection, its evidence of wear. And before any melody was clear, the familiar, relentless beat established itself. That beat that was like a skeleton shared by every member of a species, only the flesh that clung to it differentiating one animal from another.

I just listened. Despite the urge to move, the music's insistence on dancing, tracing its rhythms in three dimensions, I stood still in the middle of the room, listening. I'd heard all the songs before. I'd grown up with them, at high school dances, on the car radio when I was learning to drive. At the time, I'd felt that the music belonged to my generation. I didn't imagine that men a decade older were dancing to it through all hours of the night, united by its rhythms, forging a community between those beats. Back then, disco seemed more of a dividing mark than a unifying one. The other boys in school hated it, preferring to turn their attention to more "serious" bands like Led Zeppelin and Lynyrd Skynyrd. Only the girls liked disco, the girls who had no recourse but to dance with each other in the auditorium, because none of the boys had learned the John Travolta steps. I, too, had to pretend not to like it, had to keep from tapping my feet as I stood against the wall with the other boys, at once a part of the experience and completely separate from it. We all went there to scoff at the idea of dancing, but within some of us, at least, lurked a desire to be called onto the floor by someone, to let the music overtake us for at least a moment.

> I've got all my life to live,
> And I've got all my love to give.

I imagined Martin on a dance floor somewhere, a huge cavern with a disco ball casting flecks of light over the jerking bodies beneath it. High on MDA, they would dance through the night every Saturday, moving from the regular clubs to the after-hours spots, finally, at dawn, ending up at "church," yet another club that opened at six. The drugs were only a means to keep them awake through the night, to keep them dancing. Dancing itself was the real drug—the beat pounding in their legs more life affirming than the hearts that beat in their chests. Dancing was a release, an escape into pure physicality—

like sex. On the dance floor, in bed, at the baths, they left their minds and hearts behind. Simply bodies, they were ironically innocent, as pure and innocent as animals, whose only goal is to eat and fuck.

As Gloria continued to warble in the distance, her creamy voice sometimes at odds with the incessant beat, I walked around the apartment. I suddenly felt like a spy, observing things so much more closely than when Martin was around. His absence made me more curious, and I found myself wanting to piece the objects of the room together to somehow reconstruct him. As if he'd been lost forever, as if these things were all that was left.

He had surprisingly few framed pictures—family, one or two close friends, only the wide lapels and jewelry dating the photos. I imagined his closets full of albums and boxes stuffed with loose photos, memories he'd tucked away, out of sight, and drew out from time to time to relive the moments that in his daily life he struggled so hard to forget. For all I knew, though, the objects themselves were constant reminders. What other explanation for the mismatched candlesticks on the mantel, the antique blue vase so out of place beside the computer? Perhaps they'd been gifts from people who were no longer around—less disturbingly reminiscent than photographs, yet more comforting in their tangibility.

I resisted the urge to open doors, to peer into desk drawers. I'd kept secrets of my own lately—the doubts about Zach, my casual forays into that world Martin kept tucked inside the past, or at least its weak imitation. I hadn't told anyone about that, the strangers who'd caressed me, whispered in my ear, the momentary imitations of intimacy.

Lost in thought and the pounding of the beat, I didn't hear the door until it clicked shut again. "Gloria?!" Martin's voice cried in disbelief. "What's gotten into you?"

I ran to shut off the stereo. "Martin! What are you doing back so soon?"

"I didn't need to stay so long, after all," he said, settling his suitcase gently by the door. In his other hand, he held a white box, taped securely on every side, the seams invisible, inviolate. He carried it into the bedroom.

I replaced the record in its sleeve. When he returned, without the box or his jacket, I was attempting to squeeze it back onto the shelf. "I had no idea you were into disco," he said.

"I'm not," I said, "not really." With a little push, the record shimmied into place. "I just had a sudden craving."

"I try to resist those," he said. He opened a door of the glass-lined cabinet and pulled out a bottle of whiskey. "Care to join me?" he asked.

"Martin, it's four o'clock in the afternoon."

He settled a tumbler on the sideboard and poured. "Well, it's happy hour in New York, and I'm still on East Coast time."

"New York?"

He spun the cap back on the bottle and turned to face me, glass in hand. "Oh, I didn't tell you where I was going, did I?"

"Or why."

He took a sip and walked toward the window. "Why'd you shut the music off?" he asked.

"I thought you'd rather not—"

"No, it's okay." He looked down at the street. The fog was creeping in; Washington Square was growing hazy.

"So—New York."

"Yeah." He tapped his fingers against the glass. "It's cold there. I almost ran into Saks to buy a wool coat."

"You left awfully abruptly."

He took another drink. "And I was still too late," he said, searching the horizon.

"For what?"

"Kevin. He was already dead by the time I got there."

I'd never heard of Kevin before, never known that Martin had any friends in New York. Another piece of the puzzle, filled in though it was already gone.

"Who—"

"Kevin was . . . beautiful. Not just physically. In fact, he wasn't much to look at, really. He just had something, you know? He understood so much. Especially—especially when he started to get sick. It just changed him, the way confronting death often does, if you let it. Suddenly, he—he just turned into this . . . wise man. A sage or something. Kevin's the one who made me believe in God again."

Though his face was turned away, its reflection began to appear dimly in the windowpane, diaphanous as a ghost. He wasn't crying. I couldn't really read his expression at all. "I'm sorry," I said, moving forward.

"I hadn't seen him in nearly a year. This was supposed to be our chance to say good-bye. It wasn't supposed to happen this fast."

"You never mentioned him before."

"No. I don't like talking about it, Neal. I'm sick of talking about it. To tell you the truth, sometimes I wish they were all gone. I wish Kevin was the last friend in my life, just so I wouldn't have to go through this again."

I laid my hand gently on his shoulder, the soft brown wool of his sweater soothing as fur. He inhaled deeply, closing his eyes. "I'm sorry," he said, reaching across his chest to pat my hand. "Stupid thing to say."

"No. Not at all."

We stood together quietly for a long moment, both watching the fog settle on the street outside. Inexorable, the fog overpowered the skyline, casting the world in a single color, thickening until nothing else was visible. I remembered the terrifying moment when I'd first crossed the Golden Gate Bridge in the fog, its vermilion girders and cables disappearing into the mist, leaving the illusion that not twenty feet ahead of me the other half had broken off in some unfelt earthquake, the remnants hanging perilously suspended over the abyss.

"Thanks for coming over," Martin said. "I probably ruined your Saturday." He broke away and carried his empty glass into the kitchen.

"No, I had no plans."

Martin returned and began fluffing the pillows on the sofa. "Where's Zach?"

"I don't know. Home, I guess."

"Don't you guys have plans for tonight?"

"Nothing special. Maybe I'll call him when I get home."

Martin stopped and dropped himself onto the sofa. "Sounds like trouble."

"Not really." I ran my finger across the back of an armchair, bouncing over each tarnished silver tack. "I think things are changing. I'm tired, Martin. I don't know what's left."

"Is he still—"

I sighed. "Yeah. It changes daily. One minute he's fine, then he's depressed, then he's manic. I can't keep up."

"So you're *giving* up." He stared forcefully at me, the old determined expression back once more.

"That's blunt."

He shrugged. "The truth usually is."

"What do you suggest I do, Martin? Ride the roller coaster with him? Keep a tourniquet handy for the next time he tries to off himself?"

Martin smiled, or what passed for a smile today—his lips pressed smugly together. He was as tired as I was. "Do you love him?"

"Is it that simple?" I leaned over the back of the chair. "Martin, I don't know what *love* means anymore."

"I don't know what you want, Neal. It sounds like you want Zach to be predictable, all organized according to your expectations. No problems, no burdens, no surprises. Just everything neat and tidy. Forever."

I pulled back, lifting myself from the chair, holding it firmly between us, like a shield. "No, I just want to know he's okay."

"And what if he's not?"

"I don't know."

"I repeat: Do you love him?"

"What does that have to do with it? Is that the answer to everything?"

His hands lay still on the cushions beside him. "Yes."

"I don't understand, Martin. You're the one who's been telling me to leave him, to take care of myself."

"Right. And you've been telling Zach that you would take care of *him*. Well, I'm sorry, but you can't have it both ways. If you're responsible for him, then you're responsible for him. If you're going to love him, then he shouldn't have to fly through any hoops. If he has to *earn* your love, Neal, then it's not really love at all."

"Martin, don't you know what I'm going through with this?"

He got up suddenly, rolled his eyes. "Oh God, what *you're* going through, while your boyfriend's slashing his wrists and spending the winter in a loonybin! How hard *your* life has been!" He hefted his suitcase from beside the door and went down the hall to the bedroom.

Stunned, I stood quietly for a moment before following him.

I watched him from the bedroom doorway. The suitcase lay spread open atop the comforter. He was tossing dirty clothes from it into the hamper beside the closet. He spoke without looking up. "Neal, you have absolutely no idea what other people go through every goddamn day of their lives. Watching their lovers shrink before their eyes, zone out from medication and dementia. Bathing skin and bones, nursing every little bruise, wiping their asses, cleaning piss off the mattress. No, *your* life is too hard to handle. Well, good. Get rid of him, Neal. Before you're *really* tested."

He marched back and forth to the dresser, putting away clothes he hadn't gotten the chance to wear. "You see this?" He pointed toward the dresser, the white box so placid beside a tiny vase of dried orange flowers. He stroked the top of the box gently, the gesture completely out of sync with the tone of his words. "Do you have any idea what this is?"

I didn't answer, but my eyes were drawn to the box, the way it bulged in the middle, the stringy ends of the gray tape like split hairs.

"This is all that's left, Neal. When they take away everything you own, and everyone you know, and every experience and memory you've ever had, this is what's left. It all fits here, in this pathetic little box." He laid his elbows on the dresser and rested his forehead on one hand. Finally, he wept.

If I had asked, he might have told me about Kevin sooner. If I had asked, the sight of Martin now might not have come as such a surprise, this side of him—vulnerable, frightened, small. Martin was my shaman, the big brother who knew the lay of the land, who set down the footprints for me to follow, who offered his shoulder when I got tired. But that wasn't who I saw before me now. Those weren't the shoulders that now trembled in this chilly, silent room.

I clutched him from behind but couldn't steady the trembling. I pressed myself closely to him and let my arms fall until they embraced him, crossed before his chest, and drew him tightly toward me. I lay my head on his shoulder, one eye closed against his neck, and felt his trembling pass into my own body. He sobbed now, openly, loudly, and each sob shuddered through his back and into my chest, along my spine. I held him until the last sob died and silence came back to embrace us both.

I'd hardly ever gone to bars in Boston—only when friends dragged me along. Adam had hated the very idea of bars—the institutionalization of casual sex, he called it. He preferred to meet his tricks more spontaneously—at museums, on the street, in line for a movie. The few times he'd dared to venture into a bar, he'd spent the entire evening panicking about whether he might be spotted by someone who knew him—or worse, someone who knew his girlfriend.

I'd started going regularly to the bars in San Francisco several weeks ago. I could call it lust: Zach had been in the hospital for over a month by then. I could call it curiosity: after Uri, I wanted to test my newly discovered attractiveness. I'd always felt awkward in such situations before—on display, certain my every flaw was glaringly visible, no matter how dim the lights. My awkwardness, of course, ensured that the flaws showed; it called attention to them by the very effort to hide them. I might as well have worn a sign.

Beer helped. As soon as I made my way inside, I headed straight for the bar. I needed that first relaxing rush of beer. More important, I needed something to do with my hands.

I preferred the Midnight Sun because of the videos. On large screens at either end of the room, the images vibrated. Some people treated the videos as mere background, but it was equally acceptable to focus your attention on the screen, as if you'd come in just for the show.

The bar extended the full length of the room, with men sitting at the stools and spilling out toward the far wall, some gathered at high tables in the center of the room. There were always several groups huddled together around the tables, friends who were just out for a night of relaxation, making fun of the singles who took it all so seriously. At other bars, the ratio was reversed: hardly anyone seemed to know anyone else, and if not for the relentless music, the room would be coated in silence. In those bars, everything was in the eyes, the persistent, predatory scoping.

I feigned interest in the videos, even the music I'd never heard before—which was most of it. Already, barely thirty, I felt completely out of the loop.

I began to wonder if the absurdity of the videos was deliberate—a grand plot conceived by the owners of pick-up bars—because so often, it provided the opening line. "What on earth does a volleyball game have to do with this song?" someone said to me once, gesturing toward the screen with his beer. Several figures were dancing on either side of a net, their taps on the ball choreographed in time to the music.

"Damned if I know," I said. And that was the end of the conversation. He continued to stand beside me, watching the screen in disbelief. It was my turn to say something witty. I stared at the screen, searching out some other bizarre image I could deconstruct, but nothing would come to me. I actually thought about asking "Come here often?" but just as quickly dismissed the notion. A minute later, he disappeared into the crowd, in search of another beer, or a drinking companion who wasn't completely catatonic.

On other occasions, the witty line would come effortlessly, but in the end, I wouldn't have the nerve to whisper it into the ear of whoever stood beside me. What if he didn't get it? There was nothing worse than a joke that fell flat. And my humor tended to be rather intellectual; I had to tread carefully. Jokes about James Joyce probably didn't go over well in a place like this.

But I kept coming back. Practice makes perfect—I'd learned that from the cello. If I came often enough, I thought, eventually I'd feel comfortable here.

The Midnight Sun was a pretty bar—that is, it was full of pretty boys. Young gym bunnies, the occasional preppie. And they all knew how pretty they were; that was the worst part of it. You had the feeling that they'd spent two hours picking out their outfits, greasing their hair down in the perfect approximation of a natural curl. Or, worse, they hadn't spent any time at all on their appearance; they really *were* that beautiful—effortlessly, like a sunset, or Brad Pitt.

Meanwhile, I would tug obsessively at one lock of hair that kept curling over my ear, or readjust the position of the bottle in my hand. I dreaded finishing my beer—the terror of empty hands, the ludicrousness of holding an empty bottle, the danger in ordering another. Every option was equally horrifying. Instead, I drank slowly, short sips just to keep my throat from getting too dry. In case anyone did speak to me, I didn't want to destroy all potential by croaking out a hoarse reply.

The crowd hissed when the Jacksons—Michael and Janet, though by now it was hard to tell them apart—appeared on the screen, dancing around a spaceship in crisp black and white.

A tall blond stood beside me, leaning on the bar. I'd caught his eye a few minutes before and had moved closer. Physical proximity had become my modus operandi; that in itself was an invitation, let him do the hard work. "Now that makes *me* want to scream," he said, still watching the video.

"At least there are no little boys in it," I said.

"Thank God for small favors."

"That's what Michael said."

He laughed. Score one for Neal. "Just when you thought it was safe to turn on the radio," he said, "Michael returns."

"Well, I can't complain. He's one of the few singers these days I can recognize."

"That's because none of them lasts more than a month. 'People come and go so quickly here,'" he added, tossing a slight falsetto into his voice.

His eyes were dark and probing, as if everything he looked at were under equal scrutiny. And he didn't smile at his own joke—which immediately impressed me. "But you've been around for a while," he added.

"What do you mean?"

"I've seen you here. A few times."

My efforts had paid off, I thought; I'd become a regular. And a noticeable one, at that. "Well, every once in a while. Just to get out of the house."

"Uh-huh." He laughed now, nodding in mock agreement. There was a lascivious undertone to his voice that threw a soft shiver along my legs. "I'm Tony."

"Neal," I said, taking his offered hand. Mine was still damp from the beer bottle, and I instantly regretted not wiping it off first.

Tony didn't seem to notice. "So what kind of music do you normally listen to?" he asked.

"When I'm not standing in a crowded bar watching androgynes do the twist on a big screen?" I sighed. "All kinds, really."

He smiled slyly. "You look like the classical type to me."

"Well, I—yeah," I confessed. "If I were trapped on a desert island and had to choose just one."

"I'd choose Madonna," he said.

"Twenty-four hours a day?"

"No, I'd shut her off every once in a while. But when you need a little pick-me-up—and believe me, you would, on a desert island—there's nothing like the Material Girl." His wide lips closed around the beer bottle, and I watched his Adam's apple dance as he swallowed. I imagined myself kissing it, following it with my tongue. Bobbing for apples.

Tony lived, conveniently, in the Castro. I followed him up to 19th Street, keeping a step or two behind to avoid bumping into him when he made an unexpected turn. It was nearly 2:00 now, and men were starting to gather around Collingwood Park, all looking around hungrily. We passed through them silently, Tony not even casting a glance in their direction. With his hands pressed into the pockets of his leather jacket, his elbows swayed slightly as he walked. The jacket ended just below the belt loops of his jeans, accentuating the tight curve of his ass. I resisted an urge to cup one cheek with my hand as I caught up to him.

He turned suddenly into an alley off of Eureka and held the low gate open for me. He skipped down a few stairs to a basement apartment. "It may not get any light," he said, grimacing as he pulled keys out of a tight jeans pocket, "but at least it has its own entrance."

I followed him inside and shut the door. "Pardon the mess," he said, turning on a halogen lamp by the couch.

The light flickered for a moment and Tony readjusted the setting. The lamp revealed a small room, crowded with furniture—a gray couch by the door; a bed in the far corner, the covers thrown back in an approximation of neatness; a mahogany dresser, a white shirt hanging over the edge of an open drawer. A counter in the back separated the living space from a tiny kitchen, the window over the sink revealing what looked like a flower garden.

Tony, still in his leather, was picking newspapers up off the floor and piling them on the coffee table. "Can I get you something?" he asked, finally standing up and brushing off his hands. "A beer?"

"Another one? I don't know if my liver can stand it."

"Sure it can." He smiled and pulled me forward with a cold hand behind my neck. He kissed me quickly, lips soft and wet. He pulled away, but kept his hand on my neck, one finger flickering under my hair. "Besides, you don't want me to think you're a cheap date."

"It's a little late for that, isn't it?"

He had a dimple in only one cheek, the left one—just off-center. "Be right back," he said. He took his hand away, and my neck felt suddenly colder than before he had touched it.

I unzipped my jacket and folded it over an arm of the couch. Beside the newspaper on the coffee table, I spotted a pile of magazines—the *New Yorker* fanned out over the *Advocate*, *Vanity Fair* barely visible at the bottom. Glass clattered in the kitchen as Tony pulled beer bottles out of the fridge. While he scouted through drawers, apparently in search of an opener, I peered around the room.

Everyone has their own technique for analyzing a person through his possessions. Tabloid reporters search garbage cans. Diana had been caught several times peering into medicine cabinets. Martin swore by books; the first thing he did in someone's house was scan the bookcase. (The first time he came to my apartment, he pronounced me worthy by mere virtue of the fact that Proust and Hawthorne adorned the shelves.) Tony didn't have a lot of books, and I still wasn't quite sure where the bathroom was. But I felt that I had everything I needed right here: an eclectic pile of CDs on the floor, tilting as dangerously as the Tower of Pisa; a framed sheet of Marilyn Monroe stamps on a shelf; an assortment of colognes clumped on the dresser; photographs of smiling men (himself included) just inches away from the posed scowl of a middle-aged woman, undeniably his mother.

Martin said that most of his boyfriends had started out as one-night stands. I'd always wondered how you could know that quickly—how you determined by the morning whether you wanted to exchange numbers, whether this was the kind of person you ever wanted to see again for more than sex, let alone spend your life with. I scanned the room, searching for clues. I felt suddenly as if my entire future were compressed into this moment; the key was here somewhere. I had only this moment to figure out who this man was and where he and I would be in ten years.

"Here you go." A bottle of Anchor Steam bubbled beneath my eyes, foam just cresting at the lip.

"Thanks." I looked up, into Tony's eyes. He'd taken his jacket off; it was draped over a stool in front of the kitchen counter. He clicked his bottle against mine, the necks meeting like crossed swords before a duel. We drank, and he touched me again, his hand drifting now from my neck to my back, coming to rest gently at my waist, his thumb gliding naturally into a belt loop. He led me to the couch and set his bottle on the coffee table, pushing the pile of magazines over to the far edge.

We didn't bother with conversation. We'd gone over as much as we needed to in the bar—small talk mostly, but enough to know that we liked each other, that we clicked somehow, at least for tonight. I believed that he'd already told me as much as he could; the rest I would have to gather on my own. As we kissed, my eyes darted open from time to time. My hands swirling through his hair, I found myself wondering how many other fingers had been in the same spot, how many other eyes had noticed the fine brown strands that lay beneath the blond. And how had he felt about them? How easily did Tony say "I love you"? How could he possibly have learned to say it, if that crone staring at us from the bookshelf had been his emotional teacher?

I tried to quiet the questions, to shut off my mind. But the effort simply called attention to the phenomenon. It was like trying not to think of a pink elephant: suddenly, your mind is full of nothing but fuchsia trunks and salmon tusks.

Zach had told me I thought too much about everything—especially sex. "It's not your mind I want to fuck," he said once. "Keep it the hell out of the bedroom."

I shut my eyes now and tried only to feel—Tony's tongue probing my mouth, his hands riding along my chest, reaching for a button, his crotch straining against mine. I opened my mouth wider, spread my legs for leverage in pushing back, reached between us to help him with the buttons. He moaned into my mouth and pulled away, his lips traveling across my cheek, tongue flicking toward my ear before his teeth closed gently over it. My own moans escaped now, and I writhed beneath him on the couch.

It was surprisingly tender sex, considering the speed with which we yanked off each other's clothing. By the time we slipped between the sheets, naked, I had developed an intuition that I could completely trust Tony, that I knew he was incapable of hurting me. I knew him at some other level—beyond the photographs, the cologne bottles, the stacked newspapers. My body knew him, and my body couldn't care less about details.

He fell asleep in my arms, nose twisted against my chest, snoring gently. Lying back on the pillow, I savored his warmth. He'd shut off the lamp when we moved to the bed; I couldn't see the details anymore, only shadows, silhouettes of his life. I couldn't even put into words what I was sensing. I tried not to think of words.

I'd held Zach like this in the beginning, cradling him like an innocent, like a clean slate. I'd craved his mystery then, willingly lived in his darkness. But mystery was fraught with danger, because the truth just won't sit still.

Tony stirred beneath me, as if he'd sensed the train of my thoughts—as if we were traveling together through the night. He held me tighter, squeezing my shoulder to test its strength, its solidity.

And later, slipping out of sleep in the warm darkness, drained of the sexual tension that had brought us together, we held each other and talked. The details of his life, I learned, were different from mine, but there were bridges everywhere. He was from the East Coast, too—upstate New York, where the winters were even harsher than Boston's, the cold air blowing off Lake Erie and freezing everything in its path.

"I had to get out of there as soon as possible," he said. "So every college I applied to was in California. Eighteen years of wool was enough for me."

He majored in comparative literature at Stanford and fell in love with the Bay Area. Conveniently, he was jut coming out of the closet when he graduated, so he made the hour-long trip to San Francisco to settle. Now his literature degree gathered dust somewhere while he worked at a start-up software firm in the Multimedia Gulch south of Market.

We were two would-be humanists lost in cyberland.

We slept fitfully through the night, alternating who held whom, sharing the deadness of the fourth arm. (Only three can ever be comfortable, the fourth inevitably lying beneath someone's back or twisted beside a thigh.) We made love again, talked about Mahler and Proust (Tony had actually read the whole thing—in French—while for me, it just looked good on the shelf). We seemed to pass a lifetime in that double bed, in that single night.

In the morning, Tony offered to make coffee. His hair disheveled, tumbling over his brow, he leaned over me in bed and planted a kiss on my lips, another more gently above each eye. "Stay for breakfast?" he asked.

Smiling down at me, he was beautiful in the daylight, his errant cowlick only making him more human. I lay back against the pillow, not caring what I looked like in the morning, because his eyes told me it didn't matter.

The phone rang, and abruptly Tony turned away. "Stay right there," he said, dropping a finger tenderly onto my nose. As he got up, I found myself slipping toward the edge of the bed. He picked up the phone and mumbled a greeting. "My mother," he mouthed, cupping the receiver. I smiled and drew the covers away, immediately reaching for underwear to sheath my nakedness. I was dressed by the time he got off the phone. I thanked him for the offer of breakfast, but I had to go.

"Wait," he said as I stood by the door. He scribbled something down on a pad by the phone and brought it to me. He was still naked, his cock hanging solidly between his legs. His pubic hair was strawberry blond, growing darker in the line that flowed up to his chest. He handed me the paper. "My number," he said. "Call me."

I smiled and folded the paper into my pocket.

He kissed me—gently, not seductively. He was willing to let me go. He trusted that it wouldn't be forever.

He stood back as I opened the door, afraid of the morning air or the prying eyes of nosy neighbors. "Have a good day," he said.

"Good-bye." I had to pull the door sharply to get it to click into place. The morning was chilly. Grateful for my warm jacket, I zipped it up and dashed through the alley to the street. I ran all the way to the bus stop.

The SAT registration deadline came and went. Zach never got around to sending in his check.

"I have plenty of time," he told me on the phone. "I could even wait until October."

"If you need to take it only once," I said.

In the pause that followed, I could imagine the look on his face—the look he'd had when a movie sold out while we were still in line, the same look he would have if Martians landed in Union Square. "Why would I need to take it twice?"

"Some people do. But don't worry," I assured him. "You'll do fine."

He was quiet for a moment longer, while I struggled for a different topic. These silences had grown more common lately. In the old days, in person, I could always cut into them with a touch or a kiss, but now, on the phone, they lingered, feeding on themselves, threatening eternity.

"They're moving me back out onto the floor next week," he announced. "Mrs. Simpson said it was a waste to have me doing inventory."

"That's great. You'll get your commissions again."

"Yeah. Things are looking up. I can't wait, really. I just know I'll be even better now. I feel so energetic, you know?" He laughed. "I think I could sell sandals to an Eskimo!"

He'd been in the stockroom for weeks now. I'd never said anything to Zach, of course, but I suspected that they were afraid to put him back out on the floor, until they'd had a chance to see for themselves that he wasn't going to do anything foolish—mumble incoherently to himself and jerk off in front of the customers, stab someone with a spiked heel. I couldn't really blame them. Before this, I hadn't known anything about mental illness, either. For all they knew, there was no difference between a nervous breakdown and the psychosis of a serial killer.

"He's turned into Super Salesman," I told Martin a week later. The day before, I'd stopped by Macy's on my lunch hour to watch Zach operate. I'd never seen him move so quickly, with such a sense of purpose. He barely acknowledged me as I stood at one of the display tables, pretending to admire a pair of Rockports. He gave me the same polite smile I saw him flash at the real customers as he knelt before them and slipped a shoehorn behind their heels.

"He's better than he was before. Before he got sick, I mean. It's like ending up in the hospital was the best thing for him—like baptism by fire or something."

"That's great, isn't it?" Martin lifted the plastic cover from his latte and sipped. "The last time we talked, you were complaining about the mood swings."

We were drinking coffee on a bench in Aquatic Park. The bridge sparkled in the distance, not a touch of fog yet darkening the sky.

"Great?" I said. "I don't know."

"Are you telling me you liked him better the old way?"

I smiled and swirled my cappuccino. "I don't know. It just doesn't feel right. I mean, he pops a few pills and suddenly he's headed for Employee of the Year? Maybe I should try it: by next month, I could be sitting in the corner office."

"Are you sure," he said, "you aren't just annoyed because he doesn't need you so much anymore?"

"That's ridiculous," I said. "He didn't need me in the beginning. It's just that now he's . . . I don't know, a Stepford wife or something."

"Is he making you meatloaf?" Martin had returned to his normal self, never letting anything get in the way of the irresistible joke.

"Just the opposite," I said. "We hardly ever see each other anymore. He always has some project. First it was school. Then he wanted to take tennis lessons. Of course, he hasn't actually done any of it; he just talks about it, sits at home, and maps it out."

"How much planning can it take? You call a tennis instructor, you make an appointment."

I sighed. "Well, not for Zach. It's a major research project for him. He has to find the best instructor in town, buy the right outfit . . ."

"Delaying tactics."

The cup tilted to my lips, all I got was a mouthful of steamed milk; the coffee was still inches away. "You're right. It's like he *wants* to want all these things. But he doesn't really . . . want them."

"What *does* he want?"

"Damned if I know." I took a long gulp, finally managing to get some coffee in my mouth.

"And you?"

When I turned, Martin was staring out at the bay, as if the question were so casual—or so profound—he didn't need to look me in the eye. "What do I want?" I repeated. I borrowed one of Zach's pauses. "Damned if I know."

We finished our drinks, both looking absently out at the bay. A sailboat glided past, slicing a determined course toward the bridge. I could barely detect a ruffle in its sails, only sleek, flat whiteness.

"Look," Martin said suddenly, piercing the silence, the magic of the lone, placid sail, "I'm sorry about the other day. I didn't mean to belittle what you're going through. It was just that, after Kevin, I wasn't really seeing clearly."

"No, Martin. Maybe you were seeing more clearly than ever." I clutched the empty cup, craving the warmth that had escaped so quickly.

"You've done a lot for Zach," he said. "I know that. It's unfair of me to accuse you of shirking your responsibility."

I hadn't told him a thing. I'd kept it all inside. The sailboat continued, raced around the bend. I swiveled my head, away from Martin, to follow it. "Even if I have?" I said.

"What?"

I crumpled the cup. It imploded too easily. "Betrayed him. Thought about leaving."

"How could you have betrayed him? This is not your fault."

"You don't understand, Martin. You were absolutely right that day. I don't have what it takes to commit to someone. The going gets tough and—" I rose from the bench, searching for a trash can.

"It's all right," he said, catching my arm as I tossed away the empty cup. "Do you know how many times I've wanted to run away? And I did sometimes. Neal, there are friends I didn't even say good-bye to because I simply couldn't bear the sight of them at the end. It scared me, and I couldn't look. I protected myself instead. Now I could beat myself up for that. Or I can look at all I *have* done, and forgive myself."

I ducked my head, but nothing could stop the tears. "I've been seeing other men," I told him. "Just here and there, to combat the stress. To remind myself that there's more to me than just Zach and his . . . problems."

"Of course there is." Holding both my arms now, Martin forced me to meet his eyes. "That's what bothers me most, Neal. I'm afraid you'll forget how special you are. Zach is not the only man who will ever love you."

I felt as though something had lodged painfully in my chest. "Maybe." I lifted my head, eyes closed against the sunlight. When I looked down again, into Martin's eyes, the tears had stopped. "I did meet one guy. It was just one night, but—I don't know, it felt like something happened. I just can't. Not now, not while Zach is still . . ."

"What? He's fine. You just said, he's taking care of himself."

"But for how long, Martin? I don't trust it."

He gently massaged my shoulder. "Are you getting what you need? That's all I care about, Neal. I want *you* to be okay."

"I'll be fine." I squinted in the sun, tried to smile.

"What about this other guy?"

"I don't know. I can't deal with that right now."

"Well, maybe you should. I mean, you don't have to change everything overnight. And you certainly don't want to make more of this than it is. But it might be good for you. It's nice to be wanted."

We laughed together. "No, Martin. I have to deal with Zach first, figure it all out. I feel so guilty."

"That's useless," he said. "Instead of wallowing in guilt, ask yourself why you did it. What was missing? And what does this guy supply that Zach doesn't?"

"It's not fair to compare them."

"I'm not asking you to. You don't know this—"

"Tony."

"You don't know Tony. But maybe you know what he represents." He squeezed my shoulder and finally released me. "Think about that."

The cello can weep. As a child, I had always found instrumental music too abstract; I needed words to let me know what a piece of music was about. Only the human voice, I thought, could truly convey feeling. And then, in the opening bars of Elgar's *Concerto,* I heard the cello weep.

I had listened to that recording a dozen times a day, until my parents, tired of it, bought me another, which was similarly overplayed. Inside of a month, I had an enviable library of music, most of it focused on the cello. Finally, out of sheer exasperation, they bought me the real thing. I suppose they figured that with the instrument in my hands, I could create endless variety, even if most of it was completely cacophonous.

One Sunday evening, on a whim, I retrieved the cello from the storage room where it had sat since Zach's ill-fated attempt to move in. Pulling it out of the case for the first time in months, I admired the polished wood, shiny, protected by its velvet-lined bed. I laid a score on the music stand—Bach; I'd been listening to the recording for weeks—and began. After a few initial missteps, it miraculously came back to me, like the proverbial bicycle. I'd never been Yo-Yo Ma, but occasionally I could achieve a kind of smoothness in playing, more than just getting the notes in the right order. It had always surprised me, when I'd rehearsed enough that I could stop concentrating on the notes and let them carry me instead. When it was over, I would emerge into the silence like a man waking from a dream: after the fact, the music seemed sketchy, its colors unreal, as if I'd been at once a part of it and a casual observer.

I don't know how long the phone had been ringing before its buzz actually registered in my head, cutting into the music like an unwanted, out-of-tune foreign instrument deep in the orchestra pit—Schönberg's atonal screech attacking Bach's formal structure. I stopped, the bow still pressed against the strings, which vibrated like live creatures against my hesitant fingers. I swooned slightly as I lifted my head, as though the blood had grown unaccustomed to traveling so high. I leaned the cello against a wall, the bow against its belly, climbed onto the bed, and reached for the phone on the nightstand.

Zach cleared his throat before saying anything. "Hi."

"Hi." I pulled the pillow from the other side of the bed to lean against.

"What are you doing?"

"Nothing." Finally settled, I glanced across the room at the abandoned cello. The wood gleamed on one side.

"Oh." He sounded sleepy. I checked the alarm clock beside the phone; it was just after ten.

"What's up?" I tried to predict the next obsession. Modeling? Sailboats? Maybe he planned to join the police force.

"I heard from my friend Roy last night."

"Who's Roy?"

"We dated briefly," he said. "Over a year ago." Suddenly, I remembered the thin guy at Café Flore. That clammy hand, the nervous shuffling from one foot to the other.

"You never mentioned that you'd dated him."

"I never mentioned a lot of things." There was more impatience in his tone than anger. He had other things on his mind.

I tried to sound casual. "Why did he call? Does he want you back?" I wondered suddenly which answer I really wanted.

"He's sick," Zach said, hissing the word like a slap.

Again I stared at the cello—the silent strings, the gentle curve of the neck.

"Are you there?"

"What's wrong with him?" I asked.

"Nothing much yet. He went into the hospital for strep throat and the next thing you know he has pneumonia. So they ran a few tests. You can figure out the rest."

"I'm sorry." It was all I could think to say.

"We could all be sorry soon."

The jealousy jumped in my belly, somersaulted into something else. "What do you mean?"

"Well, I was last tested in Seattle, ages ago, before Roy. And with the incubation period . . ."

"But you were safe with him, right?"

"That's my business."

I tried to fold my legs on the bed, but they felt paralyzed. "No, Zach, I think it's my business, too. *We* weren't safe all the time; I have a right to know."

"If we weren't safe, Neal, that's your responsibility. Roy has nothing to do with it. We're all responsible for our own actions." The Twelve Steps again—a versatile system, both crutch and weapon. *Now* he extols the virtues of taking responsibility, when *I'm* the one reaching out for a lifeline.

"So what are you going to do?"

"I'm going to get tested. What else can I do?"

"Jesus." I looked down toward the foot of the bed. Zach pulling away, come glistening on his cock, dripping between my legs.

"Don't panic," he said.

What I wouldn't give for a bottle of Prozac, I thought, if it would grant me that smugness, that complete lack of affect.

We were both silent now, the telephone suddenly more of a palpable link than an aural one. I thought of the wires coursing through the wall, over the sidewalk, around poles, crisscrossing the city, up and down hills, crackling as pigeons sat there for a rest, vibrating with the voices of thousands and the silence of us.

The Shed at Tanglewood is open on all sides. Sitting in the middle of it, my back solid against the hard wooden seat, I would savor the cool breeze drifting in from the surrounding wilderness. As though in conscious exchange, the music from the stage wafted over me and made its way out, toward the trees. It was clear to me then, as it had never been when I listened to my records at home or practiced in some square-framed studio, that music was indeed a gift. It was man's gift to God, recompense for nature's beauty.

At the time, I focused more intently on another gift. There, on the stage before me, in the midst of the other strings, Adam leaned into his cello. We had met just a few days before, when he'd been assigned as my tutor. I'd saved up for months to take the summer off and spend it here, absorbing the music and the clear blue sky, giving my dream one last chance.

I didn't fall in love right away, though I still remember the tingle that raced up my arm when we first shook hands. At the time, I was more nervous than randy. I recognized Adam's name from the symphony roster; meeting him in the flesh was challenge enough.

At that point, the music was all that mattered. I was there for the music and to learn all that I could.

From my seat in the Shed, I studied his playing—the deftness of his fingers sliding from one note to another, the elegance with which he glided the bow across the strings. He held the cello against himself like a lover, reaching around as he might to guide her through a golf swing, or simply to clutch her to his chest. His eyes were inaccessible—studying the score before him or gazing up at the beams above our heads, but most often shut tight—as though the emotion of the music guided his hands, the conductor's baton rendered impotent, unnecessary.

I listened for the cello, isolating its plaintive song from the noise of the surrounding orchestra—further still, seeking to distinguish Adam's playing from his colleagues'. Each instrument has its own voice, he'd told me during our first lesson. Like the human voice, no two cellos are exactly the same, and the beauty that comes from each is unique, incomparable.

The bow rode gently through the air, caressing the cello as Adam's lean fingers lay softly upon its neck. The sun glowed orange behind him, deep inside the trees that lined the hill. The cello seemed the sunset's voice, growing fainter as the colors faded, sinking into the horizon as though drowning in earth. And I fell in love—with the music, with the breeze, with the handsome man whose eyes lay shut but whose fingers gave voice to the world.

I told this story to Tony, that night in his bed. I had never described it to anyone else before. I think I'd actually forgotten what it felt like—watching Adam, listening as the strings sang to me in a new and powerful language. Tony's arm behind my neck, his fingers

curled softly around my shoulder, I gazed into the night and wondered where this memory was coming from, why the feeling had returned, unbidden and so vivid.

The strangest part was how natural it felt to be telling him all this.
Despite the warmth of his skin, the hairs on his leg that tickled my ankle, the gentle sound of his breath, it was as if I were alone in the
room, in the dark. I had said "I love you" countless times—to Adam,
to Zach—but this seemed immeasurably more intimate.

And he hadn't even asked.

The clinic was only a few blocks from the hospital where I'd visited
Zach. I thought I had escaped this neighborhood, thought I'd never
have to tread these broken sidewalks again. I had always felt like a
stranger among the sick and the suffering, as though there were
something disrespectful about entering their world when my only discomfort was the awkwardness of being around them.

I walked blindly along the street, following Martin with the mind-
less obedience of a baby duck waddling behind its mother. Even
though I'd been here before, just two weeks ago, walking away with a
few cc's less of blood, I'd forgotten the address, the precise path to the
clinic. I'd been in even more of a stupor then. It was just a couple of days
after Zach's phone call, when the whole world seemed engulfed in a
haze as thick as the summer fog that hugged the Marin Headlands,
vowing never to let go. Then as now, I'd trusted Martin to know the
way. He'd been here before—for himself, for his friends. He'd held
their hands, sweaty with fear, as they waited for the results. He'd com-
forted them afterward, scooped his arm around their shoulders as he led
them back outside. He knew exactly where he was going.

I hadn't wanted to call Martin. He'd been through this too many
times before. I'd always had the feeling that part of his attraction to
me lay in my youth and relative inexperience: here, he must have
thought, was someone he wouldn't have to worry about, a friend who

wouldn't die on him like the rest. Yet here I was, dragging him through it all over again.

He was surprisingly stoic. After that first night, when I'd been unable to sleep a wink, tossing, turning, finally pacing the floor in the silent darkness, scouring the refrigerator and the bookshelves futilely for distraction, I'd had no choice but to call him. In the morning, bleary-eyed from terror and lack of sleep, I'd picked up the phone and told him everything. He listened quietly, revealing only an occasional murmur of understanding and sympathy. Perhaps, I thought, it was by now a script for him; all he had to do was fill in the blanks—like a jaded romance novelist, rewriting the same plot but giving the characters different names.

Martin had anchored me throughout the past two weeks—not by openly reassuring me, but just by listening, being there. While I screened my calls, dodging Zach at every turn, Martin was the only person I really spoke to outside of work—certainly the only one I confided in.

Before Zach's diagnosis, it had occurred to me that his mood swings could be AIDS related. I'd heard so many stories about dementia—the virus crossing the blood-brain barrier and wreaking havoc, causing erratic, puzzlingly irrational behavior. I had no idea whether Zach's symptoms were typical, and I didn't have the courage to ask anyone. I attributed my suspicions to paranoia and tried to forget them.

The waiting room was silent, just a few people scattered on the chairs that lined each wall. At the desk, Martin gave my name to the receptionist, who told us to take a seat. I sat on a cold plastic chair near the desk, where the long corridor to the examination rooms began. Directly across from me, a safe-sex poster blared orange against the industrial green of the wall. The words were in Spanish—*SIDA* in darker, larger letters than the rest. How much prettier it sounds in Spanish, I thought, how lacking in irony. I wondered if there were a homonym in Spanish as absurd as its English equivalent. Perhaps, before disease had coopted it, *sida* had meant "hope" or "life" or "joy." Now it was emblazoned on ugly walls in dilapidated buildings where people waited for vials of blood to pronounce them dead or alive.

Everyone in the room wore the same stony expression. Near the door, a middle-aged Latina fumbled with the bag on her lap, clattering its wooden handles rhythmically together like oversized castanets. A younger man and woman sat together, the man perched on the edge of his seat, elbows resting on his knees, fingers knotted together, bouncing in time to the Latina's beat. The couple didn't acknowledge each other, didn't touch. It was the pose, I guessed, you might see in an abortion clinic, the man out of place, uncomfortable with the cloak of responsibility while feeling himself a victim as well.

Only the fortyish man in the corner seemed at all free of apprehension. His gold hoop earring glinted in the fluorescent light as he turned to look up impatiently at the clock. His expression implied that this was all routine for him—his six-month ritual—and he was more concerned with the rest of his day. He had things to do, people to see. He didn't have time for this.

Nobody, I thought, has time for this.

I ignored the rack of flyers at my side—leaflets in rainbow colors. I knew what they said. I'd heard it all before—safe sex, needle exchange, the benefits of early intervention. None of it was new to me. I found it hard to believe that anyone still needed a leaflet to tell them how to stay alive.

But if we did know better, if it was simply a question of knowing what you should and shouldn't do, then why was I here? Why did that man in the corner find himself here every spring, every fall, as if he'd really learned nothing? There had recently been a study published in the paper suggesting that HIV was more likely to be transmitted between lovers than tricks. In the beginning, it had been those furtive, nameless encounters that killed people. But by now we'd learned: we protected ourselves from strangers. But when we loved, we removed the barriers. That's what love was all about—breaking down walls. Now it was love that killed.

They left the waiting room one by one, shuffling down the long corridor, disappearing behind the harsh click of the office door. The gay man was first, emerging from the room after only a couple of minutes, bopping back out with the same casual indifference he'd had going in. Heading back to his life, marking his calendar for another visit in September.

The Latina was next, returning to the outer office with an expression no less inscrutable than before, though her bag was now silent. The glass door seemed to stick, perhaps from the wind that tossed scraps of paper in eddies on the sidewalk. She pushed hard against it and was promptly swallowed by the wind, her flowered dress flattened against her knees as she turned down the walkway to the street.

I hadn't spoken to Zach since that night, the phone call that had started all this. He hadn't said much then about getting tested, and I was afraid to hear. I wanted to know my results before his, to avoid having that much more anxiety added to the pile. Other couples, I knew, went through this ritual together. It was as standard in our community as premarital blood tests were for straight couples. We could have been sharing this moment, vowing to help each other through it, whatever "it" ended up being. But somehow, I couldn't picture Zach beside me right now. This moment, somehow, was too real, too intimate. It didn't belong to us.

When the young couple had vanished down the hall, Martin and I were alone in the room. I wiped my hands on my jeans, rubbing off the sweat. It was my turn.

But this time, the door stayed shut for a long while. The others had been in and out in just a few minutes, but fifteen had already passed and there was no sign of life in the corridor.

I looked at Martin. Our eyes met briefly, and he smiled. Not much of a smile, just sealed lips lifted slightly at the edges—a polite smile, almost formal. We might have been strangers at a bus stop, using empty gestures to combat the frustration of delay.

Perhaps, I thought, empty gestures were all we had left. Once the fear had taken over, all of our conversations focused on the mundane—indifferent *How are you?*s, even less sincere *Fine*s. We rehashed movie plots or exchanged idle gossip. All serious topics were tacitly banned. They threatened to pierce the shell of numbness that had become my sole defense.

I played back the answering machine these days with dread riding my shoulders. If no news was good news, I prayed to find no light flashing on its surface when I entered the apartment. Zach called every other day, usually when I was home. I would stand in the middle of the living room, just a few steps from the receiver, and listen to the disembodied voice coming through the machine. *Where are you?* he asked each time, though no accusatory tone was ever discernible. He didn't seem to mind that I was avoiding him. After the first few calls, he even began to fill me in on his day—as if the machine itself were his new companion, waiting for updates.

And as the numbness settled, his voice unnerved me less and less. The ringing of the phone became a mere fact of life, no more insistent or unexpected than the stream of traffic on the street or the thudding footsteps of my upstairs neighbor, or the ticking of the clocks. The numbness was better than a tranquilizer. I slept soundly each night, enveloped in dreams I couldn't recall in the morning, except for the distinct impression that I had never dreamed so vividly in my life.

When the couple finally reappeared, I had lost track of time. It was the opening of the door that brought me back, a rusty creak that suddenly seemed more appropriate for a horror film.

They came out together, the young woman leaning against her boyfriend, whose half-smile sat with uncomfortable effort on his face. As they passed us, her blonde hair splayed against his black jacket, everything seemed at once sped up and slowed down—like the distortion of time you get from pot, that sense that what clearly happened only five seconds ago might have been last year. When the door finally slammed behind them, a cool draught floated toward me, washing over my ankles.

The receptionist called my name, and Martin and I made our way down the hallway at last. The counselor greeted us at his office door, around a corner at the end of the hall. Tall, thirtyish, handsome, he held out his hand and shook mine confidently. His businesslike smile suggested that there was no crisis here. We were gathered simply to discuss a transaction, to conduct our business and move on.

I sat beside his desk, in an oddly comfortable leather chair that gave luxuriously with my weight. Martin took a wooden seat beside me, his chair turned to put the three of us into an acute triangle.

"How are you doing?" the counselor asked. His name, I suddenly remembered, was Bob. I remembered because at the time it had struck me as an odd name for a gay man—casual, blunt, completely different in tone from Robert or even Rob. Bobs were straight, I thought. Bobs were men who watched football in Barcaloungers, who mowed the lawn on Saturday morning and left their underwear on the floor for their wives to pick up.

"Okay," I said. "At least I'm sleeping these days."

Bob smiled. "Good." He pulled a folder from the standing file on his desk. A simple manila folder with an arbitrary number on the flap, no name. They didn't use names here. I could have lied about my name; Bob wouldn't have cared. A name was only an arbitrary means of identification, no more or less definitive than a number.

"Now, would you like to see the results of your test?"

I paused, glanced at Martin for a moment. "Yes," I said.

"First, I want to remind you what we talked about when you came in before. The test will reveal only whether you've been exposed to HIV; having the virus doesn't mean you're sick. There are precautions you can take, and if that's the case, I recommend that you go to your doctor and talk about treatment. The earlier you start, the better your chances of fighting the virus."

I nodded. Another familiar part of the story: the authorities were always telling people to get tested, even if they weren't worried about anything in particular. Like that man in the waiting room. But who wants to take the chance? I'd always thought. Why choose to find out you have a death sentence? No matter what you might be able to do—which was highly questionable, I thought, given the virus's ability to mutate and fool every drug they'd ever tried against it—you'd still have to live with that knowledge. There was this thing in your system that wasn't going to go away. Not until it had ruined every cell of your body. When your heart stops and your brain shuts off and your lungs implode, the virus is still alive, still bursting through cells for as long as it takes the system to shut down.

"Second," Bob went on, "these results represent your status three to six months ago. So even if the results are negative, that doesn't mean you're home free. You'll need another test six months from now to be sure."

Unless I keep having sex, I thought. Then I'll never be sure. Maybe I'll just stop having sex.

"In any event," Bob said, "it's essential, for your sake and your partners', that you practice safer sex every time. You have our brochures, right?"

"Yes." I was watching Bob's hand, the hair on the knuckles dancing as he tapped his fingers against the folder to emphasize his points.

"Okay. Shall we?"

I looked into his eyes at last. Green eyes. Green, I thought, is the color of life. "Yes," I said. "I'm ready."

"Do you have the form I gave you last time, to verify?"

I fumbled into my shirt pocket and pulled out a small slip of paper. It had been torn from a perforated sheet, both sides bearing the same six-digit number. It was a safety measure—more for the patient's sanity than any other reason. If you didn't trust the results in the file, you could double-check the numbers. I clutched the slip in my right hand, my wrist resting on the cold wooden desktop.

With my free hand, I reached blindly toward Martin's chair until my fingers were suddenly caught in his, his grip tightening around them so that I could feel the tension in each knuckle. When he lightened his hold on me, the throbbing of blood in my fingers made them seem even more alive, resting gently against his palm.

Bob opened the folder and pulled out a large sheet of paper, the mate to the slip in my hand.

I stared at my own paper, just to keep my eyes away from his, perhaps to hold off the inevitable moment. What if, I thought, and suddenly I pictured a series of misshapen spots popping out on my hand, purple lesions encrusting the twisted fingers that so tightly clutched the paper, sweat nearly smudging the all-important numbers.

Bob took the slip from me, compared the numbers, and nodded. And then he flipped the sheet around to face me and laid it on the desktop.

I remember the scene as if I had witnessed it from above—the paper, the desk, my hands, my shoulders, the top of my head, neck bent impassively. I had separated somehow, lifted from the experience. It was someone else's life I observed, someone whose problems were far removed from mine.

The wrist that had held the slip of paper began to tremble, and I felt myself tumble back, back into my body. I watched my hand, fingers dancing nervously, formlessly, in the air. Something—just air, I thought, it was that empty—rose in my chest and spread out toward my shoulders as I dropped my head and allowed my glance to stray toward the paper, toward Bob's finger, which pointed at a block near the middle of the page, a long word in all capital letters. NEGATIVE.

The bubble burst in my chest and immediately my eyes filled. The paper grew hazy, as though someone had spilled water on the fresh ink, making it run across the page. The response had been building; it would have come no matter what the result. Dead or alive, I would still be crying.

And instantly, embarrassed by the tears, I started to laugh. Laughing at myself for crying. Laughing at the tension that had just broken inside me. For that instant, that slow-motion moment that lasted an hour, it seemed that every emotion I had ever felt existed at once, side by side, on top of one another, within one another. That was why it seemed to last so long: no single moment could contain so much feeling.

I pulled the paper off the table and passed it to Martin. He nodded, barely glancing. It was as if he didn't need to look, as if the answer were completely inconsequential. Either way, his hand would still be gripping mine. Either way, nothing in this moment would be any different.

"Thank you," I said when the fear of sobbing had passed. I wasn't even sure who I was speaking to—Bob, God, my own blood.

"I was afraid you might leave without looking," Bob said. He was smiling now. My eyes had cleared enough to see that, the shine of his teeth between thin lips. "I peeked before you came in. I wasn't going to let you go without finding out."

I sat back and took a deep breath, guided by the squeeze of Martin's hand.

"Of course you should get tested again in a few months to be absolutely sure," Bob went on, "but from what you've told me, I think it's pretty safe to assume that this result is accurate. It's been six months since the incident you described, and it did happen just once, right? You were safe the other times?"

I nodded. "Yes. Just the once." Again I saw Zach pulling away, his face all nonchalance, nearly disinterest.

"Then relax." He paused. "But please, always use a condom from now on, okay?"

I nodded. Finally, my lips curled into a smile, as though simply to mirror his.

"And if you have any questions," he said, pushing his chair away from the desk, "call us." He stopped the chair, the wheels squeaking as he got up. "Do you want to be alone in here for a minute? I'll—"

"No," I said. I turned to Martin, caught his eye at last. "No, I think we should go. I just want to . . . walk."

We said good-bye to Bob, and I walked beside Martin along the corridor. It seemed shorter now, only a couple of seconds until it opened into the waiting room. More people waiting, some with backs stiff against the chairs, eyes lost in some middle distance, others hunched over their knees, gazing at the floor. Enclosed in their corners of the room, careful to look at anything except one another.

I walked steadily past them all and through the door to the street, where a breeze suddenly swirled around me. And outside, enveloped by the blazing sunlight, my legs grew weak, as though the bones had crumbled and there was no structure left to hold me up. I slumped against a pillar and allowed my back to slide down the granite until I was sitting, knees bent, bowed out. A shiver rumbled through me, as if something had just passed out, spinning away, beyond my shoulders, up and gone.

Martin stood before me. I looked down at his shoes, sensible loafers. "Are you all right?"

I nodded sharply. "Yeah." I couldn't explain. For the moment, I was through with explanations. There didn't seem any need for them anymore.

I was alive.

We walked together silently, Martin just a step or two behind, allowing me to lead. I had no idea where we were going; I just needed to walk. There was something reassuringly real about walking, feet pressing solidly against rough concrete. Buses and streetcars were sterile by comparison, cocoons to protect you from the outside world, spilling you off at your destination as if all the places in between didn't count.

If not for the changing light, I would have lost track of time as well as space. The sun, low on the horizon when we started from the clinic, was shining almost directly overhead when we reached downtown. Nearly noon on a spring Saturday, and Union Square was full of weekend shoppers. I stopped on Geary, just across from the park, and let them wash by me in both directions, a raft anchored in a turbulent sea.

Martin stopped beside me, turned to face me. "Are you all right?" he asked.

I smiled. "I'm fine," I said, looking over the crowd, toward the trees crisscrossing their way through the square.

We climbed Powell, the cable car clattering down the hill beside us, tourists hanging from the posts, Gap bags swaying out over the street. The conductor clanged the bell as the car reached the intersection, a crisp sound that seemed to silence the rest of the urban noise.

I turned on California, some sixth sense drawing me through the heart of Nob Hill. This had been the first neighborhood in San Francisco I'd fallen in love with. On that first visit, I'd wanted only to ride a cable car, and this was what I had seen. This would forever be San Francisco to me.

Finally, I began to feel a throbbing in my calves. After so many silent miles, my muscles at last were beginning to complain. Martin plodded along beside me, his breath still steady, as if this amount of exercise were completely normal to him, no effort at all.

The cathedral sat placidly on the crest of the hill, dominating the city. Like Chartres or St. Paul's or Florence's Duomo, it seemed the heart of the city, the source of all that grew around it. The stained-glass rose above the huge doors was in full bloom, the cathedral poised for any contingency—rooted to the ground, daring it to sway.

Except for a wedding or two, I'd barely set foot inside a church since high school. As I entered through the doorway, the cool air held in by gray stone walls chilled my skin, turning the sweat on my forehead to ice. Only now did I realize how warm it was outside.

"Do you mind?" I whispered to Martin. We'd never really discussed religion. Some people are offended by the very idea.

"Of course not," Martin said. "This is one of my favorite places." He laid a hand gently on my shoulder, my shirt sticking like glue between us for an instant. When he lifted it away, I smiled again and walked alone toward the nave.

I passed the labyrinth carpet, a few barefoot pilgrims marching slowly along its twisted, symmetrical path. Some wore the embarrassed smile of those caught crying at sentimental movies, others looked straight ahead, as if their feet could find the path all by themselves, without the help of their eyes.

My mother had taken me to church every Sunday for ten years or so, until adolescence had stolen away my interest. I rebelled against church as I rebelled against everything in those days. Other things—Brussels sprouts, soap operas, Mozart—I eventually came back to, mostly in college. But by then, the reality of religion had gotten in the way—the moral indignation of an immoral rabble, declaiming individual lines from the Bible as if the verses were from personal letters addressed to them alone, and they were free to pick and choose at will. By then, I associated religion with hatred, a hatred directed primarily at myself, at the way I chose to love, the way that love had chosen me.

But all along, I'd felt the attraction nonetheless—the grandeur of these spaces, the way they stood so silently and powerfully against the very world that tried to control them. I'd lost myself at Notre Dame, at St. Peter's. And whenever I did venture to a service, mostly with my mother on Christmas Eve, certain hymns would bring tears to my eyes, embarrassing tears I would bury behind the hymnal, or in a Kleenex as I pretended to nurse a cold.

There was no need for pretense today. As I genuflected in the aisle, then scooted over into a pew, I felt all the pretense draining away. This was real, I thought, as real as the pavement beneath my feet all the way up Nob Hill, as real as the sun that had made my ears sting.

I knelt on the cushioned rail and rested my elbows on the pew before me, hands folded firmly before my lips. And for the first time in years, I prayed, the words coming as easily as if I'd last spoken them an hour before. But now, somehow now they felt weightier, heavy with meaning, linked to a reality I could no longer leave outside those oversized doors. And when I had spent all the words I knew, one more echoed in my head, as loudly as if it were bouncing off the walls around me. *Thanks.*

My hands were wet with tears when I finally lifted my head. Standing, I decided to let the tears dry on their own, in streaks that lined my face. It felt good to cry. Everything felt good now, everything about being alive.

Suddenly, as I stood and headed back down the nave, I was aware of the music. The organ pipes, deep and rich, boomed through the cathedral, the chords flowing effortlessly one into another, swirling, filling the space. The sound was so powerful, it felt as if the pipes hung from every wall, as if I were within the very soul of the music.

When I reached the end of the nave and stood again at the head of the labyrinth, Martin was still there, near the entrance, softly smiling, silently urging me on. And way above his head, the stained-glass rose let in the late morning sunlight, splintering it into an array of colors, a rainbow that made the gray stone come alive.

There was no answer at Zach's place. The first couple of times I left a message, but after that even the machine wouldn't pick up. Perhaps he was just paying me back for the past two weeks, when I'd refused to take his calls, when I'd stood in the middle of the room, frozen by the ringing of the phone.

I didn't know exactly what I wanted to say, anyway. Or at least not how to say it.

Words were failing me these days, revealing their inadequacy at every turn. I'd always been aware of thinking in words—my mind typing them like subtitles under the images of life before me, one letter at a time. If I couldn't see the words, I wasn't accurately interpreting the experience, or feeling the feeling. Words gave everything shape—a framework without which it would all be a hopeless jumble, untranslatable.

But now, quite suddenly, the words fell away. And, even more surprisingly, nothing crumbled as a result. In fact, what remained seemed even stronger—focused somehow, emboldened by its unexpected ability to hold itself up. Instinct, intuition, a gut feeling—whatever I chose to call it at any given time, it sustained me. I learned to trust it—the silent voice that guided me as I walked along the street, telling me which store to browse in, which bus stop to wait at, which book to read.

I walked regularly now—long walks after work, getting off the bus a mile or more from home. Climbing the inevitable hill, I felt the pavement through my feet, stopped at the scent of lilacs bursting from the trees. I didn't care so much about the destination—collapsing onto the couch to unwind from the day. I didn't want to leave the day behind, to wish time away. This was time, too. This was the day.

Nearly a year ago, I'd tagged along behind Martin, following his pointing finger, learning all about *his* history. But I knew the city myself now. Somewhere within its depths, it held a piece of my history, as well. Each moment that went by was a part of it, the present continuously rolling into the past. That didn't stop it from being. The present was always present. It was all that could be.

It was still light out when I got off work now—the only real sign that winter, at last, was dying. By the time I got to Market and Castro, the sun was just beginning to fall behind Twin Peaks, bleeding a faint orange through the encroaching fog. I stopped midway up the hill to watch it, the light slanting down over the street, absorbed by the cream walls of the theater, whose neon sign flickered gently into life.

I was still staring, bracing myself awkwardly against the hill's slope, when a familiar voice shook my reverie. As though conjured up, an accessory to the postcard vision, Tony called to me as he came down the hill. "Hey, stranger!" he said, blond hair falling over his brow as he made his way.

"Tony. How are you?" We hadn't seen each other in several weeks, since that morning I'd slipped out, left him to his telephone calls and his life.

I can't say I hadn't thought about him, the phone number that lay tucked into the back of my daily planner, between business cards and scraps of miscellaneous notes. I didn't want to think about him—not yet, not until I knew what to do about Zach. I hadn't gone out again since that night—no forays into bars or clubs, no wandering the hungry streets. The panic of the past few weeks had cast a new tone on everything. A chapter was coming to a close. It wasn't time yet for the next one.

We chatted for a while, the familiar flirtation brightening the most mundane comments. "Call me," he said, cocking his head with a gentle smile. I remembered his face in the moonlight that spilled over his bed, the animation of his features as we talked long into the night, about art and music and something deeper, something unspeakable between the words.

"How are you?" Zach's voice echoed across the wire, as if he were calling from an empty auditorium or the hull of a ship.

"Where have you been?" I asked. I sat at the foot of the bed, tapping the bow against my knee. The cello stood propped against the wall, waiting.

"I've been working on some stuff," he said.

"What stuff?" Maybe he'd enrolled in that SAT class, I thought, started the tennis lessons, enacted the hundred and one other dreams he'd professed with such ardor.

He paused. Something rattled in the background. "I checked myself in this time," he said.

I slid the bow across my knee. This, I thought, this is how the cello feels.

"I got scared, I guess." He was whispering, and I remembered how public the phone was at the hospital—in that open space, just beside the nurse's station. "Nothing happened, but I know the signs now."

No scissors, I thought, no stockpile of pills. Thank God for that.

"How are you?"

"I'm okay. Just tired." He paused again. When he spoke, the feigned nonchalance was transparent, heartbreaking. "Will you come visit?"

"Same place?"

"Yeah." He laughed. "But they gave my old room away. The new one's even smaller, if you can believe that."

"How's tomorrow?"

"Great," he said. A hesitation crept back into his voice. "I've missed you."

"Take care of yourself, Zach. I'll see you tomorrow." I dropped the phone into its cradle and bent forward, over my knees. The bow tapped gently against the floorboards, scratching out an old melody.

I remembered each step—the chipped paint of the handrail, institutional green; the still, cold air that seemed to turn the stairwell into a postmodern antechamber, like the airlock between a spaceship and the black vacuum outside. I'd walked slowly up these steps before, counting them as in childhood I'd counted imaginary sheep. And though I climbed, it always seemed as if the world had been reversed and I was really descending—with each turn at a landing, spiraling deeper into something otherworldly, a place that couldn't accommodate the outside, that would feel contaminated by even a gust of air.

We had been together for five months when Zach ended up in the hospital the first time; after that, less than three before he'd brought himself back. Our relationship seemed to have a half-life, dividing, disintegrating before my eyes. Half-lives are chemistry's clock. You can tell how old something is by how much of it is left.

Wanda was on duty today. She greeted me with the old familiarity, as if we'd last seen each other just a day or two ago, as if I'd merely been on vacation and now was finally home.

"He's in his room," she said, and walked with me through the common area. I recognized a few faces, but most of them were new. It was encouraging to know that at least some had made it out. But obviously, the new ones kept coming. Without that turnover, this place would have gone out of business years ago.

Wanda stopped beside the Ping-Pong table and pointed toward the far corner. "That's where he is now," she said. "Right at the end."

I nodded, dumbly thanking her. I turned abruptly, to ask her how he was—hoping for a clue, some sense of what had gone wrong this time. But she had already turned on those spongy white shoes, was already floating her way back down the hall.

I knew I had already seen the worst. The initial shock had passed months ago. But still I felt more nervous now than on any of my previous visits. Then there had been hope, and the drive to understand. But now, the mere fact that I had been called once more to these cold, hollow halls bespoke only failure. I felt as if I were finally seeing this place for what it was: a core of disappointment and shattered dreams, a place where hope goes to die.

Once again, he was sitting by the window when I knocked on the open door—a new window in a new room, but the view was only slightly different. He smiled as I approached, eyes shining beneath a new baseball cap. He looked beautiful—a little pale and uncertain, but beautiful.

He rose from the chair and opened his arms, tentatively. I leaned into his embrace and kissed him softly. I was still clutching my sunglasses, having pulled them off in the dim stairwell. Sitting down in the armless chair by the bed, I placed them gently on the nightstand. The blond wood turned green behind the round lenses.

Zach pulled his chair closer to mine and folded his hands in his lap. "I'm sorry to drag you here again," he said. "You probably thought you were all through with mental hospitals."

I smiled the remark away. "How are you doing?" I asked.

"Fine." He nodded emphatically. "Just ironing out the wrinkles."

His demeanor was different. Not at all as despondent and self-contained as he'd been at the depth of his illness, nor as transparently happy as at the height of his "cure." The self-pity and the armor were both gone.

"Things were getting weird there for a while," he told me. "I got scared . . . that it was happening all over again."

"You didn't—?"

"No." He sat back with a sigh. "No, I didn't let it get that far." He laughed. "That's an improvement, at least. Catch it before there's a mess to clean up."

I needed to change the subject. "How's Roy?" I asked.

"He's okay," Zach said. "He got through the pneumonia, and he's fine."

I hesitated, gauging his composure. "And you?"

"I didn't bother taking the test," he said. "I have too many other things to worry about right now."

I wanted to tell him my own results. Perhaps that, at least, would take some of the fear away. But he didn't ask. He stared through me with those deadly blue eyes, and he didn't ask.

"I wanted to talk to you," he said. He was looking down at his hands. *This is the church, this is the steeple . . .* "Things have been so up in the air lately. . . . I just thought we should set it all straight."

He lifted his head slowly, revealing his face beneath the cap's wide visor. "I know this has been hard for you. I've kind of . . . dragged you down with me. And . . . well, I'd understand if you didn't—" He fumbled through the words, as though dashing from one strategy to another. "I mean, I don't want to keep you from your life. This is hard, and I don't want to put you through it anymore."

He was being noble, generous. He wanted me to refuse. To be grateful for the offer, but to refuse.

I studied his face in the shadow of the cap. His sideburns rode in wisps just above his cheekbones, which sloped gently to give his face a handsome but still innocent quality. He *was* beautiful.

"Zach, what are you saying?"

"I mean, you don't have to feel obligated anymore. If you don't want to deal with me, with—*this*—I'll understand." He fidgeted, as though attempting to throw off something—his illness, perhaps, this thing that he still considered somehow separate from himself, an enemy he could fight off like a virus.

It was too easy. He'd made it too easy.

"It's not just that, Zach," I said. "Don't think it's just because I'm not willing to stick it out." I leaned forward, resisting the impulse to reach for his hand. "Even without this"—I pulled my head back slightly, circling him with my eyes as though tracing an aura he threw off, the aura of his disease—"we never had much of a chance, you know? The truth is, I think we jumped into this so fast we didn't really see the whole picture. Love is blind, right?"

He attempted a smile. "Maybe. Dr. Porter says I'm overly spontaneous."

"It's one of your more charming qualities."

We sat quietly for a long while, catching each other's glance from time to time. Zach was always the first to turn away, as though threatened, as though I were seeing too deeply, seeing too much.

We rose together eventually and embraced once more, arms loosely around each other's body. As he began to draw away, a kind of panic tumbled in my stomach, and I abruptly pulled him closer, hugged him to me as though we both might collapse without the will of my arms. He returned the embrace, though not quite as fiercely. I closed my eyes and the feeling passed, washed away somehow, carried to safety. Slowly, we disengaged and I backed out of the room. "Call me if you need anything," I said, and he nodded silently.

The first breakup never takes, they say. Afterward, in the grip of grief and loneliness, it's too easy to jump back in—when the familiar, however painful, however impossible, seems the only thing that will do. But eventually, you run out of half-lives. Eventually there's nothing left.

Outside, I walked the length of the block in the hospital's long shadow. At the corner, I crossed to the sunny side of the street. I reached into my pocket for my sunglasses, but they were gone. I stopped by a newspaper box and checked every pocket, finding only ChapStick and a few gum wrappers. I'd left the glasses in Zach's room, folded beside the bed. They were cheap, I told myself. I could replace them at a drugstore.

Squinting, I continued along the street, the sun warm on my face. It felt strong, potent on my cheeks—raw, unmediated. I relished the heat, the blood that rose to the surface of my skin.

The bugs danced in lopsided formation, hovering in the air as though suspended on an invisible mobile. Most often gliding gently through the air, they would occasionally bump into one another and spin out of control, dive-bombing in miniature kamikaze attacks. Mosquitoes, flies, or some other frenetic species—they were too tiny, too fast-moving to identify. Despite their frantic, erratic behavior, they simply coexisted, and we walked through them as carelessly as if they were the branches of trees that we pushed out of the way to continue along the path.

Martin led the way, climbing up and down muddy hillocks, over stones that had acquired a certain sheen from the tread of a thousand footsteps. His pace was slow, steady, as all the while he clutched the urn in one hand against his chest.

No doubt, Kevin wasn't the first person who'd made such a request, and he wouldn't be the last. I suspected it was illegal to spread ashes here—akin to littering somehow—but I didn't object. If anything, I thought, spreading ashes would sanctify the place.

Martin had shown me photos of Kevin, most taken during their days in New York, just after college. He was younger than me in those pictures, a happy twentysomething seeing life as little more than an adventure or a cosmic joke. In one photo, they were standing together on the steps outside the Metropolitan Museum, Kevin's arm draped over Martin's shoulder, Martin's wrapped around Kevin's waist. They were laughing—perhaps at the photographer for taking so long to compose the picture. Poised on the edge of a step, they seemed perilously close to falling. I couldn't tell whether the strength of their embrace was actually the cause of their peril or their attempt to buffer it.

Kevin hadn't spent much time in San Francisco. He had visited only a few times, never for more than a month. But Land's End had somehow become a special place for him. It had provided his first view of the Pacific Ocean, and there was a kind of magic in the very name—the notion that this was as far as you could go, one more step and you were entering an unknown world. It seemed an appropriate place to spend eternity.

We proceeded through the brambles, the caves created by arching trees. Above us, on the far hillside, the windswept trees looked like oversized bonsai, their rigidity too perfect, too focused—all reaching toward the land, pointing east as though trying to escape the ocean's power. Martin walked onward without seeming to notice. Even in this wilderness, he knew where he was going, and I suspected he could have gotten there with his eyes closed.

But when he stopped, it was sudden. His foot raised for the next step, he turned to face the water that churned fifty or so feet below us. His face bore an attentive expression, as if he were listening—to the ocean, the wind, perhaps the buzz of the flies. And I realized that he hadn't been heading for any particular place, after all. He was simply waiting for the place to make itself known.

"Let's sit," he said, digging into the dusty ground with the toe of one sneaker. Just ahead, a large flat stone projected over the cliff face. He crouched upon it and dangled his legs over the side, the urn now cradled in his lap. I sat beside him and looked down at the waves crashing toward shore. Around the bend, only the very tips of the bridge's towers were visible, the sole sign of man's invention.

I had worn shorts for the first time all season, and already I could see the pink rising to the surface of my skin. I pressed a finger into my thigh and watched the white circle disappear as I lifted it away.

"I feel like I should say something," Martin muttered, "a prayer, or a eulogy." He stroked the lid of the urn, settled his hand warmly on the belly. "Kevin didn't believe in God. He said religion was just a collective fantasy to get us through life, a way to pretend that there was some reason, some order."

"And what do you think?" I asked. The wind was strong up here, bringing goosebumps to my arms, blowing my hair toward Martin, the longest strands nearly grazing his shoulder.

"I'm not sure. I think I like the mystery."

We hadn't talked about that visit to Grace Cathedral, the reason I'd felt compelled to go there that day, how it had somehow focused everything, put it all into perspective, given me back my life.

"That's all there ever is," I said. "That's why they call it faith. If God proved Himself, it wouldn't be any fun."

Martin laughed, still looking out at the ocean. "Don't you think He ever shows Himself?"

I remembered the booming of the organ, the light scattering through the rose window. I remembered Martin waiting at the end of the nave. "Sure," I said, "now and then."

We sat silently for a time, the two of us suspended over the cliffside. If I just gazed ahead and ignored the juts of land on either side of my peripheral vision, I could imagine that we were hovering miraculously over an abyss—detached from both land and sea, free as the gulls that darted over the water in search of lunch.

I remembered our first trip out here together, when my imagination had enlivened this landscape with a completely different set of fantasies: men waiting in the bushes, leaning against trees in haughty invitation. Those fantasies now seemed merely naive, broken under the weight of expectation I'd laid upon them. I'd come to San Francisco with visions of a life I'd thought I'd missed—and now, barely a year later, I'd managed to touch that life, or what remained of it fifteen years into the plague, and it all seemed so simple. Like every other fantasy, it had crumbled somehow into a core of reality—the essence without the charming halo visible only from a distance. Despite the disappointment of lost innocence, I was surprised to find that I actually preferred the reality. I was here—a living, breathing creature, bordering on vertigo as I hung suspended over the roiling ocean. I was alive, and I was right here.

It had been more than a month now since I'd last seen Zach. I'd been tempted to call, just to see if he answered, if he was out of the hospital yet, trying the real world out once more—but each time I'd let my hand fall away from the buttons on the phone. I'd gone to Macy's on my lunch hour once, but turned around at the foot of the escalator and decided to wander the first floor in search of bargains.

Martin had barely reacted to the news of our breakup—as if it were old, long overdue. More important, I thought, I hadn't needed to talk about it. Somehow, silence was enough. Everything had been said long ago.

A couple of weeks later, I had begun taking private cello lessons, the first time I'd formally studied since Adam. At the moment, I was working on a particularly difficult piece by Dvorák. Each night, I sat with the cello in my bedroom, listening for the right notes, sensing the vibration between my legs, trying to feel it in my chest. My new teacher, Elsa, told me that that was the true source of the music: You had to feel it in your chest first. It was the vibration in the chest that really caused the vibration in the instrument. Without that, the greatest music in the world would be tin.

My playing was better now. It seemed that nearly a year in hibernation had released something in the cello, or in me. Elsa wasn't the taskmaster that Adam had been: she didn't obsess over the precise curl of my fingers or the occasional note that fell flat. She encouraged me to play for pleasure. We both knew I'd never be great at it. And finally, that didn't matter. The music mattered, even if no one but the two of us ever heard it.

Martin fidgeted now at my side, still cradling the urn, still gazing at the horizon, where the sun had started to fall, orange, toward the sea.

"I never got to say good-bye to Kevin," he said, his words bitten by the wind that whipped around us. "He died just before I got there. It felt so incomplete, you know? Like, it couldn't really have happened because the script wasn't right. Remember the end of *Terms of Endearment,* where they just look at each other? At least that, I wanted at least that." He sighed, throwing his head back, into the shade of the trees. "And then, the night I got back, with the ashes, I set the box on my dresser—you know, the one by the door, on the other side of the room from the bed. And I went to sleep. A deep sleep, the kind I hardly ever have these days. And I remember waking up in the middle of the night—it was black all around. Except the dresser. The box—" He broke off, nervously laughing. "The box was glowing," he said flatly. "This orange light was all around it." He laughed again. "It was like the burning bush talking to Charlton Heston." His back arched suddenly. Something clicked in his throat, and I saw the tears. "Only it was Kevin, talking to me. He didn't say anything, I didn't hear his voice. But for that moment, I believed it was him—the light. And I wasn't scared, and I didn't think anything of it. In the light of day, I would have thought I was going crazy. But then, I just smiled. I felt so at peace. The light was still shining when I closed my eyes and went back to sleep."

He wiped his eyes, caught the teardrop hanging at the bottom of his cheek. "I suppose I might have dreamt the whole thing, but I don't even care. Whether it was a dream or not, it happened. Kevin said good-bye."

I clutched Martin's hand, our fingers entwining upon his lap, just beside the urn held tightly between his legs. The tears fell silently, and his features grew calm again. He looked out over the ocean, into the horizon, the ever-changing light. He seemed to be meditating, methodically drawing in breath, his eyes lying gently on the distance, resting rather than seeing. There was a passivity in his features now, a detachment that somehow strengthened them. Even his hand in mine felt stronger—not from any exertion in his grip, but from some inner stability.

"Let's go," he said after a few minutes. And he rose up from the ledge and led me along the cliffside, down the rocky path toward the beach.

Watching him ahead of me, I feared that he would lose his balance. I imagined the urn hurtling from his hands and crashing onto the rocks. But Martin walked with a surprising steadiness, taking each step as if he had trod it a hundred times before, as if he knew each stone, each twist along the path and the safest spot to set his foot. So intent upon his meanderings, I barely watched my own feet and stumbled more than once, righting myself at the last moment by clutching an exposed tree root or jumping onto a rock. As we got closer to the beach, the spray of the water began to dance on my face, the cool, salty air enveloped me. I felt goosebumps rising on my exposed arms.

This particular stretch of beach was surprisingly deserted. It was too early in the season; the weather was unreliable, and most people were unwilling to brave the journey down here only to find the fog stealing in. The few who had ventured to the beach were already on their way home; we'd passed most of them in the parking lot. A lone man remained, sitting in a corner by the cliff's face, fully dressed, arms wrapped around his knees. We moved quietly past him and toward the pounding waves that beat around the enormous boulders marking the shore.

The tide was falling, the sand still wet beneath our feet, though the waves were weaker now, not quite reaching us. A few scattered seashells lay half-submerged in the chocolate-gray sand, and a tiny crab scuttled toward the receding foam.

Martin stood just at the water's edge, the tide occasionally lapping at his feet. He embraced the urn in the crook of his arm and pulled at the lid. It gave with a slight pop, revealing the safety of its snug fit. He held the lid toward me, and I took it into my hands and stepped back. The lid was highlighted in gold leaf, the pattern vaguely Egyptian—delicate hieroglyphs mysterious, untranslatable.

Martin peered into the urn for a long moment. Then, serenely, he looked up, out at the water, and reached inside. Watching only the waves, he pulled his hand out, cupped now, the fingers closed in straight lines over his palm, and extended his arm. In a single sweeping gesture, he spilled the ashes into the next wave that broke around his feet.

I had never seen human ashes before. Varying shades of gray, some even bright white, they ranged from soft powder to harder, pebble-sized pieces, brittle remnants of bone. Leaving Martin's hand, a few glittered in the fading sunlight, others floating for a moment in the air—lighter than air, borne briefly by the wind before settling to the ground. The water drank them in, greedily snatching the ashes into the waves with each handful that Martin spilled through the air.

His gestures acquired a fluid rhythm, fingers cupping each handful the same way, arm making the same semicircular arc to disperse the ashes, to give Kevin over to the sea. He tipped the urn further each time his hand dove inside. When he had completed a dozen or so movements, he clutched the urn to his chest and closed his eyes as though in prayer. Opening them at last, he lifted the urn itself out over the water and tilted it vertically. A final cloud emerged, immediately sucked into a sudden breeze that blew half of it stealthily back to shore.

I walked backward, my eyes still on the shore, the water that lapped around Martin's feet, the ashes that had merged indistinguishably with the darkening sand. A few pebbles glinted, like diamonds spilled from an incautious hand. I wondered if I was stepping over pieces of Kevin, if the hard ashes of other strangers had made their way to this tiny stretch of beach to mingle with his.

This, I thought, is what it all comes down to. After everything—the alternating boredom and drama that we call life—we come back to this, the elemental forms of ash and bone. Chemistry is about reactions, two elements coming together and creating something new. Constant transformation. Kevin—the vibrant, funny man Martin had loved—was now mingling with the sand, the water, the bits of kelp that floated to shore. Everything connected, everything eventually a part of something else. Two elements come together, and neither is ever the same again.

ABOUT THE AUTHOR

Lewis DeSimone's work has appeared in *Christopher Street,* the *James White Review,* and the *Harrington Gay Men's Fiction Quarterly.* He lives in San Francisco.

Order a copy of this book with this form or online at:
http://www.haworthpress.com/store/product.asp?sku=5501

CHEMISTRY

_____in softbound at $22.95 (ISBN-13: 978-1-56023-559-0; ISBN-10: 1-56023-559-4)

Or order online and use special offer code HEC25 in the shopping cart.

COST OF BOOKS_____

☐ **BILL ME LATER:** (Bill-me option is good on US/Canada/Mexico orders only; not good to jobbers, wholesalers, or subscription agencies.)

☐ Check here if billing address is different from shipping address and attach purchase order and billing address information.

POSTAGE & HANDLING_____
(US: $4.00 for first book & $1.50 for each additional book)
(Outside US: $5.00 for first book & $2.00 for each additional book)

Signature_____

SUBTOTAL_____

☐ **PAYMENT ENCLOSED: $**_____

IN CANADA: ADD 7% GST_____

☐ **PLEASE CHARGE TO MY CREDIT CARD.**

STATE TAX_____
(NJ, NY, OH, MN, CA, IL, IN, PA, & SD residents, add appropriate local sales tax)

☐ Visa ☐ MasterCard ☐ AmEx ☐ Discover
☐ Diner's Club ☐ Eurocard ☐ JCB

Account # _____

FINAL TOTAL_____
(If paying in Canadian funds, convert using the current exchange rate, UNESCO coupons welcome)

Exp. Date_____

Signature_____

Prices in US dollars and subject to change without notice.

NAME_____

INSTITUTION_____

ADDRESS_____

CITY_____

STATE/ZIP_____

COUNTRY_____ COUNTY (NY residents only)_____

TEL_____ FAX_____

E-MAIL_____

May we use your e-mail address for confirmations and other types of information? ☐ Yes ☐ No
We appreciate receiving your e-mail address and fax number. Haworth would like to e-mail or fax special discount offers to you, as a preferred customer. **We will never share, rent, or exchange your e-mail address or fax number.** We regard such actions as an invasion of your privacy.

Order From Your Local Bookstore or Directly From
The Haworth Press, Inc.
10 Alice Street, Binghamton, New York 13904-1580 • USA
TELEPHONE: 1-800-HAWORTH (1-800-429-6784) / Outside US/Canada: (607) 722-5857
FAX: 1-800-895-0582 / Outside US/Canada: (607) 771-0012
E-mail to: orders@haworthpress.com

For orders outside US and Canada, you may wish to order through your local
sales representative, distributor, or bookseller.
For information, see http://haworthpress.com/distributors

(Discounts are available for individual orders in US and Canada only, not booksellers/distributors.)

PLEASE PHOTOCOPY THIS FORM FOR YOUR PERSONAL USE.
http://www.HaworthPress.com

BOF06